LET'S GIVE IT UP

FOR GIMME LAO!

LET'S GIVE IT UP FOR
GIMME LAO!

A Novel

SEBASTIAN SIM

EPIGRAM BOOKS
SINGAPORE · LONDON

Epigram Books UK
First published in 2017 by Epigram Books Singapore
This Edition published in Great Britain in May 2017
by Epigram Books UK

Copyright © 2016 by Sebastian Sim
Cover Illustration by Yong Wen Yeu

The moral right of the author has been asserted.

A CIP CATALOGUE RECORD FOR THIS BOOK IS AVAILABLE FROM THE BRITISH LIBRARY.

ISBN	978-1-91-209867-5
PRINTED AND BOUND IN	Great Britain by Clays Ltd, St Ives plc
	Epigram Books UK
	55 Baker Street
	London, W1U 7EU

10 9 8 7 6 5 4 3 2 1

www.epigrambooks.uk

To My Mother

ONE

THERE WERE THREE things Gimme Lao did not know about himself.

The first occurred at his point of birth. The second happened way before he was born. And the third repeated itself many times over his life.

Strictly speaking, the third was not about him. It was about the pivotal impact he had on other people, which he never found out about.

Take for example Yik Fan. Gimme Lao and Yik Fan went to the same primary school. Being two years apart, they were not in the same class, nor did they end up in the same extracurricular sports team. As far as he was concerned, Gimme Lao never knew Yik Fan existed.

Yik Fan, on the other hand, would never forget Gimme Lao.

Specifically, Yik Fan would never forget the spectacle of Gimme Lao's public humiliation on stage during school assembly. Not the fierce sobbing of the subject of ridicule, nor the malicious smirk of the disciplinary master as he made the boy put on a frock and applied cherry red lipstick on his lips. The entire assembly was collapsing in riotous laughter, and no one noticed that Yik Fan was trembling with fear.

When Yik Fan reached home that afternoon, he quickly retrieved the lipstick he hid in his socks drawer and threw it down the rubbish chute. For the following two Sundays, he refrained from slipping into his mother's high heels and prancing around the house like he usually did after she left for the market. By the time the third Sunday rolled around, the suppressed urge had become an unbearable itch. The boy succumbed. But the thrill of slipping his feet into the familiar comfort of his mother's high heels was sullied by a new apprehension. He saw his eventual downfall with clarity and certainty. It was only a matter of time before he would be paraded on stage, a subject of ridicule for the entire world's entertainment.

Yik Fan countered the fear with pain. He brought out his mother's nail clipper and clipped deep into his toe, tearing off a tender chunk of skin and flesh along with a sliver of toenail. His mother chided him for being careless.

The boy continued to be careless. As a teenager, he was always scraping his heels against the spikes on his bicycle chainring. When he was riding his first motorcycle, the exhaust pipe must have seared his legs a dozen times. After he got married, his wife was shocked at how easily Yik Fan could hurt himself. There were always razor blade cuts on his lips and bruised nails where he had stubbed his toes. She sighed and accepted the fact that her husband was hopelessly clumsy.

Yik Fan accepted the penalty of pain for the right to continue with his secret fetish. After his firstborn arrived, his wife was so preoccupied with the baby that she left him very much to himself. That was when Yik Fan became emboldened. He bought a new kimono cardigan, a crepe gown and a split dance dress in sultry red to expand his repertoire. On Sunday afternoons when his wife brought the baby to the in-laws, Yik Fan decked himself out in elaborate outfits and enacted scenes of fantasy. He was supposedly a damsel in distress chained up in a dungeon on that fateful afternoon when his mother-in-law came in unannounced to retrieve the tin of baby formula. He panicked at the sound of the key at the front door and dropped his key to the handcuff. The look of horror on his mother-in-law's face searing into his psyche was many times more painful than the multiple burns from the motorcycle exhaust pipe. After she left, he extricated himself from the bondage and sat in a daze for a full hour before realising that it was all over. The last image he saw before he applied the blade to his wrist was that of Gimme Lao on stage at the school assembly 20 years ago, sobbing fiercely as the crowd roared with laughter.

Gimme Lao did not know that. Neither did the disciplinary master who humiliated him on stage. Both of them went on living their lives, oblivious to the fact that their actions planted shame and fear so deep in a little boy's psyche, it led him to end his own life 20 years later.

The second thing that Gimme Lao did not know about himself happened way before he was born. Both his parents decided it was better that Gimme Lao not know. Grandma Toh, the only other person who knew, was sworn to secrecy.

Grandma Toh was a widow who lived next door to Gimme Lao's parents in their single bedroom flat unit. She was entrusted with babysitting duties while Gimme Lao's parents worked. She understood the gravity of the secret she was supposed to keep and agreed wholeheartedly that Gimme Lao should never be told. But the secret grew like a throbbing tumour in her throat. It was a relief to her when Aunty Seah, who lived two doors away, accidentally scraped her foot against the lid of the secret and proceeded to pry it open with curiosity.

"Don't you find it strange that the boy's grandparents never visit?" Aunty Seah mentioned casually when she came visiting one afternoon.

Grandma Toh bit her lip as she rocked the baby suckling the milk bottle in her arms. She prayed that Aunty Seah would veer off the topic and not tempt her.

"When the young couple moved in a year ago, I thought it was nice to have newlyweds join us in the block. The husband was especially amiable. Mild-tempered fellow. Can't say the same for the wife though. I am pretty sure she's the one who wears the pants in the house." Aunty Seah continued with the gossip. "But what irks me is that the couple is so secretive. No one in the block knows about their past or their background. Seriously, what is the big secret that they cannot share?"

Grandma Toh felt an actual, physical constriction in her throat. It was such a torture to know and be forbidden to tell.

"And then when the young wife got pregnant, all the neighbours were happy for them. We kept a lookout for the inexperienced couple and gave them all the help they needed. You even volunteered to be her confinement nurse after the baby was born. But don't you find it weird that the couple receives no visits whatsoever from their parents or their relatives? I mean, how would the couple cope if you had not stepped forward to take over babysitting duties when they went back to work?"

"Well, I did promise my cousin I would look after the young couple," Grandma Toh muttered.

"How did your cousin come into the picture?" Aunty Seah asked, confused.

Grandma Toh sighed. It was simply too difficult to hold her tongue. "My cousin works as a maid for the Lao family, the one that owns the Three Rifles fashion brand. They have a massive mansion on Grange Road."

Aunty Seah's eyes widened. "Wait a minute. Are you telling me that Lao Sheng Yang, the father of this baby, who works as an administrative clerk in an insurance company, comes from one of the richest families in town?"

Grandma Toh nodded. It was so satisfying to be in a position to dispense secrets by the spoonful into a willing ear and watch the amazement grow.

"Was he kicked out of the house and disowned by the family because they were against his marriage?" Aunty Seah ventured a guess.

Grandma Toh frowned. It was a letdown when the listener was too quick to guess the ending. "It is a long and complicated story."

"You have to tell me."

"You have to keep it a secret."

Aunty Seah nodded eagerly.

"My cousin has worked for the Lao family for decades. She

practically watched Lao Sheng Yang and his two brothers grow up. She was there too when the boys' mother succumbed to tuberculosis and became bedridden for many years. That was when Huang Rhoo was brought into the family as a goddaughter to look after the ailing mother."

Aunty Seah's eyes widened again. "You mean to say Huang Rhoo, the baby's mother, was Lao Sheng Yang's godsister? That is kind of scandalous."

"There is more to it," Grandma Toh continued. "Huang Rhoo's father, who worked for Sheng Yang's father, was a compulsive gambler. He had to beg Sheng Yang's father constantly to cover his debts. In a way, he was selling his daughter to the family. Tuberculosis is contagious, and Sheng Yang's father would rather have had someone from outside his family look after his wife."

"So that was how the couple met and fell in love," Aunty Seah nodded.

"Both were in their mid-teens then. Huang Rhoo was doing very well in school before she had to quit and take on the nursing role. She begged Sheng Yang to continue tutoring her in the evenings. In fact, my cousin told me that between the two, Huang Rhoo was the smarter one. She could tell because whenever the two played Chinese chess, Huang Rhoo often lost her temper and chided Sheng Yang for making badly calculated moves. It's a pity she never went back to school. Otherwise she could easily get a better job now, instead of the pharmacy assistant job she currently holds."

"Don't we all know about her temper," Aunty Seah raised

an eyebrow. "Remember the time she kicked up a big fuss with the family living upstairs who hung their wet laundry out over hers and dirtied her drying bedsheets? This is one woman with a fierce temper."

"Well, not unexpectedly, the young couple developed feelings for one another over time." Grandma Toh ignored the rude digression from the story she was telling. "When the mother eventually passed away two years ago, they decided to inform the family of their intention to get married. That was when all hell broke loose. My cousin told me that Sheng Yang's father chased the girl out of the house and gave his son an ultimatum. Either he break off the relationship, or he would be disowned and cut off from the family inheritance. That was how the couple ended up fending for themselves in our neighbourhood. Now you should understand why the two are so secretive about their past. And remember that you gave your promise. Keep this secret to yourself!"

"Of course I will," Aunty Seah said. "But what I do not understand is, what is the big deal about the marriage? Granted the girl is poor and her father is a compulsive gambler. But is that reason enough to disown the son?"

Grandma Toh bit her lip hard. She was hoping to get away with sharing only half the secret.

"Is there more to the story?" Aunty Seah was as sharp as a brand new pair of scissors.

"I have told you that Huang Rhoo's father is a compulsive gambler. Why do you think Sheng Yang's father keeps him on the payroll and covers his debts?"

"Why indeed?"

"Because they are half brothers. The patriarch of the Lao family has more than one mistress hidden outside. So Sheng Yang's father has no choice but to keep him and two other half brothers on the family business payroll."

Aunty Seah's eyes widened for the third time. "Which makes Lao Sheng Yang and his wife cousins? That is incestuous!"

"Which is why you must keep this secret to yourself," Grandma Toh reminded her in a hushed tone. "The baby must not know. Ever."

Aunty Seah looked at the suckling baby with sympathy. "Poor little bastard. He could have inherited such a huge family fortune but for the sins of his parents."

Grandma Toh slapped Aunty Seah on the thigh and warned, "Enough! Don't make me regret telling you this."

Aunty Seah did deliver on her promise. Gimme Lao grew up not knowing that he was born rich, yet robbed of his inheritance by true, defiant love.

The first thing that Gimme Lao did not know about himself occurred on the day he was born. That was the day half the population on the island was glued to the television. Not their personal set at home, for most of them could not afford one back in 1965. They were hanging around various community centres, where communal television sets were mounted on wooden pedestals, from which arced stone benches fanned out. Rumour was abuzz that the prime minister was going to announce a momentous piece of news at any moment.

The other half of the population was engaged in their quotidian affairs: clipping their nails, picking their teeth or scratching that persistent itch in their ass cracks. Positioned at the outer circle of the rippling shock wave, they received the terrible news an hour or two late. Some of them had the audacity to question the news bearers. Did they hear it right? Did the prime minister really mean something else? But the news bearers were indignant in their own defence. The prime minister choked and shed a tear on national television. There was no doubt about it.

The entire population on the island had been unceremoniously kicked out of their own country. They were no more a part of Malaysia. The Mother had disowned them.

For some strange reason, Gimme Lao the unborn baby must have experienced prenatal cognisance. He refused to be purged from his mother's womb. For nine whole hours, his mother shrieked and howled, scratched his father till she left claw marks on his arm and at one point even punched the nurse who was screaming at her for making too much noise. Eventually, Gimme Lao had to exit. He emerged looking bewildered, unsure whether the world that awaited him was hostile or benign. But the nurse was mad at the mother and took revenge by giving the baby a merciless pinch on the thigh. That was the moment Gimme Lao recognised hostility and bawled.

Gimme Lao's father was a soft man who shed tears easily. He whimpered with pain when his wife's nails dug deep and drew blood on his arm. He snivelled with joy at the sight of his firstborn bawling his tiny lungs out. He would later choke up with emotion when he found out that the island would no longer be flying the Malaysian flag.

In the midst of all the excitement, Gimme Lao's father did not realise that his was the first baby to be born in independent Singapore.

At that point in time, this significant little detail caught no one's attention. Gimme Lao's mother was too exhausted, his father too excited and the doctor who delivered him too caught up with the next three babies arriving on his shift.

Three days had passed before a journalist finally called up the hospital and wanted to know which baby was the first born past midnight on 9 August. The hospital administrator flipped through the nurses' schedule and summoned the nurse who was on midnight shift. "Go check the records on your shift and let me have the name."

The nurse was annoyed to discover that according to the records, a Chinese baby named Lao Chee Hong was born one minute past midnight on 9 August to a mother named Lao Huang Rhoo. She was pretty certain that this was the woman who had punched her in the face.

Flipping to the next record sheet, the nurse saw that a baby girl was born six minutes past midnight. That was the moment the idea struck her. She extracted a Zebra-brand ballpoint pen from her pocket, tested to make sure the ink matched and carefully added a horizontal stroke to the numerical one. Gimme Lao became the second baby to be born, seven minutes past midnight.

It was by this insidious horizontal stroke that Gimme Lao was robbed of his rightful title of the first baby to be born in independent Singapore.

No one ever found out the truth.

TWO

GIMME LAO DID not like Grandma Toh at all. He did not like the fact that she made him eat when he wasn't hungry, bathe when he wasn't ready and sleep when he still wanted to play. He hated it when Grandma Toh shovelled piping hot minced pork porridge into his mouth with an aluminium spoon so large it stretched his lips till the corners hurt. He disliked the brute strength Grandma Toh employed when she wrapped a hand towel round her palm, ran a damp bar of soap over it and scrubbed his skin with a total absence of mercy till it turned raw and red. And when it came around to the early afternoon soap opera on the radio, he would be made to drop his toys, lie on the sofa and rest his head on her lap. What he detested most was the suffocation he had to fight when Grandma Toh rocked and pressed her ample bosom onto his face. If he fussed, Grandma Toh would shush him fiercely. Nothing must disrupt the storyteller on the radio spinning yet another hypnotic, mesmerising yarn.

Gimme Lao was also keenly aware that it was Grandma Toh who tore him wailing and clawing from his mother's arms every morning before his parents disappeared down the corridor. The tearful ritual used to drag on for five minutes or more in the beginning, when Grandma Toh and the young parents restricted their methods to gentle coaxing and persuasion. They soon realised that not only was this ineffective, it also often left the mother's blouse stained with snot and tears. Grandma Toh then decided to employ drastic measures. She wrapped one arm around Gimme's waist and pinned his kicking legs to her stomach with the other. As Gimme continued to claw at his mother and wail hysterically, Grandma Toh leaned close to his ears and whispered firmly that he ought to let go at the count of three. She then counted aloud. At the third count she secretly secured one of his toes and pinched it hard with the sharp ends of her nails. Gimme would scream, let go of his mother and swing around to pound his tormentor with his tiny fists. At this point, the young parents were free to scuttle down the corridor and make a run for the bus. Eventually, Gimme learnt to let go before the count of three to spare himself the physical agony. His parents never discovered Grandma Toh's clandestine tactic and would in later years crow over her magical touch in taming the petulant toddler.

For the rest of the morning, Gimme Lao would be strapped to a squat bamboo contraption which served as an innocent box stool upright, but when flipped on its side, instantly morphed into its evil twin, a devious seat with holding bars that pinned down the toddler's legs and made it impossible to disentangle from without aid from an adult.

It was not that Grandma Toh derived pleasure from sadistic modes of infant care. She had to secure Gimme Lao safely in one corner of the kitchen while she worked. Grandma Toh cooked and sold sambal chilli for a living. Her specialties were sambal belachan and sambal jeruk. The morning routine began noisily as she threw handfuls of red chilli into the mortar and, using a pestle, pounded them furiously till the skin broke and the seeds were crushed. Once the chilli had been ground into a flaming red paste, she added in a handful of garlic, half a large onion and her own secret recipe of belachan. This last ingredient Grandma Toh concocted once a month by steaming sun-dried krill, mashing it into a paste and allowing it to ferment over several weeks. Her secret was to add in copious amounts of shallot paste and sugar right before she toasted the belachan to unleash the flavour. The spicy mix was then introduced into a preheated pan with a thin layer of vegetable oil. For the rest of the morning, Grandma Toh would patiently stir the belachan batch by batch until the mix absorbed the oil and morphed into a heavy paste that was both menacingly dark and alluringly red. For sambal jeruk, she added in kaffir lime to give it that tongue-teasing sting.

It took Gimme Lao many weeks to get accustomed to the oppressive aroma of the sambal that permeated the kitchen every morning. Eventually, he stopped crying and choking from the overpowering smell and continued playing with his toys nonchalantly even when the toasting was at its peak. Grandma Toh scheduled his toilet breaks in accordance with her own. She would disengage Gimme from the bamboo contraption, carry him to the toilet, remove both his diaper and her pants and position herself and him over the squat toilet. Strangely enough, Grandma Toh's pee cascading into the ceramic receptacle never failed to trigger a corresponding release from the toddler. Once, when Grandma Toh was in a cheeky mood, she experimented by regulating her pee in tiny little squirts and giggled herself silly when Gimme Lao copied her rhythm. It was a pity there was no one else around to share the comedy.

It would be past noon when Barber Bay came in for lunch. The barbershop occupied a corner unit on the ground floor of their apartment building. The shop used to belong to Grandma Toh's husband before he passed away. Barber Bay, who had graduated from apprenticeship to a business partnership with the husband, promised him he would help take care of Grandma Toh and their daughter Elizabeth. In exchange, he became co-owner of the shop space with the widow. Every day at noon, Barber Bay would pull down the shutters to the shop, climb the seven flights of stairs up the building and join Grandma Toh for lunch. There was a lift that served landings four, eight and twelve, but Barber Bay claimed he needed the exercise.

There was no doubt that Barber Bay was a hardworking man by nature. After Grandma Toh's husband died, Barber Bay terminated the services of the cleaning lady and took over the tasks himself. He arrived an hour early every morning to give the place a meticulous sweep and mop before the first customer sauntered in. After the last customer for the night left, he boiled water to soak and wash the face towels and left them to dry overnight under the ceiling fan. He made use of the lull in between customers to go through the barbering tools with a toothbrush, removing hair and beard follicles from between the sharp metallic teeth. Once a week he also climbed onto a stool to dust the ceiling fan and spray-wiped the mirrors with window cleaning detergent. In fact, the barbershop became cleaner and brighter after the cleaning lady stopped cleaning the place.

Grandma Toh prepared a simple lunch for the two of them that repeated itself every seven days. On Monday, it was steamed rice with crispy fried ikan bilis, roasted peanuts and a thin egg omelette. On Tuesday, it was Teochew porridge boiled to the consistency of glue, with a salted egg and pickled vegetables. Wednesday was the day Grandma Toh splurged a little and cooked minced pork porridge. Thursday saw a return to steamed rice, accompanied by stir-fried bean sprouts with salted fish. On Friday and Saturday, Grandma Toh permitted their palates a little variety by switching to bee hoon, served with fish ball soup one day and fried with sambal chilli the next. She made it a practice to cook excess on Saturday, so that she had leftovers for Sunday, when she ate alone. On Sunday, Barber Bay attended church together with her daughter Elizabeth.

Barber Bay was an easy man to cook for. Though he did not like porridge in any form and detested the taste of bean sprouts and salted fish, he was too much of a gentleman to risk upsetting Grandma Toh. So for three days a week, he humbly endured a lunch that did not please his palate. He quietly chewed his food and watched as Grandma Toh clamped Gimme Lao between her thighs and shovelled food into his mouth. Though he secretly winced when he saw the toddler struggle with the humongous portion per shovel, he was too polite to criticise Grandma Toh's judgement. What would a bachelor of 40 years and counting know of infant care?

After lunch, Barber Bay would pick up the twin sets of multitiered woven cane containers, within which Grandma Toh had packed labelled jars of sambal belachan and sambal jeruk. Balancing them using a bamboo pole resting on his shoulder, Barber Bay followed a circular delivery route within a 20-block radius. There were a dozen hawkers selling laksa, fried rice and soup noodles who depended on Grandma Toh as their sole sambal chilli supplier. The consistency of her product and the reliability of Barber Bay's delivery schedule had secured their trust and loyalty for over a decade.

Unfortunately, Barber Bay's humble nature also encouraged devious hawkers to take advantage of him. The original agreement was to have them return the empty jars from the preceding day washed, dried and ready for refill. The laksa hawker tested the ground one day by presenting Barber Bay with unwashed jars, claiming that his wife had sprained her wrist and could barely cope with the washing of the bowls and chopsticks. Being the benign and compassionate soul that he was, Barber Bay wished her a speedy recovery and accepted the jars in their dirty condition. But when the wrist in question failed to recover after a week, Grandma Toh balked. She gave specific instructions for Barber Bay not to accept any more unwashed jars from the laksa stall. A fresh batch of sambal chilli would only be delivered in exchange for washed and dried jars.

Barber Bay found himself caught in a dilemma. He was a foot soldier sent to the battlefield unarmed and unready for confrontation. When the laksa hawker waved away his fumbling threat and demanded a fresh batch of sambal chilli, he gave in very quickly. The mission having turned out a total fiasco, Barber Bay dreaded the imminent tongue lashing from Grandma Toh. In fact, he dreaded it so much he decided to stop by the barbershop and quickly wash and dry the incriminating jars himself. Grandma Toh was thus led to believe that the laksa hawker had succumbed to her threat and the situation was back to normal.

But the situation got worse. When the chicken rice hawker and the fishball noodle hawker saw what was happening, they decided to ride on the recalcitrant's coattails. Horrified at the spreading mutiny, Barber Bay had to implement damage control. He quickly altered his circular delivery route and adopted a twisted butterfly pattern, such that the mutinying trio would be served last, and no one else could copy their insurrection.

Grandma Toh began to suspect something was amiss when Barber Bay returned from his delivery duty close to an hour late every day. She did not quite believe him when he told her that he had volunteered to deliver lunch to the fishball noodle hawker's frail old mother in her home. So one fine day, she forewent her favourite radio soap opera and went downstairs to tail Barber Bay on his round. She was furious when she discovered the truth. Although Barber Bay was made miserable by the chiding, he was secretly glad Grandma Toh finally took control.

The following Saturday, Grandma Toh carried Gimme Lao in her arms and made her way to the market. Stopping at the laksa stall, she ordered six packets of laksa to go. She stared down the laksa hawker when he laid out his palm for payment. "I am the one collecting payment here," she growled. "These six packets are in lieu of the washing fees for your sambal jars. I will be back next Saturday for more."

As Grandma Toh predicted, the laksa hawker decided it was not worth the weekly harassment, and his wife's wrist instantly enjoyed full recovery. Grandma Toh celebrated her inspired suppression of the lead mutineer by inviting Aunty Seah and Gimme Lao's parents to join herself and Barber Bay for a laksa treat. The last packet she kept for her daughter Elizabeth when she returned home that night. The next Saturday, they all had chicken rice. The last mutineer, however, surrendered before time and deprived them of their anticipated treat of fishball noodles.

Grandma Toh trusted Barber Bay to handle the barbershop accounts by himself. At the end of every month, she would wave him off when he tried to show her the account books after handing her an envelope containing her share of the earnings.

"Do you see me popping in to the shop every day to check on the customer flow? I don't, because I trust you. So did my late husband. If we didn't, we would offer you our daughter's hand in marriage, so that we could make you part of our family and remove any reason for you to cheat. You understand?"

Barber Bay blushed and lowered his head to focus on his bowl of rice. He wondered if Grandma Toh was aware he had a crush on her daughter Elizabeth. She was only 13 when he first apprenticed for her father. Over the years, she had blossomed into a fine young lady. He looked forward to the evenings, when Grandma Toh made Elizabeth deliver his dinner to the barbershop on her way out. He would freeze in the midst of his occupation and let the unfolded razor knife rest on the stubble, or the blending shears hover over the frizz, or the scoop end of the digger lean in against the ear canal—and watch silently as Elizabeth glided over to the far end, placed the dinner container next to the sink and glided out again just as gracefully.

Barber Bay sighed. He wished he knew what Elizabeth thought of him.

Back when Barber Bay was an apprentice under her father, Elizabeth was tasked to fetch their dinner. Her father made it a routine to grill the girl about her academic progress and the friends she mixed with. Listening in, Barber Bay became enmeshed in her school life. He knew she excelled in music and art and frequently topped her class in English language. He also knew she struggled hopelessly with mathematics and found physics and chemistry lessons a torture. He knew the names of the two girls who were part of her clique in school and was secretly glad she was too shy for boys.

Once, when Elizabeth mentioned that her music teacher had encouraged her to take up piano lessons, her father snorted. Where would they get the money to buy a piano? There were 168 families who occupied the single bedroom units in the apartment building they lived in. As far as he knew, none of the families owned a piano. An electric rice cooker was the luxury item every family was striving for. A television set might follow. But a piano was miles off the wish list.

Barber Bay lost sleep over the look of disappointment on Elizabeth's face. But lying in bed one night and cooling himself with a straw fan, he was struck by a brilliant idea. Every Sunday morning he had to visit his brother, who was then serving a five-year sentence in Queenstown Remand Prison. There was a church near the prison, and he often heard the piano accompaniment as the congregation sang the hymns. Might not the church pastor be agreeable to letting Elizabeth use their piano for practice on some afternoons?

The following Sunday, Barber Bay loitered near the church after his prison visit and waited till service was over. Though normally timid and reticent, Barber Bay stepped into the vestibule with uncharacteristic boldness and asked to speak to the pastor. He was stumped, however, when the cassocked man brought to him turned out to be Caucasian. Barber Bay spoke no English.

"Do you speak Hokkien?" There was a sparkle of mischief in the pastor's eyes. He never failed to enjoy that look of astonishment when locals first heard him speak their dialect.

Relieved, Barber Bay made known his request. The pastor pondered for a minute, then looked up and smiled, "We might have agreed to the arrangement if the request came from our church member. Why don't you bring the young lady to church next Sunday? Our service starts at eight thirty in the morning. I will see you both then."

The next morning, Barber Bay intercepted Elizabeth on her way to school. As he unfurled his plan, her initial apprehension and confusion cartwheeled first into astonishment at his enthusiasm, then excitement at the resurrection of a lost hope and finally a deeply felt gratitude. She had no idea this apprentice working for her father was such a kind-hearted soul.

It went without saying that this ought to be kept a secret from her parents. Elizabeth told them that she had been roped into the school choir and had to attend weekend practice. On the following Sunday, she sneaked downstairs at sunrise to meet Barber Bay. He was waiting for her outside the barbershop, dressed in a freshly ironed Crocodile International branded shirt, his hair neatly parted at the left and glossed over with Brylcreem and his hands holding on to a brand-new bicycle he had bought two days ago.

"I thought we were going by bus?" Elizabeth blushed slightly as she balanced herself riding pillion.

"If we are going to take the bus every Sunday, it is going to add up. This bicycle will cost us less in the long run."

It was a 45-minute cycle to the church. Elizabeth found it wobbly and frowned. Barber Bay cherished the intimacy of her hands on his waist and smiled. He imagined the warmth of her proximity next to him on the pew and looked forward to the church service. In fact, he was already looking forward to the series of Sundays ahead with sweet anticipation.

Upon arrival at the church, they were led to the reception table at the vestibule. After registration, the woman behind the table asked for their preferred language. Barber Bay was slow to realise that the innocent question was pivotal in derailing his plan of church-based courtship.

"Not to worry, sir." The woman looked at Barber Bay benevolently. "Although Pastor Clarence delivers his sermons in English, we have translators upstairs who do concurrent interpretations in Hokkien, Teochew and Cantonese. If you will just follow Brother Miak here, he will lead you upstairs to the Hokkien sector."

Stunned, Barber Bay watched sorrowfully as another usher led Elizabeth down the main aisle. From where he was positioned upstairs, he was unable to see the larger congregation downstairs. Neither was he able to focus on the translator, who was earnestly interpreting the ongoing sermon. A sense of despair overcame Barber Bay. It was apparent that the God of this church had a very different plan for him.

Barber Bay was glad when the session finally ended after three torturous hours. He rushed down the stairs and waited for Elizabeth. His heart sank when he saw her emerge in the company of two other girls. They were Elizabeth's schoolmates, and she was going to take the bus home together with them.

Pastor Clarence was stationed at the door to greet the congregation on their way out. He was slightly alarmed when he saw the look of dejection Barber Bay wore. Barber Bay declined his invitation to stay back for a chat and mentioned that he had to visit his brother in prison. A warm glow engulfed Pastor Clarence's chest. It was pure miracle. A love for music was planted in a girl's heart. A love for the girl brought this man to step into the church, in the hope that the girl could practise on the church piano. And the man had a brother in prison who awaited salvation. God always did have a plan.

Barber Bay, on the other hand, did not like the way God tampered with his plan. He wanted to spend time with Elizabeth every Sunday, but God had planted a hundred worshippers between them. He bought a bicycle so they could enjoy the morning breeze together riding to church, but God provided Elizabeth with companions for a bus ride. It was not till years later, when his heart was softened by God's grace and his mind enlightened by God's wisdom, that he was able to look back and realise that God was answering the bicycle seller's prayers.

Three Sundays later, Elizabeth became Elizabeth. She made Barber Bay continue to call her Toh Yee Wen at home, as she was not ready to reveal to her parents that she had accepted Christ. Pastor Clarence agreed to let her practise on the church piano two afternoons a week, so she was able to take up piano lessons in school. As far as her parents were concerned, she was engaged in choir practice.

In later years, Elizabeth would recall the Monday morning that Barber Bay intercepted her on her way to school and proposed the idea of playing on the church piano as the first instance of God's grace at work in her life. Why else would the taciturn apprentice at her father's barbershop behave in such an uncharacteristic manner? The young man had never caught her attention before and after introducing her to church, again faded silently into the background. He was there to anchor the barbershop business when her father succumbed to cancer of the liver several years later. He took over the barbershop operations after her father passed on and lent her mother a hand when she started cooking and selling sambal chilli for income. He was again there to smooth out the sour discord when her mother finally discovered that she had secretly accepted Christ. Deep in her heart, Elizabeth saw Barber Bay as the silent angel God had sent to look after her. That God's grace knew no bounds moved her deeply.

Elizabeth never did recover from the clash with her mother over her secret faith. Grandma Toh had a Goddess Kuan Yin altar in the kitchen, to which she offered joss sticks every morning to pray for health, wealth and safety. According to the Bible, any other form of idol worship was an abomination. Elizabeth felt guilty that she had to hide the shine of her faith that was true and beautiful. The gold chain with the cross pendant had to suffer the darkness in the purse till she left the house. She felt awful whenever Grandma Toh was busy and instructed her to offer the joss sticks at the altar, which she could not rightfully refuse. In a way, she was glad when Grandma Toh finally discovered her secret. The torrent of verbal abuse Grandma Toh bestowed upon her only served to justify her rebellion. She now had permission to stand up and fight for her faith.

At dinner, Grandma Toh would rummage through her shallow chest of history and dish out grievances against Western atrocities. It took her many weeks, but she eventually concocted a personal version of Chinese sufferings under the westerners that freely disregarded chronological order and accuracy. Prior to China's Boxer Rebellion at the turn of the century, the Western powers introduced both opium to weaken the will and Christian missionary teachings to confuse the mind. When the Chinese decided to rise up in rebellion, eight imperialistic Western nations ganged up and sent in their troops. That led to the Rape of Nanjing, where up to a million Chinese were beheaded, mutilated and sexually violated. Eventually, when the great Sun Yat Sen forced the bullies to the negotiating table to invalidate the unequal treaties imposed upon China, he was ruthlessly assassinated.

In the beginning, Elizabeth made a heroic effort to address Grandma Toh's historical inaccuracies and logical lapses. Opium and Christian teachings were not conspiring addictions, the Rape of Nanjing was committed by the Japanese in a totally different war decades apart and the great Sun Yat Sen was never assassinated. But when it became apparent that Grandma Toh was not malleable, Elizabeth learned to tune out and shut up.

At church, Elizabeth chose to confide in Pastor Clarence. She had expected the comfort of solace and encouragement. But Pastor Clarence surprised her.

"This is God's challenge for you. Bring your mother to church. Do not leave her to drown."

Elizabeth froze. She could not imagine her mother receiving grace in the house of the Lord. In her mind, Grandma Toh belonged to the crass landscape of chilli pounding, neighbourly gossips and radio soap opera addiction. Elizabeth herself sought an escape from that landscape of unpolished manners and petty concerns. Why would she want to bring it along with her to church?

Elizabeth began to avoid Pastor Clarence. Whenever that was not possible, she pre-empted by asking Pastor Clarence for advice. How should she deal with the many challenges at work? She hinted at male superiors who cornered her with unwanted attention, female colleagues who ridiculed her for her repetitive wardrobe and the unreasonable workload piled on her by her bullying boss. It came to a point when Pastor Clarence was truly worried for the young lady. He spread the word among the congregation that Elizabeth needed help. Soon, help started to pour in.

Elizabeth found herself swathed in goodwill. A strong referral landed her a job selling Yamaha pianos near C. K. Tang Department Store along the new Orchard Road shopping belt. A timely connection linked her up with a British family who was looking for a piano teacher for their child. Church ladies passed her clothes they couldn't fit into anymore after childbirth. In fact, the flurry of camaraderie attesting to God's grace satisfied Pastor Clarence so much that the lone, unsaved soul of Grandma Toh buried under a mound of joss stick ash was all but forgotten.

For the first two years that Elizabeth worked at Yamaha, she was happy. The colleagues she worked with were civil, and the customers she served cultured. Her English became polished as she adopted the intonation of the many foreigners frequenting the showroom. She enjoyed sitting down to play a tune and drawing customers to her like hummingbirds to nectar. She knew in her heart that some customers purchased the pianos because they dreamt of playing as gracefully as she did. That realisation made her proud.

During her breaks, she pretended to be a shopper and strolled along Orchard Road all the way till she reached Orchard Market. She tried on scarves and winter jackets as though she were planning for a holiday where there would be snow. She picked and examined cuff links and ties as though she were going to surprise a boyfriend. Once a fortnight she would splurge a little to tease her palate with something new and alien at the Cold Storage Milk Bar. Peach slices encased in gelatine moulds. Pineapple upside down cakes. Mincemeat tarts and lemon meringue pies. There was so much delight to be had.

By the end of the second year, the realisation finally seeped in that there was no winter vacation to look forward to and no boyfriend to pick cuff links for. The clothes she received from the church ladies went quickly out of style. The novelty of sitting alone at the Cold Storage Milk Bar savouring a new item was replaced by the painful awareness that she was pampering herself only because no one else in her life was doing so. On her scheduled rest days on Tuesdays, she hated awakening to the pounding of pestle against mortar and the nauseating aroma of sambal chilli. And Sunday church had become a chore now that she had to rush off to the busiest shift of the week right after service. God's grace had all but disappeared from her life.

Elizabeth became secretly desperate. She was all of 25 and had never gone on a date before. There were simply no eligible candidates. She would not consider anyone with a lower education, or anyone who did not speak good English. That practically ruled out all the young men within a mile. There were men at work who might be eligible, but they did not seem to pay her any attention. There were men in church who looked promising, but she did not know how to approach them. Her despondency sharpened when a young couple moved in next door. They were both two years her junior, and it irked her whenever she spotted them strolling leisurely through the night market, hand in hand. Her desperation peaked when the young couple gave birth to a baby boy. She suddenly realised that she might never have anyone to call her own; not a husband, not a child.

Elizabeth became bitter. If she had to end up alone, she would need money to take care of herself. She calculated and decided it was too slow to save up based on her meagre pay. She asked the British family whose child she was tutoring to recommend her. Once she had secured enough piano tutoring assignments, she quit her job selling pianos at Yamaha to become a full-time tutor. She took on students with a vengeance. She would tutor three students in the day, go home for dinner and then head out for yet another night lesson. She gave herself no rest day.

Within a year, Elizabeth was earning five times what she used to make at Yamaha. As her savings account grew, her bitterness abated. She began to give herself a little treat in the afternoon between classes. She would spend a leisurely hour flipping through fashion or interior décor magazines at the MPH bookstore along Stamford Road, or munch on a peach tart and sip from a cup of milk tea while seated comfortably in the cosy dimness inside Jack's Place Steakhouse, or catch an afternoon matinee at Capitol Theatre. It was during those afternoons of leisure that God's grace re-entered her life.

Elizabeth loved foreign movies. She caught *Mary Poppins* and *The Sound of Music* and embraced Hollywood musicals as her personal antidote to counter the harshness of reality. She watched *Guess Who's Coming to Dinner* and found herself identifying with the rebel in Sidney Poitier. When she learnt that Sidney Poitier had been the first black actor to win an Oscar, she passionately adopted him as an idol. In fact, she was so inspired she convinced the young couple next door to name their toddler, who was assigned to her mother's care, Sidney.

It was, however, a challenge to teach the toddler his new name. He was born Lao Chee Hong, which translated to Grand Ambition. When Elizabeth coaxed him to enunciate Sidney, the mumbled echo that emerged was Teenee. Further cajoling brought forth Heenee, then Nimee and finally Gimme, by which time Elizabeth lost patience and gave up. Grandma Toh, too, found the name Gimme much easier to master than Sidney and so the name stuck. This was how Gimme Lao came to pioneer a new English name.

Elizabeth was not particularly fond of children. She tolerated Gimme Lao's presence in the house only because he occupied Grandma Toh and staved off her desire for a grandchild of her own. Elizabeth entertained a rather vague vision of herself as a mother. In contrast, the vision of herself as a wife was infinitely sharper. She knew exactly what kind of a wife she would make, how the furniture in her house would be arranged, down to the last detail of the curtain across the window and the cutlery on her dining table. She was only waiting for the right man to show up for dinner.

And then he came into her life. Sidney. Sidney McKellen.

She first heard his voice. She had just finished demonstrating a tune to a new student when she heard the door down the hall open and a booming voice announce itself, "Darling, I am home."

As footsteps approached, she turned to greet the person whom she imagined must be her new student's father. But her voice was caught in her throat. Instead, she gaped at the bluest pair of eyes she had ever come across. Fortunately, the new student, a plump girl of eight, hurled herself at her father and provided Elizabeth a window of several seconds to recover herself.

"Good afternoon! You must be Doreen's new piano teacher. I am Sidney McKellen. Pleasure." The man said as he extended his right hand, a sparkling smile sprouting simultaneously on his lips and in his eyes.

"Captain Sidney McKellen, British Air Force!" Doreen announced giggling, her arms wrapped round his neck and hanging from it like an obese little chimpanzee.

Elizabeth smiled weakly as Captain Sidney McKellen gave her a firm handshake. She noticed instantly that he had a chiselled chin with a cleft, not unlike Sean Connery, whom she had seen in the James Bond flick *You Only Live Twice* recently. Almost instinctively, she recalled the scene in which the secret agent 007 enjoyed a shampoo and lather rubdown by three Japanese sirens in a large wooden tub. She felt knots in her stomach.

This was the man she had laid out her dinner table for.

She could distinctly see it in her mind. Captain Sidney McKellen seated at the table, his thick palm holding her silver fork and delivering a sliver of duck confit to his luscious lips angled at the precise gradient of his cleft chin, the sky blue in his eyes reflected in the ocean blue of her table napkin. Even his tie was in a colour complementary to her curtains.

Elizabeth suddenly felt like shopping. Over the next few days, she bought herself three new dresses and tailored them for a better fit. She also bought two pairs of earrings, a necklace and a bottle of Chanel No 22. The following week, she showed up for Doreen's piano lesson in a sleeveless shift dress in striking indigo. Doreen's mother gasped and avowed that the item was most stunning. When Elizabeth agreed to share her tailor, Doreen's mother took to her immediately. But Captain Sidney McKellen did not show up that day.

When Captain Sidney McKellen failed to show up over the next few weeks, Elizabeth began to panic. She decided she needed to gather more information. After the piano lesson was over, she would stay behind and chat with Doreen's mother and fuss over her younger daughter Madeline, a toddler with eyes as blue as the captain's.

It took Elizabeth two months' worth of investigative interrogation disguised as innocuous chatter to pin down the critical piece of information. Every Sunday morning, Doreen's mother took Doreen along with her to attend the weekly gathering of her gardening interest group. The captain would be left alone to babysit Madeline. Elizabeth's heart pounded. She garnered her courage and casually mentioned that on Sunday mornings, she had to relieve her mother of her babysitting duty so that her mother could do her marketing. It was exhausting to look after a bouncy toddler all by oneself, for one simply could not afford anything less than full concentration.

In full glory of God's grace, Doreen's mother picked up on the bright idea Elizabeth implanted in her mind and happily suggested Elizabeth bring her toddler over on Sundays as Madeline's playmate. That way, the two adults could take turns and not tire themselves out.

Elizabeth shopped again. This time round, she bought black lace panties.

Back home, Elizabeth stumbled when Gimme Lao's mother responded to her enthusiastic suggestion with a puzzled look. "That is very kind of you." Her tone was courteous, but cold. "But I work five and a half days a week, and Sunday is really the only time I get to see my child."

Elizabeth paled. She could have slapped herself. In her haste, she had forgotten what she had learnt at Yamaha. The way to sell an expensive piano was to sell the music.

"I just thought it would be a wonderful opportunity." Elizabeth spoke slowly, but thought quickly. "They have bought all these educational toys for their girl. She is the same age as Gimme, but she can already spell and read simple picture books. They even have an ingenious card game that teaches her how to count, add and subtract. If Gimme plays with her, he gets to learn all these too."

Gimme Lao's mother liked the sound of the music, and the piano was sold.

The following Sunday, Elizabeth skipped church for the first time in over a decade, and Gimme Lao met his playmate Madeline for the first time in his life. Captain Sidney McKellen served a chilled glass bowl of pineapple punch and a silver platter of assorted English biscuits. Elizabeth did not touch the biscuits for fear that the crumbs would wedge themselves in between her teeth and disfigure her smile. Gimme Lao had no such concerns and grabbed one freely.

Madeline seemed to take an instant liking to her new playmate. She abided by the captain's gentle persuasion to be generous and offered Gimme Lao a choice selection from the platter on an open palm. Gimme Lao spotted the offer, dropped the biscuit he held in his hand, rushed forward to seize the offering and effectively slammed Madeline off her feet. It was a good thing that the floor was heavily carpeted. Madeline simply looked dazed to find herself suddenly seated.

Elizabeth howled. She threw herself on the carpet and hugged Madeline as though she were trying to protect her from a falling beam. The captain laughed and remarked that it was perfectly all right for toddlers to play rough. He said to leave the kids alone and let them work out their dynamics. Elizabeth blushed to think she might have made a fool of herself. But she caught a glimpse of her black lace panties showing where her hemline had folded upon itself and decided the foolery of falling onto the carpet was worth it.

Over the next few Sundays, Gimme Lao and Madeline worked out their dynamics. Madeline took on a nurturing role and expended tremendous effort trying to teach Gimme Lao the alphabet and simple arithmetic using her chest of educational toys. When her playmate did not display any measure of interest, Madeline turned to household appliances and demonstrated how to flush a toilet, or activate the garden hose, or climb onto a rattan chair to flick a switch and watch the garage door rumble downwards nosily. These lessons fascinated Gimme Lao. He especially loved switching on the garden tap, stepping onto the wriggling hose and wrestling with the water spurt till the two of them were completely drenched. The water adventure often left the two giggling themselves silly, till Elizabeth stepped in to halt the fun and chide Gimme Lao for his mischief.

Gimme Lao did not like Elizabeth. She put a cap on the fun he was having and never failed to step in just as the fun peaked. When he lost interest doodling in the colouring book and started applying the colour markers on Madeline's face, Elizabeth stopped him. When he picked up a piece of Lego brick and attempted to stuff it down Madeline's throat, Elizabeth stopped him. When Madeline reached out to wipe a crumb off his face and he defended his muffin from what he interpreted as an attempt to snatch it by biting Madeline on the finger, Elizabeth screamed and stopped him.

Gimme Lao finally figured it out. Madeline was the switch that triggered responses from Elizabeth, much like the switch that triggered the rumbling descent of the garage door. When Gimme Lao handed Madeline a soft toy, Elizabeth ruffled his hair as a sign of approval. When Gimme Lao hugged Madeline and planted a kiss on her cheek, Elizabeth cheered and applauded.

Once the cause and effect was established, Gimme Lao wised up. He would rush to the tart platter and pick one that he did not fancy to offer Madeline. While Madeline was distracted and Elizabeth fooled, he would return to collect the one with the strawberry topping he wanted for himself. The strategy was simple and effective.

Sometimes, when Elizabeth annoyed him by capping his fun, he would run across to Madeline and bite her on the shoulder. The ruckus of Madeline bawling, Elizabeth picking her up to cuddle and soothe, Madeline screaming for her father, the captain embracing the crying child and Elizabeth not letting go and leaning herself into the captain's embrace tickled him. Gimme Lao learned from experience that Elizabeth would chide, but not physically punish him, when the captain was around. Only in the captain's absence would Elizabeth pinch or slap him.

Gimme Lao liked the captain, if only because Elizabeth paid him less attention when the captain was around. She would play the piano for the captain and laugh heartily when he applauded at the end of the performance. Then she began to insist that the captain sit down so she could lean over his shoulder to teach him a tune. Sometimes they would sit side by side and attempt a duet. When the captain fumbled, a giggling Elizabeth would slap his arm and grab his palms to position them. Soon, Gimme Lao witnessed the captain retaliating by grabbing Elizabeth on the waist and tickling her till she turned blue. And then suddenly, they stopped playing the piano. They would disappear for long stretches on Sunday mornings and leave Gimme Lao and Madeline to their own devices.

For the several months that followed, Gimme Lao benefited from the perpetual cheerfulness that seemed to enwrap Elizabeth. She bought him toys of all shapes and make from the night market; a blue rubber float outlined like a flattened duck, a wooden rocking horse with a pink mane, a bolster in the shape of a giraffe with orange square dots, and a plastic drinking cup sculpted like a kangaroo with a gigantic pouch. Gimme Lao's mother eventually had to urge Elizabeth to stop.

She was pampering her boy unnecessarily.

Elizabeth did eventually stop. Not because the mother urged her to, but because her cheerfulness came to an abrupt end.

Gimme Lao had no inkling that fateful Sunday morning when the door down the hall unlocked itself softly, that his play dates with Madeline were officially over. Both of them looked up, startled, to see Madeline's mother step in, signal them to be quiet and tiptoe down the passageway. Pandemonium erupted almost instantly. The opening shrieks and screams were followed by an interminable stream of wrangling, until Elizabeth finally emerged from the bedroom in shameful tears. She grabbed Gimme Lao and her handbag and stumbled out the door. The last thing Gimme Lao remembered was a glimpse of the tart with the strawberry topping, sitting untouched on the platter because he was saving it for later.

Gimme Lao noticed that Elizabeth began to spend more and more time with his mother. She would let herself in through the door shortly after dinner, and Gimme Lao's father would want to bring Gimme Lao for a stroll around the night market. Upon their return, they sometimes heard tiny sobs emerging from the bedroom. It would be close to midnight when Elizabeth emerged, her eyes often puffy and swollen.

At one point, Gimme Lao's father bought a roll-up mattress and told Gimme Lao that the two of them would have to sleep in the living room for a while. Elizabeth would be returning from the hospital and recuperating in the bedroom. When Gimme Lao asked if Elizabeth was ill, Gimme Lao's father said no. She had simply made a mistake and needed the doctor at the hospital to help remove the mistake. That was also the reason Elizabeth wasn't sleeping next door. Grandma Toh was furious with her, and the two should not see too much of each other for the time being.

Even Gimme Lao could tell that Grandma Toh was in a consistently foul mood. He did not quite understand the tirade Grandma Toh launched in the presence of Elizabeth, nor her bemoaning in the company of Aunty Seah. He kept hearing the term 'Red-Haired Ape' mentioned repeatedly and so learnt to mumble it under his breath until he mastered the intonation and started spitting it out vehemently in the manner of Grandma Toh. Aunty Seah shushed him fiercely. When he did not stop, Grandma Toh grabbed him by the arm and pinched him hard with the sharp end of her nails. Through the confusion of his howling and weeping, he thought he heard Grandma Toh threaten to drown him in the water barrel along with the blue-eyed baby Elizabeth was carrying.

THREE

When Gimme Lao was six, he fell in love with his kindergarten teacher. Her name was Foo Swee Peng, and she told the entire class she thought Gimme was the best student she had ever taught. Before the year was over, Miss Foo secretly wished she hadn't.

It all started when a nursing officer from the Ministry of Health came down to the kindergarten to conduct an outreach programme. The children were made to sit on the straw mat in front of a chalkboard, and all were allowed to pick a toothbrush of their choice from a mug that was being passed around. Gimme Lao picked an orange one.

"Children, a show of hands please. How many of you brush your teeth at home on a daily basis?"

Of the 26 students in the class, six hands sprouted upwards. Gimme Lao was one of the six.

"Very good," the nursing officer said. "I shall now invite these six children to do a demonstration."

Miss Foo and the nursing officer lined up the six children in a row and swivelled them to face the crowd. Of the six, a girl in a ponytail found the 20 pairs of eyes staring up at her too intimidating and grimaced as though she was about to cry. Miss Foo quickly approached to allay her fear. In her effort to hold back her tears, the girl lost control of her bladder and her pee streamed down her legs. The cleaning lady had to be summoned to bring the bundle of frayed nerves to the toilet to salvage what remained of her pride.

"Next, I am going to pass this tube of Colgate toothpaste around and you will show your friends how to squeeze a little bit of it onto your toothbrush. Can you do that for me?"

As it turned out, two of the five could not. Apparently their mothers took charge of the squeezing procedure back home. The pair of discredited demonstrators were asked to join the 20 uninitiated children on the straw mat.

"Now we shall watch how the three of them get ready to brush their teeth." The nursing officer beamed.

Both Gimme Lao and the girl next to him managed to dispense the requisite glob of toothpaste onto the bristles. The last boy, however, squeezed too hard and the toothpaste streamed down onto the floor. The audience broke out into a paroxysm of giggles.

"I use Darkie toothpaste at home," the boy proclaimed loudly, in defence of his botched demonstration.

"It doesn't matter," the nursing officer said. "You need to control your strength so that you do not squeeze too hard. Look how the other two did it."

The Darkie user felt insulted and crossed his arms to adopt a sulking posture. Unfortunately, the tube of Colgate toothpaste was pinned between his arm and his chest and the content squirted out onto his shirt. Half of the audience spotted it and broke out into riotous laughter. The other half was infected and laughed too, despite not knowing what exactly it was that they were laughing about. Miss Foo had to summon the cleaning lady again to execute damage containment.

"Tell the class your names," the nursing officer prompted the two who remained standing. Gimme Lao thus came to be introduced to Janice Ong, his only worthy opponent in the class of dentally challenged children.

"Now Janice and Gimme will demonstrate the correct method of brushing their teeth," the nursing officer announced.

Gimme Lao kept his eyes on Janice, while Janice kept her eyes on the audience. Both of them started brushing on the front-facing surface. When Gimme Lao moved on to the back of the teeth, Janice was still rotating her bristles in the front. By the time Gimme Lao was brushing horizontally across the chewing surface of his molars, he knew he was teeth-brushing champion. Janice Ong never moved beyond the front.

The nursing officer made the pair rinse their mouths and promoted Gimme Lao to class monitor for the upcoming public health programme. The children were issued a plastic mug each, and the brushing of teeth would become a daily class routine. Janice Ong was tasked to assist Gimme Lao as his deputy.

Gimme Lao couldn't wait to get to school every morning. After Miss Foo led them through the Singapore national anthem, he would station himself at the cabinet and distribute the mugs and toothbrushes to the children. Janice Ong then led them to the toilet in a wiggly line. After the first dozen took up their positions in front of the elongated trough, Gimme and Janice would start from opposite ends and assist to dispense the requisite glob of toothpaste onto the bristles of the multicoloured toothbrushes. Both would supervise the collective brushing and rinsing and then repeat the process with the second lineup of children. Only when everyone was done would Gimme and Janice brush their own teeth.

Miss Foo was impressed with Gimme Lao. Unlike Janice Ong, who stood and watched and made no comments even when some of the children did it the wrong way, Gimme Lao was hawk-like in the standards of precision he demanded. If a child thought he could get away with one or two cursory swipes across the back of the teeth, Gimme Lao made him do it again. If a pair giggled and teased one another with their mouths full of foam, Gimme Lao shushed them harshly. If they ignored him, Gimme would reposition the two in the lineup so that they would be separated by other serious tooth brushers. Miss Foo did not have to lift a finger to discipline the rowdy children.

When the same nursing officer came down two months later to promote a second health campaign, Miss Foo did not hesitate to reappoint Gimme Lao as the class monitor. She told the nursing officer, in front of all the children, that she thought Gimme Lao was the best student she had ever taught. That was the moment Gimme Lao fell in love with Miss Foo Swee Peng. It became clear to him that he was right when he demanded proper behaviour from the other children. He must not fail Miss Foo's expectations.

The nursing officer showed them several posters to illustrate where germs lurked. The children strained their necks and gaped. They had not known that purple and green discs with malicious eyes and evil grins danced on toilet flush handles and doorknobs. The nursing officer explained that if people who prepared food did not have the habit of washing their hands after using the toilet, these germs would hitch a convenient ride onto the food and into the victim's stomach. That was how people fell ill.

What the nursing officer wanted the children to do was to wash their hands regularly. Gimme Lao, as the reappointed monitor, would assist Miss Foo and help the class cultivate the habit.

His new duty required Gimme Lao to station himself at the washing trough after the collective toilet break to supervise the washing of hands. By the third day, he came up to Miss Foo wearing a look of serious concern and declared that there appeared to be a problem.

"When Janice flushed the toilet, the germs got onto her hands," Gimme Lao explained to Miss Foo. "When she turned on the tap, some of the germs got onto the tap. After she washed the germs off her hands, she turned off the tap. Wouldn't the germs on the tap then get onto her hands again?"

Miss Foo stared at her star student with wonderment. She now believed there was no limit to how far this boy could go in life! She sat down with Gimme and devised a solution. It was eventually decided that Gimme would take on the added duty to turn off the taps for all the children. When it came time for Gimme himself to wash his hands, Miss Foo would do the honour of turning off the tap with her hand wrapped in her handkerchief. The problem was thus solved.

Two months later, the nursing officer visited again. This time round, she brought along posters depicting a leaking tap and explained that it was important not to waste water. Singapore did not have enough water for its people to drink and use. The country was dependent on its neighbour, Malaysia, to supply water. This was why it was launching a national campaign to save water. Every precious drop must be fully utilised.

Miss Foo's new instruction for the longest serving class monitor was to ensure that all taps at the washing trough were securely turned off. But Gimme Lao again surprised her. After studying the washing pattern for three days, Gimme Lao approached Miss Foo and proclaimed that they were wasting too much water. All the children must use only one tap.

"But that would not change the volume of water used," Miss Foo explained patiently. "It would simply mean the class would take much, much longer to finish washing their hands."

Gimme Lao shook his head and asked to do a demonstration. He made Janice Ong pretend to wash her hands under an imaginary tap. Gimme himself used an invisible bar of soap to lather his hands, then placed them directly under Janice's pair of hands. He then nudged Janice out of the picture, moved his hands higher up, continued the washing motion and asked a third child to place his supposedly lathered hands underneath his. Miss Foo's eyes almost popped out of their sockets.

The following week, a reporter from the tabloids was invited to visit the kindergarten. Miss Foo was proud to showcase an innovative approach to saving water. The children lined up in three columns in front of the washing trough. They had one week to practise and were generally confident when they demonstrated the tiered method of sequential hand washing pioneered by Gimme Lao. The reporter was highly impressed.

When the article appeared in the tabloids, Gimme Lao's parents and their neighbours went wild. His father bought five copies of the tabloids, four of which he allowed the neighbours to circulate. The last copy he wrapped in plastic and sealed airtight using Scotch tape. He intended it to become part of the family treasure to pass on to future generations. Gimme Lao's mother asked Aunty Seah for some discarded fabric from the factory she worked in. She copied the tagline from the campaign poster so that she could embroider the words 'Water is precious. Save every drop' onto a new cotton blanket she was going to sew for Gimme. Unfortunately, Gimme Lao's mother did not speak or write English, and her scribbled letterings on a piece of paper left much to be desired. The initial embroidery read 'Wateri spreious. Saveery drop'. Elizabeth from next door had to make her remove the stitches and do it again.

Grandma Toh was especially proud of Gimme Lao. She hijacked one of four copies of the tabloids in circulation and toted it on her round of the neighbourhood gossip circuit. She told the provision shop owner that Gimme must have benefitted from all the afternoons keeping her company while she listened to radio soap operas. There was so much life wisdom for the picking in storytelling. She shared her suspicions with the fishmonger that early exposure as a toddler to the stimulation of toasted sambal chilli might even have triggered brain development in the child. It paralleled the theory that pregnant women listening to soft music awakened the cognitive intelligence of their unborn baby. By the time she reached the incense shop seven blocks away, Grandma Toh had elevated herself to become a talent developer extraordinaire of gifted children.

Barber Bay asked to be given a copy of the tabloid so that he could cut it out and paste it onto the space between two of the mirrors in the barbershop. He positioned it directly underneath an old newspaper clipping of Pastor Clarence giving a sermon in church. In that article, Pastor Clarence was featured as an oddity because he was a Caucasian pastor who spoke good Hokkien. When a regular customer remarked that the eyesore of a yellowing clipping ought to be taken down and retired to the dustbin, Barber Bay smiled wryly but said nothing. Nobody else but Barber Bay could spot it—a tiny dot over the pastor's right shoulder, the back view of Elizabeth playing the piano.

Gimme Lao experienced the spoils of fame for the first time. At the night market, the toy hawker recognised him and allowed him to pick one of the matchbox collectibles for free. Gimme Lao felt the tingling of excitement as he examined the extensive range of tiny automobiles neatly packed in four-inch boxes and finally picked a red truck sitting on an imposing set of military tank wheels. Neither the toy hawker nor Gimme Lao's parents could figure out the strange configuration. Gimme Lao's father urged him to pick some other recognisable automobile, but Gimme Lao shook his head determinedly. He didn't know what it was, but he knew he wanted it.

The mystery was solved the following Sunday when Elizabeth brought him to the MPH bookstore along Stamford Road and guided him through a *Children's Encyclopaedia of Automobiles* as thick as a fist. Gimme Lao had picked a Snow Trac for himself. For an entire hour, Gimme sat on the carpeted floor and flipped through the pages, enthralled. There were more than a hundred pictures depicting strange automobiles set against alien backdrops of snow, boulders and rivers. When Elizabeth returned from the Romance section to pick him up, Gimme was reluctant to go. Elizabeth decided to give them another half an hour to indulge. An hour soon passed. When Elizabeth eventually conceded that the child's love for automobiles and their steely mechanics far exceeded her love for gorgeous men and their steely muscles on book covers, she decided to buy him a gift. Thus Gimme Lao returned home triumphant, with the *Children's Encyclopaedia of Automobiles* that was to keep him entertained for many weeks to come.

Back in the kindergarten, Gimme Lao encountered a problem. He had brought along his Snow Trac in his school bag and was itching to show it to his friends. Problem was, Gimme Lao had no friends. None of the children liked him. Kindergarten life was generally fun except for the segments Gimme Lao took charge of. On their scheduled toilet breaks, Gimme Lao desired a straight line-up marching to the washroom. Whenever the line wiggled, Gimme Lao barked at them. If the recalcitrants ignored him, Gimme Lao would rush forward and stomp on their shoes. At the washing trough, the mischievous among the children would giggle as they engaged in stealthy flicks of water to catch one another unaware. When that happened, Gimme Lao would step forward to switch off the tap, stare down the child's dwindling grin and supervise as the child learned to take the washing of hands seriously. Gimme Lao had no patience for buffoonery.

Miss Foo Swee Peng found herself caught in a dilemma. She was aware that her star student adored her and performed his monitor duties as a tribute to her. On her part, she had rewarded him with public commendations and private pats on the back. In retrospect, she realised that these acknowledgements had probably reinforced his drive to overdeliver. By the time the standards of discipline he demanded had calcified to a near-military benchmark, it was too late for her to interfere without hurting his feelings. Miss Foo simply averted her eyes and prayed that no child would get hurt.

When Gimme Lao realised that none of the children would be interested to hear him discuss his Snow Trac, he approached Miss Foo instead. Once again, Miss Foo was impressed. It had never crossed her mind to implement a Show and Tell module, believing it was beyond the capacity of kindergarten children. But she was willing to give it a try for her star student.

The next day, Gimme Lao was ready to impress the class. He brought along his *Children's Encyclopaedia of Automobiles* and his matchbox collectible Snow Trac. He explained how a very smart man in a snow country wanted to go fishing in winter and so designed and built a truck that ran on tracked wheels, like those of a tank. And because the tracked wheels ran so well over soft snow, it was made and sold to many other snow countries. Subsequently, it was discovered that the tracked wheels also ran well over sand, so it was made and sold to sand countries as well. Eventually, soldiers realised that Snow Tracs were lighter than tanks and they could operate a machine gun on top. So they also used it in war countries. Unfortunately, Singapore was a country with no snow, no sand and no war, which meant the class would never get to see a real Snow Trac. The end.

Miss Foo asked if anyone had any questions for Gimme Lao. No one did. She then led the class through an appreciative round of applause and thanked Gimme Lao for sharing his knowledge. She was about to switch back to the original curriculum, when Gimme Lao asked when he could next present. There were 117 types of vehicles featured in the *Children's Encyclopaedia of Automobiles*, and he could do one a day.

Miss Foo secretly sighed. She glanced at the other 25 children and asked with despondence if anyone would like to have a go at Show and Tell next week. None would. Miss Foo ignored Gimme's outstretched hand and turned to ask Janice Ong if she had any hobbies, or pets, or favourite cartoon programmes on television or anything at all worth presenting. Mercifully, Janice Ong kept some goldfish in an aquarium at home. It was settled then. The children would all learn about goldfish the following week.

The class was delighted when Janice Ong's mother arranged for their domestic help to bring along a pair of goldfish in a portable plastic tank. Miss Foo allowed the children to approach the exhibit in groups of five to examine it at close range. After everyone had a chance to gawk and giggle, Miss Foo signalled for Janice Ong to begin.

Janice Ong had six goldfish. They all lived happily in a big fish tank. Sometimes, Janice Ong's father lifted her onto a bar stool so that she could break crumbs from a loaf of bread to feed the goldfish. When the water became murky, Janice Ong's father would order the domestic help to clean the aquarium. Janice herself would transport the goldfish one by one into a pail of water using a net. After the aquarium was clean again, Janice reintroduced the goldfish and they swam happily in the new, fresh water. The end.

When Miss Foo invited questions from the audience, Gimme Lao's hand shot up. "Why are goldfishes called goldfishes?"

Several hands shot up from among the audience in a frenzied attempt to steal the question from Janice Ong. The once-disgraced Darkie user flouted the rules by shouting out the answer before Miss Foo had time to pick anyone. "Because they are golden in colour!"

"That is not true," Gimme Lao insisted. "There is a stall at the night market that sells aquarium fishes, and they have goldfishes in black."

Some of the audience began to giggle at the idea of a black goldfish. The Darkie user had an epiphany and shouted, "Maybe it is an Indian goldfish!" That triggered riotous laughter from the rest of the class. Janice Ong interpreted it as a favourable reception of her presentation and beamed happily.

"Actually, I do remember seeing some goldfish in black too." Miss Foo waited till the class calmed down before she did her sharing. "My guess is all goldfish were once golden in colour. But after hundreds of years, some of them take on a different colour. They are like roses. There are red roses, yellow roses, white roses, but all are called roses."

None of the children could understand the mysterious link

between goldfish and roses, but decided collectively to give their teacher the benefit of the doubt and did not ask her to clarify. Gimme Lao however directed a second question at Janice Ong. "Where do goldfishes come from?"

Janice Ong quickly recalled a picture book she owned that showed many different types of fish coexisting in a very big blue sea. Without hesitation, she ventured to educate Gimme Lao, "Goldfishes come from the sea."

Miss Foo bit her lip and attempted to soften the blow, "Actually, goldfish do not come from the sea. Only salt-water fish live in the sea. Goldfish are fresh-water fish, so they can only live in lakes and ponds."

Some of the audience snickered. Janice Ong hung her head in shame. Gimme Lao raised his hand to ask a third question but Miss Foo announced abruptly that the presentation was over and that everyone should give Janice Ong a round of applause for a good presentation.

"But she didn't give a good presentation," Gimme Lao protested. "She only answered one question and she gave a wrong answer."

The Darkie user was struck by another bolt of inspiration and started chanting very loudly, "Janice Ong. Always wrong. Janice Ong. Always wrong..." The other children burst out laughing and quickly joined in the chant. Horrified, Miss Foo moved in and wrapped her arms around Janice Ong to protect the poor girl from the lynch mob. The domestic help standing at the back of the classroom gasped, but it was too late to warn Miss Foo. She could only watch helplessly as Janice Ong, as always when she became upset, grabbed the nearest limb and bit hard. Miss Foo shrieked in pain and flung her arm back, inadvertently upsetting the portable plastic tank and sending the pair of goldfish flying out of their fresh-water abode onto the straw mat laid out on the floor.

The children started screaming and hopping around madly. The Darkie user valorously approached the floundering pair of goldfish and tried to kick them back into the tank. His sweeping foot caught one on the third attempt and sent it flying in an arc towards Miss Foo, who shrieked and instinctively tried to hop out of the way. Unfortunately, the goldfish landed and flipped itself right under one of her heels. The collective shriek that followed was so shrill, the cleaning lady heard it all the way at the back of the building and thought to herself that Miss Foo really ought to tone down the games for the children.

The same evening, when Gimme Lao's father asked about his day in school, Gimme crinkled his nose and reported that Janice Ong did not do her homework well. If she did, she would have answered all the questions correctly, no one would be screaming and hopping about, and her goldfish would still be alive.

Janice Ong did not turn up for school for the next two days. The class, however, spotted her domestic help, who arrived with an important-looking man in a dark suit and waited outside the classroom while the man held a prolonged conversation with Miss Foo. The children did not understand terms like 'traumatised' and 'scarred', but they caught and understood 'crying all night'. They also observed that Miss Foo looked pallid and kept apologising. Before the visitors left, Gimme Lao thought he saw the domestic help point her finger at him surreptitiously. He also thought the man threw him a parting glare that was none too friendly.

The following week, the children were pleasantly surprised when Miss Foo announced that the class was going on an excursion. All of them were given a cap and a plastic water bottle with a strap they could sling over their shoulders. On the bus journey, Miss Foo explained that they were going to visit Van Kleef Aquarium, where they would get to see myriad marine creatures. She also highlighted that the excursion was made possible by the generosity of Janice Ong's father, who had sponsored the aquarium entrance tickets, the bus, the caps as well as the water bottles.

Janice Ong was waiting for the class at the entrance to the aquarium with her mother. She was initially shy, but the children had practised their collective greeting on the bus, and upon Miss Foo's signal, waved their hands and shouted merrily, "Good afternoon Janice, we missed you!" Janice grinned with delight and was happy to rejoin her class.

The Van Kleef Aquarium was an amazing place. The children gawked at a gigantic clay sculpture over the entrance, that of a blue turtle carrying a yellow seahorse and an intertwined pair of fish on its back. Once they streamed past the hanging curtains, they entered the chilled interior of what resembled a stone cave. Along the walls were huge tanks illuminated from within, where marine creatures of all shapes and sizes swam languorously. There were fish that sat unmoving like brown rocks, seahorses with kangaroo pouches that entwined their tails gracefully with swaying stems, sea snakes that wiggled from one end of the tank to the other and undulating jellyfish so thin the children could almost see through them. What took their breaths away was the crocodile that squatted on a rock and bared its teeth in a menacing snarl. Some of the more imaginative children could even hear their own bones crunch and snap.

When the children were assembled and waiting for the bus, Miss Foo made them thank Janice's mother, Mrs Ong, collectively. Mrs Ong beamed and told the children that Janice had a wading pool and a trampoline in her garden, and that she had given Janice permission to invite some of the classmates over for play dates. Especially well-behaved children who were nice to her. In time to come, Janice's father might even organise another outing to someplace interesting. The brand new Jurong Bird Park that had just opened in January, for instance. Wouldn't the children like to visit the largest aviary in the whole wide world?

Back in the kindergarten, Miss Foo implemented some changes. Gimme Lao, the longest serving class monitor, would be relieved of his duties. Instead, monitor duties would be divvied up and rotated on a daily basis. On any given day, an appointed monitor would be tasked to distribute mugs and toothbrushes, a second monitor dispense toothpaste, a third monitor turn off the taps and yet a fourth ensure all toilets were flushed. Every single child, regardless of capability or inclination, would get his turn to perform monitor duty.

Gimme Lao could not explain the sense of loss he felt. He

watched miserably as lenient monitors permitted foolery and laughter during teeth brushing sessions. He bit his tongue when he spotted giggling boys cross swords using their arcs of urine. He bristled with irritation when mugs were returned to the cabinet in nothing that resembled tidy rows. But worst of all was the wait.

Every child was waiting for an invitation from Janice Ong.

The invitation came every Wednesday. Janice Ong picked three or four at a time. If their parents agreed, her father would dispatch his driver to ferry them after class on Friday to his house which was, according to the first few batches invited, almost as huge as the Van Kleef Aquarium. Not only was there a wading pool and trampoline as promised, there were dogs! A Pekingese that was short and dumb, and a Golden Retriever that was tall and smart. When the children changed into their swimming costumes and jumped into the wading pool, the Golden Retriever would hop in and burrow his muzzle into the children's crotches, tickling them into bursts of guffaws. The Pekingese would waddle near and look around in a puzzled way for invisible raindrops when the children teased it with flicks of water. Mrs Ong arranged for the domestic help to clean the aquarium on Fridays so that Janice's guests could take turns to scoop out the goldfish with the tiny net. There would be ice cream served at three and a selection of board games in the playroom followed. By five, Mrs Ong would pack the children into the car and dispatch them home right up to their doorsteps. All the children who went asked to go again.

Gimme Lao kept count. As the weeks went by, the pool of

children who were not invited shrunk. Some of those who were invited became bitterly disappointed when their parents refused to grant permission. They could only watch with envy as Janice transferred their invitations to repeat guests who were blessed with benign and understanding parents. Eventually, only two were left: Gimme Lao and Mei Mei, the girl who missed Gimme's inaugural demonstration of teeth brushing because she had been brought to the washroom to clean up after peeing in her panties.

Janice Ong did not hold any grievances against Mei Mei. She had simply forgotten about her. Mei Mei's mother did not braid her hair and pin on hairclips decorated with yellow butterflies or red strawberries. Mei Mei kept quiet and did not raise her hand like the others when Miss Foo threw the class a question. In any game they played, Mei Mei preferred to stand on the sidelines and watch, while the rest went berserk on the play mat. In other words, there was no reason for the children to pay her any attention at all.

Miss Foo, too, noticed that the pair had been left out. So when one of the invited boys returned on Thursday with a sour face and announced that his parents wouldn't let him go because they had a family gathering, Miss Foo gently reminded Janice Ong that Gimme Lao and Mei Mei had yet to be invited. Janice Ong took one apprehensive glance at Gimme Lao and immediately handed Mei Mei the invitation card. Gimme Lao bit his lip hard to hide the quiver.

Gimme Lao's mother was quick to notice that the boy was not himself at dinner. He held his chopsticks like an ice pick and poked at his favourite barbequed pork slices with disinterest. When she asked him about his day at school, she was alarmed to see him shake his head with melancholy. She kept pressing, until Gimme finally relented and spilled the beans. He was no more the star student in class. Miss Foo had relieved him of all his earlier duties. The other children snickered and said horrible things about him behind his back. They said he was too arrogant and stringent as a monitor. They even came up with a nickname for him—Pretend Teacher. Worst of all, Janice Ong would not extend the play date invitation to him. He had heard so many magical accounts from the other children and really wanted to go!

Gimme Lao's mother felt her heart shatter. She had simply assumed that her boy was both the star student and the adored role model of a monitor in class. It did not cross her mind that petty jealousy existed among kindergarten students too. When she reported for work at the pharmacy the next day, she asked to take the afternoon off. She was going to surprise Gimme by turning up unannounced and whisking him off downtown for ice cream and a visit to his favourite MPH bookstore. She was even prepared to buy him another one of those children's encyclopaedias he seemed to love so much.

There were still 10 more minutes before the dismissal bell rang when Gimme Lao's mother arrived. She stood outside the classroom and watched as Miss Foo made her final announcements. Three little girls were summoned to the front and asked to lay out the contents of their school bags for inspection. When Gimme Lao's mother spotted the tiny swimming costumes, she understood that these were Janice Ong's invited guests for the week.

Miss Foo was satisfied with the layout and asked the girls if they were excited. Mei Mei watched with a blank expression as the other two girls nodded vigorously. Both started chatting excitedly about their last visit, and how much they enjoyed the wading pool and the Golden Retriever doing the hilarious nose shovel. Miss Foo crinkled her nose and asked what exactly did they mean by the term 'nose shovel'. The entire class erupted into a brouhaha trying to explain to the uninformed teacher what the girls were referring to. Miss Foo had to shout for the class to silence itself before she turned to the two girls and suggested they do a demonstration.

The first girl was quick as she bundled her fists into a make-believe muzzle and announced that she was going to play the Golden Retriever. The second girl screamed and started running round the table while the fisted muzzle chased after her. The children burst out into riotous laughter. Miss Foo was still confused and asked at the top of her voice what did it all mean. The first girl suddenly decided that the stationary Mei Mei would make a better target and so turned abruptly and jammed her fisted muzzle into Mei Mei's crotch. Mei Mei let out a shrill shriek of terror. The first girl was delighted at the response and continued to imitate the Golden Retriever's persistency as she intensified the assault. By the time Miss Foo physically intervened and pulled the enthusiastic pantomimist away, Mei Mei was wailing hysterically and had once again wetted her panties.

The pandemonium took a while to die down. By the time Mei

Mei was led away by the cleaning lady and the class was quiet again, several parents had arrived to pick up their children. Miss Foo spotted Janice Ong's mother and quickly explained that there had been an accident and thus one of the girls on the guest list would not be going. Mrs Ong beamed and said it was quite all right and turned to ask the rest of the children if anyone would like to take her place. Several hands shot up. Gimme Lao was desperate as he jumped onto his feet and shouted at the top of his voice, "Take me! Please! I really want to go!"

Mrs Ong was tickled by Gimme Lao's display of desperation and asked with a smile if his parent was around to give approval. Gimme Lao pointed at his mother, who waved amiably and nodded to indicate her consent. Mrs Ong was about to extend the invitation when Janice Ong tugged at her hemline and whispered softly. Mrs Ong bent down to hear her daughter out. When she next straightened up, there was a cold look of dismissal on her countenance. In a clear voice so everyone could hear, she remarked, "So, this is that very rude boy who made fun of you. Why would we want to invite him, indeed? We shall only invite your friends."

Miss Foo was alarmed and decided she had better intervene before the situation got ugly. She chuckled dryly and told Mrs Ong that squabbles between children were quite common and really shouldn't be taken too seriously. Mrs Ong arched her brow and turned to ask her daughter what were the exact words Gimme Lao used when he teased her. Janice Ong hung her head and replied very softly, "Janice Ong. Always wrong."

Miss Foo and Gimme Lao quickly recovered from their

surprise and wasted no time redressing the accusation. Miss Foo readily vouched for Gimme Lao that he made no such comment. Gimme Lao simply pointed a finger at the Darkie user.

Mrs Ong was slightly perplexed as she recognised the Darkie user from the play date two weeks ago. Janice Ong herself was confused. After all, memories of the episode of major embarrassment several weeks ago had begun to recede. She was pretty certain that Gimme Lao was the one who triggered the onslaught of mass teasing, but couldn't say for sure if he contributed that horrible rhyming tease. Unable to ascertain, Janice Ong looked up at her mother for help.

If only Gimme Lao's mother could have given Janice Ong's mother a moment to consider, things might have developed differently. But she didn't. She was quick to grasp that her son had been wrongly accused, and an instantaneous fury engulfed her. She stepped forward and spoke to Mrs Ong in a severe tone, in Mandarin, "Do you know my son felt miserable because your daughter invited everybody but him for the play date? And now she is accusing him of something he did not do. You really ought to teach your daughter better behaviour!"

The burning flush on Mrs Ong's face was indication that she understood the outburst coming from Gimme Lao's mother, but for some reason she turned to Miss Foo and asked haughtily, still speaking in English, "Who is this lady? Can you tell her that I do not tolerate rudeness from anyone?"

Before Miss Foo could respond, Gimme Lao's mother cut in again. "I may not understand every English word you say, but I understand your attitude. And now I am beginning to understand how your daughter got to behave so badly. Children copy their parents. Period."

Miss Foo trembled as the two mothers exchanged looks of daggers. She had been trained as an educator to handle and counsel children if they fought. Her training did not prepare her for the current scenario. Fortunately, Mrs Ong decided to stick to her original strategy of non-direct confrontation and turned to address Miss Foo again.

"My husband was generous enough to sponsor a school excursion to the Van Kleef Aquarium. I myself opened up my house to host play dates for the children. And what do I get in return? Disrespect and insults from a fellow parent. Do you think this is fair, Miss Foo?"

Miss Foo hunched herself and mumbled an apology. She said she was sorry for what was happening but she was sure the matter could be amicably resolved by all parties involved.

Mrs Ong arched her brow and said, "I accept your apology. I would like an apology from the other parent too. Otherwise, I will advise my husband not to go ahead with the school excursion to Jurong Bird Park he was thinking of sponsoring for the year-end holidays. I myself will also put an end to the weekly play dates."

The entire class understood the terms and gasped. Some of the girls began to whimper. The Darkie user glared at Gimme Lao and hissed fiercely, "This is all your mother's fault!" All the children who heard it turned and focused their collective glares of hatred on Gimme Lao. His cheeks burning, Gimme Lao stood up and walked towards his mother. There was an ambivalent look in his eyes as he asked his mother in a whispery voice, "Do you want to apologise?"

Gimme Lao's mother's eyes were red with anger, but her tone was firm and decisive when she said, "No, we should not apologise." Gimme Lao bit his lip and nodded in silence. There was a flash of understanding between mother and son as they held hands and strolled out of the classroom. They could hear muffled comments and discussions behind their backs and knew the remarks would not be friendly. But it didn't matter. What mattered was that they stood their ground.

The two of them took a bus down to Cold Storage Milk Bar at Orchard Road and had ice cream. They shared a banana split, taking turns to scoop from the three balls of vanilla, chocolate and strawberry flavours. Lost in their respective thoughts, neither spoke. Afterwards, they strolled over to the MPH bookstore at Stamford Road. Gimme Lao found a *Children's Encyclopaedia of Birds* and spent an hour browsing through melancholically. When Gimme Lao's mother asked if that was the book he wanted, Gimme nodded. He would have to be content with the illustrations now that there would not be any school excursion to the Jurong Bird Park. Not quite the real thing, but they would have to do.

Gimme Lao's mother saw her boy looking downcast and fury surged in her chest again. This time, the anger was no longer directed at the snobbish woman who thought she could dictate which child would get to have fun and which child would not. Truth was, she could. That woman could effectively ostracise her boy and deprive him of what he craved for. And Gimme

Lao's mother was furious that she herself was unable to protect her child from the pain and the hurt.

That very moment, Gimme Lao's mother made a momentous decision. She would find the money to sponsor the school excursion to Jurong Bird Park herself.

Gimme Lao's mother was under no illusion about their financial standing. Her husband worked as a clerk in an insurance company and brought home a fixed pay of 180 dollars a month. She herself earned 120 dollars a month at the pharmacy. They could afford the house mortgage, but not a car. They could bring their boy for a day trip to the zoo, but an overseas holiday was out of the question. To pay for entrance tickets for 26 children and a teacher to the Jurong Bird Park, hire a bus to ferry them to and fro and possibly buy them lunch, could easily add up to their combined take-home pay for the month. There was no way she was going to dip into the family savings.

The money would have to be additional earnings.

Three days later, Gimme Lao's mother deposited Gimme at Grandma Toh's place after dinner. Her husband was surprised to see her putting on lipstick.

"Where are you going?" he asked, while getting ready to leave for his weekly session of Chinese chess. Despite the fact that he wasn't very good at it, Gimme Lao's father was a fanatic. When they first got married, he engaged his wife in the game two to three nights a week. Over time Gimme Lao's mother lost interest; her husband's moves were tediously slow and his strategies embarrassingly transparent. She was glad when he met a fellow chess enthusiast of similar calibre at his workplace, a sales manager called Harrison Pua who lived six bus stops away. The pair had stuck to their weekly matches for several years now.

"I need to talk to Harrison," she remarked. "I know he is constantly recruiting new sales staff."

"But we have discussed this before," Gimme Lao's father was unable to hide the whine in his voice. "I can't do sales. I know Harrison says anybody can be trained but…I am just not ready."

"I am."

Harrison Pua was indeed on the constant lookout for new talent, and he immediately spotted the steely resolve in the woman's eyes. Although Harrison Pua had occasionally proposed Gimme Lao's father join his sales team, it had never progressed beyond a mere suggestion. Harrison knew his chess mate well. The man was gentle and amiable, but lacked drive. The only time he could summon aggression was in their games of Chinese chess.

The wife was a different creature altogether. When Harrison explained that it took six weeks to undergo training and sit for the certification examination, the woman frowned and asked why should it take so long.

Harrison veiled his grin with a look of concern as he enquired cautiously, "Are you in urgent need of money? I can always give you a loan first, to tide things over."

"I need money to organise a school excursion for my son." Gimme Lao's mother saw the look of worry on her husband's face and decided to be frank about her intentions. "Thank you for your offer, but I want to do this myself. Just sign me up for the training, Harrison."

Two months later, Barber Bay was surprised to see Gimme Lao's mother walk into his shop in the evening. He allowed the unfolded razor to laze against a lathered chin as he gave her a visual frisk and tried to determine what it was that looked unfamiliar. It wasn't the wavy perm in her hair, nor the bold crimson on her lips, although he was seeing these for the first time. It was the look in her eyes. There was a focused shine in them.

If her unannounced visit merely surprised him, her behaviour shocked him. After greeting him amicably, Gimme Lao's mother sat on an adjacent chair and introduced herself to the customer whose chin he was shaving. For the remaining 20 minutes while the man was trapped, Gimme Lao's mother chatted about the unpredictability of life, discussed the responsibility of a man to his family, emphasised the importance of life insurance coverage and asked for an appointment to show the man what her company had to offer. Sustained by a tiny flask of herbal chrysanthemum tea she brought herself, Gimme Lao's mother engaged the next five customers while they remained immobilised in the barber chair. By the time the last customer left, she had secured two follow-up appointments for herself.

One month later, Gimme Lao's mother received her first commission cheque from the insurance company. The next day, Gimme Lao was proud to submit a note to Miss Foo Swee Peng. The note stated that his mother would be glad to sponsor a school excursion to Jurong Bird Park for the entire class.

Including Janice Ong.

FOUR

WHEN GIMME LAO was 11, his mother showed him her new name card. In the delicate cursive of Apple Chancery font, the card pronounced her to be Mary Lao, Sales Manager of the Overseas Assurance Company. She also told him that she was well on her way to qualify for the coveted Million Dollar Round Table industry award.

The seven sales agents recruited by Mary Lao knew her story well. It all started with a rude awakening, when the child she loved was made miserable because she as a parent did not wield as much power and influence as the next parent. She was infuriated with herself when she realised she had been lazy with her calling as a mother. It was a jungle out there, and she had picked a role as tame as a mouse deer. As a result, she was defenceless when her offspring was threatened. Fired up by the awakening, she took drastic steps to change her role. She passed the insurance certification examination at the first attempt and closed four cases quickly within the first month. That she was able to sponsor a school trip for her child and his classmates to Jurong Bird Park marked the turning point. She was grooming herself to be a tiger in the jungle. That became the first of Mary Lao's Five Rules of Success.

Pick your role.

Her agents were invariably shocked when Mary Lao talked about her husband's failings with brutal honesty. She likened him to a stubborn mouse deer, content to earn a meagre salary even when she had demonstrated how she could earn in a month what he earned in a year. If one chose to wear the skin of a mouse deer, one could never grow claws.

Mary Lao always ended her sharing by reiterating that it was meant as an illustration, not ridicule. In truth, she wasn't so sure herself.

Back when she closed her first case five years ago, she was ecstatic and roaring to celebrate. She took her family down to Queen Elizabeth Walk and showed Gimme Lao where she and his father used to go on dates. She described how the hired trishaw dropped them at the Merlion statue, the towering sculpture fusing the head of a lion with the tail of a fish. From there, the two of them strolled along the embankment and took in the nectarous fragrance of the frangipani. Stars dotted the night sky as far as the eye could see, merging with the flickering lights of the cargo ships parked along the seafront. At the end of Queen Elizabeth Walk, they often stopped for supper at the Satay Club, an open cluster of hawkers roasting skewered beef, chicken, pork and mutton on charcoal grills. The air would be thick with succulent enticement. They would order 10 sticks of satay and a block of chewy rice wrapped in coconut leaves to share. Until Gimme was born, those nights were the high points of her life.

Mary Lao was glad that Gimme was in sync with her gaiety.

She could tell the boy was as exhilarated by the promised school trip as she herself was by the bright future of her budding career. What perplexed her was her husband's brooding silence. Mary Lao waited till their order of satay arrived and Gimme was preoccupied with the rare treat before asking him in a soft tone, whatever was the matter.

"What you are doing is not very nice."

Mary Lao was astonished, both by the admonishing tone of voice and by his readiness with the reproach. He had obviously been harbouring the resentment for a while now.

"The way you barge into the barbershop and bombard the customers with no regard to how Barber Bay feels is rude, to say the least. Does it not concern you that you may scare away some of his customers?"

"Has he complained to you?" Mary Lao was curious.

"No, Barber Bay is too decent a gentleman to complain. But that doesn't give you the right to bully him."

Mary Lao knotted her brows as she studied her husband. He was not given to quick temper, and this outburst was uncharacteristic of him. It was especially puzzling because he was not even on close terms with Barber Bay. "Why are you so upset when Barber Bay himself did not make a complaint?"

"Because I hate to see nice people bullied." Her husband pressed on. "Remember the incident when Barber Bay was bullied by the laksa hawker and had to wash his sambal chilli jars for weeks? It's not right. And poor Barber Bay would still be washing the jars if Grandma Toh hadn't intervened. I hate to see you doing the same thing to him."

Mary Lao reminded herself to soften her tone as she explained what she thought was painfully obvious, to her husband. "First of all, I don't see myself bullying anybody. Barber Bay offers his customers hair cutting services, while I offer them insurance service. Many people don't realise they need insurance, so I make the fact clear to them. Eventually, when their families collect insurance benefits, they too will thank me. They thank me, not because I am nice to them, but because I provided a necessary service to them. In fact, I am confident that before the year ends, I will sign Barber Bay up for his first insurance policy too."

"If he ends up buying a policy from you, it is because he is too nice to say no," her husband rebuked.

Irked by his bullheadedness, Mary Lao raised her voice, "This preoccupation with being nice and decent is precisely the problem with you, Mr Lao Sheng Yang! You can't stand people not liking you. And you find it more important to be nice and likable than right and effective. Guess what? If you choose to be nice in life, you will end up washing other people's sambal chilli jars. I don't aspire to be nice. I do what is necessary to get what I want. If others don't like it, it's their problem, not mine."

What occurred next caught Mary Lao and her husband off guard. His tiny cheeks bulging with a chunk of half-masticated mutton, Gimme suddenly waved his satay stick in the air like a wand and in a mumbled outburst, regurgitated what he just heard, "I don't aspire to be nice. I do what is necessary to get what I want. If others don't like it, it's their problem, not mine. Kekeke…"

That ended any serious discussion for the night.

Although Mary Lao did not enjoy arguing with her husband,

his dissension did help to delineate and entrench her stance. She did not need her prospects to like her. She just needed them to realise that they needed life insurance. Her role was really very simple. Once they heard her out, any sensible person would want to sign on the dotted line to acquire an insurance policy.

Or so she thought initially.

As the weeks went by, Mary Lao became increasingly amazed by how few people were willing to face the truth or have their comfort zones challenged. Many people did not like to discuss death, or accidents or illnesses. Since that was what Mary Lao generally discussed, they had a tendency to avoid her. If they found themselves in her company, they made it obvious that they were willing to discuss the unbearable heat of the day, or the horrendous price of vegetables, but not the unbearable tragedy of illness and death, nor the horrendous hardship that widows and orphans suffered. Such topics made them uncomfortable.

"Have you not noticed that the rowdy fishmonger who used to shout and beckon to you at the market doesn't do that anymore?" her husband remarked. "He doesn't even want your business!"

Mary Lao did not like the snide undertone in his voice. She suppressed the urge to start an argument and told herself that she could do better than an attempt to convince. She would prove her point.

The following Sunday, Mary Lao picked the busiest hour at the market to pay the fishmonger a visit at his stall. The fishmonger, besieged by the weekend throng, easily ignored her. Over two hours, he noticed Mary Lao watching him and regularly scribbling on a notepad. When the throng eventually thinned out, he could no longer contain his curiosity.

"What are you doing, Mrs Lao?"

That was the break Mary Lao had been waiting for.

"I was doing some calculations," she said. "In the last two hours, you sold more than 40 fish. Each fish sold required you to chop it up using that massive, unwieldy cleaver of yours. It must be hard on your wrist."

The fishmonger raised the cleaver, waved it around dexterously and laughed, "Twenty years of practice. Practically part of my arm now!"

"I wonder if your wife can do the same?"

"Have you seen my wife?" the fishmonger sniggered. "She won't last an hour!"

"What if you went on vacation without your family, a really long one, and she had to do it?"

"Why would I want to go on vacation without my family?" The fishmonger was puzzled.

"Well, Grandma Toh's husband did, many years ago. And he never returned, leaving Grandma Toh alone to fend for herself and her daughter."

The fishmonger's face turned ashen. He attended to one of his customers and pointedly ignored Mary Lao. But Mary Lao pressed on with her monologue. She took calculated advantage of his physical entrapment and kept hammering at the shield of resistance to reach the rational mind behind. It took a long while, but the fishmonger eventually saw that Mary Lao was not discussing his death, but his wife's livelihood following. In the end, Mary Lao left the market with a discounted silver pomfret and a sales appointment scheduled for the same night.

The experience with the fishmonger developed into the second of Mary Lao's Five Rules of Success.

Give yourself permission.

Mary Lao gave herself permission to behave in ways that did not endear her to others. She accosted the laksa hawker during his mid-afternoon hiatus and switched off his radio so he could hear her better. She surprised her tailor with a packet of his favourite ginger tea, but distressed him for an entire afternoon with her sales talk. She went to the provision shop to buy a bottle of vinegar and refused to leave until the shop owner granted her a sales appointment.

Although her prospects generally found her approach annoying, they started listening once she abraded their layer of scepticism. For the women, Mary's reminder that they would be in trouble if the breadwinner in the family no longer provided for them struck fear. For the men, Mary's appeal to their sense of responsibility as husbands and fathers bolstered their ego. When the required signature was finally inked on the dotted line, Mary Lao never thanked them for the business. She always made it a point to thank them for taking good care of their family.

As the months went by, Mary Lao's husband became increasingly bewildered by her success. He was rattled when his chess mate, Harrison the sales manager, repeatedly referred to Mary Lao as the company's star discovery of the decade. It went against his grain to accept that his wife could win the trust of her clients when she conducted herself in such an abrasive manner. Yet the truth could not be denied. Barely a year into her new career, his wife was earning three times his salary. Once, when she revisited the possibility of him switching into insurance sales, he stiffened and would not discuss it. Heaving a sigh of resignation, she asked if he would ever give himself permission to succeed in life. That was the first instance he felt hatred towards her.

When Mary Lao started making good money consistently, she began to indulge the family. She was proud to bring them to dim sum lunches on Sundays at the swanky Mayflower Restaurant and thought nothing of buying her boy a set of the *Encyclopaedia Britannica* for his birthday gift. She failed to notice that awkward moment of embarrassment every time the bill was wrongly delivered to her husband, and she had to snap her fingers to redirect the waiter. Neither was she aware that her son had ceased asking her husband for permission, favours or advice. The child had sensed the shift of power in decision-making and had leaned in her direction accordingly.

Mary Lao had no idea her husband was struggling with the anguish of displacement. Although she was dimly aware that they did not seem to be enjoying a lot of sex, she was not overtly concerned. The novel excitement of fast and furious income was her new route to orgasmic gratification.

Harrison, her sales manager, was the one who triggered the formulation of two more of Mary Lao's Five Rules of Success. He related how his former sales manager challenged him to be frank about his utmost fear as an insurance agent. It turned out that he was fearful of approaching English-educated prospects who refused to speak Mandarin, for he himself had a poor grasp of English. The sales manager then challenged Harrison to secure a sales appointment with one English-speaking prospect at the beginning of each week. Until then, he was not to allow himself any other sales appointment for the rest of the week.

"But why would you want to accept that challenge?" Mary Lao had asked, not comprehending. "Your income will suffer for no good reason."

"Look around you. Ninety percent of our sales agents are Chinese-educated chaps like you and me. They are dipping their fingers into the same pie. Hardly anybody is approaching the English-educated prospects, out of fears that are similar to mine. But because I made it compulsory for myself to overcome that fear, I had to. Once I picked up the English language, my market expanded quickly. That was the key factor that catapulted me to sales manager status ahead of my cohort. If you give yourself the same challenge, I see you making sales manager within two years."

Mary Lao bit her lip in a head rush of invigoration and trepidation. Like many from her generation, she feared the alien language spoken by the Westerners. Unlike many from her generation, she almost never backed down from a challenge. The next evening, Mary Lao approached Elizabeth from next door and made her an offer. If Elizabeth could coach her in English, she would share half of the commission she earned from the first 10 policies she sold to English-speaking clients.

For Elizabeth, Mary's offer couldn't have come at a better time. She had been eyeing a new entertainment gadget she had spotted in one of her student's houses. It was a videocassette recorder that was recently launched in the United States, but not yet commercially available in Asia. The price was exorbitant, but the promised commission-sharing from Mary Lao eradicated her concerns. She made her student's father promise to buy her one on his frequent business trips to the United States.

In less than two weeks, Elizabeth's ultra-modern entertainment gadget arrived. She was the first person within a 30-block radius to own a Philips videocassette recorder. The student's father also generously allowed Elizabeth access to their collection of videotapes. Elizabeth picked *Mary Poppins* and designated it as Mary's tuition material. The two, together with Gimme Lao, watched the videotape every evening for seven days straight. Elizabeth made mother and child practise the dialogues and learn the songs by heart. The trio had a fabulous time lip-synching the songs from the soundtrack. Gimme Lao fell in love with the magical nanny and insisted that his mother name herself Mary too. That was how Mary Lao acquired her English name.

Elizabeth was smart to pick musicals from the private collection she was given access to. After *Mary Poppins*, they moved on to *The Sound of Music*, *Fiddler on the Roof*, *The King and I* and *My Fair Lady*. Not only could these musicals withstand repeated viewing, it was easy for Mary and Gimme to pick up the language, humming the assortment of catchy songs till they were etched in their minds. Elizabeth teased mother and child and reflected that had she jumbled up the sequence of her selection, Gimme would have named his mother Maria Lao, Golde Lao,

Anna Lao or Eliza Lao.

By the time Mary Lao found herself humming to the tune of "Loverly" as she spread kaya and butter over a slice of bread for Gimme's lunch box, she knew she was ready to tackle her first English-speaking client. And she already had a target in mind.

There was an Indian family of 12 living in a unit directly above the barbershop. They were prominent only because nobody could figure out how they had managed to squeeze a dozen people into the single bedroom apartment. Mary Lao had never spoken to them, but had observed their routine and counted no less than eight children. Every evening at seven, without fail, the eldest daughter would bring her siblings to the playground and supervise them as they went wild on the jungle gym. A month ago, Mary Lao would have crossed the family off her prospect list for two reasons. One, they spoke no Mandarin and she herself spoke no English. Two, a breadwinner with so many mouths to feed was not likely to have enough savings to kick-start an insurance programme. But in accepting the challenge that Harrison had issued her, Mary Lao decided to tackle the impossible. She was going to talk the head of the family into buying the protection his family so obviously needed.

After dinner the next evening, Mary Lao left the dishwashing to her husband and brought Gimme downstairs to the playground. Ten minutes later, the Indian brood arrived. One of the younger girls pointed at Gimme hanging from the top bar of the jungle gym and started chatting excitedly to the eldest sister in Tamil. Mary Lao approached them with a broad smile and asked if the girl knew Gimme in school. The girl nodded shyly. She was in the adjacent class in the same year.

"I have seen you and your husband before, but I didn't know you speak English." The eldest sister sounded pleasantly surprised. "I am Sabitha Subramaniam, and this is my little darling Omala."

Mary Lao was glad that Sabitha was friendly and chatty. In fact, Sabitha did most of the talking over the next hour, providing elaborate answers when Mary Lao asked about the Subramaniam family. As it turned out, little Omala was really Sabitha's cousin and their fathers were brothers. When Sabitha's father died of a heart attack several years ago, Omala's father took in Sabitha's mother and her brood of four. Since Omala's father had a brood of four himself, and adding to that Omala's mother and grandmother, he became responsible for an extended family of 12.

"Very, very hard for your uncle!" Mary Lao exclaimed. "So what work he do?"

Sabitha was heartened by Mary Lao's empathy and chose to disregard her jumbled English tenses. She hesitated a little before she replied, "My uncle works as a prison warden. I know it is tough for him. But he is a responsible man and he loves us dearly."

From the corner of her eyes, Mary Lao could tell that the neighbours strolling past were hurling curious glances in her direction. Although there was a sprinkling of Indian and Malay families living in the same block, they tended to keep to themselves. Since most of their Chinese neighbours spoke no English, they might nod and smile as they crossed paths along the corridor, but would be ill-equipped to carry out a conversation. The spectacle of Mary Lao carrying a conversation with Sabitha for over an hour was so out of the ordinary that an obese Chinese woman stepped up close, folded her arms and watched intently as though it were a television programme.

"This woman lives directly above my family," Sabitha became uncomfortable and whispered to Mary Lao. "She is never very friendly. Can you ask her what she wants?"

The obese observer pointed at Sabitha and spoke to Mary Lao in Hokkien. "Tell her that her mother should close the windows when she cooks curry. Otherwise the smell travels up and in through my window and stinks up my kitchen."

Mary Lao flushed. The Hokkien word for curry was a phonetic translation and there was no way Sabitha could have missed it. Sabitha immediately became agitated and enquired, "Is she complaining about the curry smell? Tell her she should mind her own business. In fact, tell her she should wring her laundry properly before hanging them out to dry. How many times has her dripping laundry dirtied ours? And she has the nerve to complain about our curry smell!"

"What did the Indian girl say?" the obese woman wanted to know.

Mary Lao refused to be embroiled in what could easily escalate into a quarrel. She told the obese woman firmly that she was discussing business with Sabitha and told Sabitha they ought to ignore the obese woman. The obese woman shrugged her shoulders and remained where she was, watching the conversation with mild interest, as though she were watching a foreign language movie without subtitles.

"My neighbour cook sambal chilli every morning. I no problem with that," Mary Lao declared.

"Sambal chilli is really too mild," Sabitha boasted. "My mother makes a wicked curry. The first time you try it, I guarantee you tears will stream down your face."

"Really?" Mary Lao laughed, her mind churning quickly. "Why not we test? I ask my neighbour make hot-hot sambal chilli. You ask your mother cook hot-hot curry. Saturday I come your place. Dinner."

"The challenge is on!" Sabitha laughed.

The obese woman recognised the word curry and decided that the two couldn't possibly be discussing business. Once again she prompted Mary Lao to remind Sabitha to close her kitchen windows. To sidestep the minefield, Mary Lao quickly bid Sabitha goodbye and summoned Gimme to go home.

When Saturday rolled around, Mary Lao and Gimme paid Sabitha a visit armed with a jar of Grandma Toh's sambal belachan. Mary Lao panicked when she saw the sumptuous spread Sabitha's family laid out for her. There was chilli parotta, chicken salna, sambar idlis, kadala curry, pineapple rasam and Chettinad-style chicken curry. Blushing deeply, Mary Lao apologised for her miserable jar of sambal belachan. Sabitha laughed and explained that this was the first time they had had a visit from a Chinese neighbour in the 10 years that they had lived there. It was an honour.

The Subramaniams laughed heartily when Mary Lao and Gimme both choked and shed tears over their curry dish. In contrast, Sabitha's siblings and cousins scooped spoonfuls of

Grandma Toh's sambal belachan into their mouths and rolled their eyes giggling. The contest was unceremoniously over.

What surprised Mary Lao more than the family's hospitality was the opulence of the household furnishings. A majestic wooden carving over one metre tall of Lord Ganesha riding a mouse dominated one wall. This was framed by drapes of saffron satin that ran from the ceiling all the way to the floor. Three smaller but intricate Tanjore paintings of Krishna, Balaji and Lakshmi hung from the opposite wall. Gimme Lao was fascinated by the shine of precious stones on these paintings and stood staring long and hard with his mouth agape. The women wore gold bangles, while the head of the household wore multiple gold rings. Mary Lao simply could not figure out how a prison warden could afford such luxuries for the family.

It wasn't until Mary Lao had to use the toilet that she solved the mystery. There was a built-in cabinet in a corner fully stocked with cartons of cigarettes. That was Mr Subramaniam's secret: as a prison warden, he doubled up as a supplier of cigarettes and other items the prisoners were willing to pay for. It would not surprise her if Mr Subramaniam dealt in drugs too. It was necessary for the Subramaniams to keep a low profile, thus they continued to squeeze themselves into the tiny one bedroom apartment and hide their jewellery from sight. But Mary Lao's unprecedented neighbourly visit was too much of a temptation, so they decided to deck themselves out in their finest gold.

Mary Lao was dizzy with delight when she stepped out of the toilet. For the rest of the evening, she continued to worm her way into the Subramaniams' confidence. By the end of the second week, she had Mr Subramaniam sign on the dotted line for four insurance policies: one life policy for himself and three endowment policies for his three sons. In her heart, she was humming the tune to "Loverly".

All seven of Mary Lao's sales agents were familiar with the Subramaniam story. Mary Lao used it to illustrate the third and fourth of her Five Rules of Success.

Gnash your hottest chilli. The one that brings tears to your eyes and triggers a coughing fit so severe your windpipe feels like bursting. For once you learn to handle the hottest chilli, you can feast on dishes that are out of reach to those who cannot handle their chilli.

That was the third rule.

Had Mary Lao assumed the Subramaniams could not possibly afford to buy insurance and chosen not to approach them, she would not have been able to close four cases in one go. In fact, Mr Subramaniam subsequently referred two of his fellow prison wardens, to whom Mary Lao sold three more policies.

Thus the fourth rule: do not judge a covered dish.

After the tearful introduction to the Subramaniam brand of spicy curry, both Mary Lao and Gimme became enamoured with Indian spices and dishes. Every other week, Mary Lao and Sabitha's mother would bring one another dishes to sample. Gimme Lao became fast friends with Omala in school too. During lunch break at the canteen, Omala would slip Gimme Lao a piece of Dharwad pedha from her lunch box, and Gimme would share his ang ku kueh. When they moved on to year three, both children enrolled in the school band and became recorder buddies. While waiting for the school bus home, the pair would whip out their hard plastic recorders and practise their band pieces together. The girls in their respective classes mocked them by calling them a "kopi susu"—black coffee with white milk—couple. Peeved, Gimme Lao and Omala simply launched their counter-offensive and called the girls various demeaning nicknames.

Although the two often joined each other for lunch breaks, Gimme Lao almost never got to see Omala during the morning tea break. That was when Omala retreated to the secluded corner of the garden behind the janitor's storeroom to play zero point. Gimme Lao played various games with the boys. There was hantam bola, police and thief and the ever-popular hopscotch. But none of the boys played zero point. It was a girl's game; one that Gimme Lao secretly wished to play.

Zero point was a game played using a rope made of intertwined rubber bands. Two girls, acting as height markers, held one end each and stretched the rope taut at ankle level. The rest of the girls took turns to straddle the horizontal rope and perform a set of skipping manoeuvres with incremental complexity, using their legs to draw patterns out of the rope. Once everyone had a go, the rope was brought up to knee level, and the game replayed. By the time the rope reached waist level, most of the weaker players would have been eliminated. The last girl standing won the game.

For weeks Gimme Lao hid himself behind the janitor's storeroom to watch and study the game. Omala was quick on her feet but too short to tackle the rope at chest level. Two of the best players were in year five—tall, rangy girls who dominated the game. Of the two, the one with a mole on her chin was a harrier. She ordered the other girls around, decided the queuing sequence and determined forfeits and penalties. Her name was Gan Ah Sai, but the girls called her Garnasai, or "like shit" in Hokkien, behind her back. The other girl, Kai Li, was Garnasai's loyal sidekick. The two had the last say when it came to the game of zero point.

Eventually, Gimme Lao could not bear it any longer. He stepped up to the two of them and announced that he wanted to play too. Garnasai gave him a dismissive glance and shook her head. Kai Li added, "Zero point is for girls only. No boys allowed."

"But I want to play," Gimme Lao persisted.

"You can play if you are a girl. Are you a girl?" Kai Li teased. Some of the other girls started giggling.

Gimme Lao kept quiet but would not leave. He stood to one side and watched as Garnasai executed a flawless pattern with the rubber band rope held at chest level. When she finished, Gimme Lao announced stubbornly, "I can do that too."

Garnasai glared at him and snorted. Omala decided to put in a good word for her buddy, "Let him play. He can take my turn and I will just watch." Kai Li objected, "No, he cannot take your place. Only girls can play this game." Omala threw up her hands and challenged the other girl, "But why?"

Before Kai Li could answer, Gimme Lao remarked coldly, "Because they are afraid I will beat all of them."

For a while, a frozen silence descended on the group.

Garnasai glared at Gimme Lao, who stood a full head shorter than her. When Gimme Lao returned her glare and did not flinch, Garnasai decided to issue him a challenge. "You can be the first boy to play zero point if you can beat me. Until then, you will play as a girl. Omala can lend you her frock."

All the girls broke out into paroxysms of laughter. Even Omala laughed, until she suddenly remembered Gimme Lao was her buddy and quickly hid her grin behind a cupped palm. Gimme Lao himself frowned, silently contemplating the challenge. When he eventually made up his mind and nodded his agreement, all the girls gaped in astonishment. Even Garnasai found it hard to believe Gimme Lao actually accepted her challenge.

"Quick, let him have your frock, Omala!" Kai Li urged gleefully. Omala looked doubtful, but Gimme Lao nodded to reassure her. All the girls wore the same white shirt and blue shorts the boys wore, but had an additional pleated blue frock worn over the first layer. Gimme Lao took over Omala's frock and quietly slipped it over his head. All the girls started to giggle hysterically. Gimme Lao folded his arms, bit his lip and waited patiently till the game resumed. The moves he had observed and studied from afar were not as easily executable as he had imagined. By the time recess ended, Gimme Lao had never once managed to move past the waist level. Garnasai snorted at him and pointed her thumb downwards. The other girls scuttled back to their respective classes and eagerly spread the news that Gimme Lao had worn a frock to play zero point.

When Gimme Lao returned the next morning to the secluded garden, there were a handful of boys from the other classes who were gathered there leaning against the wall of the janitor's storeroom. They alerted one another once Gimme Lao approached and cackled loudly. Gimme Lao felt the deep burn of his own blush. He did not know then, but there was a betting pool among the boys as to whether Gimme Lao would have the guts to put on a frock in their presence.

"Are you going to join us, Princess Gimme?" Kai Li teased. The girls giggled and the boys cackled.

Gimme Lao strode over to the girls but shook his head when Omala gestured to ask if he needed her frock. For this morning, he would just observe the game. He was certain the boys would grow impatient and leave soon. But Garnasai understood his strategy and shred it asunder by throwing him an ultimatum. If he did not put on a frock and play zero point right away, he could forget about playing the game ever again.

Gimme Lao bit his lip and thought hard. The boys by the wall started a chorus of wolf whistles. The girls giggled. Omala was about to put in a good word when Gimme Lao suddenly turned to her and held out his hand. The boys erupted into spontaneous cheering as Omala took off her frock uneasily and handed it over.

His face tense but determined, Gimme Lao strode over to the group of boys, glared at them belligerently and quietly slipped on the frock. At first, the boys laughed out loud. Gimme Lao remained silent but took a step closer. Some of the boys became unnerved by the proximity and belligerence of their subject of ridicule, and their laughter quickly dwindled. An awkward silence ensued. The head of the gang finally realised that Gimme Lao had effectively robbed them of their fun and with a scowl, gestured for the rest of the gang to retreat.

The game of zero point was constantly interrupted for the rest of the session. Every time curious onlookers came to gawk or ogle, Gimme Lao would stride up to them and stare them down till the element of fun was completely eroded. In no time, the girls were so frustrated with the interruptions they began to shoo the onlookers away before Gimme Lao had a chance to react.

By the third day, word had gotten around to the teachers. The principal, together with the disciplinary master, decided to investigate the matter. They recruited a mole from among the zero point players and received confirmation before they launched their surprise visit to the secluded garden. All the girls froze and looked worried.

"Why are you in a frock?" the disciplinary master asked in a severe tone.

Gimme Lao turned pallid. The disciplinary master had a reputation for ruthlessness when he dealt with recalcitrant students.

"Boys do not wear frocks," the disciplinary master declared. "Only an Ah Gua would wear a frock. Do you want to put on lipstick and wear high heels and become an Ah Gua?"

Some of the girls giggled. There were a handful of effeminate boys in school that were badly teased and labelled as "Ah Gua". The disciplinary master quickly singled out Omala, who was conspicuously missing her frock.

"And why did you lend him your frock?"

Omala looked around helplessly. Gimme Lao had his head

bowed, while the other girls remained silent and unsupportive. Garnasai glared at her ferociously, daring her to mention her name.

When the disciplinary master realised he wasn't going to extract any confession from the pair of recalcitrants, he decided to escalate it to the next level. "I want both of your mothers to see me tomorrow morning before the assembly."

On the ride home in the school bus, Omala nudged Gimme Lao and asked if he was going to comply with the instruction. Gimme Lao shook his head. It was embarrassing enough to be called an Ah Gua by the disciplinary master in front of a group of girls. He did not want his mother to hear that too. Omala thought about it and decided she would meet the disciplinary master's injunction midway. She would bring her cousin Sabitha, but keep her mother out of it.

Omala's strategy did not work. When the disciplinary master saw Sabitha, he simply waved her away. "I asked to see your mother. Not your sister, not your cousin. Which part of my instruction was unclear?"

At the assembly that followed, the disciplinary master took to the stage and summoned the pair of misfits. To Gimme Lao's horror, he made Omala remove her frock and hand it over. "Since you obviously like it, you will wear it in front of the whole school."

The giggles and cackles in the assembly rippled from the front row to the back as those behind stood on tiptoes or leaned sideways to catch a glimpse of the spectacle. Riotous laughter erupted when the disciplinary master produced half a dozen clothes pegs and proceeded to pinch small tufts of Gimme Lao's hair upright. By the time he whipped out a lipstick and drew on Gimme Lao's lips, the assembly grid had collapsed. All those behind were pushing their way forward to get a better glimpse. Some of the teachers laughed too, although there were a few who looked perturbed.

The disciplinary master allowed the students to have their fill of laughter before ordering them back into their assembly grid. Pointing his finger at Gimme Lao, who was by then sobbing with acute humiliation, he delivered his message through a loudspeaker, "This is how an Ah Gua looks like. If you are a boy, dress like a boy. Boys do not wear skirts, or frocks, or gowns or dresses. Only if you want to be an Ah Gua, then you dress like Gimme Lao. Do you want to be an Ah Gua? Do you?"

The disciplinary master kept pressing until the entire assembly gave him a resounding "no". He then turned to Gimme Lao and proclaimed, "Let this be a lesson to you, Gimme Lao. There are boundaries you do not cross. You are born a boy. You will grow up a man. One day in the future, you will recall this day of humiliation and thank me for stopping you in time before you turned into a wayward Ah Gua."

Gimme Lao was weeping inconsolably when the disciplinary master had a teacher help remove his frock and lead him to the toilet to wash up. For the rest of the day, he hid his head in his folded arms on his desk and sniffled intermittently. His class teachers let him be. On the school bus going home, Omala sat next to him and ferociously stared down anyone who dared hurl a snigger at her buddy. Gimme Lao was too distraught to put up any form of defence himself.

By the time the bus deposited them below their block, Gimme Lao and Omala had come to an agreement. This episode of humiliation would be kept a secret from their families. The two sealed their agreement with a tug on their little fingers, not knowing that the bird was already out of the cage. Unbeknown to them, Sabitha had stayed back and witnessed their humiliation from the far end of the assembly field. Both the Subramaniams and the Laos had learnt all about it.

Over dinner, Gimme Lao was grilled by his parents. Both Mary Lao and her husband wanted to know the details. Strangely though, the two interrogators had entirely different focuses. His father wanted to know why on earth he put on a frock, while his mother wanted to know exactly how the disciplinary master had punished him in the assembly. As the dinner came to an end, the two interrogators arrived at vastly different conclusions. Gimme Lao's father concluded that Gimme Lao had it coming and hoped that the public humiliation would dissuade him from ever crossing the boundary again. Mary Lao however stared at her husband in disgust.

"Have you not been listening to our boy?" she gasped. "He had been issued a challenge, and he took it up. That was why he put on a frock!"

"And you think that makes it right?" her husband retorted, incredulous.

"I am saying he had a reason."

"He has to learn to do the right thing."

"If we all had to do the right thing, the two of us wouldn't be married in the first place, would we?" Mary Lao snapped and almost immediately regretted it. They both blushed deeply and stole a furtive glance at Gimme Lao. The boy did not appear to have caught what she said. Mary Lao heaved a sigh of relief and muttered to herself, "I need to speak to the disciplinary master."

"About what?" her husband asked, alarmed.

"About calling our boy an Ah Gua!"

The next day, Mary Lao timed herself to arrive just as the school bell rang. She collected Gimme Lao and marched him to the principal's office. Gimme Lao felt a heady mix of apprehension and excitement. He knew his mother was fearless and felt a secret pride that she was pitting herself against the principal for his sake.

The principal had to summon the disciplinary master upon Mary Lao's request. Once he arrived, Mary Lao asked him point-blank if he had called her son an Ah Gua in front of the entire student body. The disciplinary master sniggered and replied derisively, "Your boy was wearing a frock. What else do you expect me to call him? A good example?"

Mary Lao reached into her tote bag, extracted two library books and slammed them onto the table. She flipped through the first volume until she came to a chapter on the attire worn by ancient Chinese emperors. Tapping her knuckles on the page, Mary Lao glared at the disciplinary master and challenged, "From Tang dynasty to Ming dynasty to Qing dynasty, tell me what the emperors are wearing? Are you calling them Ah Gua? Is that what you are teaching the students in class?"

The disciplinary master frowned at Mary Lao's belligerence. Before he could reply, Mary Lao flipped through the second volume until she came to a chapter featuring Elizabethan attire for men and asked again, "Are you telling me these men are Western Ah Gua? All of them?"

The principal saw that the disciplinary master was flushed with anger and decided to step in quickly. "Mrs Lao, perhaps we shouldn't have used the term Ah Gua on your boy. For that I apologise. But we do have rules in school. Boys are simply not allowed to wear frocks."

"Show me then."

"Sorry?" The principal looked confused.

"Show me where it is stated that boys are not allowed to wear frocks in school," Mary Lao requested stubbornly.

The principal had to hide his look of agitation as he turned to reach for the volume of school rules and regulations. His agitation quickly turned into embarrassment as he realised there was no statement in the volume that spelled it out. It was simply understood as a hidden rule.

"So you are telling me my boy was punished for breaching a rule that does not exist in your school rules and regulations," Mary Lao stated coldly. The principal and the disciplinary master exchanged looks of silent fury. They knew they were right, but simply could not prove it.

Mary Lao glared at them a little longer before she swept the two library books back into her tote bag. Turning to Gimme Lao, she spoke in a clear voice so the two could hear her. "What did the disciplinary master tell you again? That there are boundaries you do not cross? Remember this: people who follow rules blindly are people who are too lazy to use their brains. You have your own brain. Use it. Question the rules. Question the boundaries." With that, Mary Lao stood up and left the office with her boy.

The same night, Mary Lao's husband blew his top. He was aghast at the bad example his wife set for their child. What was she thinking? How could she possibly teach the child to disrespect school authority? When his tirade gained momentum, Mary Lao sent Gimme Lao next door to play at Grandma Toh's place. But the walls were thin, and Gimme Lao did not miss a word of his parents' thunderous argument.

When Harrison the sales manager drove by to pick Mary Lao and her husband up for work the next morning, he could sense the palpable frost between husband and wife. Unwittingly, he enquired and was instantly ensnared and pressed for an opinion.

"If your boy crossed the line, I guess we should trust the school authorities to discipline him." Harrison cleared his throat uneasily. "The principal can't possibly have all the boys running around in frocks in school, right?"

"It was not stated in the school rules and regulations," Mary Lao insisted icily.

"Some boundaries are drawn with invisible ink, but respected nonetheless." Harrison attempted to make his case. "Take for example insurance sales. As a man, I can walk into the red light district at Geylang to make cold calls and suffer no consequence to my safety or reputation. As a woman, you can't do the same. There is a boundary. It may not be spelled out in our company rules and regulations, but we all know it exists, and we all respect it."

Mary Lao sealed her lips in defiance and thought hard. Despite the logic in Harrison's analogy, she was not convinced. But Mary Lao was not one who was adamant about winning an argument. She would rather prove her point. And the name that sprang to her mind was Black Cougar.

Black Cougar was a sinister character. Tawny, sinewy and taciturn, he prowled the corridors in the ungodly hours between midnight and sunrise when most of the neighbours were fast asleep. Just before first light broke, he would stamp out his sixth cigarette butt and retire to bed. It would be close to dinner time before he re-emerged, another cigarette pinched between his fingers and a can of beer clamped in his palm. Leaning against the parapet, he maintained a languid gaze into the distance and ignored the neighbours who strolled past him. He did not see the distaste on the women's faces as they frowned at his exposed torso, leaving nothing to the imagination except what was shrouded in a white pair of cotton briefs. He did not see the wonderment in the children's eyes as they strained themselves to study the various tattoos on his limbs and his back. A mermaid and a skull pierced with daggers adorned each arm, while a ferocious black cougar and a nymph caught in an erotic entanglement with a python graced each thigh. His broad back provided an ample canvas for a menacing dragon to roll and rumble in and out of tufts of heavy clouds. There was a sixth tattoo, a tiny calligraphy of a Hindu mantra inked half an inch above the base of his manhood, meant to enhance his sexual prowess. Among the neighbours, only Aunty Seah had seen it. She first saw it up close 25 years ago, when they were newly married and Black Cougar made her give him fellatio. Five years later, when Black Cougar stopped bringing home money, Aunty Seah refused to engage in his favourite sport. That was the last she had seen of the mantra tattoo up close.

Black Cougar worked as a bouncer at the Apollo Night Club along Havelock Road. At 50, he was the oldest bouncer in the team. He was not the strongest, but his thirst for blood made him one of the most fearsome. Other bouncers stopped once they threw the troublemakers out the back door and sent them scurrying away with bloodied lips. Black Cougar brought them to the back alley and manhandled them till they could hardly recognise themselves in the mirror. He was especially brutal to men who were rough on the hostesses. He simply could not stand the sight of any girl bruised, crying, or in pain. It reminded him of his sister.

As a child, Black Cougar was close to his sister. His earliest memory was that of himself clinging on to her for dear life when the twirling saucer at the funfair spun so fast he feared his head would detach itself from his shoulders. After that, his sister would buy a sticky candy and both of them would lick it to the bone while they watched the other children shriek their way through various rides. They could not afford a second ride, not with the coin their father gave them. Their father worked as a bricklayer, and he gave them a coin for the funfair only during dry seasons, when work was plentiful. Black Cougar and his sister enjoyed the funfair for many dry seasons, until the day their father's employer, a man they called Boss Kwok, brought news that their father had lost his footing and fallen off the scaffolding from a height of five storeys.

After their mother was done with the funeral and the crying, she went back to Boss Kwok to beg for work. Boss Kwok arranged for her to work at the construction site transporting bricks between floors, but she was too frail for the job. Boss Kwok then switched her to cleaning and cooking, but the women at the kitchen were of a different dialect group and did not take to her. They ganged up and made life so miserable for her that she went back to Boss Kwok and begged him to take in the three of them. Although Boss Kwok was a widower, he was not inclined to start a new family. At her wits' end, she whimpered and made an offer. Black Cougar's sister would become his goddaughter. As the godfather, it was understood that he had full command of their obedience.

Black Cougar was nine and his sister 13 when they packed their bags and moved in with Boss Kwok. He slept in the kitchen on a thin mattress rolled out next to his mother. His sister got to sleep in the bedroom with Boss Kwok. The first night, his mother pressed the pillow over his ears and urged him to sleep quickly. He couldn't, not when he could still hear the muffled shrieks and whimpers coming through the wall. The next morning, once Boss Kwok had left for work, his mother hugged his sister dearly and explained to her that it was now her duty. If she did not perform her duty, all three of them would end up sleeping on the streets.

Black Cougar watched helplessly as his sister lost the lustre in her eyes. There were always bruises on her body. Their mother told her not to fight it, but the bruising continued despite her adopted compliance. It finally became apparent that Boss Kwok was turned on by the struggles. Over the next five years, she became pregnant thrice. Each time it happened, their mother brought her to the clinic to have an abortion. On the third occasion, the operating equipment must have been contaminated, for she came down with a fever that lasted for a week. Even after the fever subsided, she appeared enervated. One night, Boss Kwok lost his patience and reached for her under the blankets, blatantly ignoring her feeble protests. He only stopped when Black Cougar barged into the bedroom and bashed the headboard with a cleaver. The next morning, his mother packed a bag and forlornly told Black Cougar he had to leave before Boss Kwok threw the whole family out.

One of the bricklayers took pity on the teenager and referred him to a relative who ran an import and export business at Boat Quay. Black Cougar moved in, slept in a corner of a granary at night and unloaded grain sacks from bumboats in the day. Over the next few years, he grew taller and his scrawny frame packed on muscles like a bull's. After he saved up enough money, Black Cougar went back to look for his mother and his sister. It was his intention to rescue the two from the tyranny of Boss Kwok, but not before he reduced the man to a pulp with a good trouncing.

Black Cougar was prepared for bloodshed. What he was unprepared for was the serene spectacle of his sister breastfeeding a newborn while Boss Kwok played a game of five stones with a laughing toddler. His mother was delighted to see him. She took money from Boss Kwok and went downstairs to buy fish head curry to celebrate the occasion. Throughout dinner, though they were kept busy feeding the children, Boss Kwok and his sister listened cordially as his mother caught up with his life over the missing years. For Black Cougar, it felt surreal and disorientating. He found it hard to believe that none of the three remembered how he was thrown out of the house as a teenager.

Prior to the reunion, Black Cougar was an angry young man harbouring a focused and targeted vengeance. But the altered dynamics of the family had robbed him of his target. Frustrated, he lost his focus and began to pick fights randomly. It did not take much to trigger his rage. As his battle scars accrued, his fighting skills sharpened. He began to attract the attention of the triads, who wanted to recruit him as their fighter. Alarmed, his mother quickly arranged for his marriage, in the hope that conjugal joy would release his tension and tone down his belligerence.

The strategy worked. The newlyweds enjoyed conjugal bliss for the first few years. As a young bride, the chatty and affable Aunty Seah thawed and mollified the dark and taciturn Black Cougar. All the neighbours were invariably fond of Aunty Seah, and Black Cougar remained comfortably silent in her shadow. Although his towering frame dwarfed his wife, he looked tame standing beside her, as an ominous and brooding cougar would, standing beside its trainer. The two came across as an odd couple blessed with a perfect match.

Things changed after Aunty Seah suffered her miscarriage. During her subsequent spell of depression, the uncommunicative Black Cougar was ill-equipped to lend her the emotional support she needed. The couple began to quarrel bitterly. Black Cougar quickly regressed to a surly state and started to pick fights at work. Before long, he was asked to leave. His brother-in-law, Boss Kwok, realised that Black Cougar could not function in a congenial environment. He spoke to someone he knew at the Apollo Night Club and landed Black Cougar a job working as a bouncer.

For the first time in his life, Black Cougar's combativeness became his strength. Not only did he win respect from the other bouncers, he won the admiration of quite a few hostesses. They began to pamper him and brew him herbal soup with black chicken or fusion tea with powdered deer penis. In contrast to the ongoing cold war with his wife, these warm gestures from the ladies proved too much of a temptation. Black Cougar soon took up with one of them. When it became necessary to reciprocate with gifts of jewellery and chilli crab suppers, Black Cougar stopped bringing money home. That marked the point of no return for his dwindling marital bliss.

Over the next two decades, Black Cougar learned to compart-mentalise his life. Between sundown and midnight, he was a carnal creature and respected bouncer at the Apollo Night Club. In broad daylight, he regressed to a shadowy existence at home, detested by his wife and ignored by his neighbours. He could not remember the last time he had a proper conversation with any of them. That was, until Mary Lao suddenly decided to start one.

Black Cougar's initial confusion and suspicion quickly diminished as Mary Lao made clear her proposal. She wanted him to introduce her to the hostesses at Apollo Night Club. For his effort, Mary Lao would compensate him with a commission cut for every policy she sold.

Brows furrowed, Black Cougar took a long, hard look at Mary Lao. He could detect a fire in her eyes, a hunger for money and success. Beyond that, he could not imagine how she could possibly connect with the ladies at Apollo Night Club. They were of an entirely different world. Wordlessly, Black Cougar shook his head. She would only be wasting her time.

Mary Lao persisted. She stayed up late and waited for Black Cougar to return from work. A freshly brewed cup of tea in one hand and a chilled can of Tiger Beer in the other, she proceeded to join him for his night smoke. Mary Lao kept talking, but Black Cougar kept quiet. By the end of the second night, Mary Lao was reduced to begging. Still, Black Cougar said no.

"Can you at least tell me why you won't give me a chance?" Mary Lao pressed.

"Because," Black Cougar sighed, "you will only end up embarras-sing yourself."

"What makes you so sure?"

Black Cougar jiggled his can of beer and gestured at Mary Lao with his cigarette. "Let's say I agree, and I bring you to the supper place where the girls go after their shift. They will offer you a cigarette, but you will say no. They will order a jug of beer to share, but you will choose to jiggle your tea bag over your cup of boiled water. Do you think the girls will warm up to you when you make no effort at all to blend in? You will only be embarrassing yourself."

Mary Lao was stunned. It felt as though Black Cougar had just hit her with a hammer and cracked open her skull to let in necessary light. It was also suddenly clear that the man was willing to help her.

The next two nights saw Mary Lao come prepared with a six-pack and her own packet of Marlboro Light. Her initial attempts left her choking and coughing, and she saw Black Cougar guffaw for the first time. The noise they made woke some of the neighbours. Mary Lao spotted them adjusting the window sashes and peeping through the gaps. She knew her behaviour and the company she kept would no doubt trigger a scandal among the neighbours. But she chose not to be concerned.

The following week, Black Cougar arranged for Mary Lao to join him at the open-air seafood eatery near Apollo Night Club shortly after midnight. Mary Lao was surprised when Black Cougar introduced her as his goddaughter. But the reason soon became apparent. The ladies from Apollo warmed up to her immediately, offering her cigarettes and constantly refilling her beer mug. They teased Black Cougar and interrogated him over how many more ambiguous 'goddaughters' he had hidden all over the island. It was all in good fun.

Mary Lao heeded Black Cougar's advice to keep quiet and listen. The ladies gossiped about their clients, boasted about the gifts of jewellery they received and cursed the misers who tipped badly. They bantered about the newest bouncer to join the team, a tense and shy young man, and jestingly challenged one another to tame the stud and diffuse his tension. There was no lack of laughter throughout the supper. Mary Lao did not get a word in about insurance, but enjoyed herself thoroughly. At the end of the night, the ladies warmly bid Mary Lao farewell and asked her to join them again.

Mary Lao did just that. She took time to get to know the ladies. By the time she revealed that she was in insurance, they were already fairly comfortable with her as a friend. Mary Lao had also learnt to speak their language. Instead of discussing death and illness, Mary Lao discussed buying $20,000- to $30,000-jewellery in instalments, leveraging on the mechanism of an endowment policy. Over the weeks, Mary Lao became the person they went to for advice on how to invest in a jewellery fund.

Mary Lao's husband was unhappy that she stayed out till four in the morning and slept in late. He was also uncomfortable about her spending so much time with the sinister Black Cougar. He complained that she was setting a bad example for Gimme Lao by picking up drinking and smoking. Was she even aware that the neighbours were gossiping about her?

Mary Lao sighed silently and made a tired attempt to make her husband understand. The reason all the neighbours were gossiping was because they were ordinary people living ordinary lives who abided by ordinary codes of conduct. Mary Lao herself had no intention to be ordinary. Neither did she want her child to be. If anything, she would be disappointed if Gimme Lao turned out to be an obedient student who abided by all the school rules. She would rather train him to challenge the status quo and grow up to be a thinking man.

That became the fifth of Mary Lao's Five Rules of Success. Always question the boundaries.

As her husband unfurled the morning papers and hid his look of anger behind the news headlines, Mary Lao suddenly felt sad. She was certain that she was destined to reach new heights in life. She just wasn't certain that she could bring both her husband and her son along with her.

FIVE

GIMME LAO AND Omala swore to be friends forever. The two shared the best bites in their lunch boxes, reserved buddy seats on the school bus and kept one another's secrets. No one but Gimme knew that Omala was already betrothed. No one but Omala knew that Gimme had committed murder.

Omala's father had two brothers. The older one who had fathered Sabitha and her siblings had passed away. The younger one had never married, but devoted himself to serve at the Hindu Temple of Krishna at Waterloo Street as a keeper. His name was Anandan, and as far as his nieces and nephews were concerned, he was the greatest storyteller ever. Once a week, Omala and Sabitha's mothers left the children at the temple while they did their night shopping. For an hour or two, Uncle Anandan would entertain the children with mythological tales. He allowed them to sit, sprawl or lie down on the cool cement floor and pointed his finger upwards to draw their attention to the many painted portraits that lined the ceiling. He swirled his finger around in random patterns while the children giggled in anticipation, until he suddenly straightened his arm and pointed at one of the portraits. The child that could shout out the name of the deity won himself the privilege to lie down with his head on Uncle Anandan's lap. Omala was the quickest among the children. More than anyone else, she loved to bury her cheek in Uncle Anandan's folded thighs and hear him spin his tales.

Among all the Hindu deities, Hanuman the Monkey God was their collective favourite. Uncle Anandan serialised the Hanuman tale and spun it over the course of many weeks. From his very first act of mischief, plucking the sun out of the sky, to his amazing courage and wit battling mighty demons in the epic *Ramayana*, Hanuman was an inspiration to the children. The boys took turns playing Hanuman as they re-enacted the Battle of Lanka and led an army of monkeys to defeat Lankini, Lord of the demons. When Omala grew tired of playing the captive Sita awaiting rescue, she asked to play Hanuman. But her brothers and cousins would not hear of it. Whenever they ran short of female roles, they allowed the girls to play soldiers or demons. But never Hanuman the Monkey God.

When Omala complained to Uncle Anandan, he chuckled and confessed that there was a limited choice of heroic roles for little girls in Hindu mythology. Powerful goddesses, like Saraswati and Lakshmi, were invariably the wives of even more powerful male deities, like Brahma and Vishnu. Kali, the goddess of time and death, was a trifle dark and violent, while Durga, who had 10 arms and rode a tiger, was too fierce. "Why don't you like playing Sita? She is a very nice lady, and Lord Rama loves her very much," Uncle Anandan added.

"But Sita does nothing useful!" Omala whined.

"She does," Uncle Anandan defended the poor Sita. "She is the humble wife of Lord Rama. I am sure she cleans and cooks and looks after her husband like your mother looks after your father. That keeps her busy and useful."

"But I don't want to clean and cook," Omala frowned. "I want to join in the battle, like Hanuman does."

"You can join in the fun after you finish washing the dishes," Uncle Anandan teased. "It is the duty of all wives to keep the household clean. Of course, you will be lucky if you are the wife of Chandra the Moon God. He has many, so they can take turns washing the dishes."

"How many wives does Chandra have?' Omala enquired, her eyes as round as dinner plates.

"All of 27!" Uncle Anandan laughed. "They were all princesses of King Daksha Prajapati. Chandra the Moon God visits one a night, which means you are only kept busy one night per month serving your husband. You are free the rest of the month to do whatever you want."

Omala did not get that Uncle Anandan was teasing her. One week later, she leaned close to Gimme Lao in the school bus and whispered, "Don't tell anyone, but I just got married. I am now the wife of Chandra the Moon God." When Gimme Lao gave her a blank look of incomprehension, Omala had to explain herself. She had spent several nights thinking about it. If she only had to wash the dishes once a month, she would have so much time to do what she wanted. She could have all the adventures denied Sita, the lovely but useless wife of Lord Rama. So she found out from Uncle Anandan which portrait belonged to Chandra and in a private and unsupervised moment mimicked a quick ceremony to betroth herself to the deity-husband she needed to see only once a month. Gimme Lao was the only person she disclosed her secret to. He was to keep it to himself. If he betrayed her, she would unleash her fury on him with the violence of Kali the Goddess of Death and strangle him with the 10 hands of Durga, the one who rode the tiger.

Gimme Lao paled upon hearing Omala's threat. He had been consumed with guilt over a dark secret for the past two days. This threat by Omala was all it took to break down his defences. Gimme Lao took in a deep breath and told Omala he would be the keeper of her secret if she promised to reciprocate likewise. Two days ago, he had committed murder.

The chain of events was triggered several weeks ago, when a regular customer suffered a fatal heart attack while Barber Bay was shaving his sideburns. By the time the paramedics arrived, the old man was unequivocally dead. Barber Bay knew that the old man occupied a single bedroom unit in the adjacent block all by himself. None of his neighbours had seen anyone visit him, so there was no way his relatives, if there were any, could be contacted. In the end, the town council took over and dealt with the burial and property disposal matters. In the midst of the confusion, Barber Bay neglected to inform the town council that the deceased had left a caged bird at the barbershop. It was a hopping little yellow eye finch that sang incessantly. By the time he remembered, the town council refused to take in the extra item of trouble.

Barber Bay was a kind and considerate man. It was his habit to keep the radio on the entire day for the stream feed of news and music, and he felt that the yellow eye finch would not enjoy the noise. He imagined that if Grandma Toh took in the caged bird, the daily toasting of sambal chilli in the kitchen would be torture to the poor creature. In the end, he approached Gimme Lao's father for help.

The novelty of having a singing bird in the house intrigued Mary Lao for two days and Gimme Lao for two weeks. By the third week, the duty of feeding the yellow eye finch and cleaning the cage became the exclusive responsibility of Gimme Lao's father. Unlike the other two, Gimme Lao's father grew increasingly attached to the yellow eye finch. He located a coffee shop in the neighbourhood that provided a trellis framework for hanging birdcages and made it his Sunday routine to bring the yellow eye finch along for a breakfast gathering with other bird lovers. Mary and Gimme joined him once, but failed to discern the music from amidst the cacophony of competing vocals from two dozen singing birds. Thus, the Sunday routine remained his alone.

The yellow eye finch could have lived the rest of its natural life in the cage in Gimme Lao's household, were it not for the quarrel Gimme Lao's parents got into over dinner one night. Mary Lao had again urged her husband to sit for the certification examination for insurance, so that she could enlist him as a sales agent. She did not even require him to do actual sales. She would close the sales herself but park the cases under his account, so that the company would pay them twice, once under his direct sales commission and once more under her managerial cut. But Gimme Lao's father stubbornly refused. Everyone in the company would know he was a dummy agent and laugh at him behind his back.

Frustrated, Mary Lao launched a tirade. How could he, at the age of 36, harbour no ambition whatsoever? Was he content to settle for the meagre pay of an administrative clerk for the rest of his life? Did he not notice that all the other bird lovers who gathered for their Sunday routine were either retirees or bums who would amount to nothing in life? Did he understand the meaning of 'wan wu sang zhi'?

Gimme Lao did not understand the meaning of 'wan wu sang zhi'. By the blush on his father's face, it could not be anything but a derogatory term. The next day, Gimme Lao asked his Chinese language teacher in school about the term.

The teacher took the opportunity to explain to the entire class the historical background to the idiom. There once was a Chinese emperor who was so enamoured of cranes, he reared a school of them in the palace gardens. Not only did the emperor spend all his time admiring the cranes to the point that he neglected his duties, he declared that the cranes had the right of way when they crossed paths with the ministers and generals. By so doing, the emperor unwittingly incurred the silent wrath of his subjects. Eventually, when the northern barbarians launched an invasion, the generals refused to obey the emperor's order to take up arms. As a result, the poorly trained army, led by the incompetent emperor, was swiftly crushed and defeated. Historians picked up the lesson and condensed it into the idiom 'wan wu sang zhi'—one who is excessively enamoured with one's hobby will neglect one's true calling in life and amount to nothing respectable.

"The generals should have killed all the cranes before the emperor got too involved," Gimme Lao opined. "They could have saved the country."

"Oh no, that would be an unnecessarily cruel thing to do!" the teacher exclaimed. "The generals could perhaps have released the cranes into the wild. That is the humane thing to do. But then they would incur the wrath of the emperor and bring danger to themselves and their families. Politics is really too complicated."

Gimme Lao contemplated the teacher's solution and decided it could be applied to the problem at home. He waited patiently till he found himself alone one night when his father was out for his weekly chess game and his mother had left for an insurance sales appointment. Gingerly unhinging the birdcage from the hook in the ceiling, he brought it to the kitchen window and lifted the cage door. The yellow eye finch had to be coaxed to abandon the comforts of the cage and head out into the unknown. Gimme Lao then hung the cage back and proceeded to do his homework in the living room.

It took Gimme Lao's father all of two minutes after he stepped into the house to discover the horror of the empty birdcage. He let out a shriek and retraced his steps into the living room. "The bird's gone! Do you know what happened?"

Gimme Lao looked up with practised bewilderment and asked what was the matter.

Gimme Lao's father sat down heavily on the sofa and stared unseeing at the blank television screen. The look of shock was frozen on his face. Gimme Lao made a show of going into the kitchen to investigate. Upon his return, his father was angled forward, his face hidden in his palms.

"You must have forgotten to lock the cage door, Dad."

Gimme Lao's father shook his head slowly. When he finally removed his hands, there was a look of furious hatred in his eyes. "Never mind. I know what happened. Just do your homework."

Mary Lao did not return till midnight. She was a little surprised to see her husband reading the papers in bed, well past his usual bedtime. She quickly washed up and, hitting the pillow, requested her husband to switch off the light. She was too tired to notice that her husband was unusually silent, and that the folding and tossing aside of the papers was unusually brusque.

At dinner the next evening, Mary Lao caught Gimme making a face and gesturing at the empty birdcage. She gasped and remarked, "The bird is gone." The looks on both her husband and her son's faces told her that they had not expected her to take this long to realise it. Shrugging, Mary Lao muttered, "Maybe it's for the better. The bird was turning you into a bum. Now you can do something useful with your time." Had Mary Lao been more observant, she might have detected the dark swell of fury in her husband's silence and the look of apprehension on her son's face.

The next evening, Mary Lao was preparing dinner in the kitchen when Gimme Lao walked up to her with a weird expression on his face. "Dad has bought a new pet."

Flustered, Mary Lao wiped her hands dry and went into the living room. Her husband was seated on the sofa removing his socks. There was a 12-inch aquarium tank sitting on the table.

The sand was spread and the rocks were in place, but the tank was not filled up with water yet. Mary Lao secretly sighed with relief. A tiny aquarium was manageable.

"When do you intend to buy the fish? You should bring Gimme along and let him pick some," Mary Lao remarked as she removed the lid to get a better look. The scream that followed was so shrill, Grandma Toh came running from next door to find out what was wrong. She found Mary Lao pallid and trembling and pointing into the aquarium. Looking in, Grandma Toh spotted the tiny, luminous green snake.

"Is that one of your school projects?" Grandma Toh chided Gimme Lao as she replaced the lid to the tank. "You shouldn't scare your mother like that."

"Is that what you are trying to do? Scare me?" Mary Lao regained her voice and spit at her husband. "You know I hate snakes!"

Gimme Lao's father awarded Mary Lao a chilly glance and picked up the papers silently. He behaved as though he had earplugs on and couldn't hear the tirade that Mary Lao launched. Grandma Toh quickly grabbed Gimme Lao's hand and dragged him into her house. Children should never be exposed to the quarrels of parents.

Gimme Lao felt miserable. He had wanted to remove the subject of his father's infatuation so that the man would not stray further and further from his mother's expectations. Gimme Lao admired his mother. She had risen from the rank of a pharmacy assistant to become a successful insurance sales manageress through sheer perseverance and tenacity. In contrast, his father started off as an insurance clerk and maintained the status quo. He had snuggled deep into the comfort of mediocrity and refused to take up new challenges in life. Where once Gimme Lao had merely felt sorry for his father, he now began to despise the man. He had never imagined his father would be vindictive enough to buy a pet snake knowing that his mother was terrified of lizards and other crawlies. It was pure malice.

Gimme Lao lost sleep. The more he thought about the matter, the more enraged he became. It was bad enough that his parents were not talking to each other, and that an awkward silence enveloped the house all day. The irony of it was that nobody was paying the pet snake any particular attention. His father dutifully fed it earthworms and crickets, but ignored it otherwise. The glass tank and its silent occupant squatted on the table as a reminder of the ongoing cold war in the house.

It took Gimme Lao several days to garner his courage to do what had to be done. Once again he waited till his father left for the weekly chess game and his mother left for a sales appointment. This time round, the cranes would not be released into the wild as his teacher had suggested. They had to be murdered, left lifeless and bloody so that the emperor would tremble under the horror of the massacre. Releasing the yellow eye finch only served to intensify his father's longing for it. It would have to be a gruesome death this time.

Gimme Lao did not fancy touching the slimy creature, neither did he want to splatter the glass tank with blood. He thought drowning would be a good idea, but wasn't sure if snakes could swim. Eventually, the idea came to him. He set the kettle on the gas stove and fired it up. Once the kettle whistled, he grabbed the handle with a cushioning hand towel and gingerly carried it to the living room. Flipping open the feeding hole on the lid, Gimme Lao poured the boiled water into the tank till it was three quarters full. He set down the kettle and watched as the tiny green snake wriggled in silent agony for a few minutes until it was over. And then the lifeless body floated upside down.

It was only then that Gimme Lao started shaking. What had he done? His father would kill him! Even his mother might not condone this hideous act of murder. The snake had no place in his family, but did it deserve to die such a painful death?

Gimme Lao got out of the house and fled down the stairs to the Subramaniams. Omala and her cousins were playing five stones, or kallangal, as it was called in Tamil. For the next two hours, Gimme Lao sat unmoving and watched unseeing as the other children took turns throwing and picking the five stones in their various permutations. Eventually, Sabitha had to show Gimme Lao out the door so that the family could turn in for bed.

Back in the house, his father was reading the papers and his mother was taking a shower. The glass tank containing the dead snake was gone. Gimme Lao had no idea which of the two arrived home first to discover the gruesome murder, but neither of them questioned him about it. Soon, the lights were switched off and the family retired to bed. It was as though nothing extraordinary had happened.

Gimme Lao never did uncover the truth: that his father was the one who arrived at the scene of murder, recovered from the shock and disposed of the snake and the tank. He did not know that his father's shock was quickly replaced by relief. The man had been stressed out by the cold war with his wife, but did not know how to end it. He was secretly glad that his wife had taken it upon herself to drown the snake. The quiet disposal of the tank was him signalling that he was ready to step down from the stalemate.

Mary Lao was similarly relieved that her husband had finally backed down from his stubborn stance and gotten rid of that wretched snake. After the lights were off, she felt his hand on her waist under the blanket. She made it easy for him to remove her pyjamas, and the two engaged in conjugal intimacy that had been missing for days. The next morning, both of them woke up in extraordinarily good spirits.

Gimme Lao too felt relieved that he was able to share his dark secret with Omala. No one could break the bond between him and his buddy. He was especially thrilled when both of them were streamed into the same class in year six. The principal gathered all the Primary 6 students and impressed upon them that it was a very important year.

"Not only are all of you sitting for the PSLE, or Primary School Leaving Examination, at the end of the year, you are also targeting the inaugural bilingual programme. Only the best students who score in the top eighth percentile in the PSLE can get into the prestigious programme, offered by a mere handful of elite schools in Singapore. And it is my ambition to usher more students than any other primary school into the top eighth percentile, or TEP for short. I want all of you to make the school proud."

Inspired, Gimme Lao and Omala made a pact to study hard so that they could both make it into the TEP cohort. When Mary Lao arranged for a tuition teacher to brush Gimme Lao up on the examination subjects, he insisted Omala attend the tuition sessions too. Mary Lao was secretly amazed by the exceptionally strong bond the two children had managed to foster. When both scored brilliantly for the PSLE, she had no objections to their selecting the TEP programme in the same secondary school. In her mind, she could see Gimme and Omala growing old and sharing memories as lifelong friends.

But she was wrong. Gimme Lao and Omala turned hostile before they graduated from secondary school. It had to do with Mr Hasim Hassan, who taught them literature in Secondary 3. It was a love and hate affair. Omala was so infatuated she wanted to marry him. Gimme Lao on the other hand felt like murdering him.

No one who had crossed paths with him could possibly ignore Mr Hasim Hassan. The smooth demeanour and calm temperament one would expect from a literature teacher, much like the grace and finesse of musical notes one would expect out of a violin, were totally absent in him. Instead, Mr Hasim Hassan was as loud and brutal as a bandstand. When he was passionate, his voice boomed low like a bass drum. When he flew into a rage, his voice screeched like a runaway cymbal. And when he had an opinion or a stance to defend, he went on a rampage with his drumsticks and drowned out everybody else with his forcefulness.

The first time that Gimme Lao and Omala witnessed

Mr Hasim Hassan's fury was right after the Kishore concert incident. Kishore was one of India's most respected sitar maestros. Coming from a family of musicians that traced its pedigree back to the court musicians of the Mughals, Kishore electrified the audience when he reinterpreted classical ragas and dispensed with the traditional accompaniment of the tanpura drone. Working closely with famous sitar-maker Hiren Roy, he studied and improved on the instrument. Shortly after independence, Kishore became one of the first Indian musicians to be invited to perform in England, in a concert to showcase the subcontinent's musical heritage. Prior to 1980, the Singapore National Day Concert working committee had twice invited Kishore to fly in to perform, but Kishore had politely declined. This time round, the India International Trade Fair Organisation was negotiating for better access rights to the busiest port in the region and a Kishore concert materialised as part of the package.

In the weeks leading up to the concert, Mr Hasim Hassan could barely contain his excitement. He shamelessly pilfered 20 minutes of the classes he taught and instead of discussing the guilt that hounded Lady Macbeth as she sleepwalked and tried desperately to wash off invisible bloodstains, he brought along his private cassette tape and played a segment of Kishore's sitar performance. He told the students that Shakespeare was great but he was dead and could wait. Kishore on the other hand was a living legend and Mr Hasim Hassan himself could barely bear the agony of the wait.

The Kishore concert did not materialise.

According to the news, when Kishore arrived at the Singapore International Airport at Paya Lebar, the welcoming party ushered him to a VIP customs clearance lane that had been set aside for him. Kishore, ever humble and virtuous, declined the special treatment and insisted on joining the main queue. When his turn came, Kishore was puzzled by the accusatory look on the customs officer's face. Without a word, the man pointed to a poster on the wall, which simply read 'Singapore Customs and Immigration reserves the right to bar male visitors with long hair and unkempt manes from entering the country'.

Kishore, whose mane cascaded down his back halfway to his waistline, stood stunned while the welcoming party blushed furiously and tried to negotiate with the customs officer. The man stood his ground steadfastly. This rule had been in place for close to 10 years. Even Jimmy Page and his band Led Zeppelin had to cancel their concert because they refused to crop their long hair. Why should it be any different for Kishore?

When Mr Hasim Hassan learned about the circumstances under which Kishore was turned away at the customs, he blew his top. He completely ignored the syllabus of the day and ranted for the entire duration of the class. It was bad enough that the government ran a campaign to discriminate against males with long hair and made it legal for customs officers to impound their passports and refuse them entry until their hair was cropped. But to be so arrogant as to insist on dictating the behavioural code to foreigners? That was pushing it too far!

After 30 minutes of Mr Hasim Hassan's ranting, Gimme Lao could no longer bear it. He raised his hand for permission to speak and firmly reminded Mr Hasim Hassan that there was a poster prominently displayed at the school cafeteria reiterating that 'Males with long hair will be attended to last'. It was a widely accepted governmental policy. Why should foreigners visiting the country not be asked to abide by it? Singapore carried a death penalty for drug traffickers. Should foreigners be exempted from the rule then?

Mr Hasim Hassan's eyes lit up at Gimme Lao's opining. It was obvious to the class that he loved a challenge.

"Why do you think the government imposes the death penalty on drug trafficking, Gimme?"

"Because it is the duty of the government to protect the people. Drugs are bad for our health. Drug addiction destroys lives and families."

"Very good, Gimme. Now my next question: do you not agree that alcohol and cigarettes are bad for our health too? And that drunken violence and secondhand smoke harms the family? Why do you think the government does not impose a ban on these?"

Gimme Lao hesitated a little before putting up a defence, "Because the impact of drug addiction is a hundred times worse."

"Good point." Mr Hasim Hassan raised his brows and turned to the rest of the class. "Gimme brought up a very important word. Impact. Drug addiction reduces a person to a useless member of society. He will not be able to hold a job, and he may even resort to vices or crime to fund his addiction. Mass drug addiction can cripple a society. The government cannot allow that. Do we all agree with the argument so far?"

No one in the class objected.

"Alcohol and cigarettes on the other hand, though harmful for the consumer, do not directly harm the society at large. In fact, these commodities are heavily taxed, thus providing a steady stream of income for the government. Make no mistake, boys and girls. The government is mandated to take care of the people's welfare. But the government is also a living organism primarily concerned with its own interest and survival. It needs its people to function as economic beings. You can smoke and drink and still work and pay taxes, so the government allows it. But if you take drugs and stop contributing, you become useless to the government. That, it will not allow."

The class was stunned. No other teacher had ever openly critiqued the government.

"Let us now come back to the policy of discriminating against males with long hair. Why do you think the government does that? Enlighten us, Gimme."

Gimme Lao sat up straight and spoke in a clear voice. He had been handpicked to be part of the welcoming team when the Minister of Home Affairs visited the school last month. He recalled very clearly what the minister shared when she toured the school cafeteria and discussed the various campaign posters on display.

"It is a campaign against the decadence of Western influence and hippie culture. Hippies wear their hair long, listen to pop music all day long, smoke cocaine and heroin and engage in wild sex. We do not want that in Singapore."

The class erupted into paroxysms of giggles. Someone

whispered that they didn't mind the wild sex part.

"And what is it about the hippie culture that is so decadent?" Mr Hasim Hassan raised a single eyebrow at Gimme Lao.

"What I just mentioned." Gimme Lao frowned. "They don't work. They just want to have fun."

"Exactly!" Mr Hasim Hassan clapped his hands together and exclaimed. "They don't work. They just want to have fun! That is not acceptable to our government. Our government needs all of us to be workhorses. Work 50 out of 52 weeks a year. Work five and a half days out of the seven-day week. You are only valuable if you contribute economically. You are groomed and trained to be workhorses. All these campaign posters you see distributed by the ministries, they work like cookie cutters. Their function is to mentally mould you into the exact shape that the government wants. Do you get it?"

Many in the class squirmed in discomfort. Never had a teacher challenged the authorities in their presence. A handful, Omala among them, bit their lips. They could savour the undercurrent of excitement in their blood as they experienced a paradigm shift. They watched as Mr Hasim Hassan whipped out a cassette tape from his bag, popped it into the player and pressed 'play'. Sitar music wafted out and enveloped the classroom. Mr Hasim Hassan gestured for the class to remain silent and to just enjoy the music.

The recess bell rang as the piece came to an end. Mr Hasim Hassan sighed with great satisfaction and remarked, "This music is a piece of heaven right here on earth. Such a genius as Kishore will not survive in Singapore. His talents will be ignored and the man will be trained to be a workhorse like everybody else. Boys and girls, there are independent spirits among you: of that I am sure. Do not be defeated by the system. Play your own music, even if it is different from the others. Especially if it is different from the others."

At the school cafeteria, Gimme Lao bought two bowls of laksa and sat waiting for Omala for a full 20 minutes. When she finally arrived, he grumbled irritably, "What took you so long?"

"I went to talk to Mr Hasim Hassan. I asked him out on a date."

"What?!"

"Kidding!" Omala chuckled. "I asked him if I can meet up with him sometime after school."

"Whatever for?"

"I want to hear him talk about real life, not books. The Kishore discussion just now was exciting!"

"I thought you enjoyed literature?" Gimme Lao frowned.

"I do!" Omala mumbled as she manoeuvred a spoonful of noodles into her mouth. "I love the riches of Yeats and Shakespeare, but Mr Hasim Hassan is right. These guys are dead and can wait. In the meanwhile, real life is happening outside the school gates. I want to grab that!"

"And he said yes?" The frown never left Gimme Lao's forehead.

"Yes. Saturday afternoon. He is rehearsing for some experimental stage play at a venue called The Substation, at Armenian Street. He asked me to swing by."

Gimme Lao felt uneasy about the arrangement. Firstly, he

did not trust Mr Hasim Hassan. The man did not play by the rules. Gimme Lao trusted rules. He himself excelled within the framework of rules. He had emerged champion in the annual mathematics quiz two years in a row and was recently elected to be chairman of the Students Mathematics Club. He loved that there was no ambiguity about mathematics. All answers could be arrived at through logic and intelligence.

Literature, on the other hand, allowed for ambiguity and interpretations. Mr Hasim Hassan drove the class to dig deep and uncover their respective interpretations. The man claimed that there were no right or wrong answers. That alone was enough to unnerve Gimme Lao. He secretly suspected that Mr Hasim Hassan lacked due respect for the parameters of what constituted right and wrong. He found the man as incomprehensible as the subject he taught and instinctively distrusted him.

Secondly, he did not trust Omala to behave herself. She had a tendency to disregard rules and authority and often landed herself in trouble. When they studied biology in year one, they had had to dissect a rabbit in the laboratory. Omala had annoyed the biology teacher by insisting that the class be allowed to vote to sacrifice their learning in exchange for the release of the rabbit. In year two, Omala was upset when she read in a *Life* magazine article that child brides in Yemen as young as five or six, betrothed to husbands who were 20 to 40 years older, tended to suffer from physical abuse and fatal miscarriages. Shortly after, she embarrassed the school authorities by going on stage during the annual ministerial visit and questioning the minister as to why Singapore was not listed in the International Human Rights Watch list of countries that had voiced their opposition to the practice of child brides in Yemen. The visiting minister fumbled clumsily for an answer until the principal came to his rescue. Following the incident, the school authorities made it compulsory for students to submit their questions for vetting before they were selected to participate in the annual ministerial dialogues.

Gimme Lao's foreboding became entrenched when Omala's Saturday visit to The Substation extended into weekly sessions. She had enrolled herself as a stagehand for the play in development.

"What is the play about?" Gimme Lao wanted to know.

"Can't tell you. Theme and content are embargoed till opening night." Omala grinned and added with a wink, "I can sneak you in for the rehearsal though. It will be an eye opener, I can promise you that!"

On Saturday afternoon, Gimme Lao caught a bus down to the National Library building at Stamford Road and strolled over to the adjoining Armenian Street. He located The Substation easily. It was a red-brick building that used to serve as a power substation up till two years ago. While it awaited redevelopment, it was rented out to the performing arts community as a rehearsal and performance space.

Omala galloped down the stairs at three sharp. "Full rehearsal starting in five minutes. I will sneak you in. You got to leave before they turn on the lights. Mr Hasim Hassan doesn't need to know you're here."

The theatre was dark enough that their entrance went

unnoticed. Omala ushered Gimme to a bench where he could get an angled view of the stage. Five chairs were lined up in a row on stage, illuminated by five sets of spotlights. He was surprised to see all the seats in the mini-theatre taken up. It was most unusual to have a turnout of over a hundred people attending a rehearsal.

Someone in the back stage tapped on a percussion triangle to invite silence from the audience. The stage lights went off. Several seconds later, two sets of spotlights came back on, descending onto two seated figures on stage. A Chinese in a white tee shirt sat bent over on the left, his face hidden in his hands. The second was a Caucasian wearing a brown suit, who sat staring at the audience with a startled expression, his left hand holding a cup suspended in the air.

"Karl..."the Caucasian whispered. The Chinese did not answer.

"Karl...the coffee..." Still, the Chinese did not move.

Then, the Caucasian let the cup drop. It crashed onto the floor, shattering the silence with the impact of breaking porcelain. The Caucasian stood up, tottered, then slumped down onto the floor. Dead.

The hands that covered the face crawled down to the neck, revealing eyes that were stunned, sad, in pain. The stage lights extinguished. In the ensuing darkness, an announcement was made in a monotone, devoid of sentiment.

"Deceased: male, 36, Caucasian, married, father of one, super-market operations manager. Cause of death: poisoning. Case classified as murder. Name of Brian Brown."

"Suspect: male, 24, Chinese, single, supermarket supervisor. Charged with first-degree murder. Name of Karl Li."

"Relationship: manager and employee."

"Suspected relationship: homosexual lovers."

"Motive for murder: not established."

The lights came on. The body on the floor was gone. The murder suspect sat in the centre, flanked on both sides by four angry, shouting men. No one could make out what was being said amidst the overlapping arguments and rants. The Chinese suspect cupped both ears, face grimaced in agony, body twisted. "Stop!" he pleaded. "One at a time, please…"

All but two spotlights extinguished. One focused onto the Chinese suspect, the other onto a bespectacled Malay man on the left. Gimme Lao gasped as he recognised Mr Hasim Hassan.

"I am your psychiatrist, Karl Li. You must believe that I am here to help."

"What can you do for me?" the Chinese suspect asked, slowly putting down his trembling hands.

"The deceased's lawyer has a strong case on his hands. You must cooperate with me if you want to clear yourself of the murder charge."

"Clear?" the Chinese suspect snorted. "I told them. I poisoned Brian."

"Now, now, now…we don't know that yet. Your family doesn't seem to think so. Your uncle is willing to go to great lengths to clear you of the charge."

"My family? They don't speak to me anymore. They cannot accept the fact that their son is…gay."

"But your uncle loves you," the psychiatrist insisted.

The Chinese suspect snickered. "He does? How can he, when I am such an inconvenience? Do you know that he is a prominent grassroots leader in his constituency? He cannot afford a scandal."

"Karl! Look at me, Karl!"

The spotlight over the psychiatrist was extinguished. A second spotlight traced the angry voice and illuminated a balding, middle-aged Chinese man seated on the right. The Chinese suspect cringed.

"You are a disgrace, Karl!" the uncle fumed. "What happened to you? You were such a sweet child."

"I was…a sweet child," the Chinese suspect echoed.

"You broke your mother's heart. You totally disappointed your father," the uncle accused.

"I disappointed my father…" Another echo. "What did he expect of me?"

"Why…that you should grow up a fine young man just like everybody else."

"Just like everybody else. But I can't be. I am not just like everybody else."

"Nonsense! You can and should be just like everybody else."

"Everybody else finishes school, gets a job, gets hitched, gets married and starts a family. I finished school, got a job, got… fell in love and then… There is nothing after that. There is no marriage, no family for me. I don't know what to do next."

"You fell wayward. You got into bad company. You must tell the judge that. The man, that white man, destroyed your life."

"That man's got a name. He is Brian," the Chinese suspect announced coldly. "He did not destroy my life. I did not have a life until I met him. And neither did he. We gave each other a new life when we came together. It was painful, very painful, but we were ourselves with one another."

"You don't know what you are talking about!" the uncle bellowed. "Why can't you give your mother less pain? She loves you so."

"She feels pain because she cannot accept me as a gay child. She would rather hang on to the stubborn belief that I am an innocent child gone wrong, corrupted by the decadence of the West, than suffer the agony of realising that she doesn't really know me. In her pain she is dignified and righteousness is on her side. She asks to feel pain."

"How could you say such a thing about your mother?" The uncle uttered, horrified, before dissolving into darkness, "You need help."

The spotlight once again descended on the psychiatrist.

"Karl, I want to help. Will you talk to me?"

"What would you like to know?"

"It's best if we start from the beginning. Tell me how you came to meet Brian Brown."

"He was the manager at Cold Storage Supermarket. He interviewed me when I applied for the job three years ago."

"And how would you describe your working relationship with Brian Brown?"

"Good. I was hardworking and willing to learn. He was happy to guide me. Within a year he promoted me to supervisor."

"And you liked him a lot?"

The Chinese suspect let a nostalgic smile creep up as he lost himself in recollection.

"He was always good to me. We used to go for lunch breaks by ourselves, just the two of us. And we talked. We talked a lot."

"About?"

"About his family, his wife. About myself, my family. About our lives."

"He talked about his wife. So you knew he was married."

"Yes, he told me a lot about his wife. Her name was Sue."

"Why do you think he talked to you about his wife?"

"Because I asked."

"Why?"

There was a pause.

"I was curious."

"Why were you curious?"

"I guess…" The Chinese suspect bit his lip. "I wanted to know if she was a good wife. If he was happy with her."

"Did he tell you he was unhappy with his marriage?"

"No." It took a moment of reflection. "But I know he was happy with me."

"How can you be sure about that? Did he tell you?"

"I sensed it."

"How?"

"I just know!" The Chinese suspect was getting irritable.

"All right…I believe you," the psychiatrist coaxed. "Tell me, Karl, when was the first time he made a pass at you?"

There was another pause. The expression softened. The

irritability disappeared, replaced by a dreamy haziness. "He didn't. I made the first move."

The psychiatrist persuaded very gently, "Tell me."

"It was…in December. My first Christmas at Cold Storage. I had never been that swamped before. Festive promotions. Christmas jingles. The cash registers kept ringing. And the stocktaking drove me crazy! The never ending stocktake…"

A tall figure in a brown suit moved silently into the sphere of spotlight. It was Brian Brown. The dead man. The murdered.

"I will never finish this!" Karl exclaimed in exasperation.

"You don't have to finish it today," Brian consoled. "There is plenty of time tomorrow."

"Brian, you are the manager. You should be the last to tell me that!" Karl chuckled, slapping Brian on his thigh. "Besides, I noticed that someone worked on my stocktaking last night after I left. It was you, wasn't it?"

Brian grinned shyly. "I don't want you to overwork yourself."

"You should have told me." Karl smiled warmly. "I would have stayed on and we could have worked together."

Brian shrugged. "I am working overtime tonight."

Karl stood up, his eyes lit with irrepressible joy. "I will go and get us some dinner." he said, retreating out of the spotlight.

"Is there anybody else working overtime?"

"What?" Brian swivelled around, jolted, only to realise it was the psychiatrist who spoke.

"Is there anybody else working overtime?" The question was repeated.

"No. No one else."

"So you will be alone with the boy?"

"Yes…with Karl." Brian fidgeted with discomfort.

"What were you thinking of, Brian? What were you thinking?" The psychiatrist clicked his tongue in disapproval.

"What are you trying to say?" Brian snapped, confused, embarrassed, annoyed.

"Did you say something?" Karl asked, stepping into the sphere of spotlight.

"No…I am just tired." Brian stumbled, craning his neck.

"You need to relax." Karl stood behind the chair and began to massage Brian's neck. Brian shut his eyes and sighed in contentment.

"Feel better?"

"Heavenly."

"What you need is a fresh cup of strong coffee," Karl remarked, giving his ear a loving pinch before retreating out of the spotlight. Brian was left alone, softly caressing the spot that was pinched, lost in thought.

"You liked that, didn't you?" the psychiatrist interjected.

"What?"

"When he pinched you on the ear, you enjoyed the touch, yes?"

"I-I don't know."

"Yes, you do," the psychiatrist insisted. "You were very much aware of what was going on. What happened next, happened because you wanted it to happen."

"What happens next?" Brian asked, trembling a little.

"What happens next is you take time off the bloody

stocktaking to enjoy your coffee," Karl announced as he appeared and handed Brian a cup. He looked on lovingly as Brian sipped the coffee. "Does Sue know you will not be home for dinner tonight?"

Brian almost choked, spilling coffee onto his pants. Karl knelt down quickly to wipe off the stain with his handkerchief. Brian gazed at him, confused. "Why do you always mention Sue, Karl? You do it every time we are together."

Karl slowed down on the wiping. "I am just curious... I have never met her, but I believe she must be a remarkable woman to have a man like you love her so much. You do love her, don't you?"

The hand that held the cup was shaking slightly. "Of course I do. I am her husband."

"That is good." Karl's remark was almost inaudible.

"There is no need to be jealous, Karl. You are a good boy. You will someday find someone who will love you more than I love Sue."

"More than you love Sue?" Karl looked up, with hope in his eyes. "Do you love someone more than you love Sue?"

"I...I didn't say that," Brian stuttered. "I am sure I didn't say that."

Disappointment registering on his face, Karl slowly withdrew to his own chair and sat down.

"What is it, Karl? Is it something I said?"

"No, it is something you did not say."

There was a long pause. Brian fidgeted. Karl remained silent. The psychiatrist watched.

Eventually, Karl broke the silence. "If there is someone who loves me more than you love Sue, let him speak. For I know that I will love him as much as he loves me. I do know that I love him already."

Brian trembled when Karl looked up and gazed into his eyes. But he could not tear his eyes away.

"Kiss me, Brian," Karl finally said.

"I heard that!"

It was a shout, emitting from the dark space next to Brian. A spotlight came on and illuminated an Indian with a moustache. The lights on Brian and Karl went off.

Fuming at the interruption, the psychiatrist jumped on the newcomer, "Who the hell are you?"

The Indian with the moustache hurled the psychiatrist an arrogant glance and announced haughtily, "I am the lawyer for the deceased, Mr Brian Brown. And I saw and heard it!"

"Saw and heard what?"

"Saw and heard and witnessed the accused seducing and entrapping the deceased in the emotional entanglement that would directly lead to his murder two years later."

"Bullshit!"

"Watch your words. I could sue you."

"I am not going to waste my time with you," the psychiatrist decided. "I want to speak with my client Mr Karl Li."

"So do I," said the lawyer.

"What is it?" The spotlight descended onto the Chinese suspect Karl Li. Brian the deceased was nowhere in sight.

"Mr Karl Li, I have some questions for you," the lawyer promptly said.

"What is it?" Karl repeated. He appeared dazed and disheartened.

"Was the deceased, a Mr Brian Brown, your lover of two years, with whom you had an ongoing sexual relationship?"

"Sex? Yes. That we love one another? Yes too."

"Did you have any sexual partners before him?"

"No."

"Never even experimented?" The lawyer sounded incredulous. "Why?"

Karl gazed blankly into space. "I was…confused."

"Confused!" The lawyer perked up.

"Scared…" Karl muttered.

"Scared? Because you know it is wrong?" the lawyer suggested almost gleefully.

Karl shook his head.

"Speak up, Mr Karl Li. We cannot record gesticulation," the lawyer urged.

"What I felt was not wrong. It would be wrong to pretend to love a woman and marry her when you know in your heart your love lies with a man."

"In your heart your love lies with a man? And who might this man be?"

Karl was silent.

"A certain Brian Brown? Your manager, mentor, who gave you ample guidance and showed you concern when you were first starting out? Someone you look up to? Respect and admire, perhaps?"

"I know what you are driving at," Karl remarked coldly. "It

is more than that. It is…love."

"And how would you know love, Mr Karl Li, when you have never been in a relationship before this? Could you not simply be, as you so proclaimed earlier, confused?"

Karl shook his head with determination. "It is love between Brian and me. I know it."

"How would you know? By the stirring in your groin?" the lawyer challenged.

"It is more than a stirring in the groin! It is the care you feel for each other. It is the warmth and understanding you convey when you look each other in the eye. It is putting the other person ahead of yourself. It is the pain you feel when you are unsure if this will last at all. The willingness to give all, your time, your energy, your heart, your everything. God, don't you think I know love at all?"

Karl began to whimper.

"He is upset," the psychiatrist said. "Leave him alone for a while."

The spotlight over Karl dimmed, then flickered out.

"Perhaps I should talk to your client too," the psychiatrist suggested.

"What? Why?" The lawyer became alarmed. When the spotlight flickered on and Brian Brown materialised on the adjacent seat, he was quick to add, "I want my client to know that he has the right not to answer any question of yours that he or I deem irrelevant to the court case at hand."

"I am sure he understands that," the psychiatrist remarked coldly. Turning to the deceased, he began his questioning.

"Brian, were you lovers with Karl for two years?"

"Yes, I was."

"Do you love him deeply?"

"Yes, I do."

"My client only thinks he does," the lawyer cut in. "It is the accused who confused my client with his confusion. The accused is confused between emotional intimacy and homosexual attraction. My client does not love him. He has a loving wife at home."

The psychiatrist continued. "Brian, you have a wife at home, yes?"

"Yes."

"Do you love her?"

There was a moment of hesitancy. "I-I think so. I don't know."

"My client knows. He does love his wife. Why else would he marry her? They have a kid, for crying out loud!" It was the lawyer.

"Yes…I do love her," Brian conceded.

"Between Karl and Sue, which appears more the person you would honestly like to love?" the psychiatrist pursued.

"That is a ridiculous question!" the lawyer exclaimed. "The accused is nothing but a peripheral sexual adventure. I'll even take misadventure!"

"I feel sorry for Sue," Brian sighed. "But it is Karl I dread to lose."

"You did not have to answer that question, Mr Brown!" the lawyer fumed.

"I think… I know I do love Karl."

"You don't have to commit yourself here," the lawyer hissed.

"You are dead, remember?"

"I wish I had committed myself before he killed me," Brian lamented in a sad voice.

"He killed you! Yes, but spell out his name. Quick!" the lawyer urged.

"Why did he do it?" the psychiatrist probed.

"He did it because I was confused and in pain, and he wanted me out of this pain."

"We need names here, Mr Brown!" the lawyer clenched his fists.

"Names? Yes. I was going to name my second baby after him, if it were a boy."

"Your second baby?" Both the psychiatrist and the lawyer exclaimed simultaneously.

"Sue is pregnant again. It was an accident."

"How did Karl take the news?" There was compassion in the psychiatrist's voice.

Brian shook his head and started to whimper. "It was my fault. I couldn't leave Sue. I felt so sorry for her. I slept with Karl and loved him. I ceased to love Sue but slept with her nonetheless because I had no excuses. But I lied and told Karl he was the only one I slept with and loved."

"No, no, no… You are getting it all mixed up," the lawyer insisted. "It is Sue, your wife, whom you love. It may be true that you slept with Karl, the accused, but definitely untrue that you love him. You may think you love him, but that is the accused projecting his confusion onto you."

"You are confusing me!" Brian held his head in his hands

and whined.

"Stop confusing my client!" The lawyer turned to shout at the psychiatrist.

"I am not the one confusing him!" the psychiatrist retorted.

"You are confusing yourself!" An angry voice emitted from the darkness. Karl moved up behind Brian and cradled his head. "I thought you understood what we had."

"I do, Karl, I do!" Brian looked up and exclaimed.

"Then why is Sue pregnant?"

"Because...because I felt sorry for her."

Karl sat down heavily on the adjacent chair, laden with a deep sadness. There was a long pause before he finally sighed and muttered, "I love you too much to see you languish in this pain, Brian."

"But what can I do?" Brian started to cry.

"You can leave Sue and the kid and come to me."

"I can't do that." Brian shuddered.

"Or you can leave me and go back to Sue."

"I don't want to leave you, Karl," Brian pleaded.

"So what do you want to do?" Three voices asked in frustration.

"I don't know," Brian sobbed aloud.

There was a long silence. The auditorium echoed with Brian's sobs, his shoulders shaking. The spotlight dimmed on the lawyer, then the psychiatrist, next the sobbing figure and then, just before Karl was to be engulfed by the enveloping darkness, he asked, in a low, sad voice, "Shall I make you a cup of coffee?"

Darkness descended.

A jarring crash as porcelain hit the ground.

In the darkness, a newspaper report was read aloud.

"A 36-year-old man was found dead in the manager's office at the downtown Cold Storage. The police identified the deceased as the operational manager, a Mr Brian Brown.

"The informant, also an employee of Cold Storage, was there to greet the police upon their arrival. The same man claimed to have administered the poison in a cup of coffee that was the direct cause of death.

"The case has been classified as murder, first degree."

"The suspect, a 24-year-old Chinese male, has pleaded guilty."

Two spotlights came on. One illuminated the Chinese suspect's uncle, looking rightfully grieved and in pain. The second shone onto a bright-eyed young man, leaning forward in his chair with a tape recorder stretched towards the uncle.

"Good afternoon, Mr Li. I am a reporter from *The Essential Truth* news magazine. We are grateful to you for granting this interview. I understand there is more to the case than what was disclosed by the police. Can you perhaps enlighten us on the relationship between your nephew Mr Karl Li and the victim Mr Brian Brown?"

"I need to clarify something," the uncle announced. "Mr Brian Brown is the deceased, not the victim. The victim is my nephew, Karl Li."

"How is that so?" the reporter pursued.

"Karl is a sweet child. Has always been, until he started work at Cold Storage. It was there that he fell into bad company and went wayward. And the bad company is none other than he who you thought was the victim, that Brown guy."

"Can you be more specific?"

"Mr Brian Brown, in his position as the trusted manager… I shudder to use the word, sexually seduced my nephew."

"Do you have any evidence to back up your claim, Mr Li?"

"Evidence? You need look no further than my nephew himself. An innocent, filial, obedient young man, uninitiated to the sins of the flesh, who was unable to resist the sexual temptation that deviant gay man laid on him, completely destroying his life! What more evidence do you need?"

"But I was told that Mr Karl Li has identified himself as a gay man."

"Nonsense!" the uncle bellowed. "Homosexuality does not run in my family. It is western decadence and gay influence that corrupted my nephew. He is the victim, I am telling you!"

"Thank you, Mr Li," the reporter acknowledged, as the spotlight over the uncle dimmed. The reporter turned to the lawyer, who materialised under another descending spotlight. "Mr Lawyer, I believe you have a statement to make."

"That is correct." The lawyer nodded haughtily. "I represent my client Mr Brian Brown and his family, who are grieved at his untimely departure, in wishing to clear his name of some scandalous libel."

"Scandalous libel, Mr Lawyer?"

"Yes. The newspaper has been careless in reporting the case and has wrongly labelled my client as a gay man."

"Isn't it true that your client Mr Brian Brown has had an ongoing homosexual relationship with the accused Mr Karl Li?"

"There is only one gay man in this relationship, and that is

Mr Karl Li. My client was, simply, a victim."

"And how is that so?" the reporter pursued.

"Brian Brown was a good man. Had always been, until the accused, a self-confessed gay youth, started work at Cold Storage. It was then that my client fell into bad company and went wayward. And the bad company is none other than he who was to be his murderer two years later, that Chinese kid."

"Can you be more specific?"

"The Chinese kid, taking advantage of my client's trust as his mentee… I shudder to use the word, he sexually seduced him."

"Do you have any evidence to back up your claim, Mr Lawyer?"

"Evidence? You need look no further than my client himself. A loving, responsible, doting husband and father, uninitiated to the lure of deviant sexuality, who was unable to resist the temptation that deviant gay youth laid on him, completely destroying his life! What more evidence do you need?"

"Are you suggesting that in this case, there is an innocent victim who has fallen prey to the seduction of a gay man? And the victim himself is not gay?"

"That is correct!" Two voices concurred. The spotlight had again descended onto the uncle.

"And that the gay man is the cause of the tragedy, the one who brought the other party to his downfall?"

"That is again correct." Two voices answered simultaneously.

"And the one is…"

"The accused. Karl Li," said the lawyer.

"The deceased. Brian Brown," said the uncle.

The two turned to glare at one another.

"You are confused!" They insisted simultaneously.

"I am confused," the reporter confessed.

"You are all confused!" the psychiatrist announced, materialising under the descending spotlight. There were now four men on stage.

"And who might you be?" asked the reporter.

"I am the psychiatrist."

"What do you have to say about the accused, Karl Li?"

"He is a victim."

"See? That was what I said," the uncle interjected, triumphant. "The man is a professional. He knows what he is talking about."

"What about the deceased, Brian Brown?" The reporter once again directed the question at the psychiatrist.

"He is no less the victim."

"Now the man is talking!" the lawyer interjected, triumphant. "I have to give the man credit. He does know what he is talking about."

"Wait a minute, this can't be!" The reporter waved off the interruption. "We can't have two victims here."

"It's the truth."

"It cannot be!" Three voices protested.

"You represent *The Essential Truth* news magazine. It is the essential truth you want, isn't it?" The psychiatrist turned to the reporter.

"But this is unacceptable! The reader will never buy the story. We need a guilty party."

"You want a guilty party? I will give you one." The psychiatrist arched his brows. "In fact, I can let you choose. Guilty party number one, Karl's family, represented by his uncle over here."

"What?" The uncle was caught off guard.

"A family that does not recognise Karl as who he is, a gay man. A family that withholds understanding and support. A family frantic to protect itself from scandal and only too willing to blame the deceased as the cause of all evils."

"He is the cause of all evils!" the uncle disputed.

The psychiatrist ignored the remark, but pointed a finger at the lawyer instead. "Guilty party number two, the legal system, represented by Mr Lawyer here."

"What?" the lawyer bellowed.

"A legal system that denies the gay man his sexual identity. A legal system that enforces a heterosexual behavioural code on a man like Brian Brown and hinders him from living life the way he wants to. A legal system that labels the homosexual alternative lifestyle as a deviant and immoral one."

"It is a deviant and immoral one!" the lawyer argued.

"Now we are getting somewhere!" the reporter said gleefully. "There is controversy and sensationalism galore, enough to make this our star article for the upcoming issue of *The Essential Truth*."

The psychiatrist swivelled around and glared at the reporter. "I almost forgot. There is yet one more on the list."

"There is more!" The reporter was over the moon. "Pray tell."

"Guilty party number three, the media, represented by Mr Reporter, you yourself."

"Me?"

"A media that is selective and biased. A media that is too

eager to offer the public what it wishes to see. A media that thrives on sensationalism, selectively focusing on the seedier aspects of gay culture and failing to report that there are gay men out there who lead well-adjusted, fulfilling lives."

"This man is talking nonsense!" the uncle protested.

"I regret overestimating his intelligence and professionalism," the lawyer professed.

"I guess I will have to trust my journalistic acumen, sift through the recordings and retain what is publishable," the reporter snorted.

The central spotlight came back on. The wretched Chinese suspect sat with his legs folded and eyes shut. The four men began to bombard him with questions and accusations, but the Chinese suspect ignored them. He seemed to have gone into a trance. The lights on the surrounding men began to dim, and the commotion faded as they slowly disappeared into the oblivion of total darkness. A silent figure in a brown suit strolled into the sphere of light. He stood behind the Chinese suspect, not moving, not speaking. The Chinese suspect slowly opened his eyes, aware of the new presence.

"Brian, is that you?"

"Yes, Karl. It's me."

The Chinese suspect rolled his head back, his shoulders slumped. "Oh, Brian, I feel so tired…so tired."

"Come, you ought to relax." The man in the brown suit behind the chair began to massage the Chinese suspect's neck. There was a sigh of deep contentment.

"Does that feel good?"

"So much better. Where did you learn to do that?"

"What you need is a good, strong cup of coffee."

Lights extinguished.

A final crash as porcelain hit the ground.

The mini-theatre thundered with applause as the lights came back on and the six actors stood in a row to bow. Gimme Lao was feeling dazed when he felt a nudge from Omala seated next to him. "You got to go. Wait for me at the library. I will meet you in an hour."

Gimme Lao found a quiet corner at the reading room and pretended to read the Chinese papers. He remained mired in disconcertion; Omala had not prepared him for the shock.

"The audience loved it!" Omala gushed when she finally hopped in. "The standing ovation lasted more than five minutes, can you imagine?"

"I hate to tell you this but the media authority will never let them perform," Gimme Lao remarked. "Not with homosexuality as the main theme. All these rehearsals will be for nothing."

"Of course they will never let us perform. The director and his team aren't stupid!" Omala laughed. "And that is the beauty of running rehearsals at The Substation. Word of mouth got us a steady stream of audience members by the week. When the opening date comes, they will simply postpone licence application and keep running rehearsals. Why do you think so many people turn up every Saturday? This is the unlicensed performance!"

Gimme Lao frowned. He knew Omala well enough to under-stand the attraction a deviant experimental play troupe such as this held for her. "Omala, listen to me. Mr Hasim Hassan and his friends are pushing the boundaries and they will eventually get into trouble. You have to stay away from them."

"Stay away from them? Are you out of your mind?" Omala was incredulous. "These are the most exciting people I have come across! Those few actors on stage just now? Two of them run an organic farm in the Philippines, one of them volunteers at an animal shelter and the other two are collaborating with Mr Hasim Hassan to start an underground newsletter for the gay community. These are passionate people who are championing causes the rest of the sleeping population remain oblivious to or blasé about. They are doing exciting things with their lives!"

"Mr Hasim Hassan is gay?" Gimme Lao almost forgot to breathe.

"Not only that, his boyfriend was part of the cast on stage too." Omala's eyes twinkled with mischief. "Guess which one?"

Gimme Lao fidgeted uncomfortably. "There was an article in the papers just two days ago about an engineer who was caught in the public toilet soliciting a young man for sex. The engineer was thrown in jail. Did you miss that article?"

Omala paused for a moment as she suddenly realised Gimme Lao did not share her enthusiasm. "The engineer did not solicit or pay for sex. It was entrapment. The young man was an undercover police officer laying a trap for men who cruise in public toilets."

"That's not what was reported in the papers," Gimme Lao retorted.

"Of course not. You will never get the truth from the state-controlled media," Omala sighed. "I know because the engineer is a friend of Mr Hasim Hassan. They were discussing the incident last week. That is why they need to have an underground newsletter to serve the gay community. People need to know what is really going on."

Gimme Lao bit his lip as he gazed at his best friend. Already he could feel the crack between them. He knew deep down that Mr Hasim Hassan was a bad influence on Omala. He also knew she would not take kindly to any advice in her current state of infatuation. Biting his tongue and quietly observing would be the best strategy for the moment.

Over the next few weeks, Gimme Lao did not offer his opinion when Omala updated him on her wild frolics and stimulating discourse with her fabulous new friends. They went down to Bugis Street and had midnight supper with androgynous cross-dressers and transsexuals. They rented bicycles and visited charming old buildings slated to be torn down for urban redevelopment to hang handmade mini-wreaths on the doorknobs. They were at Kallang National Stadium cheering as rising football star Fandi Ahmad scored the definitive goal to win the Malaysian Cup. They debated on whichever topics struck their fancy: euthanasia, incest, conscription, marriage of convenience; nothing was taboo among the gang. Omala was so invigorated she failed to notice his silence.

When Omala's birthday swung around, Gimme Lao treated her to ice cream at Swensen's. She was bubbling with excitement when she revealed that Mr Hasim Hassan and his gang were planning a midnight celebration for her. Gimme Lao veiled his jealousy and asked where they were headed. Omala had no idea.

It was meant to be a surprise.

The next day, Omala cornered Gimme Lao at the school cafeteria and asked, "Do you know which is the tallest building in Singapore?"

"The OCBC Building by the Singapore River?" Gimme Lao ventured a guess.

"Clever boy!" Omala pinched his ear teasingly. "Guess what? They sneaked me up to the rooftop water tank area last night. We had tablecloths spread on the floor with donuts and cakes, candles lining the parapet and a glorious view of the downtown area from the highest point on the island. What a fabulous way to turn 15!"

"Isn't the rooftop locked and off limits?" Gimme Lao became alarmed.

"Not if you know the right people who hold the right keys," Omala said gleefully.

"What if you get caught?" Gimme Lao was suddenly furious. "Unlawful entry is a punishable crime. Even if the police let you off because you are a minor, the principal can kick you out of the school. Do you even think rationally anymore? Or are you happy to be led by the nose by that gang of trigger-happy rebels?"

Omala was stunned by the outburst. "Take it easy, Gimme. No one got hurt here."

"You don't see what is happening, Omala," Gimme Lao chided. "You are high on adventure and novel experiences and not realising that you are dancing near the cliff edge. It only takes a tiny misstep and you're gone."

"Maybe you are right," Omala shrugged. "But when you are

dancing near the edge, your senses are heightened and sharpened and that is when you really come alive. I realise there are risks. But the alternative is to resign myself to becoming part of the contingent of the walking dead. Not sure about you, Gimme, but I am not going to let that happen to me. Then again, I can't expect you to understand this, not when you are chained to the school fence where the rules and regulations are painted in the indelible ink of unthinking compliance."

Gimme Lao blushed with embarrassment, furious that Omala should see him in such an unflattering light. Never once had either stabbed the other with affront or derision. He had been right all along about Mr Hasim Hassan. The man was a bad influence on his buddy, and he had to do something.

The next day, Gimme Lao deposited an anonymous letter in the feedback box addressed to the school principal. In the letter, he wrote in detail about Mr Hasim Hassan's involvement in an unlicensed stage play at The Substation and highlighted the deviant theme of the play itself. He also wrote that Mr Hasim Hassan brought one of the students along to a private party held on the rooftop of the OCBC Building, an area out of bounds to the public.

A few days later, when Mr Hasim Hassan turned up for his literature class with bloodshot eyes and a grave expression, Gimme Lao knew the school principal had taken action. They were barely 10 minutes into the lesson when the class monitor asked solicitously if Mr Hasim Hassan was feeling ill. It was obvious to the students that the man was not himself.

"I am sick to the bone, yes." Mr Hasim Hassan spun around

to confront the class. The fury and anguish in his voice was unmistakable. "Sick of the hypocrisy and stupidity of the unenlightened. Sick of those in power dictating the code of conduct for the masses. Sick of the lack of freedom of expression in this miserable country!"

The class was stunned. Omala was the first to recover from the collective shock. "What happened, Mr Hassan?"

"I am involved in an experimental play at The Substation, a play with a controversial theme." Mr Hasim Hassan trembled a little as he ranted. "Someone from this school found out and reported it to the media authorities. That tip-off was enough to trigger a clampdown. Now the play has been banned and the production team put under investigation, myself included."

"That is terrible!" Omala paled. "But how did you know the informant was from our school?"

"Because the principal was questioning me about your birthday party," Mr Hasim Hassan spit. He followed Omala's horrified glance and zoomed in his glare on Gimme Lao. "Then again, I would not expect the informant to possess the courage and honesty to own up. In all likelihood he would simply hide in his stink hole and gloat in private."

His face burning, Gimme Lao stood up and professed, "I have no problem owning up. Had I lacked courage and honesty I would not expose you, would I?"

"Expose what?" It was close to a shout. Mr Hasim Hassan did not have a good rein on his own temper.

"Expose the hypocrisy of your claim that it is your mission to enlighten our minds. Your involvement with the play is nothing but an attempt to brainwash the audience. You want everyone to accept and support your deviant values and beliefs. It is a very private, very selfish agenda."

The class looked from Gimme Lao to Mr Hasim Hassan in confusion. Gimme Lao had spoken with confidence. Over the last few days he had been mentally rehearsing for just such a confrontation. Mr Hasim Hassan on the other hand was shaken. "You have no idea what you are talking about, nor the harm you have done with your actions."

"I have seen the play." Gimme Lao turned to the class. "It affirms homosexuality. The takeaway for the audience is that gay people should be accepted and embraced. Isn't that so, Mr Hassan?"

A wave of whispers rippled across the classroom. All eyes were on Mr Hasim Hassan as he flushed deeply and cleared his throat. "Yes, there is a lot of misconception about homosexuality. The play addresses those misconceptions."

"You challenged me to a show of courage and honesty earlier," Gimme Lao pressed on. "I would like to issue you the same challenge, Mr Hassan. Are you or are you not gay, sir?"

There was dead silence in the class. Mr Hasim Hassan turned pallid.

"Or do you merely hide in the stink hole and gloat in private?" Gimme Lao raised his eyebrows emphatically. It felt good to be able to turn the man's earlier insult back on him.

Mr Hasim Hassan was literally shaking when he took in a deep breath and said, "You are right. If I lack the courage and honesty to admit that I am gay, I am in no position to enlighten your minds, or to teach you anything. So I am putting this on record right now. I am gay."

Pandemonium broke out among the students. It took Mr Hasim Hassan a full 10 minutes to quiet everyone down. He had also leveraged on that interval to compose himself. "Since we have broached the topic of homosexuality, are there any questions you would like to ask me?"

Gimme Lao raised his hand. "Can you explain to the class section 377A of the penal code in Singapore?"

Mr Hasim Hassan clenched his fists. "You have obviously done your research, Gimme. Why don't you share it with the class then?"

"It is a piece of legislation criminalising sex between men, even mutually consenting adult men. Isn't that right, Mr Hassan?"

"It is a relic we inherited from our British colonial past," Mr Hasim Hassan stressed. "And it is wrong. It should have been taken out."

"Is that the message you are trying to drive into the unenlightened minds of the audience who attend your play? To tell them something that is illegal and punishable is quite all right? That to me sounds like a very personal and very selfish agenda. You can get the people you convince into a lot of trouble, my best friend included. I am not sure you are fit to be a teacher at all, Mr Hassan."

The class gasped.

Mr Hasim Hassan blinked to stem the impending tears of anger. Very slowly, he turned to pack his bag and sling it over his shoulders. Before he walked out of the classroom, he paused and addressed the class. "I am not sure if I am coming back. In case I don't see you again, please remember this. Continue to grow your minds. Always challenge what the authorities tell you, myself included. Good luck."

The class gasped again when Omala stormed over and gave Gimme Lao the slap that broke their promise to be friends forever.

SIX

GIMME LAO RAN into Omala again in 1984. He was given permission to defer his National Service in the military to pursue medical studies at the University of Singapore. He spotted her in the atrium at the Central Library building on campus, where the Social Sciences Club was putting up an exhibition. He sat cross-legged on the parapet and watched her from a distance. The two had not met since they graduated from secondary school. That was the year Gimme Lao's family upgraded to a condominium in District Nine. Although the Subramaniams were invited to the housewarming party, Omala chose not to attend. In fact, that party turned out to be a farewell party in essence, for that was the last time Gimme Lao sat and dined with Grandma Toh, Elizabeth, Barber Bay and Aunty Seah. Mary Lao had made good in her career and moved her family into more affluent social circles. The other neighbours weren't able to keep up.

Gimme Lao noted that Omala had grown much taller. She was stationed in front of an exhibition panel addressing a tiny group of students and did not spot him. The scrawny girl standing next to Omala however noticed Gimme Lao staring from afar and decided to stroll over to hand him a pamphlet. Gimme Lao quickly browsed through. The literature advocated for animal rights. The two pictures in the pamphlet depicted gavage feeding of geese for foie gras production and catheterisation of moon bears for bile extraction. Gimme Lao smiled to himself. This was quintessentially Omala.

The scrawny girl suddenly hoisted herself onto the parapet and sat swinging her legs. "Pretend we're discussing the pamphlet," she muttered. "I need a break. My feet are killing me."

Gimme Lao tilted his head and teased, "You're leaving your buddy all alone at the booth? Not a very nice thing to do."

"Don't worry about her." The scrawny girl crinkled her nose. "That's Omala we're talking about. We call her The Tornado. She has enough passion and ferocity to tear the entire campus apart."

"What do they call you?"

"Wei Wen," the scrawny girl answered matter-of-factly. "I keep a low profile. I am in the Social Sciences Club to earn extracurricular activity points, not to change the world."

Gimme Lao paused to get a good look at the girl. She was very fair, to the point of being pale. Her lips were thin, and her eyebrows were but the faintest suggestion of twin shadowy crescents. There was a sense of invisibility about her; she would be hard to notice in a lecture hall among the other girls dressed to grab attention. The only remarkable feature that left an impression on Gimme Lao would be the steely gaze in her eyes. She looked like someone who knew where she was headed.

"I am Gimme Lao. Year Two. Medicine."

Wei Wen turned to look at him. "Medical student? Half the girls in my sorority would kill to date one. I can make good money pimping for you."

Gimme Lao laughed. "What makes you think I can't get my own dates?"

"Not that you can't, but that you don't have insider information," Wei Wen explained. "As you can tell, I don't have the looks nor the boob size to be a threat to any girl. So I am harmless enough to listen in on all their gossip and confessions. I can tell you which girl goes down on her knees and which doesn't. Can save you a ton of time."

"You're a witch!" Gimme Lao pretended to be horrified. He was instantly drawn to her deadpan humour.

One week later, Gimme Lao bumped into Wei Wen at the monthly campus flea market. She waved him over to her cart and pleaded, "Get one of my tee shirts please! I haven't made enough to cover the cart rental yet."

Gimme Lao smirked and picked up a sample at random. The print on the front read 'I Am Missing The Singapore Dream'. Flipping to the back, he frowned as he tried to decipher the odd letterings: 'ash', 'redit', 'ondo', 'lub' and 'ar'. He sent Wei Wen a questioning arch of the brow.

"I am missing all the five 'C's. Cash. Credit card. Condo. Club membership. Car." Wei Wen stared at him. "You're not very intelligent for a medical student, are you?"

"You are not very friendly for a salesperson trying to close a deal, are you?"

"Buy a tee shirt and I will help you get a date. I know you have to attend a couple of networking lunches with the medical graduates who are invited back to share their experiences. A pretty date by your side will lighten things up."

"I will buy a tee shirt if you agree to be my date."

There was a pause as Wei Wen stood looking stunned.

"Say yes and say it quick. The rental cart is not going to pay for itself," Gimme Lao teased. He enjoyed seeing the blush spread over her face.

Not only did Wei Wen accompany Gimme Lao to his networking lunches, the two began to date regularly. Gimme Lao's cohort mates were generally surprised that he had chosen to settle for such a plain-looking girl. After all, medical and engineering students were considered by most of the girls on campus to be good catches. Many would overlook the lack of social graces or physical attributes of a doctor or engineer in the making for a chance to eventually be married to one. Had Gimme Lao so desired, he could have a huge pool of eligible candidates to pick from.

But Gimme Lao knew he did not have the patience to play the dating game. He was told by the seniors that once hospital attachments began in Year Three, social engagements would grind to a halt. "Get attached fast," they advised. He needed a girl who knew what she wanted and where she was headed, who understood the value of time enough not to spend an hour every morning getting her hair styled and makeup applied, who would not get upset because he failed to text her on her pager when he was bogged down by tutorial assignments and who was intelligent enough to catch his jokes. Based on his intuition and early observations, Wei Wen fit the bill.

When the two first kissed, Wei Wen asked Gimme Lao why

he had picked her.

"Because you don't spend time looking in the mirror admiring yourself. You look into binoculars, focus on what is up ahead and work towards the future. I admire that."

"That must rank as one of the most unromantic things to say right after a kiss," Wei Wen chuckled. "But I like it."

"Why did you pick me?"

"Because you're my ticket to my Singapore Dream." Wei Wen poked him in the ribs. "I expect to escape public transport by the time you make registrar and to escape public housing once you start your own practice."

As she watched Gimme Lao chortle, Wei Wen wondered if Gimme realised she was serious about what she said.

Wei Wen's childhood ended when she was in kindergarten. That was the year her mother gave birth to her younger brother. He was born with Down's syndrome. It was a good thing Wei Wen's grandmother lived with them and took on the role of caregiver, so her parents could continue running their food stall at the hawker centre. But the grandmother was adamant that Wei Wen chip in. The little girl was trained to change her brother's diapers, feed and bathe him and rock him to sleep at night. After all, the parents were not going to live forever. The grandmother drilled it into the little girl's head that her brother was her responsibility for as long as they both lived. There was no escaping it.

In primary school, Wei Wen's rapture over her teacher nominating her to join the chess club was short-lived; her grandmother forbade her to attend practice sessions. When the teacher sent her home with a note, her grandmother stormed down to the principal's office to demand that Wei Wen be exempted from extracurricular activities. There was a retarded sibling at home to be cared for. Wei Wen was secretly disappointed that the principal gave in to her grandmother's demands. She might have been really good at chess.

In secondary school, Wei Wen told the family she was going to work part-time at McDonald's to earn her own allowance. That was the only way the grandmother would let her off her caregiver duty. For the first time in her life she had independent control over her leisure hours. All she had to do was inform her grandmother that she had taken on additional shifts, and she was free to join her friends at the arcade or the movies. Life was beginning to look good, except that there was never enough pocket money, not when she was paid a miserly 2.50 dollars an hour.

At least the team at McDonald's was fun to be with, especially with Haizad around.

Haizad was the assistant manager at the outlet. The girls loved him because he was handsome, fun and generous with his money. After shifts, they would head down to Centrepoint at Orchard Road, where Haizad bought them slurpies from 7-Eleven and the gang hung out in the mall to talk shop. At the movies, Haizad supplied popcorn and supersized Pepsis. When a birthday swung around, the gang was treated to ice cream cakes at Swensen's. He was every girl's perfect manager. That was, until Zarinah came into the picture.

Zarinah was not the prettiest girl in the gang, but definitely the most bosomy. At McDonald's, she wore the uniform one size too small, so that the buttons strained themselves against the fabric and the boys queuing up to place their orders could peep between the button gaps to check out the colour of her bra. Haizad made a show of reprimanding her because it was his duty. But everyone at the outlet had caught him eyeing Zarinah when he thought no one was watching.

One day, Zarinah whipped out the newest Sony Walkman from her bag and popped in a *Best of ABBA* cassette tape. Everyone gasped and crowded around her. Walkmans were the newest craze in town, but how could Zarinah afford one? They didn't come cheap. Zarinah smiled mysteriously, said nothing and continued to bob her head to "Dancing Queen".

Ironically, once the general curiosity tapered off, Zarinah itched to reveal her secret. A scandal soon began to brew. Zarinah was now Haizad's special girl. She visited him on his rest days on Tuesdays when they locked themselves in his room for hours on end. Zarinah giggled and said she couldn't go into details about the kind of fun they had for that would get him into trouble. She was, after all, merely 15.

A chasm began to form in the gang's dynamics. When they met at the mall and argued over which film to watch, Haizad sided with Zarinah and overrode the others' picks. When they organised overnight barbeques at East Coast Beach, Zarinah dictated which cassettes were to be played in the portable player. The gang became an unwilling audience to Zarinah's public display of affection calculated to attract attention. Over the weeks, hostility brewed as the gang gossiped mercilessly about Zarinah. Everyone agreed that the girl was poison.

The hostilities began to surface at work. When Zarinah was scheduled for counter duty, the backup staff was slow to assemble her orders and conveniently forgot to top up her condiment and serviette supplies. When Zarinah took over food caller duty, special orders that omitted lettuce or ketchup or mayonnaise never came up right. Zarinah quickly realised she was being ostracised. She complained to Haizad bitterly that everyone was jealous of her. There was nothing Haizad could do except pair Zarinah up with Wei Wen for her shifts. Wei Wen was a neutral party.

As much as she was aware of the conspiracy against Zarinah, Wei Wen did not feel compelled to join in. She was minimally courteous. Zarinah saw Wei Wen's neutrality as the overhanging branch she could grab to save herself from drowning in the virulent currents of animosity. She shared her Cadbury chocolate with Wei Wen at meal breaks. She lent Wei Wen her prized cassette tapes. She even offered to pass Wei Wen her Sony Walkman once Haizad delivered on his promise to buy her a newer model on her birthday. Despite all her grand gestures, Wei Wen remained minimally courteous. The stubborn girl's anchored neutrality frustrated Zarinah to no end.

Luckily for Zarinah, she soon discovered that Wei Wen was susceptible to curiosity.

Zarinah caught that flicker of interest in Wei Wen's eyes when she hinted that Haizad was always eager to try out stuff he watched on video. He knew a clandestine supplier who brought in obscene, uncensored videotapes from overseas. That was what occupied them when they holed up in his room on Tuesdays. Some of the stuff he wanted to mimic from the videos she found revolting, but she always gave in after he coaxed and cajoled and promised to bring her shopping. When Wei Wen left her burger suspended in midair and forgot to chew the chunk she had just bitten off, Zarinah knew she had her.

One afternoon, Haizad summoned Wei Wen to his office and spoke to her in hushed tones. He was planning a surprise for Zarinah and needed her help. Could Wei Wen drop by the pastry shop below his apartment at eight on Tuesday evening to pick up and deliver a cake to his place?

Wei Wen found no reason to decline. Besides, she was curious about Haizad's collection of obscene, uncensored videotapes.

The delighted shrieks and screams that greeted the cake delivery were so exaggerated Wei Wen suspected it did not come as a surprise to Zarinah at all. Nevertheless, she allowed herself to be hugged and dragged into the apartment to share in the celebration. It turned out that it had been a hundred days since they got together. After cake and Coke were served, Haizad whipped out a wrapped gift and Zarinah obliged him with another round of shrieks. The screaming continued as Zarinah pulled out a satin nightdress in sunset orange.

"My favourite colour!" Zarinah threw herself at Haizad. "I am going to put it on right away."

Wei Wen found herself dragged into the bedroom by the enthusiastic girl. As Zarinah stripped and changed, Wei Wen looked away and caught sight of the pile of videocassette tapes strewn carelessly near the video player. Unable to contain her curiosity, Wei Wen knelt down to examine them. What she saw on the video jackets sent a tinkling thrill down her spine. Her cheeks burned.

"Pick one that you like. We can all watch it together," Zarinah remarked casually before she opened the door and sashayed out of the bedroom. Wei Wen swallowed. She could not imagine watching an obscene videotape together with Zarinah and Haizad. Neither could she imagine giving up this rare opportunity to watch one.

A moment later, Zarinah and Haizad entered the room carrying the tray of cakes and Coke cans. Wei Wen froze. She was certain they could hear the thumping in her chest. Zarinah asked if she had made her selection. When Wei Wen shook her head, Zarinah proceeded to pick one and pop it into the player. She squeezed herself in between Wei Wen and Haizad at the foot of the bed, grabbed Haizad's hand and clamped it in between her thighs.

The narrative was simple enough. Before he left for the office, a Caucasian homeowner reminded his Hispanic maid that a plumber was scheduled for a repair job later in the day. The black plumber arrived on time and started working on the clogged sink. The maid offered him a drink but carelessly spilled it onto his tee shirt. The plumber removed his stained shirt to wipe the spill dry. One thing led to another, and the plumber was soon sinking his plunger into the maid's pipe. The homeowner returned, spotted the spectacle and licked his lips as his throat suddenly dried up. With the homeowner's eventual participation, the action evolved into rowdy tag teaming.

Wei Wen was as fascinated by the filmed action on screen as she was unnerved by the live action occurring right beside her.

Although she did not dare to tilt her head to peep, she could tell that the couple went from kissing and petting to removing intervening pieces of garment. She was secretly relieved when the two finally clambered onto the bed and out of her sight. The exaggerated moans and groans on screen effectively blocked out the ruffling of sheets behind her. The two were done way before the tag team finished, and Haizad was fully clothed when he showed Wei Wen the way out.

The following week, Wei Wen could hardly believe it when Zarinah extended the invitation again. "We had a great time. You must come again."

Wei Wen recalled the thumping in her chest and the burning flush on her cheeks. It was overall rather exciting, although she was hardly part of the action. Again, she found no reason to decline.

It soon developed into a pattern.

Every Tuesday, as Wei Wen fixed her gaze on the screen and imagined the action occurring right behind her, there was always that unnerving anticipation that one of them would reach over to caress her neck and extend an invitation. Wei Wen did not know how she intended to react when that happened. Would she be bold enough to join in? Could she re-enact the performance she watched on screen every week? Was it going to be unbearably painful? Judging from the sounds of pleasure Zarinah and Haizad emitted, pain was not part of the game.

When several weeks passed and no caressing invitation came, Wei Wen's trepidation turned into disappointment. It became obvious that neither of them found her attractive enough. The couple merely wanted her presence to add a dash of spice.

Zarinah was astonished when Wen Wei told her she didn't feel like coming anymore. "But why? We are having so much fun!"

Wei Wen concocted an excuse. Her grandmother switched her weekly mahjong game to Tuesdays, so Wei Wen had to take care of her brother.

Zarinah refused to give up on her only buddy at McDonald's. She dragged Wei Wen along for shopping and movies after their shifts. She made Haizad pay for all their expenses so Wei Wen did not have to spend a single cent when Zarinah was around. On Wei Wen's birthday, Zarinah made Haizad buy her a pair of Reebok track shoes that cost over a hundred dollars.

"This is too expensive!" Wei Wen blushed in embarrassment and secret pleasure.

"Don't worry." Zarinah cupped her hands over Wei Wen's ear and whispered, "He is not paying for any of these out of his own salary. That is the best thing about being a manager. You can generate a second income by playing with the numbers on the daily cashier report."

Wei Wen gaped. She finally uncovered the hidden source of Haizad's generosity.

The following week, Zarinah again begged Wei Wen to join them on Tuesday. "We want to shoot a video of ourselves, and you are the only one we can trust."

Wei Wen found her heart thumping hard. It had been months since she last set foot in Haizad's apartment, and she had to admit she missed the thrill of voyeurism. When Tuesday swung around, Wei Wen found herself holding a Panasonic video recorder and taping the couple's sex romp on bed. Afterwards, the three played the tape and laughed hysterically. Wei Wen felt wonderful. She was finally part of the action.

Over the next few weeks, the videotaped action moved from the bedroom to the living room and on to the kitchen. Haizad and Zarinah began to experiment with sex toys and role-play. Wei Wen fine-tuned her skills and the quality of the taped videos improved tremendously. As she gained confidence, Wei Wen also accepted the fact that her role was to observe and tape the action, not to participate.

Wei Wen developed a sharp eye. In school, she could tell which of the kids had experimented with sex and which were dying to. When she spotted a girl who was undecided, she weighed in with her profound knowledge and egged her on. Over time, Wei Wen developed a reputation as the one to approach for sexual advice. Girls who had never taken a second look at her before were now whispering about her in awe. Wei Wen's pride at the clout she acquired was tinged with an underlying bitterness. No boys had yet to show any interest in her.

One evening shortly after Wei Wen turned 16, her brother gave the family a scare. His skin and lips turned blue as he struggled horribly for air. They rushed him to the hospital, where he was diagnosed with Atrioventricular Septal Defect. The doctor explained that this heart condition was common among people with Down's syndrome and proceeded to operate on the brother. The family was relieved when he was eventually moved out of the

Intensive Care Unit to the general ward for convalescence.

Back at home, conflict erupted when the grandmother demanded that Wei Wen fork out her savings to help pay for her brother's operation. Although her parents tried to convince her grandmother that they had enough savings to afford the medical bill, her grandmother remained adamant. She insisted that her brother was Wei Wen's responsibility for life. The girl had been working at McDonald's for over a year now. There was no excuse for her not to chip in and help foot the bill.

Wei Wen was so exasperated she started a shouting match with her grandmother, something she had never done before. Caught in the heat of the moment, she did not cease even after her father warned her severely. It was not till her father smacked her hard across her face that she stood stunned, unsure if she should feel ashamed or furious. Her mother dragged her into the bedroom and quickly pressed some money into her hands. She should go spend the night with her cousin so that her father and grandmother could cool themselves down.

An hour later, Wei Wen found herself standing in front of Haizad's apartment. She broke down and sobbed and spilled her misery as Haizad made her a cup of hot chocolate and did his best to calm her down. After she was spent, Haizad brought her a blanket and a pillow and told her she could sleep on the couch. But sleep did not come to her. She was trembling with trepidation as she recognised her need to be held and loved that very moment. It took her a long while, but she finally garnered her courage and tiptoed into the bedroom. She slipped into bed next to the sleeping figure and hugged him from behind. She could feel him awaken with a start. As he tossed, she reached up to search for his lips. She felt his hands grab her waist and rolled her over onto her back. She was shaking with anticipation when he leaned close and whispered into her ears, "I will go sleep on the couch. You will feel better in the morning."

Alone in the dark, Wei Wen was consumed with shame and anguish. Haizad, who did not mind Wei Wen seeing and filming him naked and screwing Zarinah a hundred times, had no desire whatsoever for her. She was that repulsive to him. He and her grandmother were really not that much different—selfish, callous people who took her for granted. The thought simmered in her mind and gradually built up to a boil. She would not allow herself to be trampled upon.

When Wei Wen sneaked out of Haizad's apartment the next morning, she had two of his sex videotapes inside her school bag.

Haizad was astonished when Wei Wen tendered her resignation two days later. The first thought that crossed his mind was that the poor girl must be terribly embarrassed about his rejection the other night. Wei Wen's detached demeanour attested to that. When she told him about her brother recovering from a major cardiac operation, he showered her with sympathy and concern. However, his concern quickly turned into suspicion when she casually asked for a loan of 5,000 dollars. She passed him a note with instructions to deposit 500 dollars per month into her bank account till the full loan was delivered. When he turned her down awkwardly, Wei Wen looked him straight in the eye and asked if he had a tracking system to keep count of all the sex videotapes she had filmed. By the time she left the office, Haizad was pallid with distress. On her part, the satisfaction that welled up within was sweet and deep.

Back home, Wei Wen showed the family the balance in her bankbook and negotiated for a compromise. She would gladly contribute a portion of her monthly income to the family fund. In exchange, she wanted to be absolved of all caregiver duties pertaining to her brother. She was not uncaring. She just needed time for herself. When her grandmother rejected her proposal with derision, Wei Wen threatened to move out. Fortunately, her parents sided with her. They understood that their teenager needed her freedom.

Over the next few years, Wei Wen continued to make money on the side. She applied to work in the cosmetics department in Robinsons on weekends so she could learn the art of makeup and build her contacts. Once she was ready, she quit the job and offered her makeup services to brides on their wedding days. She also made good money selling cosmetics that she sourced for at wholesale prices. By the time she entered university, she had a tidy sum in her savings account. In spite of that, she did not feel safe. She understood bitterly that her brother was her responsibility for life. It was only a matter of time before her parents retired and she had to take over.

Meeting Gimme Lao and pairing up with him was not part of her plan, but Wei Wen derived immense solace from it. Her plan was to get a degree in business studies, pocket some experience working for the big companies and eventually set up a business of her own. It was not her aspiration to make a fortune or a name for herself. She merely saw it as a necessity.

Her brother was part of her future, and she did not dare tie their financial security to the tyranny of a salaried job she could lose.

When she told Gimme Lao that he was her ticket to her Singapore Dream, she was not entirely jesting. Doctors earned a decent income, enjoyed esteemed social status and defied economic downturns. She also understood when Gimme Lao professed that he did not have time to play the dating game. Medical students studied intensively and had very little time for anything else. During their first year together, Wei Wen accustomed herself to spending nights working on crossword puzzles in bed while Gimme Lao pored over his books at the study desk next to her. Once Gimme Lao started hospital attachments the following year, she had to adapt herself to his erratic and uncertain work schedules and avail herself whenever he needed her. That was the period the truth finally struck her. Any prettier girl with other options might not stick around and wait for a boyfriend who could not be around half the time. Gimme Lao picked her because she was smart but plain-looking and had limited options. He knew she would stick around and wait for him.

Wei Wen was fine with the realisation. She knew Gimme Lao was serious about the relationship because he brought her home to meet his parents. She found his father, Lao Sheng Yang, to be a rather timid man. His mother, Mary Lao, was a different story. In fact, Gimme Lao told her his mother was the real breadwinner in the family. The spacious condo apartment at Pacific Mansion, the Chevrolet Cavalier that the family drove and the membership to the Singapore Island Country Club were made possible by her sole effort. Mary Lao was and continued to be his inspiration.

When Gimme Lao told her he was ready to meet her family, Wei Wen stalled. In the year that they were together, she had never once mentioned that she had a brother with Down's syndrome, who was destined to be dependent on her for life. She was uncertain how he would respond to her reality. She knew Gimme Lao was focused and ambitious; he was striving for a good life like Mary Lao did. He had told her he believed they were good for one another and that together they had a bright future. He saw them focusing on their career goals in their 20s, putting a down payment on their first property and starting a family in their 30s, bringing up children and establishing their careers in their 40s and perhaps retiring early in their 50s. He had it all mapped out. In his blueprint, there was no space designated for a brother-in-law with Down's syndrome.

Wei Wen concocted excuses. Her grandmother was schizophrenic and went berserk when there was a stranger in the house. Her parents had to set up their food stall at an ungodly hour in the morning and thus had to sleep very early. There was never a good time to arrange for a visit. It helped matters that Gimme Lao ran a tight schedule himself and chose to let it slide. Wei Wen continued to have the occasional dinner with Gimme Lao's parents, but he never did get to meet hers.

During their third year together, a major mishap occurred in her family that shook Wei Wen badly. Her grandmother was walking her brother in the park when he had an epileptic seizure. In trying to lift him up, her grandmother misjudged his strength and was yanked to the ground instead. The doctor diagnosed that she had suffered a broken hip in the fall and had to be bedridden for months.

The family sat down to discuss matters. They now had an invalid elderly and an overgrown child to take care of. Both parents were needed at the food stall, so the family would have to hire a live-in maid from Indonesia or the Philippines to help out. It was a good thing Wei Wen was in her last year of studies. Once she started work, the financial strain on the family would be greatly ameliorated.

Wei Wen felt stifled. Her work life had yet to begin and already a chunk of her future income had been confiscated. She could not deny her role or responsibility to her family; she knew they needed her contribution. What made it worse was the fact that she did not have the luxury of confiding in her boyfriend because she had not been honest with him. The stakes were even higher now. What would happen if Gimme Lao came to find out about her reality? Was it not possible that he would then decide he did not want her reality to be a part of his? After all, Gimme Lao was not born into her family. He had every right to decline shouldering any of the responsibility that she was born into.

The fear of losing him kept Wei Wen awake at night. It was in this tormented state of mind that she made a plan. She had to lock herself into his future. She picked her date carefully; it was her fertile window. She snuggled up to Gimme Lao in bed and shared that her grandmother had a bad fall. While he hugged and comforted her, Wei Wen reached down to fondle him. Gimme Lao took it that she needed to connect and rolled over to reach for the pack of condoms in the drawer. He was slightly surprised when Wei Wen pressed him back down and straddled him. In the heat of the moment, Gimme Lao did not insist on protection. He simply assumed Wei Wen was on the pill.

Mary Lao was the first to notice that Wei Wen scrunched up her face when she spotted the plate of fried chicken wings at dinner, a dish she used to hanker for. She also noticed that Wei Wen had to excuse herself thrice to use the bathroom in the course of an evening. Before the young couple took their leave, Mary Lao pulled her son aside and questioned him. It turned out that he had no idea.

Gimme Lao flew into a rage when Wei Wen confirmed his mother's suspicions. She might be two months into her first trimester. Why on earth was she so careless! It was not on their agenda to get married any time soon. A baby would only ruin their plans. There was no discussion to be had. The baby had to go.

Two days later, Gimme Lao was surprised when Mary Lao asked him to go home for a family meeting. He became alarmed when he found Wei Wen seated at the living room couch solemnly taciturn. Mary Lao wanted to know how she could help Gimme Lao and Wei Wen with their situation.

"We are not having the baby," Gimme Lao announced curtly. "We never planned for this. I don't intend to ruin my life for a careless mistake."

"I know this is upsetting," Mary Lao said. "Having your plans ruined is always upsetting. But having a baby, even an unplanned baby, is always a joyful thing. You just have to accept that it happened and include it as part of your future plan."

"What are you saying?" Gimme Lao was truly alarmed now.

"I am saying that I am against abortion. So is Wei Wen, and so are her parents," Mary Lao stated indubitably. "You have to take our stance into consideration."

Gimme Lao stared at her with incredulity. "Are you ganging up to outvote me on such a major decision of my life?"

"It is not just your life. It is Wei Wen's and the baby's too. And I am here to help, not to bully you into anything," Mary Lao explained. "Wei Wen can stay with us till the baby is born. We can take care of things until you two have the means to take over."

"Why does she have to stay here?" Gimme Lao snapped. He saw Wei Wen flinch and felt secretly vindictive.

"Wei Wen's grandmother is bedridden so her parents have their hands full. I thought it best if Wei Wen moved in here."

Gimme Lao looked across at his father, who sat timidly at the other end of the couch apparently without any opinion of his own. It suddenly crossed his mind that the men in the family were often relegated to the periphery when important decisions were being made. Without meaning to, he broke out into a cackle.

"Both of you have yet to turn 21," Mary Lao continued. "I will of course arrange with Wei Wen's parents to get you two married soonest. We will have to make it simple."

"I am not getting married with permission granted by my parents!" Gimme Lao practically shouted.

Mary Lao looked from the flushed agitation on her son's face to the pallid calm on Wei Wen's and silently reminded herself that Gimme Lao had not been given enough time to deal with his emotions. The young man was probably not ready to discuss plans. She might have to take the lead and strong-arm the young couple into the best arrangements.

"Why don't I arrange for all of us to meet Wei Wen's parents this Sunday to discuss matters? I will book a table at the Mayflower Restaurant for lunch."

Gimme Lao felt tears of anger well up. He grabbed a copy of *The Straits Times* and unfurled it brusquely to hide his furious, embarrassing weep. Despite the blurring of his vision, he could tell that the headlines were predominantly about the tragedy that shook the nation two days ago. A six-storey building housing the New World Hotel had suddenly collapsed upon itself. Thirty-three mangled bodies were pulled out from beneath the rubble as the nation wept. Gimme Lao felt as though he was being mocked. The unexpected pregnancy practically yanked the rug from underneath him and caused his plans to collapse into rubble. The bright future he saw for himself and Wei Wen was now sullied and mangled. The nation ought to weep for him.

Gimme Lao did not turn up for lunch on Sunday to meet Wei Wen's parents. Although he continued to go home twice a week for dinner, he was distant and clammed up as he dug into his food and irascible when the topic of the pregnancy surfaced. Wei Wen had taken a leave of absence from the university, so he only saw her at his parents' place. Mary Lao shared that Wei Wen's parents were grateful their daughter was being taken care of. She had not personally met the grandmother or the brother, but Wei Wen sent their regards every time she returned from her home visits. Mary Lao hinted that Gimme Lao should find time to visit Wei Wen's family with her. Gimme Lao pretended he heard nothing.

Every Wednesday, when Gimme Lao stepped into his dormitory room after his lecture, there would be a canister of herbal soup on his desk. Wei Wen still held the key to his room. As Wei Wen's belly began to show towards the end of her second trimester, Gimme Lao felt mortified. It crossed his mind that the students on campus must surely stare and gossip. Did the woman not care?

One particularly hot and humid afternoon, the lecture ended earlier than usual and Gimme Lao returned in time to spot Wei Wen making her way up the staircase. She had to stop every now and then to catch her breath and sponge off the perspiration on her forehead. That was the moment it struck Gimme Lao. The entire affair was not merely about his dashed hopes and dreams. Her future was at stake too. It could not have been easy for her to carry an unplanned pregnancy through in the shadow of his silent hostility. Watching her from afar, Gimme Lao was suddenly overcome by the swelling guilt within. He had been extremely callous and selfish.

Wei Wen was astonished when Gimme Lao came down the staircase to meet her. She began to tremble as he took over the canister and offered to hold her hand. By the time they stepped into the room and Gimme Lao turned to hug her, she could no longer hold it back. Tears streamed down her face as she sobbed fiercely. Gimme Lao continued to hug her tightly as he whispered into her ear that it was going to be all right. They were going to be fine.

Gimme Lao began to spend weekends at home with Wei Wen. They went for long evening strolls at the Botanic Gardens, shopped for baby clothes at Tanglin Mall and consumed copious helpings of ice cream to satisfy Wei Wen's cravings. They caught two matinees in one go, rushing from the oestrogen-driven showdown between Sigourney Weaver and the mother alien screening at The Capitol to the testosterone-fuelled aerial showmanship of Tom Cruise in *Top Gun* screening at The Cathay two streets away. Wei Wen underwent a phase where she craved excitement on screen almost as readily as she craved cakes and ice cream. Gimme Lao was happy to indulge her.

For a while, the two resumed having sex. They discovered that if Wei Wen positioned herself at the edge of the bed with a pillow wedged behind her, Gimme Lao could stand or kneel and not apply any of his weight on her. Or they could spoon at an angle that allowed comfortable penetration. But as the third trimester progressed and Wei Wen started to get abdominal cramps right after intercourse, the two stopped having sex altogether.

Upon Mary Lao's repeated prompts, Gimme Lao finally allowed Wei Wen to arrange for a meeting with her parents. They picked a vegetarian restaurant at Chinatown to accommodate Wei Wen's mother, who had recently turned vegetarian. In the initial awkwardness, Gimme Lao thought that diet preferences would be a safe icebreaker. "Why did you decide to become vegetarian?" He asked the mother.

"I was advised by my Buddhist friends. Forgoing meat is a

way to atone for our sins." The mother spoke softly. "Especially after all that happened in the family. First Wei Wen's brother, then her grandmother and now Wei Wen herself…"

"But Wei Wen is fine." Gimme Lao was genuinely puzzled. "We just met with her gynaecologist two days ago. Both Wei Wen and the baby are doing well."

"She is pregnant and unmarried. It is not fine," the father retorted curtly. He had earlier refused to shake Gimme Lao's hand.

Blushing deeply, Gimme Lao turned to Wei Wen and attempted to change the topic. "I know your grandmother fell and broke her hips, but what happened to your brother?"

"He had a cardiac operation several years ago. His health is generally weak," Wei Wen soft-pedalled.

"I didn't know that," Gimme Lao said. "Why didn't you tell me?"

"Why don't you tell us when are you going to marry my daughter?" the father blurted out before the mother had a chance to shush him.

Gimme Lao realised that he was not going to get away from the meeting unscathed. "I thought it would be better if we got married after the baby is born."

"You may accuse me of being old fashioned and traditional, but I think most people would agree with me that a wedding should occur before the baby shower. That is the right order of things."

Gimme Lao bit his tongue. Now that he was reconciled with Wei Wen, he did feel sorry that she had to suffer the ignominy of unwed pregnancy. But he did not like to be pressured into a hurried marriage.

"Does my daughter have no say in this?" The father was displeased with the lack of response.

In an attempt to avoid confrontation, Gimme Lao turned to Wei Wen and asked, "Do you really want to go through a wedding dinner with that huge pregnancy showing beneath your wedding gown?"

"We can always get legally married at the Registry of Marriages first and hold the wedding after the baby is born," Wei Wen replied softly.

Gimme Lao was caught off guard. Neither of them had broached the topic since the reconciliation. He simply assumed that she was agreeable to getting married after the baby was born.

"Now that my daughter has spoken her mind, I would like to hear from you," the father challenged.

Gimme Lao swallowed and stumbled. "I just thought it would be easier to wait till we both turn 21."

"Wei Wen turned 21 two months ago," the father snapped. "I was told you were born on the day Singapore became independent. Which means you turn 21 in two weeks. Since National Day is a public holiday, I am sure all of us can make time for a trip down to the Registry of Marriages. If you have no violent objections, I would like to call upon your mother to discuss the matter. I would very much prefer my grandchild to be born to legally married parents."

As much as Gimme Lao hated to be pressured into the arrangement, he could not come up with a valid objection. The next two weeks saw a flurry of meetings and coordination. There would be no invited guests. The two families would meet at Fort Canning in the morning, witness the ceremony and then proceed for lunch. The traditional wedding banquet could wait till after the baby was born.

When Mary Lao saw that Gimme Lao remained riled throughout, she came down hard on him. "You got the girl pregnant. You gave her the cold shoulder for half a year when she most needed love and support. You refused to meet your in-laws for months. Despite all this, I tried to make things work. I took in and took care of your girl and the unborn baby. I built a relationship with your in-laws. Do you not realise I am doing all this for your sake? Or do you want to be stuck in a miserable marriage with a bitter, insecure wife and hostile in-laws? Think about it!"

Gimme Lao went crimson with shame. It took his mother's brutal honesty to shine the spotlight onto his selfishness. He lost sleep thinking about what Wei Wen had to go through during the months he chose to ignore her. By the time dawn arrived, he had made up his mind. He would love Wei Wen unconditionally for the rest of their married life.

That evening, Gimme Lao took Wei Wen out for an extravagant dinner he could ill afford. He booked a table at Compass Rose on the 70th level of the newly completed Westin Stamford Singapore, which stood proudly as the tallest hotel in the world in 1986. After a four-course dinner, he unveiled a wedding ring and properly proposed to her for the first time. He told her he was sorry for all the pain and hurt he had caused her and promised her he was committed to loving her for the rest of her life.

"Really?" Wei Wen was trembling a little when she allowed Gimme Lao to slip the ring onto her finger. "Will you love me? No matter what?"

"I promise."

Gimme Lao was consumed with wedding bliss for the last three days before he turned 21. He finally understood what it felt like to prepare for a new chapter in life as a newlywed. He hand-picked the bouquet of roses and held it to his chest with pride as he watched the taxi drive up Fort Canning. He held the door open as Wei Wen's mother assisted the heavily pregnant bride out of the vehicle. From the corner of his eyes, he saw Wei Wen's father arrive in a second taxi and help a frail old lady out and onto a wheelchair. That must be Wei Wen's grandmother. Gimme Lao thought it odd that her brother did not step out of the vehicle to lend the father a hand.

When the brother finally emerged, Gimme Lao stood stunned. He was clearly a teenager with Down's syndrome. Swivelling around to meet Wei Wen's gaze, his bewilderment swiftly turned to anger. The guilt in her eyes was the answer to his question.

Once again, he had been betrayed.

SEVEN

Had Gimme Lao been superstitious, he would have believed his marriage was the curse that triggered the string of bad breaks following.

When he was 23 and undergoing internship in the hospital, a nurse swamped with paperwork passed him the wrong document. Gimme Lao failed to double-check. As a result, a surgical patient almost had a perfectly healthy kidney removed. His supervising medical officer, who had to shoulder the blame, was so livid she made the rest of his internship a torture. He was practically relieved when his turn for conscription swung around.

When he was 25 and serving as a military medical officer, he was careless and left his cabinet key dangling in the keyhole. A bored and nosy medic on clinic duty went through the dockets and discovered that two of the soldiers, although categorised as combat-fit, were nevertheless granted exemption from combat training and assigned clerical appointments. It turned out that both were "white horses", a term for military servicemen who received special treatment in camp because they came from prominent political families. A scandal began to brew. The two subjects were taunted and ostracised in camp, and their parents were furious that confidentiality had been compromised. The commanding officer had to expend copious time and energy executing damage control. When the ensuing investigation uncovered the trigger point, Gimme Lao was severely reprimanded.

When he was 26, Gimme Lao took up internal medicine at the Singapore General Hospital. The team of interns under his charge quickly learned that Gimme Lao did not approve of sentimentality. In fact, they suspected that Gimme Lao saw their display of compassion as a liability. During their daily rounds in the hospital, the interns were guided by Gimme's frown to trim their observational reports to the essentials. Gimme Lao had no patience for the irrelevant. Relationship building with patients and their families fell under that category.

None of the interns impressed Gimme Lao. He simply tolerated their presence.

On their part, most of the interns tried to stay out of his way. All except one, a flamboyant young man who called himself Divine. Divine did not hide the fact that he was gay. He painted one of his toenails with multiple colours of the rainbow and vowed to march in Pride parades in all the continents that held them. Although most of the other hospital staff found Divine endearing in a quirky manner, the intern got on Gimme Lao's nerves.

At one point, Gimme Lao gathered his team of interns before the bimonthly departmental meeting and asked if they had any issues to surface for discussion. Divine raised his hand. There was this comatose patient in a private ward whose parents barred the gay partner from visiting. How could the hospital help to solve this problem? Gimme Lao shrugged nonchalantly and said he did not see a problem there. The gay partner had no legal recognition and thus enjoyed no visiting rights. The hospital should respect the parents' decision.

Later in the afternoon, Gimme Lao had a nasty shock when an unfamiliar slide popped up on screen midway through his presentation. It was a case study of the comatose patient that Divine had brought to his attention earlier. It raised the issue of visitation rights and urged the hospital management to review policies that did not embrace the new diversity of evolving family dynamics. Apparently, Divine had gained access to his laptop during lunch break to add it in. As the management furrowed their collective brows to pore over the case study, Gimme Lao blushed furiously and stumbled. The head of department remarked coldly that the bimonthly departmental meeting was hardly the right place to review hospital policies, and that he was surprised Gimme Lao chose to bring up this case study. The secretary taking minutes was instructed to strike the item off the agenda.

Divine was waiting outside the conference room with another man when the meeting was adjourned. Before Gimme Lao could stop him, Divine marched up to the head of department and asked if the committee had the opportunity to discuss the case. The man standing behind him was the gay partner who was appealing for visiting rights. The head of department swivelled around and looked daggers at Gimme Lao.

After the appeal was firmly rejected and the unhappy man turned away, Gimme Lao was harshly reprimanded by the head of department. If he could not manage an intern, he could forget about any management post in his medical career.

Gimme Lao wanted very badly to thrash Divine, but the intern was nowhere to be found. He ended the shift in a foul mood, went home and picked a quarrel with Wei Wen over an inconsequential matter. He was made to feel guilty only when Skye, who was five, became terrified and clung onto Wei Wen's waist, crying bitterly.

There were days when Gimme Lao felt Skye was the only bright spot in his life. When Skye was born, Gimme Lao was still incensed with Wei Wen for hiding the truth about her brother's condition. He was determined to ignore the joy of the newborn, until Skye grabbed his finger and wouldn't let go. That was the instance he fell.

Skye was a delightful baby and a compliant toddler who aimed to please. Before he turned two, he was a devoted thigh hugger. He would mosey around the house, spot a thigh, shriek in delight and cling on for dear life. When the family took the occasional trip on the Mass Rapid Transit, Skye would tear free from Wei Wen's grasp and hug a stranger's thigh, all the while giggling himself silly. More often than not the grinning stranger would feel sorry when Wei Wen made the boy release his hold. Gimme Lao loved Skye's thigh hugs. He was secretly disappointed when the boy eventually outgrew them.

Once, Gimme Lao found a handmade card on his pillow. The distorted shape of a gigantic butterfly outlined in yellow crayon hovering menacingly over a tiny stick figure was obviously Skye's artwork from nursery school. Gimme Lao sat the boy on his lap and asked what the drawing meant. Skye explained that the nursery teacher asked all the children to draw their favourite animal as a 'thank you' gift for their parents. So Skye drew a yellow butterfly for Gimme Lao and another orange butterfly for Wei Wen. He kissed Gimme on the cheek and said, "Thank you," as the nursery teacher dictated.

Gimme Lao felt a lump in his throat. He could never explain to the boy how glad he was that his original decision to abort the pregnancy had been outvoted by Wei Wen and Mary Lao. He secretly thanked his lucky stars that he had been prevented from making that horrendous mistake.

Wei Wen, on the other hand, thanked her lucky stars that Skye turned out to be such a charming bundle of joy. There were days when she felt Skye was the only reason her marriage did not crumble. She could not blame her husband or her in-laws for despising her, not when she had so deliberately hid the condition of her brother from their knowledge. Over time, Mary Lao and her husband relented. After all, Wei Wen's brother did not live with them and readily melted into the periphery of oblivion while Skye captured their hearts and attention. The two became doting grandparents who were generous with their affection, and Wei Wen received the spillover.

Her husband, on the other hand, was not ready to forgive her. For the two years that he served in the military, he waived his privilege as a married medical officer to be home every night. He limited his exchanges with her to issues concerning their child and did not choose to share much else. Had she not made a consistent effort, their sex life would have dwindled to nothing over the years.

Wei Wen had a recurring nightmare. She was standing at the

edge of MacRitchie Reservoir, studying the receding waterline with consternation. She knew the Malaysian government was angry at Singapore for one reason or another and harboured malicious intent to turn off its water supply pipelines. The reservoir was drying up. The country was at the mercy of its neighbour. She was at the mercy of her husband and her in-laws. Her Singapore Dream had become a nightmare.

Wei Wen knew she had to do something. Her husband chose not to share his life with her, but she chose to share herself with him. After the lights were off, she went to work. She had watched enough pornographic videotapes and filmed enough sex romps for Haizad and Zarinah during her teenage years to pick up an extensive bag of tricks. She put what she learned to good use and kept surprising her husband. Although he remained guarded and uncommunicative in the day, he yearned for her to take charge once the lights were off. It was as though they lived life as a polite but distant couple by day, but enjoyed a sizzling, lascivious affair at night. Strangely enough, the pattern of bipolarity kept their marriage alive.

One morning, Wei Wen was alone in the house with Skye when the doorbell chimed. A gaunt, nervous looking man who looked to be in his 60s stood outside the gate. He asked for Mary Lao and her husband. Wei Wen explained that they were out for their morning taichi session and that he would do well to come back in an hour or two. The elderly man said it was all right. He would squat along the corridor outside and wait.

Wei Wen's curiosity got the better of her when her in-laws returned and received the visitor warmly. She brewed them a pot of tea and sat in at the dining table. It turned out that the elderly man was an old neighbour who used to run a barbershop and cut Gimme Lao's hair when he was a child. Her in-laws called him Barber Bay. It had been 10 years since they had last met.

After the initial round of pleasantries and reminiscing, Mary Lao finally spoke what was on everyone's mind. Barber Bay looked terrible. What was he suffering from?

Barber Bay sighed and said he had no idea. His health had deteriorated at an alarming rate over the last few years. He consulted a series of Chinese physicians and brewed countless pots of herbs, but all to no avail. One of his friends even volunteered to fly to China and help him source for the purest lingzhi mushrooms and rarest ginseng from the deepest, unpolluted mountains. These prized herbs cost an arm and a leg, but beggars couldn't possibly be choosers. Despite all the money spent, he grew more ill. Now Barber Bay was resigned to the cruel reality. He was dying, and he wanted to visit all his old friends to bid them farewell.

"But what did the clinic doctor say?" Mary Lao pursued.

It turned out that Barber Bay did not believe in Western medicine. He had always stayed away from clinics and preferred to seek help from Chinese physicians.

"Nonsense!" Mary Lao chided. "It is fine to love and defend Chinese traditional culture but when it comes to matters of health and sickness, being stubborn will kill you! I will ask Gimme to set up an appointment for you at the hospital to get tested. You are not dying anytime soon."

One week later, Mary Lao asked Gimme Lao for updates

while the family was having dinner. Gimme Lao wore a strange expression when he disclosed that Barber Bay had a very severe case of oral thrush.

"But it can be treated, right?" asked Mary Lao.

"He will have to come in for further tests," Gimme Lao sighed. "It could well be a symptom of HIV."

For a moment no one spoke. Skye looked around with curiosity as the adults at the table grappled with the disclosure. Gimme Lao's father was the first to break the silence.

"That explains why Barber Bay remained unmarried and kept to himself. I never knew the man was gay."

"We don't know that. Although we currently register more gay patients, straight men get struck by the disease too," Gimme Lao explained.

Mary Lao's mind was spinning fast. She knew for a fact that insurance policies did not cover AIDS. She understood that AIDS treatment was not merely futile but exorbitant. Barber Bay had very likely depleted his savings on bogus herbs from China. It was not unthinkable that he would approach her for loans once he was diagnosed with the condition. She would have to think of an excuse to reject him.

The following week, Mary Lao made a lunch appointment with Elizabeth. She knew the two attended the same church. It soon became clear that the church members were concerned with Barber Bay's failing health and constantly prayed for him. Elizabeth shared that Barber Bay was the one who had brought her to church and connected her to the grace of God. For that, Elizabeth was eternally grateful and kept the man in her prayers every night.

When Mary Lao gingerly asked if the church had funds to help out members with chronic illnesses, Elizabeth explained proudly that the congregation would not hesitate to raise funds for any brothers or sisters in financial difficulty.

"That is great!" Mary Lao exclaimed, relieved. "I was so worried that Barber Bay would be left to fend for himself. It would be tough for a single man with no family to look after him."

"Our church is his family," Elizabeth professed with pride.

Mary Lao's relief turned out to be short-lived. She was astounded when Barber Bay turned up at her doorstep several days later looking ashen and despondent. The truth was spilled after tea was served. The church had banished Barber Bay after they learnt that he had contracted HIV.

"But Elizabeth told me they would raise funds to help out with your medical expenses!" Mary Lao exclaimed.

"They say I have sinned beyond redemption. They say the curse of AIDS was God's punishment for me for sleeping with a man. But I did not!" Barber Bay sobbed bitterly. The poor man could not even muster the strength to be indignant.

"Did you not?" Mary Lao queried. "How else could you have contracted the gay disease?"

Barber Bay shook his head and blew his nose. "I was lonely. And I didn't want to grow old alone. My friend told me I could go over to Batam Island and find a nice Indonesian girl to take care of me. I could buy a house and she would take care of me in my old age and I would leave her the house and my money. It sounded like a good idea at that time. For the last five years

I would work during the week and hop over to Batam on a ferry for the weekend. My girl and my house would be waiting for me. I made her promise she would leave the trade and become my girl and no one else's. But I was a fool. She must have continued to work during the weekdays and contracted the horrible disease. Now I have AIDS. My church has denounced me and my girl in Batam is the only one left by my side now."

Mary Lao winced. She had heard stories of old men who visited Batam Island and splurged their life savings on young flesh. She had thought them lascivious and foolish. But she knew Barber Bay. She believed him to be a kind and gentle man. It was surely loneliness that had driven him to the arrangement. Just as the shoot of sympathy sprouted in her heart, Mary Lao heard her husband assure Barber Bay that he could come visit anytime and their door would always be open. Mary Lao winced again.

Barber Bay began to visit the family regularly. He had dropped out of church, and the neighbours must have heard the story from Elizabeth, for they steered clear of him. Mary Lao and her husband would brew a pot of tea and listen to Barber Bay gripe about his misfortune. He had lived an upright, inculpable life. He did not smoke, drink, or gamble. Until five years ago, he had never visited a prostitute. Yes, he admitted he eventually ventured to Batam for paid sex. But he did not mistreat his girl. He bought a property on the island to house her and provided her with a weekly allowance. Other than the missing marriage certificate, he treated her as his wife. Was that sin enough for God to strike him down with such a terrible fate? It was not merely the debilitating illness that wore him down. It was the unanimous ostracising by his church whom he thought was family and by his neighbours whom he thought were friends. He could not understand how God could be so cruel.

As Barber Bay's visits intensified, Mary Lao and her husband's sympathies wore thin. Often, Mary Lao would claim she needed to follow up on some insurance matters and retire to her room, leaving her husband stranded with the old man. Her husband tried to engage Barber Bay in a game of Chinese chess to take his mind off his troubles, but Barber Bay was a hopeless strategist and the uneven playing was as much a torture as the old man's sullen grouses. Eventually, when Mary Lao learnt that Barber Bay had asked her husband for a loan, she knew she had to take action.

Elizabeth was pleasantly surprised when Mary Lao called to ask for an invitation to church service on Sunday; she needed to speak to her pastor. After the service, Elizabeth arranged for the three of them to lunch at the popular chicken rice stall at Queenstown Hawker Centre. The average waiting time stretched beyond 30 minutes, which gave them time to chat.

Elizabeth had nothing but admiration when she introduced her pastor Larry Kong to Mary Lao. Pastor Kong was a tireless warrior who defended the word of God and stood up to all that was wayward within contemporary society. He understood that the temptations of greed, pride and debauchery were real and omnipresent. He guarded and protected his flock with a fierce motherliness. All who joined his congregation were blessed and safe.

Mary Lao chose to interrupt before Elizabeth got carried

away. That was the exact reason she had come to their church today. One of their members needed help. Barber Bay, who had attended their church for the last 20 years, was in a bad spot now. He had run out of money for his medical treatment, and Mary Lao was hoping the church could raise some funds for him.

"Barber Bay has betrayed our trust for the last 20 years." Elizabeth did not hide the look of disgust on her face. "He prayed among us as though he was innocent, when all the while he was engaging in unpardonable sin. He is beyond redemption."

Mary Lao turned to Pastor Kong and appealed, "Surely the church would have the compassion to forgive him and lend a hand? He has no one else to turn to."

Pastor Kong sighed heavily, "Mary, you must not think our church is lacking in compassion. When Barber Bay was ill, we all kept him in our prayers. When Elizabeth found out that he had contracted HIV, I spoke to him personally. The thing is, he is unrepentant. He refuses even to admit that he is a practising homosexual. How can I help him when he refuses to be honest? I have a flock of followers to take care of, and I cannot allow a diseased heretic to poison the innocent among my flock."

"But he claims he caught the disease visiting prostitutes," Mary Lao insisted.

"He knows how the church abhors homosexuality. He will never admit to it," Pastor Kong continued. "I understand you are compassionate and wish to help, Mary. I urge you to come join our church services. You will find many other worthy recipients of your compassion. The unrepentant do not deserve your help.

Come to church and stay away from the diseased."

That was the moment Mary Lao caught a glimpse of hope. She had come hoping that the church would take over the burden of helping Barber Bay. That door had been shut and bolted. But another door had opened instead. She could step in, and Pastor Kong could relieve her of the guilt of not helping Barber Bay. As the pastor made it very clear, the unrepentant were not deserving of help. The walls of the church would protect her from Barber Bay's predicament.

Mary Lao began to attend Pastor Kong's church. She did not extend the invitation to her husband because she did not see herself lasting very long. Mary Lao was not religious by nature. She did not believe she was born sinful and needed to atone for her sins. Jesus underwent hardship, persecution and sacrificed himself for others. Mary Lao saw no glory in suffering or sacrifice. She was, simply put, godless.

But Pastor Kong's sermons surprised her. When he quoted from the Book of Malachi and claimed that God intended his children to enjoy physical health and economic prosperity, Mary Lao pricked up her ears. When he preached that positive confession would unlock the blessings of wealth and abundance, Mary Lao sat up straight. When he encouraged the practice of visualisation to bring forth whatever one desired, Mary Lao felt her fingers tingle. Her earlier and apparently unfounded perception that Christianity was all about suffering and sacrifice was turned on its head.

"I cannot blame you for that misperception," Pastor Kong remarked when Mary Lao ventured to query him over lunch one day. "Too many church sermons linger on the topic of suffering, but that is not what Christianity is all about. God did promise prosperity and victory to Israel in the Old Testament. The same applies to us today too. All you have to do is fulfil your part of the faith contract and God will deliver abundance in all its forms to your life."

Mary Lao liked what she was hearing. She asked that the pastor elaborate.

"I have preached about positive confession. You can claim from God all that he promised you by speaking it, by believing it, by visualising it. The faith contract also requires that you give. By faithfully giving a tenth of your wealth to the church, God will return the wealth to you sevenfold. That is how generous God is. When you embrace God, it is a life of abundance without limit that awaits you."

Mary Lao did a quick calculation. The church congregation of over a thousand swelled her prospect list instantly. She was certain that once she established her network of relationships, it was quite possible to swell her insurance commission to sevenfold of her tithing.

"When you came to us to discuss Barber Bay's condition, it was God calling out to you to come home. And God needs you to do his work," Pastor Kong continued. "Your husband, your son, your daughter-in-law, your grandchild, they all need to come home too. Bring them to church, Mary. Bring them home."

Mary Lao contemplated the invitation. From her experience, her insurance prospects tended to recoil a little when they read the title of 'Senior Sales Manager' on her name card. Which was why she always made it a point to soften the edge by painting herself as a wife, a mother and now a grandmother. The church setting was ideal. She would bring her family. That would open more doors for her.

The next evening at the dinner table, Mary Lao suggested everyone follow her to church on Sunday. Pastor Kong gave brilliant, progressive sermons that would enlighten them the way they enlightened her. Mary Lao's husband did not feel like going; but he lacked the courage to raise his objection. The fact that Mary Lao was the one who brought home serious bacon had eroded his voting rights over the decades. Wei Wen did not feel like going either but the fact that she and her child lived in and enjoyed the comforts of the condominium that her mother-in-law paid for made it impolite to decline. Gimme Lao definitely did not feel like going. He simply said he wasn't interested. He made his own money, so it wasn't difficult for him to be curt. Skye was too young to comprehend what church meant. His grandmother made it sound like a performance of some sort. Skye hoped there would be some magic involved.

At church the following Sunday, not only was Pastor Kong delighted to meet Mary Lao's family, he amplified his jubilance by inviting Mary Lao on stage to give testimony. It was Mary Lao's compassion and desire to help a lost soul that brought her to church. Hallelujah! The Lord might have lost a child in the form of an unrepentant sinner like Barber Bay, but he brought four more of his children into the Kingdom. Hallelujah! God did his work in miraculous ways. There and then, Pastor Kong vowed to spread his wings over the family to protect them from the evil that lurked outside the church walls. If a grown man like Barber Bay could be lured to commit unpardonable sin, how much more perilous the journey must be, for a pure soul like Mary Lao's grandchild. The boy must be protected from the claws of deviant sexuality and other evils. Hallelujah!

When Mary Lao returned to the pew, her husband leaned in and whispered, "Didn't you explain to the pastor that Barber Bay is not gay? He has a woman in Batam."

"It doesn't matter." Mary Lao was adamant. "Barber Bay has fallen out with the church. We must not associate with him anymore."

Mary Lao meant what she said. When Barber Bay turned up at the door two days later, Mary Lao would not let him in. Her family was attending Pastor Kong's church, and Barber Bay was no longer welcome in her house. More importantly, she did not want Barber Bay to approach her husband for any more loans. His illness was God's punishment. It was not right for herself or her husband to alleviate it.

Mary Lao's husband could not see Barber Bay from where he was seated in the living room. He could only imagine the old man ashen and shaken. For the longest time Barber Bay must have felt safe and loved in the house of the Lord. God's love was all-encompassing. But now that the church had cast him out, God's vindictiveness was all-encompassing too. Neighbours turned their backs on him, friends barred him from entering their houses, medical expenses drained his savings, pain racked his body and fear racked his mind. God must be really angry with him.

Mary Lao's husband secretly thought his wife was being cruel. There were many things Mary Lao did that he did not approve of. He cringed at the insufferable persistence with which she hounded their friends and acquaintances for sales appointments. He detested her habit of snapping her fingers to summon the waiters or snapping at their domestic help when the bathroom tiles were not properly scrubbed. He felt slighted when she made big-ticket item purchases without consulting him. This latest move of hers to herd the family to church for no apparent reason irked him immeasurably. Yet, as always, he kept these gripes to himself. He considered himself a patient, understanding and tolerant man. Were he not, this marriage would not have lasted so long or so peacefully. As he heard his wife shut the door in their old neighbour's face, he heaved a heavy-hearted sigh. He truly had no choice but to be the bigger man to balance out his wife's many failings.

Wei Wen could not stand Sunday church. She had always been an atheist, and she found the congregation as stifling as the sermons. All the warm smiles and ubiquitous blessings from complete strangers unnerved her. How did these people imagine that instant trust and goodwill could materialise out of thin air? It baffled her that they were so ready to show concern when they hardly knew her. Did they know she used to watch and film sex tapes? Did they know she was excellent at fellatio? Did they imagine that among the congregation of a thousand, there would be no paedophile, batterer, or voyeur?

And then it struck Wei Wen. Perhaps that was what brought about the downfall of Barber Bay. The man was an accepted member of the congregation for as long as they imagined him to behave according to their prescribed code of conduct. That code of conduct would never land him in jail, or mire him in gambling debts or churn up an HIV positive medical status. Their offerings of warm smiles and goodwill were a form of demand for that code of conduct. Barber Bay had failed them. As Elizabeth so tersely put it, Barber Bay had betrayed their trust for the last 20 years. The congregation was the victim.

After three consecutive Sunday services, Wei Wen had had enough. She told Mary Lao that her grandmother once again switched her mahjong sessions to Sundays, so she had to be home to keep an eye on her brother. Although he was all of 23, he still could not be trusted to be alone at home. He knew how to turn on the gas to fry an omelette, but would likely forget to turn it off. There were instances when he was so distracted by the programme on television he allowed the soup to boil itself dry. That boy would always require supervision.

Wei Wen's conspicuous absence in church attracted queries from the welcome team, of which Elizabeth was an active member. Mary Lao explained that Wei Wen was burdened with caregiver duties for her brother with Down's syndrome. That disclosure quickly rippled across the pews. Well-wishers boldly stepped forward to introduce themselves, expressed their concerns and sympathies and promised to keep Wei Wen and her brother in their prayers. Elizabeth dutifully whispered into Pastor Kong's ear, who saw it fit to include Wei Wen and her brother in his blessings towards the end of his sermon. Many among the congregation, who could recognise Mary Lao from her testimony on stage several weeks ago, stopped by her pew on their way out and personally delivered their blessings.

Mary Lao and her husband were overwhelmed.

On the drive home, Mary Lao's husband confessed that he was moved. There was so much outpouring of love from the congregation. If he had his doubts when she first dragged him to church, the doubt had all but dissipated. He could actually feel the energy of positivity and hope flooding the church and flowing through him today. God's love was real.

Mary Lao remained silent throughout the drive, but her body was shaking with excitement. She had an epiphany earlier at church. It was a seedling of a raw idea, but it had huge potential. She had no urge to share it with her husband though. She had left him behind way back when he failed to share her jubilance at closing her first insurance sales. He could never comprehend how grand her ambitions were.

Mary Lao bided her time. She spent several weeks doing her market research, getting quotations, sourcing for bank loans and approaching potential investors among her more affluent insurance clients. When her initial idea finally took shape, she summoned Wei Wen for a discussion. Now that Skye was starting school, what were her plans?

"I might start looking for a job," Wei Wen stumbled. She had not expected the question and secretly prayed that Mary Lao was not thinking of recruiting her into insurance sales.

"You were pursuing a business degree before you had Skye. I just thought it would be a waste not to apply it," Mary Lao prompted. "I have a business venture in mind. How would you like to help me develop it?"

Wei Wen's heart skipped a beat, but she managed to retain her outward calm. "What kind of business venture are we looking at, Mum?"

"I spoke to some of my insurance clients with business backgrounds. They are willing to support me if I take up a Taiwanese pearl milk tea franchise. Are you familiar with it?"

Wei Wen could feel her pulse quicken. She had a gathering with her friends from university recently, and everyone was talking about the bubble tea craze. It was a new beverage developed in Taichung, Taiwan barely three years ago. Sweetened, chewy pearl balls made of tapioca were added to ice-blended milk tea and served in trendy cups sealed with plastic cellophane. The permutation of fruit flavours and tea bases allowed the product to spin into a colourful spectrum on the menu. No self-respecting teenager could bear to be spotted without one in hand.

"If I remember correctly, the bubble tea craze came to Singapore about one year ago. There was a sudden proliferation of bubble tea outlets along the Orchard Road shopping belt," Wei Wen reflected. "I guess it is not too late to enter the market. But I must say the rental rates at the prime shopping malls are prohibitive. We really ought to do our market research first."

"I did just that," Mary Lao said. "Which is why I am staying away from shopping malls and tapping into the neighbourhood market. I plan to set up five outlets within the first two years. All the outlets will be strategically positioned near train stations where commuters pass by on their way to school or work."

"That is a novel idea," Wei Wen admitted.

"Yes, but that is not the catch," Mary Lao elaborated. "I have registered the firm as 'Ai-Xin Zhenzhu Nai Cha', or 'Pearls of Love'. In every outlet, our service crew will include a supervisor guiding a special needs youth, such as your brother. That will be our mission. Providing employment for the less fortunate in our society. I was hoping you could get your brother to pioneer our first outlet, which I intend to set up near our church. Many among the congregation live in the immediate vicinity, so we can easily build up our support base in double quick time. What do you think?"

For a moment, Wei Wen found herself at a loss for words. Her mother-in-law had obviously thought the plan through. Although she was not convinced that altruism was the main motivation when her mother-in-law roped in her brother, it quickly crossed her mind that this arrangement could turn out to be a win-win situation. She could keep an eye on her brother while he was gainfully employed. If she needed time off to take care of Skye, surely her mother-in-law would understand. It was in fact the perfect arrangement.

The following months saw Mary Lao and Wei Wen working closely together. For once, the two women found themselves bonding effortlessly without Skye in the picture. Mary Lao's drive and ambition provided Wei Wen the impetus to apply herself. Conversely, Wei Wen's vigour and efficiency impressed Mary Lao. Over time, Mary Lao began to see Wei Wen less as an underperforming daughter-in-law and more as a promising young associate whom she enjoyed mentoring. Wei Wen, too, was aware of the altered dynamics in their interactions and keenly appreciated the trust and respect her mother-in-law now accorded her.

Initially, the men in the house were amused. Skye was often left in their charge while the women left the house for site recces and business appointments. Even when the women were back home, the men were expected to keep Skye occupied and entertained while the women discussed business development. It wasn't long before the two men realised they were being neglected. Mary Lao's husband first noticed that his wife stopped reminding him to take his daily medication. When he gently reminded her not to forget to remind him about his medication, his wife snapped. Gimme Lao too, realised that his wife now had a tendency to slip into an exhausted sleep once she hit the pillow. For years, she had always been the one to reach over and initiate sex. He never had to and did not quite know how to wake her up for it. After going three weeks without any form of intimacy, Gimme Lao was so frustrated he picked a quarrel with Wei Wen when Skye was caught trying to light the stove to conduct a personal science experiment unsupervised. Wei Wen felt guilty and said she was sorry she left Skye alone in the kitchen. When Gimme Lao continued to sulk, Wei Wen quickly realised the root cause of his peevishness. After they got into bed that night, Wei Wen reached over and tentatively scratched the nape of his neck. Gimme Lao's quick and ready response confirmed her suspicions. She had been neglecting him and he knew no other way of expressing his frustration. Her husband was simply throwing a conjugal tantrum.

The day finally arrived when the first Pearls of Love outlet was ready for operation. Mary Lao had earlier called up Pastor Kong and requested to give testimony. As she stepped up to the podium and grabbed the mike, she pinched her face and prayed aloud, "Lord, I ask for your forgiveness, for I am guilty of hypocrisy. When I first came to this church, Pastor Kong told the congregation that it was compassion and empathy that brought me to church. I myself believed that too. But the Lord's grace and teaching over the many months have opened my eyes. I am not a woman of compassion. If anything, I blatantly lack compassion."

Many in the congregation sat up straight. Though most of them would not admit it, they loved nothing more than a public confession of sin harboured, witnessed or committed.

"Some of you know my daughter-in-law Wei Wen. Some of you may even know she has a brother born with Down's syndrome. When she married my son, I took her into my family. But I did not take in her brother. At the back of my mind, I kept telling myself that the caregiver duty for her brother lies with her and her own family. I love Wei Wen for being a dutiful wife to my son and a loving mother to my grandchild, but I did not love her enough to share her burden. I felt that I had to draw a line.

"But over the last few months, God has opened my eyes. There is no line to be drawn when it comes to love and compassion. God does not draw a line, so why should I? If I love my daughter-in-law, should not what worries her, worry me too? Should not what concerns her, concern me too? I struggled with that thought. I struggled with the horrible realisation that

I am a woman lacking in compassion, a hypocrite sitting in the Lord's house of love and truth."

The congregation held their breath as Mary Lao cupped her mouth with a trembling palm. Some of the women dug in their purse for a handkerchief in anticipation of the emotional outpouring about to come. Some of the men could feel the lump in their throats.

It took a little while but Mary Lao eventually regained her composure.

"It finally dawned on me I have work to do. God's work. When a child is born with Down's syndrome, it is God testing us. Do we merely feel compassionate or do we exercise compassion? Do we merely keep the child in our prayers or do we reach out to help? I for one know where I stand now. I am determined to do God's work.

"After church service today, as you make your way past Block 75 to Queenstown MRT station, you will see a newly opened bubble tea outlet. The signboard reads 'Ai-Xin Zhenzhu Nai Cha', or 'Pearls of Love'. If you look inside, you will see Wei Wen's brother learning to run the outlet under the guidance of a supervisor. That is me doing God's work. I am committed to giving Wei Wen's brother a fighting chance at an independent life, to feel proud of himself because he can earn his own living. And I urge all of you to drop by, to give him not sympathy, but encouragement and support. Do not be the woman I once was, who speaks compassion but does not act on it. Be the greater person God intended you to be. Amen!"

A thunderous applause greeted Mary Lao's testimony. Pastor

Kong made a mental note to recruit her for the next batch of church elders; he could do with someone who could move the crowd in the manner Mary Lao had just demonstrated. Elizabeth swelled with pride as she watched Mary Lao make her way back to her pew bathed in admiration and glory. Here was a woman who did not speak a word of English when they first met, whom she herself tutored and trained two decades ago. Today, Mary Lao brought down the house with a powerful testimony on the pulpit. Elizabeth couldn't have been prouder had one of her students come in first in an international piano recital competition.

Church service ended at noon. By two in the afternoon, three of the 13 flavours offered by the Pearls of Love outlet had run out. At the peak of the rush, Wei Wen's brother panicked and almost sliced off his finger rinsing out the blender. That very night, he woke up from a nightmare screaming and crying about menacing blenders and severed fingers. Wei Wen had to come over in the morning and convince him to report for work.

Fortunately for Wei Wen's brother, the customers from church who kept returning soon become familiar, friendly faces. Some of them made the effort to chat with him and praised him profusely when he made them their blended bubble tea correctly. An elderly gentleman even bought him a transistor radio so he could keep himself entertained during the lull periods. Wei Wen's brother took to the music channel instantly. It was 1992 and Right Said Fred was topping the local radio charts. Whenever their song came on air, Wei Wen's brother would squeal in delight and bob his head to the beat. Tickled, the supervisor goaded him to choreograph a dance routine. Wei Wen's brother would uphold two fingers of each hand in a V sign and gyrate out of tempo as the song went "I'm too sexy for my shirt, too sexy for my shirt, so sexy it hurts". The children and youths in the neighbourhood got a great kick out of it and would drop by just to watch him dance. Soon, everyone started referring to both Wei Wen's brother and the outlet as Too Sexy. Students would arrange to meet at Too Sexy after class before heading downtown to the cinema or the bowling alley. Church members exchanged anecdotes about Too Sexy, some lamenting that he was picking up foul language from the hooligans, others updating how he was building up self-confidence and chatting with the regular customers. Too Sexy became an icon in the Queenstown neighbourhood.

Encouraged by the instant success of the first outlet, Mary Lao and Wei Wen decided to launch the next two outlets concurrently. They visited the school for students with special needs that Wei Wen's brother had once attended and asked for a list of candidates they could interview. It took them months of phone interviews and house visits before they managed to narrow the pool down to a handful. Mary Lao's criteria, though not explicitly stated, was unequivocal. These had to be youths with Down's syndrome whose parents were active members of churches. Mary Lao then instructed her property agent to focus on the immediate vicinity of these churches and find her a suitable shop space. Once the rental contracts were signed, Mary Lao asked the parents to introduce her to their church pastors. She shared with them her story of awakening and how she was now inspired to do God's work. Although neither church granted her request to give testimony on the pulpit, they agreed to feature her story in their church newsletters. The pastors also promised to mention her new bubble tea outlets during their sermons to illustrate how God inspired ordinary men to do extraordinary things for the less fortunate in society.

Unhappy that she was denied the chance to speak directly to the congregation, Mary Lao decided she had to raise the bar on her publicity. She made a few phone calls to her investors and almost immediately hit jackpot. One of them had a sister who was married to a top executive at the Singapore Broadcasting Corporation. Being the only influential media conglomerate in Singapore, the corporation held a virtual monopoly and dominated the broadcasting industry. Two strategic dinners later, it was agreed that the current affairs division would produce a short documentary on local social entrepreneurs with a heart. Mary Lao's Pearls of Love start-up would be featured as one prominent example.

On the day of filming, the crew came down to the Queenstown outlet to interview Mary Lao and shoot Wei Wen's brother in action. Unnerved by the filming crew and their ominous equipment, Wei Wen's brother paled and became horrendously clumsy mixing the beverages. To calm his nerves, the supervisor put on a cassette tape and played Right Said Fred's "I'm Too Sexy". Almost immediately, Wei Wen's brother delighted everyone by laughing and dancing to the tune. The crew reacted quickly and captured it on film.

When the documentary aired two weeks later, it was the

bonus clip of Wei Wen's brother dancing and having fun that captivated the audience. Viewership tripled when the episode was dubbed and broadcast again the following week on the English channel. The Too Sexy clip became the talk of the town, spinning off into more newspaper article mentions than Mary Lao could have hoped for. Singaporeans from the opposite end of the island took the MRT train to Queenstown just to visit Wei Wen's brother and have their pictures taken with him. The protagonist himself was not entirely aware that he had become a national sensation, but was generally happy to oblige when customers requested that he pose for the camera brandishing his Too Sexy V sign.

Mary Lao brought the family out for a celebratory dinner at the prestigious Shang Palace restaurant at the Shangri-La Hotel. She ordered individual servings of Buddha Jumps Over the Wall for everyone, including Skye, who had no idea how extravagantly expensive the soup was and complained that he did not like it at all. Mary Lao laughed and promised that if the revenue figures continued to climb, she could make this a monthly visit until Skye cultivated a taste for the delicacy.

As dessert was being served, Mary Lao turned to Gimme Lao and asked that he stop being so stubborn. Pastor Kong had been urging her to bring him to church. Gimme Lao should open up his mind, Mary Lao remarked. Witness the blessings God had bestowed on them. Her Pearls of Love business venture was an astounding success, and Wei Wen did not have to worry about her brother's livelihood the way she used to. It was all God's work!

Gimme Lao made a face and said that there was something he had not brought to their attention the past few weeks because they were all so engrossed with the filming project. Barber Bay had been admitted to hospital as a terminal case more than a month ago. He had just passed on the night before.

EIGHT

GIMME LAO WAS back at his office on a Sunday morning. He had three more hours to clear his work before he needed to pick Skye up for his swimming lesson. After that he had to preside over the monthly Youth Executive Committee meeting at Bukit Panjang Community Club. But first, he had to clear the major hurdle of the day. He was to conduct an exit interview for Pay Ming Kuang.

Gimme Lao had mixed feelings about this turn of events. Although Pay Ming Kuang was clearly his chief rival in the race to head the Communicable Disease Division of Tan Tock Seng Hospital, he would never have wished such a dishonourable discharge upon the poor man. Gimme Lao could not imagine how it must feel to have one's name splashed across the front page of *The Straits Times* in bold, ignominiously featured as one among a dozen men netted in the most notorious police sweep of 1996. The other 11 men had their names printed in size 10 font in paragraph six. Pay Ming Kuang had his name printed in bold, font size 22, headlining the article. He was not any more or less guilty than the rest. He was simply guilty of being the son of Pay Wee Khoon, the tycoon who headed Pay Conglomerate, which owned and operated, among other entities, the biggest banking group in Singapore.

It would not be stretching the truth to describe Pay Ming Kuang as mousy. The man was short and scrawny, spoke softly and had problems asserting himself. He had kept a low profile in medical school. In fact, no one would have found out about his imposing family background had Professor Eleanor Moh not let it slip when she conducted the module on communicable disease. Professor Eleanor Moh herself was a prominent figure. Not only did she head the Communicable Disease Division of Tan Tock Seng Hospital, she was married to a serving cabinet minister in Parliament. The first day she walked in to the lecture theatre, she scanned through Gimme Lao's cohort, spotted Pay Ming Kuang and waved at him with a warm smile. As the rest of the cohort watched stunned, Professor Eleanor Moh enquired after his mother and suggested Mrs Pay call her secretary to make arrangements to meet up for high tea. It had been ages since they last chatted.

It took the cohort less than 48 hours to dig up the details. Pay Ming Kuang was third in line to inherit a family fortune worth close to a billion. Both his brothers had chosen to work for their father. The eldest was engaged to the daughter of a local shipping tycoon, while the second was dating a girl whose father had made it to the *Forbes* list of Indonesia's 50 richest. Pay Ming Kuang himself was not attached. That effectively elevated him to being the most eligible bachelor in the cohort.

Prior to the revelation, Gimme Lao did not pay the mousy young man any attention. Now that he did, he began to notice a pattern. The reason Pay Ming Kuang was seldom spotted in the student cafeteria was that he was often dining at the staff cafeteria at the invitation of various professors and heads of department. Professor Eleanor Moh herself openly invited the young man to join her for lunch after her lectures. The cohort quickly arrived at a foregone conclusion. There were only two spots available for their batch at the Communicable Disease Division of Tan Tock Seng Hospital, and she had reserved one of them for Pay Ming Kuang. There was only one spot left.

Gimme Lao wanted that last spot.

A medical career looked like a great option when one was 14. Income was steady, social status was guaranteed and one suffered minimal impact from an economic downturn. But Gimme Lao had expanded his horizons over the years. He had witnessed his mother amass her fortune by leaps and bounds leveraging on her sales and business acumen. There was no way he could measure up by working as a general practitioner running a neighbourhood clinic. Serving in the army, he had witnessed how some cadets clandestinely enjoyed privileged treatment because they were from prominent families. Gimme Lao had no respect for these privileged offspring; they were where they were by an inexplicable stroke of luck. He did, however, look up to their parents, many of whom had made a name for themselves in their chosen field of endeavour. These people earned the respect of the community.

Gimme Lao would like that—to earn the respect of his community.

During his first year in medical school, Gimme Lao took time to study the alumni records. Although some had made a name for themselves regionally as top of their fields, they were known and respected only within the medical community. It was the handful who branched out into public service who had made a name for themselves among the general public. In fact, Gimme Lao was surprised to learn that doctors were grossly overrepresented among the 87 Members of Parliament. It would appear that a medical background opened doors more easily in the political arena. That realisation was directly responsible for Gimme Lao's awakening. He would eventually seek public office. That would be his calling.

Gimme Lao had no illusions about his handicap. He did not come from a prominent family and knew no one who moved in high places. On the other hand, he had absolute confidence in his abilities. He was sharp, focused, brilliant and persevering. Once he made up his mind about anything, he always made it happen.

The Communicable Disease Division of Tan Tock Seng Hospital was not a spot top that medical students vied for. There was hardly any glamour or prospect in it. For Gimme Lao, it was the perfect spot. It was small enough that he could shine easily, and Professor Eleanor Moh was on hand to discern and appraise his performance. Gimme Lao had done his background check on the professor. Not only was her husband a cabinet minister, her cousin was a serving Member of Parliament. With her connections, she could be his ticket to board the speedboat headed for his ultimate destination.

Gimme Lao knew he needed to make it easy for Professor Eleanor Moh to distinguish him from among the two hundred medical students in his cohort. An afternoon's leisurely swim at the university pool was all it took to map out his strategy. The following week, Gimme Lao dropped by Bukit Panjang Constituency Office to sign up as a volunteer for the Youth Executive Committee. When the interviewer frowned and asked why he chose to volunteer at a constituency so far from home, Gimme Lao lied and said it was near his in-laws'. The truth was, the Bukit Panjang Constituency Adviser appointed by the Prime Minister's Office was none other than Professor Eleanor Moh's husband, Dr Liew Kim Keong.

By the second meeting of the Youth Executive Committee, Gimme Lao realised he faced a hurdle. There were seven different committees under the umbrella of the constituency, and the one he belonged to was the least prominent. While the other committee chairmen aggressively sought Dr Liew's attention and favour, his chairman could not be bothered to play the political game. The man dutifully organised events and activities to engage youths, but did nothing to convert his efforts into political playing chips. The committee was practically invisible to Dr Liew.

Gimme Lao knew he had to make a strategic move. He timed himself to drop by the constituency office just as the director was leaving for the weekly session where Dr Liew met the residents and discussed their issues in his capacity as the constituency adviser. Feigning surprise, Gimme Lao mentioned that he did not mind tagging along. When they arrived, the director could only interrupt Dr Liew's session for all of two minutes to introduce Gimme Lao. There was a long queue of residents waiting for their turn to seek assistance or to air their grouses.

For the next two hours, Gimme Lao observed and took mental notes. The residents' issues ranged from the pertinent and imperative to the frivolous and absurd. A woman complained that from her kitchen window she could spot a shameless couple in the opposite building moving around their apartment naked and having sex without bothering to draw their curtains. Another woman noticed groups of Bangladeshi construction workers enjoying their siesta at the void deck below her flat and worried for the safety of her teenage daughter who had to walk past them to reach home. An elderly man was unhappy that the local supermarket hired Filipino cashiers who could not speak his dialect. Yet another was livid that teenagers were making out in the neighbourhood park in broad daylight. All were adamant that Dr Liew had to do something about these intolerable issues.

Gimme Lao knew he had hit jackpot when two elderly ladies came in together to highlight a problem. They had recently moved in to the new blocks at the northern fringe and were horrified to discover that there were no clinics within the vicinity. It was especially tough for the elderly folks, who were frail and lacked mobility, to have to take a bus down to the Bukit Panjang town centre to see a doctor. Dr Liew assured them that once all the new blocks in the northern fringe were built and occupied within the next three years, the clinics and supermarkets would sprout up too. He asked that the ladies be patient.

It took Gimme Lao several weeks to orchestrate the plan he had in mind. If things went smoothly, there would soon be a mobile clinic visiting the northern fringe twice a month. He convinced Mary Lao to fund the project by promising that

Pearls of Love would be prominently featured as the main sponsor when the media coverage eventually kicked in. He roped in doctors from Tan Tock Seng Hospital to volunteer for the mobile clinic, while Mary Lao mobilised volunteers from church to run the logistics and operation. Once the pieces were in place, he asked the constituency director to arrange for a meeting with Dr Liew so he could present his solution.

Naturally, Dr Liew was impressed. He tasked the constituency director to help source for additional funds and personally invited Gimme Lao to join him and his wife for dinner on Sunday. There was a new Peranakan restaurant they wanted to try, and he would very much like his wife to meet a promising young grassroots leader.

Once Gimme Lao entered Professor Eleanor Moh's radar, the hurdle was cleared. In time to come, Gimme Lao and Pay Ming Kuang secured the only two spots reserved for their batch at the Communicable Disease Division of Tan Tock Seng Hospital. During the Youth Executive Committee re-election the following year, Dr Liew Kim Keong pulled some strings so that Gimme Lao emerged the newly elected chairman. In return, Gimme Lao worked hard not to disappoint the adviser. He rejuvenated and led his team to overtake the other six committees to become the star performer in the constituency. By the third year, he chalked up a sufficient track record to be nominated as Outstanding Grassroots Leader of the Year for the Northwest Division.

The situation was however a little more complicated at work. Pay Ming Kuang's father, the tycoon who headed the formidable Pay Conglomerate, sat on the Advisory Board of Tan Tock Seng

Hospital. Chances were slim that Professor Eleanor Moh would rank Gimme Lao ahead of Pay Ming Kuang in the annual appraisal exercise. Although the taciturn man kept to himself and did not make any effort to network the way Gimme Lao did, he was nonetheless a competent and responsible physician. There was no faulting the man.

Until the notorious police sweep of 1996.

Pay Ming Kuang chose to keep a low profile for a good reason. There was a facet of his life he did not share with his family, friends or colleagues. They saw him as an eccentric who did not seem to crave company. None of his friends and colleagues knew his favourite haunts, and no one in his family questioned him when he habitually left the house late at night on Tuesdays and Fridays and did not return till three in the morning. His mother thought he might be out drinking. She secretly hoped it was drinking and not gambling or whoring that her son was trying to hide from her. As for the father and the two brothers, they were too busy to concern themselves with his clandestine lifestyle.

No one he knew would ever guess that he went into the forest on Tuesday and Friday nights.

Pay Ming Kuang first entered the forest four years ago. He had heard about the place through the grapevine. It was a stretch of wooded area sandwiched between the Tanjong Rhu Flyover and the shoreline along the East Coast. He remembered his first visit with heady nostalgia. He had parked his car along Fort Road and made a quick dash into the shadows. Once in the forest, the moonlight and streetlights were effectively obliterated. He leaned against a massive tree trunk and allowed his eyes to adjust to the darkness. He could hear nothing but the pounding of his heart.

After a minute or two, the blanket of darkness morphed into odd shapes and shadows. The undergrowth was sparse enough for him to make out a network of trails in the primary forest. There was the night wind rustling the leaves, and he could hear the stridulation of the crickets. Pay Ming Kuang emitted a nervous chuckle. He found it amusing that most people would describe the sound made by crickets as chirping. They were so mistaken. Male crickets stridulate by running the top of one wing along the lower serrated lining of the other wing, while spreading open the wing membranes to act as acoustic sails. Not many people knew this; at least not among his circle of friends. Then again, he had a tendency to pay excessive attention to details others did not bother with. That could be one of the reasons he had so few friends. People found him odd.

Growing up, Pay Ming Kuang was an odd child. Unlike his two brothers, who were rowdy and pesky, the boy was painfully shy. His mother was initially glad that her youngest was compliant and well behaved. The first incident that drew her attention to his oddity occurred when he was five. The two older boys had tied a coil of rope to her poor Maltese and set the other end on fire. According to the nanny, Pay Ming Kuang had shrieked with horror, stamped out the fire at the critical juncture and cradled the terrified animal while crying bitterly himself. The crying lasted three days. His mother had to instruct the nanny to sleep by his bed so that there would be someone to soothe him when he awoke from his tearful nightmares.

On the fourth night, it was the eldest boy who shrieked and hopped out of bed bawling. The nanny pulled back the blanket and uncovered a pincushion with a dozen pins sticking out like a tiny porcupine. When his mother questioned him, Pay Ming Kuang did not deny it. He simply muttered that his eldest brother ought to experience pain so he would never dish it out to others again.

Two nights later, her second boy fell victim. The nanny found him howling in pain stuck to the toilet seat with an even layer of superglue.

Pay Ming Kuang's mother gave the boy a severe scolding and instructed the nanny to keep a close eye on him. Two months had barely passed before the nanny highlighted yet another incident. Pay Ming Kuang had flown into a rage when he spotted a stray cat mauling an injured sparrow in the garden. Although he managed to chase the predator away, the sparrow was beyond salvation. After burying the feathered carcass under a hibiscus shrub, the boy was seething with vindictive fury for the next few days. The nanny thought he might be scheming some revenge. True enough, she finally found the trap he had set up behind the garden shed to lure unsuspecting stray cats. The boy had swung a toy propeller plane tied to a cord over the roof pipe and left it dangling. Underneath the bait he positioned a pail covered with a cardboard cut-out to which he secured the other end of the cord. Had any curious stray cat hopped onto the cardboard and made a jump for the propeller plane, it would have jerked away the cardboard lid and fallen right into the pail. The nanny shuddered when she removed the lid and looked inside. There was the cleaver missing from the kitchen, propped upright with two garden bricks, the sharp edge of the blade pointed skywards.

Pay Ming Kuang's mother was a little shaken. She realised that her youngest exhibited some psychopathic traits and concluded that nanny supervision alone was insufficient. So she convinced her husband that they should send Pay Ming Kuang to some renowned boarding school where the child would receive the best possible supervision and education. Her husband nodded, his mind preoccupied with a new project to build a casino in Poipet, along the Cambodian and Thai border.

For the next 12 years, Pay Ming Kuang lived away from home in the United Kingdom. When he returned to pursue a medical degree in Singapore, his mother found that her youngest had grown from a shy and odd boy to a taciturn young man who cloaked his thoughts and veiled his feelings. It felt like the family had invited a stranger to join them in the house. Although she would not admit it, she knew it was too late to connect with her youngest child. She had not the faintest idea what would excite, mesmerise or frighten him. He was in a secret world of his own.

That first night in the forest, leaning against a tree trunk studying the darkened landscape, Pay Ming Kuang was simultaneously thrilled, enthralled and terrified. He took a deep breath and followed a random trail. Five minutes into the woods, he began to spot furtive movement in the shadows. Whenever he halted and listened, he could discern, beyond the sharp snaps of twigs stepped upon, heavy breathing and faint moaning. His heart began to palpitate wildly. Soon, he passed by shadowy figures leaning against tree trunks. One or two reached out to touch him. He allowed them to move closer and feel him up. After several seconds, he gently pulled away and moved on. They were not likely to figure out what he wanted.

After more than an hour meandering in the forest, Pay Ming Kuang was despondent. Back in London, there were theme clubs one could go to for very specific needs. Roles were made explicit via codified attire and accessories. There was no need to second-guess. But here in the forest, the players were undifferentiated and unsophisticated. He found it utterly frustrating.

At one point, Pay Ming Kuang decided he had to make his preference explicit. He picked a burly man and snuggled up close. Once he ascertained that the man was receptive, he guided the man's hand to his head, grabbed hold of a considerable tuft and yanked hard. To his delight, the man quickly caught on and proceeded to rough him up. By the end of the session, his left sleeve was torn at the seams, and there were scratch marks on his back. Pay Ming Kuang was ecstatic. This was the first time he had been properly manhandled since he came back to Singapore.

Over the months, Pay Ming Kuang developed various tactics to advertise his preference. He brought a handcuff and cuffed one of his wrists to a branch. He gagged himself and adopted a submissive position kneeling on the ground, as though he was about to be executed by his captor. He blindfolded himself. There were nights he would even bag his entire head in a sack. He found those moments when he was fighting to inhale in the sack while an unseen player ravaged him extremely arousing.

In fact, that was the precise condition the police found him in when they descended upon the forest one night in an orchestrated sweep—breathing hard and oblivious to the commotion as the player ravaging him froze in terror.

A total of 12 men were rounded up in the midnight operation. It was anyone's guess how many more had managed to flee the forest. When the police issued their first public statement to invited media, they withheld names. They simply claimed that the operation to clamp down on a stretch of forest known to be a gathering spot for gay men who cruised and engaged in outdoor sex was successful. All 12 offenders would be charged in court.

Two days later, the withheld list of names was leaked. The front-page headline in the morning papers read 'Pay Ming Kuang, youngest son of Pay Conglomerate tycoon Pay Wee Khoon, nabbed in the police sweep of the notorious gay cruising ground'.

The entire Tan Tock Seng Hospital staff was in shock. The executive director held a closed-door contingency meeting to deal with the publicity disaster. Professor Eleanor Moh was to grant Pay Ming Kuang an indefinite leave of absence and reject any media request for comments. The executive director would leave it to the Public Relations Department to implement damage control. It was uncertain if the Advisory Board of Tan Tock Seng Hospital would require Mr Pay Wee Khoon to step down. Till the tornado blew over, everyone was to be on their toes and say and do nothing that would land themselves or the hospital in trouble.

When Pay Ming Kuang eventually tendered his resignation,

Gimme Lao was not surprised that Professor Eleanor Moh tasked him to conduct the exit interview. It would be too awkward for her. After all, she knew his mother on a first-name basis. Gimme Lao himself felt no such pressure. He scheduled it on a Sunday morning, the quietest slot at the Communicable Disease Division, so that Pay Ming Kuang was least likely to bump into administrative and nursing staff. That was the least he could do for the poor fellow.

Gimme Lao had mentally rehearsed for various scenarios. He could be sensitive and empathetic if the man needed sympathy, or courteous and matter-of-fact if the man would rather pretend the entire matter was nothing extraordinary. Yet he found himself caught by surprise when Pay Ming Kuang turned up for the exit interview beaming. It was as though the man had a tip-off that he would be promoted.

"So what are your future plans?" Gimme Lao felt obligated to ask after the interview was over.

"Go home," Pay Ming Kuang smiled warmly. "To where I belong."

Gimme Lao had to pause for a second. "You mean London."

"Yes, I mean London. Where everybody gets to breathe," Pay Ming Kuang said. "Here in Singapore, breathing space is almost entirely reserved for the mainstream. You are guaranteed breathing space only if you are straight, educated, career-centric, married or planning to and willing to toe the line. Someone like you, Gimme. You are practically the poster boy for the nation. You get to have all the breathing space you want."

Gimme Lao would have thought he meant it sarcastically

but Pay Ming Kuang had the look of sincerity.

"Your space gets drastically compressed once you deviate. Take me, for instance. Anyone who reads about my case in *The Straits Times* gets the impression that I am a sexual deviant. And there is simply no space here in Singapore for people like me. Never mind that I am a competent physician and an activist for animal rights and victims of domestic violence. As long as I don't do sex in the generally approved manner, I don't get to breathe here."

"I didn't know you were a social activist," Gimme Lao remarked, more to veil his discomfort than to satisfy any genuine curiosity.

"Yes, I am," Pay Ming Kuang nodded emphatically. "Back in London, I joined advocacy groups and took part in nonviolent direct action to champion causes close to my heart. That is a facet of me, as much as my sexual preference for men and sadomasochism. I need to live in a city where I get breathing space to live out my entire spectrum as a complete human being. Singapore is not the place for me. In a perverted way, I am lucky to undergo this public humiliation. I needed the shaming and the push to get out from this miserable place. I deserve better."

After the man left the office, his words lingered. Gimme Lao had always attributed his personal achievements to his resolution, capability and effort. Could luck have played a central role? Was he simply lucky that who he was, what he wanted and where he was headed happened to be aligned with the mainstream? How much more difficult would it be if his values and endeavours deviated from the majority?

Gimme Lao was still lost in his thoughts when he rolled into Pacific Mansion. Skye hopped off the curb and sprinted to the vehicle. "Quick, or I am going to be late!" The boy yelped once he squeezed in to the passenger seat. "Coach Moose is very strict about punctuality. Anyone who is late has to do two circuits of duck walk around the pool as a punishment. It is embarrassing!"

The swimming coach was really a young Malay man by the name of Mustafa, but the kids coined the nickname Coach Moose. Gimme Lao knew this because Skye could not stop talking about him at the dinner table. Coach Moose had trained as a commando in the army and could do single palm push-ups with his feet elevated on a bench. Coach Moose measured 40 inches across the chest, 28 across the waist and attained a perfect six-pack abdomen with a body fat percentage of seven. Coach Moose had dived with hammerhead sharks in Sipadan and trekked the Gondogoro range in Pakistan. As far as Skye was concerned, Coach Moose was the most awesome guy to walk on the face of the planet.

Gimme Lao understood the situation. The boy was 10, and Coach Moose was his hero. Gimme Lao used to be his hero. When Gimme Lao bought him a remote control helicopter for his sixth birthday and taught him how to fly it at the park, Skye thought he had the most awesome dad in the world. When Skye was eight and Gimme Lao brought him on a whale-watching trip to Kaikoura, New Zealand, Skye thought he had the most awesome dad across the seven seas. But ever since Skye started swimming lessons six months ago, Gimme Lao's throne of awesomeness had been usurped. Not that he minded. Between the growing demands of the hospital and the Youth Executive Committee, Gimme Lao did not have much time for the family. He was glad Coach Moose was shouldering part of his portfolio.

"When is Mum coming back?" Skye asked. "What do you think she will surprise me with this time round?"

"She's flying in on Tuesday," Gimme Lao said. "Did you ask her for anything in particular?"

Skye shrugged. "I don't even know what they have in Vietnam."

"Well, I am guessing Mum will either buy you the newest Speedo swimwear or find you a beautiful young bride from Vietnam."

"Don't! That is disgusting!" Skye cupped his ears and grimaced.

Gimme Lao laughed. He knew Skye had yet to come to terms with his mother's newest venture. "You still think what Mum now does is disgusting?"

"Grandma seems to think so."

"Do take your grandma's opinion with a pinch of salt. She is feeling sore that neither your mum nor I gave permission for your baptism at church. That was why she and your mum had a falling out sometime ago."

"I thought that was because Grandma fired Uncle Too Sexy?"

"And that too."

Gimme Lao recalled that period of brewing maelstrom in the family none too fondly. It was probably the first time Wei Wen had stood up against Mary Lao. Business at Pearls of Love had been spiralling downwards badly since a plague of copycat bubble tea outlets sprouted up in the neighbourhoods like wild fungi on rotting wood. Mary Lao had to close down two of the five outlets and trim manpower. Wei Wen was shocked when Mary Lao quickly decided that all the special needs staff, including her brother Too Sexy, would be the first to let go. Apparently, the profit margin was too thin for Mary Lao to continue doing God's work.

When Wei Wen came to Gimme Lao to discuss setting up her own business, not only was he supportive, he went so far as to suggest that they should think about getting a place of their own. He had noticed how Mary Lao insisted on bringing Skye to church every Sunday and had no doubt she was feeding the boy Christian values and moulding his outlook on life based on the Bible. As an atheist, Gimme Lao felt extremely uncomfortable about that.

Mary Lao was caught by surprise when Wei Wen made known her intention to leave Pearls of Love to set up her own business. The family was having dinner at home, and a moment of awkward silence followed the announcement.

"Considering that Pearls of Love is going through a tough period, I am surprised you choose to bail out at this critical juncture. That is not what family does to one another, Wei Wen," Mary Lao finally remarked, her tone a delicate balance between reprimand and sarcasm.

"Please don't make me feel guilty, Mum. As it is, I feel guilty enough that I can't help my brother retain his job at Pearls of Love," Wei Wen replied, secretly hoping that the underlying sarcasm would sear through her mother-in-law's façade of righteousness.

Mary Lao detected the enmity beneath the civility and quickly decided it would be unwise to try to retain Wei Wen. "All right then, maybe it is time you venture out on your own. Have you decided what to do?"

"Yes, I have registered my new company. Find Love in Vietnam," Wei Wen said. "It is a matchmaking outfit."

"What is a matchmaking outfit?" Skye interjected, curious.

"Well, some men in Singapore are unable to find wives. So I bring them to Vietnam to look for wives." Wei Wen pretended not to see the look of disapproval on Mary Lao's face and focused on explaining her new business model to Skye instead. "Many young Vietnamese women live a life of poverty in remote villages and shanty towns. They have to toil in the fields and use dug-out toilets and carry water from the wells every day. It is a hard life. Some of them want out. To get married to a Singapore man and move over here for a better life is a dream come true for them. That is what my business does. Help make their dreams come true."

"But why can't the Singaporean men find wives here in Singapore?" Skye wanted to know.

"Women here generally prefer to marry men who are financially stable, so those with a good career, who have money, will not have a problem finding a wife," Wei Wen elaborated. "But there are men who do not earn a lot, or are much older or handicapped, and women don't want to marry them. That is where the Vietnamese women come in."

"But why are the Vietnamese women willing to marry these men when they don't earn a lot?" Skye persisted.

"Because there is running water and air-conditioning in Singapore," Gimme Lao jumped in with a wicked grin. "They don't have those in the villages, and those are very important to Vietnamese women."

"Shut up." Wei Wen pinched Gimme Lao in the arm, laughing.

"I hope you have done sufficient research," Mary Lao remarked coldly. "Don't be careless and get into trouble with the authorities for suspicions of vice operations or human trafficking."

"I will heed your advice, Mum." Wei Wen smiled warmly before launching her next projectile. "By the way, Gimme and I are looking at some apartments. You and Dad will have more space once we move out."

As Mary Lao and her husband looked up in astonishment, Skye yelped in delight and reminded Wei Wen they ought to move into a condominium with a swimming pool because he would be taking swimming lessons soon. Wei Wen smiled and obliged, secretly pleased to spot the look of displeasure on her mother-in-law's face.

"Dad, do you think Mum will help Uncle Too Sexy find a Vietnamese wife as well?"

Gimme Lao was jolted out of his recollection by Skye's unexpected question. He swung his vehicle into the sports complex driveway and came to a halt near the entrance. "You can throw your mum that question when she returns. Run along now. You don't want Coach Moose to make you do the duck walk, do you?"

Everyone was present when Gimme Lao stepped into the meeting room. He took one glance at the agenda and decided he would hand the reins over to the vice chairman. The only item worth expounding was the annual bursary award ceremony, and everyone was familiar with the standard operating procedure. Gimme Lao expected the meeting to be short.

And then Sally Bong raised her hand. Everyone's hearts sank.

"I would like to revisit the hospice project."

"Yes, Sally?" Gimme Lao tried to keep the impatience out of his voice.

"The project was such a success. Why did we stop?"

"The project was scheduled to last only six weeks. We brought in two foot reflexologists who trained us to give foot rubs to the hospice residents. For our last session, we invited our constituency adviser Dr Liew Kim Keong to visit and watch us in action. That brought the project to a satisfactory close."

"So what we really wanted was the media coverage? Once we have our photos taken and splashed across the pages of the constituency newsletter, we stop? What about the hospice residents?" Sally Bong demanded to know.

Gimme Lao sighed aloud. "Sally, you must understand that we are not volunteering our time as foot reflexologists. We volunteer ourselves as grassroots leaders. We set an example. Once there is coverage in the media, there will be youths who will be inspired to do the same. So we move on to other projects."

The vice chairman added, "Sally, if you feel strongly about this, you can always form your own team of volunteers and continue the hospice project. Let the rest of us move on!"

Gimme Lao wished the young lady wasn't so obstinate. The irony did not escape him that the Youth Executive Committee needed more bleeding hearts like Sally Bong. Gimme Lao knew why some of the other key appointment holders were there. The vice chairman needed to serve two terms so that he could qualify for the Priority Queue scheme and secure his firstborn a spot in the premium primary school in Bukit Panjang Constituency. The general secretary was a property agent looking to expand his network of clients. The treasurer needed the free parking privilege disc for his delivery business. These were the ones who came in and took up leadership roles with an agenda. In contrast, bleeding hearts like Sally Bong were glad to contribute their time and energy as members without the privileges. Although Gimme Lao was often impatient with her idealism, he knew in his heart that the organisation needed more people like her.

After the meeting was over, Gimme Lao swung by the sports complex to pick Skye up. As usual, the boy was in high spirits after the swimming lesson. Coach Moose had given him a pat on the back for mastering the butterfly style ahead of the rest. Skye was determined to intensify his own training so he could attain impressive abdominal external obliques, exactly like what Coach Moose had.

"Can I start gym training?"

"Ten is a little too young," Gimme Lao remarked. "Maybe in another four or five years' time."

"But that will be too late!" Skye whined.

"Too late for what?" Gimme Lao laughed. "The girls can wait."

"Yucks! I am not even talking about girls. Chatty,

petty nuisances."

"Just wait and see. Sooner or later a girl will appear and you will think of no one else but her," Gimme Lao smirked.

Skye did not like the direction the conversation was veering in. He extracted a comics magazine from his bag and began to flip through. That was his signal of disengagement. Whenever Skye did not like what was happening, he would dip into his world of comics.

And it was not entirely true that Skye found all girls to be a nuisance. As much as he admired the machismo of the DC Comics heroes, it was Wonder Woman he most admired. Back when he picked up his first copy of a Justice League comic at the age of seven, he immediately became enthralled by the brooding magnetism of Batman. As the years went by, his allegiance underwent serial transfusion from the Dark Knight to Superman, Green Lantern and The Flash, until it finally settled down on Wonder Woman. He admired the way she embodied both the courage and strength of a hero and the beauty and femininity of a heroine. In his adrenaline-fuelled fantasies of superhero battles, Skye saw himself as Wonder Woman, warding off the combined attacks of Cheetah and Poison Ivy with his golden lasso and deflecting the laser beams of General Zod with his indestructible gauntlets. In a parallel universe where malevolent villains roamed, Skye fought for peace and justice as Wonder Woman.

When Skye started swimming lessons at the age of nine, he met his first superhero in real life. Coach Moose was Aquaman incarnate. The man was king of the underwater world of Atlantis, and Skye entertained many nights of fantasies where

Wonder Woman had to be rescued from the clutches of villains by Aquaman. He imagined a shimmering coat of scales attached to the contours of Coach Moose's muscled torso and mooned over the magnificent spectacle. He was happily drowning in his bottomless tub of infatuation.

When Skye was 12, he observed that many of his classmates miraculously gained several inches in height almost overnight and became secretly anxious. After dinner every night, he would go down to a quiet corner in the garden and jump rope for 45 minutes in an attempt to spur his own ascension. It was there that he re-encountered his first crush.

Skye first spotted him sitting in the garden pavilion, a lighted cigarette pinched between his fingers. The man had a fierce beard and sharp, piercing eyes. He did not smile when their eyes locked, but maintained his heavy glare. This brooding melancholy reminded Skye of Batman, and his heart skipped a beat.

Skye never found out his name, although it quickly became apparent that he was a condominium security guard on permanent night shift who made it his routine to steal a puff at the garden pavilion. For more than a year Skye enjoyed his silent company several nights a week. Although they never spoke, Skye knew the man watched him train. There was a hint of sensuality as Skye imagined Batman's unfathomable eyes staring wordlessly, his dark cape blending into the shadows of the shrubs. The Wonder Woman in him felt her knees weaken from the constant gaze as much as he himself felt his calves ache from the skipping.

Eventually, Batman disappeared. Skye felt a sense of loss. He never did find out that Batman made a decision to fly back to his village in Tamil Nadu to be with his wife and two children once his work permit expired.

When Skye was 15, he made it to the swim team in secondary school. It was there that Wonder Woman fell under the spell of Green Lantern. The team captain Jason Chan was tanned and fit like Coach Moose and wore a sleek pair of Speedoes the colour of fresh green moss. Watching Jason dive into the pool was like watching a shiny breakfast knife slice into soft butter, smooth and silky. The sight of water shimmering off his back as he re-emerged from the pool never failed to make Skye's stomach churn.

At night, after the lights were switched off, Skye shut his eyes and summoned the sight of Jason showering after swim practice. He followed Jason's hairy forearms wet with suds as the bar of soap traversed the contours of his torso. Skye sustained that vision as he reached underneath the blanket to pleasure himself. Jason's shower lasted as long as was necessary till Skye climaxed. Afterwards, Skye tiptoed to the bathroom, cleaned himself up silently, returned to bed and fell into a deep, restful sleep.

When Jason graduated the following year and left for junior college, Skye was devastated. He could not summon the same enthusiasm for swim practice he once had. The fact that another school booked the time slot after theirs for a girls' swim team further annoyed him. The girls would arrive early, change into their swimwear and wait by the pool. They would whisper among themselves and giggle as they watched the boys practise. Soon, one of the girls passed him a note with a phone number scribbled in orange luminous ink. Skye scrunched it up and threw it into the dustbin with irritability. He missed Jason badly.

Three months after Jason left, someone else caught Skye's eye. It was a boy his age who sang in the church choir. Although Skye was no longer living with his grandparents, Mary Lao insisted that he join them for church every alternate Sunday. Skye did it to please Mary Lao. He found Pastor Kong's sermons generally boring and would more often than not be daydreaming while the pastor preached. The only segment of the church service he enjoyed was the choir singing Christian songs of praise. Some of the renditions were so emotive they reduced him to tears. It was during one such moment that Skye spotted Eugene through teary eyes.

Eugene was shorter than the rest of the choirboys. Had he not stepped forward to sing the solo, Skye would never have spotted him. Eugene sang with a pristine voice that took on an ethereal quality whenever he hit the high notes. It was unlike anything he had heard before. Seated near the back of the church, Skye would often shut his eyes and immerse himself in the suspended moment of serenity and wonderment.

Skye ferreted out Eugene's appointment as the treasurer in the Youth Ministry and quickly got himself involved. He volunteered in their fundraising project to build an annex to an orphanage in Mae Sot, Thailand. He joined their monthly outreach programme and guided the residents of a nursing home to do simple strength training using resistance bands. Despite all his efforts, Skye did not get any closer to knowing Eugene. The boy was taciturn in meetings and uncommunicative during outings. He kept very much to himself. In Skye's mind, he was Nightwing; aloof, mysterious, alluring. Skye yearned to lash out with his lasso to trap and elicit a response out of him.

Skye knew Eugene was aware of his overtures. He had more than once caught Eugene studying him with a silent intensity, but then Eugene would quickly look away when their eyes met. Skye was nevertheless encouraged. He decided that Eugene's aloofness was nothing more than bashfulness in disguise. He had to be bold and make the first move. So he scribbled a note and dropped it into Eugene's backpack when the latter wasn't looking.

The next evening, Skye sat waiting nervously at Orange Julius sipping a root beer float. He had two tickets to *Harry Potter and the Chamber of Secrets* inside his pocket. If Eugene turned up, he would get hold of the movie poster and hide it for 10 years so that he could surprise him on their 10th anniversary. If Eugene did not show up, he would watch the movie alone and keep the unused ticket in a shoebox to mark his second lost love. He already had a pair of goggles with a broken strap that he had scavenged from the dustbin next to the pool minutes after Jason Chan threw it in. Skye hoped the shoebox would not fill up anytime soon.

Skye was about to give up when he spotted Eugene stepping in through the door. Grinning widely, Skye stood up and said he was glad Eugene made it in time. The movie was starting in five minutes so the two of them would have to scramble. But Eugene shook his head and said he wasn't here for the movie. He wanted to talk.

"I didn't want to come," Eugene said, after Skye bought them a piña colada Julius each. "But I knew I had to. If God wants me to undergo this test, I will do so."

Skye could feel a chill running down his spine. He had wrongly assumed that Eugene's turning up could only mean a happy ending.

"I understand what you are going through. I have been there. Shame tormented me endlessly when I felt what you are feeling now. You mustn't feel unworthy. This attraction for men is not your fault."

Skye bit his lip. He wanted to jump in and tell Eugene he never felt ashamed or unworthy. But he decided to let Eugene have his say.

"I confessed my sinful thoughts to Pastor Kong one year ago. He promised to help me through reparative therapy. It is tough; I cannot deny that. I still succumb to sinful thoughts during my weakest moments. But I am confident that with God's help, I will eventually be cured."

"You are referring to conversion therapy, aren't you?" Skye asked, his hands cold. He had read about what it entailed.

Eugene nodded. He suddenly shut his eyes and mumbled a short prayer.

"What is it?" Skye pursued, curious. "Why are you praying?"

"I was praying for forgiveness. I had thought...that your note was the Devil's work... That you were sent to tempt me. But I am wrong to think that."

Skye badly wanted to giggle, but he could tell Eugene was serious. "So now you think I am not an agent of the Devil?'

"Of course you are not. It was God who sent you. This is God's way of telling me I am now strong enough to help others. I was egoistic to think that this is about me. It is not. It is about you!" Eugene's eyes were bright when he reached over to hold Skye's hands. "You can join me for the reparative therapy."

Skye was silent for a moment. It was amazing how quickly his attraction to Eugene had dissipated. The mysterious and alluring Nightwing had all but vanished. He found himself looking at a confused teenager too afraid to acknowledge his own sexual orientation and too ready to settle for the church's mechanism of denial.

"How does the conversion therapy work?" Skye wanted to know. "Do you apply electric shocks to yourself when you watch porn?"

Eugene blushed and shook his head.

"So what do you do?"

There was a moment of hesitation before Eugene replied, "I stick my finger in my throat till I retch and vomit."

Skye cringed and withdrew his hand abruptly.

"It is only a method," Eugene hurriedly added when he saw the look of disgust on Skye's face. "We conduct regular prayer and Bible studies once a week. Pastor Kong will be there to help you every step of the way."

Skye paled. It had not crossed his mind that Eugene might tell on him. "Does your family know about you, Eugene?"

"Pastor Kong gave me his word that he would not tell them," Eugene confessed. "I wanted to do this on my own. I don't want my parents to bear this burden."

"Good. I won't tell your parents if you do not mention my name to Pastor Kong."

Eugene was a little taken aback. "Don't you want to be cured?"

Skye grabbed his bag and stood to leave. "I am fine the way I am. Goodbye, Eugene. I will always remember how beautifully you sing."

Skye told his grandmother exams were coming up so he would have to skip church to focus on his studies. He felt sorry for Eugene. It must have been terrible to carry the burden of guilt for what was natural to him. Skye grew up trusting his own feelings. He felt no attraction to girls, only to men and boys. It made no sense whatsoever to deny it just to conform to the majority.

For a teenager of 16, Skye had an amazing lack of self-doubt and an astonishing licence of self-confidence. The 'why-do-you-think' game his grandmother used to play with him had a lot to do with it. When Skye was younger, his grandmother would take him for long walks after dinner while his mother stayed behind to do the dishes. During these evening strolls, Mary Lao would encourage Skye to tell her something about his day. Did anything out of the ordinary happen in school? Or did his teacher or classmates say or do something interesting?

After Skye told his tale, Mary Lao would play the 'why-do-you-think' game? Why do you think the teacher did not allow that? Why do you think little Jiahui cried? Why do you think big bully Kong would want to behave in such a nasty manner? Skye would stop to think about it and come up with a possible reason. Mary Lao encouraged him not to stop at one, but to explore multiple possibilities. Over time, Skye became adept at the game. He learnt to spot the coward in the bully, identify the frustration behind the tears and comprehend the reasons why people behave the way they do. He began to question instructions from teachers and rules set by the school. That behaviour did not endear him to many teachers, but Skye had by then outgrown the craving to be liked by teachers.

As Skye grew older, Mary Lao began to share family stories from the past. She told him about the time his father Gimme Lao was publicly humiliated for wearing a frock and how she stood up to the principal and the disciplinary master. One ought to always question the boundaries. She described how Skye's grandfather was known as Mr Nice Guy around the neighbourhood, while she was abhorred as the relentless saleswoman who simply would not give up. In the end, she managed to serve many in the community by enhancing their financial security, while his grandfather provided no service whatsoever. The yearning to be well liked reflected a weakness. You should give yourself permission to be great, not merely likeable. She told him about her own awakening when she was upstaged by a snobbish fellow parent who had the clout to make her child miserable. The world did not owe you anything. You had to pick a role, make a stand, claim your spot and make life happen. Otherwise, your tombstone would simply read 'Unrealised'.

That word, 'unrealised', etched itself into Skye's psyche as the definitive devil to avoid. It had pushed him to arduous pool training in the hope of making it to the secondary school swim team while his classmates hunched over the terminals at LAN shops to play *Diablo* or *StarCraft*. It had given him the courage to drop the note into Eugene's backpack to invite him for the movie. Skye did not feel bitter that the date with Eugene did not end well. The failing was not his. He had learnt his lesson when Jason Chan spun out of his orbit before he gathered his courage to make a move. He would not let that happen again.

As it turned out, Skye was given a second chance. He did well enough in his O levels to enter the junior college of his choice. It was there that he met Jason Chan again.

The reunion seemed to bring Jason tremendous joy, and he lost no time recruiting Skye into the JC swim team. Now that he was no more the team captain, Jason was not obliged to divvy his time and attention equally to all team members. He asked if Skye was willing to be his training buddy.

"Really?" Skye was secretly pleased. He wondered if it was merely his imagination that the taller and brawnier Green Lantern had re-entered his orbit shining a different light.

The two coordinated their weekly schedules so they could commit to two sessions each in the gym and the pool. Once they stepped into the gym, Jason was all about tough love. He tormented Skye on the crunch machine and whipped him mercilessly on the treadmill. After gym session was over, Jason chose to hang out with him. They shared earphones and listened to the latest hits or talked shop over protein shakes. As the weeks went by, Skye began to pick up on clues that indicated Green Lantern might see Wonder Woman as more than just a fellow defender of justice. There was a soft glow of affection that seemed to shine on no one else.

As a foreign student from Malaysia, Jason was allotted a room at the JC dormitory. It was in that room, snugly crushed against each other on an oversized beanbag, that the two first kissed. Tyrese was playing on the radio, and it seemed the most natural thing for Skye to lean over and kiss Jason on his lips. Jason kissed back, hard. Skye's earlier hunch was verified. The admiration was mutual.

It was a magical time for Skye and Jason. Up till then, neither of them had ever gone past secret infatuations. But with their first kiss, they elevated their adolescent desire to a connection that was complex and satisfying. There was tenderness as they ran their fingers over one another. There was trust as they surrendered themselves without resistance. There was warmth as they held each other close afterwards. Often, they dozed off with their limbs entwined.

The blissful romance seemed perfect except for one thing. Skye had to keep it a secret. Jason did not want anybody to know.

The occasional arguments they had pertained to Jason's expectations of how the two of them should behave in public. Once, Skye forgot himself and reached over to brush some lint off Jason's cotton tee while they were seated in the student cafeteria. Jason jerked and shrank away.

"Why do you have to do that?" Jason demanded to know once they were back in the dormitory room.

Skye shrugged, "There was lint. I removed it. What's the big deal?"

"People are watching!" Jason made no attempt to hide his

exasperation. "It's the same thing in the library. You have this habit of leaning against my shoulder to read the same copy of newspaper I am reading. Why?"

Whenever this happened, Skye would sulk for a day or two. But he always relented and crept back into Jason's embrace. After all, there had to be compromises made in any relationship. If Green Lantern wished to keep the glow of their love hidden from others, Wonder Woman would just have to stop polishing her golden gauntlets.

Luckily for them, none of the guys in the college swim team suspected. There were a lot of back slaps and shoulder punches going on in the changing room, and everyone accepted these as sporting camaraderie. Whenever Skye pinched Jason on his neck and squeezed till he yelped, the others laughed. It was merely good fun between teammates.

All was well until the incident with KC Kok.

Neither Skye nor Jason had paid KC Kok any attention until their teammates made the observation that the boy was taking clandestine shots of them in the pool using a zoom lens. Initially, everyone made a joke out of it. It was just another muscle-worshipping faggot. As long as the creep did not slide his hand into their swim trunks, they were fine with him staring at their crotches all day long.

Although Skye was uncomfortable with the team's callousness, he chose not to voice it out. But his discomfort turned to horror when he witnessed Jason partaking in the pack's malicious teasing with vigour. It further perturbed him that Jason could shrug it off nonchalantly when he brought up the issue in the privacy of their dormitory room.

For the first time, Wonder Woman noticed a dark and sinister flicker in Green Lantern's light.

One afternoon, Skye chanced upon a group of his teammates huddled together in the changing room. One of them waved him over and clued him in on their discussion. Apparently, someone had slipped an envelope into the team captain's locker. Within the envelope was a 5R blow-up of the team captain frozen in the midst of an upper back stretch. This had to be that creep's way of declaring his twisted adoration. When the group started discussing how they should teach KC Kok a lesson, Skye stood up and walked away in disgust. He wanted no part of it.

The next day, Skye spotted KC Kok at a corner of the student cafeteria having lunch alone. Thinking that he ought to warn him before his teammates sprang any surprises, Skye approached and sat down opposite him. He had barely introduced himself when he noticed that KC Kok's lower lip was swollen. Alarmed, Skye asked if the guys from the swim team had roughed him up. KC Kok lowered his head and refused to reply.

Skye was still pressing the teenager for an answer when he felt a tap on his shoulder. It was Jason, and he wanted to speak to Skye in private.

"What are you trying to do?" Jason asked once they were back in their room.

Skye stared at Jason in disbelief. The accusatory tone in his voice was unmistakable. Surely it was not possible that Jason did not see how wrong the group's action was? Skye felt a chill as a thought crossed his mind. He had to know. "Did you throw the punch?"

Jason hesitated a little. "He would have gotten punched sooner or later. The way he went around taking candid photos of guys. He's a creep."

Skye did not know what to make of what was happening. He had blindly fallen for this boy who not only denied his own gay identity, but would go to the extent of harming another boy just to prove he wasn't gay.

"What if—" Skye bit his lip. It was a dangerous question to ask, but he needed to know. "What if the guys asked about us? What would you say?"

"Why would they ask? We haven't given them any reason to suspect anything," Jason insisted.

"What if I don't feel like hiding anymore?"

When Skye saw the fear and horror in Jason's eyes, his heart sank. He listened in a daze as Jason threw a tantrum. Why would Skye want to jeopardise their relationship? There was an army of bigots out there who would tear them apart if they made their relationship known. Why court hardship when they could stay in the comfort and safety of these four walls? What was he trying to prove?

Skye felt a wave of fatigue wash over him. He was too exhausted to hold any thought in his mind. After Jason stormed out of the room, he crawled under the blanket and shut his eyes. Sleep did not come, but he made himself lie still till the digital clock flashed 5pm and it was time to head home for dinner.

Slumped in his seat on the bus, Skye realised that things had irreparably changed. The Green Lantern he thought he knew had crossed over. As much as he loved Jason, he could not imagine a future with him. He would have to end the relationship. He was aware that the other passengers were watching, but he could not hold back his tears any longer. He cried into his T-shirt and mourned for the loss of his first love.

Skye stopped by the changing room at the pool to wash his face before he took the elevator up. He knew his eyes were still puffy. If his mother asked, he would have to come up with a story. But there was a chance that she might not notice. Wei Wen had successfully paired up two clients with their Vietnamese brides on her last trip and was in high spirits when she got back the night before. Skye knew he could expect steamed salmon fishhead for dinner. Wei Wen always cooked his favourite dish when she wanted to celebrate.

The phone rang just as Skye stepped into the house. It was his father.

"I need you to help me pack my toiletries and enough clothes for a week. Leave the suitcase outside along the corridor. I don't want to step into the apartment. I will swing by after midnight to pick it up. Don't wait up for me."

Skye froze. He found Wei Wen in the kitchen busy preparing dinner.

"Dad called. There is an emergency at the hospital, so he can't make it back for dinner."

Wei Wen shrugged, "That's too bad. But you should be used to his surprises by now."

"There's more." Skye wore a frown of deep concern. He repeated Gimme Lao's request to have his suitcase packed and saw Wei Wen's back stiffen.

"Did he say why?"

"He said he was in the midst of an urgent meeting and couldn't explain."

Neither of them spoke as they sat through the solemn dinner. Skye studied his mother. She was plain-looking to begin with. Although the success of her Vietnamese matchmaking agency had given her an air of confidence as a businesswoman, it had also distracted her from her grooming and exercise routine. She had put on considerable weight around her waist, and her face looked stretched and tired. It would not surprise him at all if his father had a woman on the side. If this were the case, Skye knew his mother would need his moral support to tide over the crisis. He had to stay strong, both for himself and his mother.

Wei Wen wondered if there was another woman. This was not the first instance she had been plagued by the suspicion. Her business venture had kept her busy and fulfilled for the last few years. Weeks could go by before she realised she hadn't had sex with her husband. In the past, Gimme Lao would grow irritable when intimacy was missing from their routine. He would likely pick a quarrel over the most insignificant issue and keep up the tantrum until Wei Wen recognised the root cause and made her move. The fact that his tantrum was long overdue worried her. Wei Wen wanted to believe that her husband was as distracted by a demanding medical career and his promising political ambition as she was by her business venture. It couldn't possibly be the age factor; they were both merely 38. Then again, they had been married for 17 long years.

Wei Wen and Skye kept themselves awake watching a Hong Kong drama series on DVD. It was close to one in the morning when they heard Gimme Lao's familiar footsteps approach. Skye sprung to open the door.

"Stop. Do not step outside. Stay where you are, Skye."

Wei Wen and Skye felt a collective chill as they stared at Gimme Lao, who stood a distance away with his hand held up to discourage them from approaching. He was wearing an ominous looking decontamination mask.

"Why isn't my luggage in the corridor?" Gimme Lao sounded stern.

"I told Skye to keep it inside. It might get stolen if we leave it out in the corridor," Wei Wen explained, worried. "What is it? Are you down with some virus?"

"At this point I do not know for sure, but I would rather be safe than sorry," Gimme Lao sighed. "One of my junior doctors diagnosed a patient running a fever as a possible case of atypical pneumonia, a virulent strand that we were earlier alerted to by the World Health Organization. The hospital is putting together a team to prepare for the worst-case scenario. It may escalate to become a national emergency. I will be staying in the hospital over the next few days. Now I want you two to step back to the balcony so that I can come in to retrieve my luggage. I do not want either of you within one metre of me."

Wei Wen and Skye watched from behind the curtain as Gimme Lao collected his luggage and waved goodbye. Both of them felt unworthy. There he was, their husband and father, taking precautions so that his family would not catch the virus from him.

Yet the first suspicions that crossed their mind was that he was having an extra-marital affair. The two felt deeply ashamed.

It was another two days before they read about it in the papers. SARS. Severe Acute Respiratory Syndrome. Three Singaporean ladies had returned from vacation in Hong Kong, unaware that they had caught the deadly virus from an infected elderly Chinese doctor staying on the same floor in their hotel. One of the three turned out to be a super-spreader. By the time her condition was correctly diagnosed, she had infected 17 others, including 10 healthcare workers at Tan Tock Seng Hospital.

The Ministry of Health immediately designated the hospital as SARS Battleground Zero. The Emergency Department was shut down and all ambulances were instructed to divert their emergency cases elsewhere. Tan Tock Seng Hospital was to focus solely on combating SARS. Architects and building contractors were hastily engaged to construct a huge, open-air screening tent in the adjacent field and tasked to convert four blocks of dormitory wards into isolation wards almost overnight. All the healthcare workers were given strict instructions to don the N95 mask throughout their shifts. Initially, some found the stifling masks unbearable and would steal a moment or two in the toilet or storeroom to remove them for a breather. But when the infection rate among the hospital staff inched up and the first doctor succumbed to it, everyone panicked and realised it was a brutal battle they were confronted with. That stolen moment of relief removing the mask in the toilet might prove potentially fatal.

The death of the doctor was not reported in the media.

The Ministry of Health decided it could not afford nationwide panic. But Wei Wen knew. Gimme Lao had been sending her texts and emails to update her daily. She knew the doctor who succumbed was a junior doctor barely one year into his induction in the Communicable Disease Division. His name was Gordon. Gimme Lao told her that Dr Gordon was all of 28 and had just begun dating a nurse in the division. His death was devastating for the morale of the team at the hospital.

Wei Wen waited with trepidation for these texts and emails from Gimme Lao every day. Hours could go by without the inbox icon flashing, and Wei Wen would have to convince herself that Gimme Lao was too caught up with his overwhelming workload to text. Even when he did, Wei Wen had her misgivings. For all she knew, Gimme Lao could be running a fever and not be telling her. It drove her crazy that there was nothing she could do to help share his burden.

At night, her thoughts ran wild as she lay sleepless in bed. Unlike the rest of the population, who were cushioned by the calculated omission of details that trickled down via the state controlled media, Wei Wen was fed raw daily updates by Gimme Lao. She learnt about the horror of battling a brutal, but unfamiliar, disease. Gimme Lao confessed that the team was practically stumbling about in a maze of confusion, blindfolded and shackled. There was internal panic when several patients with no apparent SARS infection were diverted to other hospitals, only to subsequently develop symptoms and go on to infect others. By the third week, these cases of late-developing symptoms had resulted in infections in four other hospitals. It was especially disheartening when frontline healthcare workers crossed the battle lines and became casualties.

As the infection rate and death count inched upwards, fear spread among those working in the battlefield. The staff canteen operator had to deal with kitchen workers who refused to turn up for work. Deliverymen from suppliers unceremoniously dumped their load outside the hospital gate and drove off. Healthcare workers were worn down by the emotional strain of dealing with loved ones who begged them to quit their jobs. Patients in denial clamoured to discharge themselves at their own risk. There was simply no let up to the tension and exhaustion.

Wei Wen hoped that Gimme Lao could perceive her deep concern when he read her email replies. In their 17 years of marriage, the two had never been apart for this long. The irony did not escape Wei Wen that this was the closest she had ever felt towards her husband in a long while. Through his daily updates, Wei Wen could sense his palpable fear and frustration. She encouraged him and told him how proud she was that he was manning the gates against an enemy that could annihilate the entire nation. She shared that Skye had initiated a project at his college to collect words of encouragement for the hospital team in the form of a quilt. In the media, it was reported that Singapore, together with Hong Kong and southern China, were the hotspots for SARS outbreaks. Gimme Lao needed to know that the entire international community was behind his team. He needed to have faith.

The turnabout came two months into the crisis. The infection rate peaked at a headcount of 7,000 to 8,000 worldwide before it slowed down drastically. By the end of the third month, the World Health Organization declared Singapore free of SARS. The battle was finally won.

When Gimme Lao stepped into the house for the first time since the crisis began, Wei Wen broke down and sobbed with bitter relief. For five whole minutes she hugged him tightly and would not let go. Gimme Lao chuckled and ruffled her hair with affection. It was all right. She was not destined to be a SARS widow after all.

The entire nation celebrated wildly. SARS was the most threatening epidemic to hit Singapore since its independence nearly 40 years ago. The Tan Tock Seng Hospital team was hailed as an exemplary warrior in the battle. During the crisis, while hospitals in Hong Kong and Vietnam had to operate at half the usual strength because many healthcare workers refused to turn up for work, the Singapore team stood strong and committed. Although the prime minister was sombre as he led the population in mourning the 33rd and last SARS fatality, Nurse Hamidah Ismail from Tan Tock Seng Hospital, he reminded everyone there was much to be thankful for. He promised that the frontline warriors who had toiled and made sacrifices would receive due recognition.

Tan Tock Seng Hospital made plans to throw a celebratory party. The prime minister was invited as the guest of honour. Gimme Lao urged Wei Wen to shop for a proper evening gown and hire the services of a professional makeup artist. He wanted to reserve a surprise for her, but she ought to be prepared for a little media spotlight.

The celebratory party was held at the prestigious Ritz Carlton Hotel. Wei Wen, Skye, Mary Lao and her husband were astounded to find themselves seated right in front of the stage, adjacent to the prime minister's table. Professor Eleanor Moh came over and personally shook Wei Wen's hand. She ought to know that her husband Gimme Lao had done the nation proud. There was a surprise coming up during the award segment, but Gimme Lao had made her promise not to tell. She could only reveal that Wei Wen was about to become the most envied woman in the ballroom that night.

The four of them were kept in delightful suspense throughout the night. After the seventh dish of the 10-course feast had been served, the prime minister was invited on stage to honour the team at Tan Tock Seng Hospital. He waxed lyrical about their sacrifice and contribution and mourned those who fell victim to the enemy. After handing out several awards to top management and frontline staff, he mentioned that the next recipient was someone special. Not only was Dr Gimme Lao the very doctor who had correctly identified and diagnosed the first SARS patient in Singapore, he was a valiant warrior who spearheaded the critical task force that successfully tracked down all the 238 cases of infection before they could further spread the epidemic among the population. Were it not for his efficiency, the SARS crisis could have blown up into a pandemic and the death toll possibly tripled. Born the same year that Singapore attained its independence, Dr Gimme Lao was truly a remarkable son of Singapore. The prime minister professed that he would be neglecting his duty if he did not rope in such a talented and committed warrior to serve the nation in a bigger capacity. He had personally invited Dr Gimme Lao to join his political party and was thrilled to have him accept his offer. He was thus proud to announce that Dr Gimme Lao would be groomed and fielded for contest in the next general election before his own impending retirement as the second prime minister of Singapore.

As the ballroom thundered with congratulatory applause, Wei Wen could feel tears of pride welling up. Although she knew her husband had political ambitions, she never imagined that his prospects could escalate so dramatically. To have the prime minister of Singapore personally announce Gimme Lao's upcoming candidacy could only mean that the cabinet had big plans for him. Wei Wen looked across the table and saw that both Mary Lao and her husband were similarly shaken. She felt Skye take her hand and squeeze it. Wei Wen returned the squeeze. This was possibly the happiest moment she had ever felt collectively with her son and in-laws.

"Mum, your mascara is running," Skye cautioned with a mischievous grin.

Wei Wen burst out into a paroxysm of giggles. She grabbed her purse and sneaked out of the ballroom before the spotlight could follow Gimme Lao back to their table. Rounding the bend, Wei Wen slipped into the powder room. She smiled apologetically when a young lady in front of the mirror looked startled at her cosmetic disaster.

Moments later, as Wei Wen cleaned up and began to reapply the mascara, she suddenly realised that the young lady was still staring at her in the mirror. Wei Wen grinned and mused aloud, "There are moments in life you need shock-proof mascara. Especially when your husband fails to warn you of the magnitude of the surprise in store."

"You must be very proud of your husband, Mrs Lao."

Wei Wen looked up startled. "Do you know my husband?"

The young lady gave a faint nod. "I am Nurse Shemin. I work for your husband."

There was a morbid cheerlessness about the young lady that Wei Wen found unnerving, but she decided there was no reason not to be cordial. "I can only imagine how tough it must have been for all of you during the crisis. It is a blessing that the team pulled through. You deserve all the commendation and awards bestowed tonight."

"Not all of us pulled through, and some are not totally deserving of the accolades either," Nurse Shemin said deliberately. "Did your husband ever mention a certain Dr Gordon, Mrs Lao?"

Wei Wen was slightly alarmed. She was certain she detected a measure of animosity in the young lady. "Is that the young doctor who died of SARS? Did you know him well?"

There was a glimpse of pain as Nurse Shemin blinked fiercely and said, "We were dating. I guess you can say we were close."

Wei Wen relented. The poor girl. "I am so sorry."

"I feel sorry for Gordon too," Nurse Shemin said. "He was the one who identified and diagnosed the first SARS patient. Had it not been for his timely diagnosis, the epidemic could have been uncontainable. And yet because he is gone, the top management decided to confer the honour to your husband. It is a win-win situation for both parties. It helps to catapult your husband's political ambition, and the hospital is guaranteed a patron when your husband eventually makes it to the cabinet. I understand how it works, but I have to say I feel sick about the whole arrangement."

Wei Wen felt a knot in her stomach. She vaguely recalled Gimme Lao mentioning that the young doctor was indeed the one who identified the first SARS patient.

"At least for Dr Zhang Lei's case there was an agreement. For Gordon's case his honour was simply stolen," Nurse Shemin said bitterly.

"Who is Dr Zhang Lei?" Wei Wen felt compelled to ask, even though she was almost certain she did not want to know the details.

"Dr Zhang Lei is the one who headed the task force that successfully tracked down all the 238 cases of infection." Nurse Shemin watched Wei Wen coldly. "But he was from China on contract employment and had no use for the accolades. So Professor Eleanor Moh struck a deal with him. Dr Zhang Lei was promised a contract extension. In return, Dr Gimme Lao became the hero who spearheaded the tracking task force. It is all neat and tidy politicking, and it makes me sick to the bone."

Wei Wen found herself blushing fiercely in a mix of both anger and shame. Up until she stepped into the powder room, she was bursting with pride and joy. Within minutes this young woman, whom she had never met before, had managed to destroy what could have been the happiest day for her in the last 10 years. Yet she could think of no reason why Nurse

Shemin would want to fabricate such a tale. It chilled her to think everything the young woman disclosed could be true.

Nurse Shemin continued to unnerve Wei Wen with her glare. "There is something else I think you should know about your husband, but I am not sure if you can take it now."

Wei Wen collected her cosmetic kit and turned to leave abruptly. She would not let this woman have the satisfaction of another stab at her ignorance. But as she reached the door, she could hear Nurse Shemin call out from behind. "Go home and ask your husband. Ask him about the woman who meets him at Hotel 81 in Chinatown. You really ought to know where your husband is on the nights he is not home."

NINE

Gimme Lao blamed it on Gordon. Were it not for Gordon, he would never have gotten into an affair with Tan Ai Ling.

Dr Gordon Hoh joined the Communicable Disease Division one year before the SARS outbreak. His arrival created a ripple effect that swept across the seven levels of Tan Tock Seng Hospital like a tiny tsunami. The staff nurses who spotted him on the first morning couldn't wait to meet their lunch buddies at the staff cafeteria. They had breaking news. It was time for Dr Vance from Gynaecology to be dethroned from the top spot in the unofficial, but respected, list of Ridiculously Hot Bachelors of TTSH. A new king had arrived.

There was a shared hunger among the staff nurses for any scrap of information they could get on Dr Gordon. The man had an accent; he picked it up during his years in Boston Children's Hospital. There was a massive scar on his forearm; he survived a rock climbing accident at Yosemite. Someone spotted an abdominal roller wheel in his locker; he stuck to a grilling routine to maintain his six-pack abs. This was practically a fitness model masquerading as a doctor.

Loyal fans of the dethroned Dr Vance were quick to cast aspersions on him. One could always detect a whiff of fresh cologne on Dr Gordon; was he trying to mask some body odour? The man must spend hours every week at the gym to have such a physique; could someone who splurged so much love on himself have any more left for a girlfriend? His hairstyle was impeccable; might he not bat for the other team?

There was no need for any admirers to defend Dr Gordon. The man behaved in such a winning manner that it was impossible not to fall for his charm. Not only did he take time to chat with the cleaners as they mopped the wards, he remembered the anecdotes they shared about their children. Whenever he left the building for lunch, he would packet fresh sugarcane juice on his way back and pass it to the old man who sold tissue packets near the entrance. He smiled and greeted all the staff nurses equally, granting no one special treatment. Those who worked in the Communicable Disease Division shared a faint but unmistakable sense of loss when Dr Gordon's rest days rolled around. Everyone had gotten used to enjoying his presence.

Gimme Lao liked Gordon. The man was proficient and easy to work with. When Gordon suggested they team up to play badminton doubles for the annual interdepartmental games, Gimme Lao was slightly surprised. He reached down, patted the bulge on his waist and lamented that he was out of shape. Gordon laughed; all the more reason why they should train for the event.

Gordon continued to surprise Gimme Lao during their weekly training sessions. Where Gimme Lao coached him professionally as his mentor, the roles were reversed on the courts. Gordon proved to be an excellent coach. He struck a good balance between admonishment and encouragement and pushed Gimme Lao to get back in form quickly. By the time the games rolled around, Gimme Lao was fitter than he had ever been in the last 10 years. There was a further surprise during the match. A team of staff nurses kept up a battle cry that roused support for 'GG'. When the two lost the last match by a thin margin, the cheerleading nurses let out a collective groan and stomped their feet in dismay. Gimme Lao was touched. It was just as well that he never found out the truth. 'GG' did not stand for Gimme & Gordon as he had assumed. It was short for 'Gorgeous Gordon'.

Three months before the SARS outbreak, Dr Gordon broke his arm on the ski slopes of Niseko while on vacation in Japan. Within 48 hours upon his return, the cast he wore transformed itself from a pristine, snowy white to a spectacular web of get-well messages scribbled with colour markers in myriad hues. That was the moment it hit Gimme Lao. The man had wormed his way into the hearts of the hospital staff in a manner he was incapable of. Had Gimme Lao himself broken his arm, all he could expect to receive would be a get-well card signed by the few staff nurses working in the Communicable Disease Division, the cost equally divided among them. His cast would remain unsullied.

"You are a popular man!" Gimme Lao remarked.

"And you are jealous!" Gordon laughed.

Gimme Lao shrugged. "But why should I be surprised? You are young. You have got the looks, the charm; the whole package. You were born to be popular."

Gordon frowned at Gimme Lao and asked, "You really think that is the reason people like me?"

"You are telling me I won't be equally popular if I have your looks and your charisma?" Gimme Lao challenged.

Gordon paused for a moment. He leaned back on his swivel chair, tilted his head and scanned the reception counter outside his office. There was a staff nurse standing on a stool extracting some files from the top shelf of a cabinet. Gordon pointed at her and asked, "Do you know her name?"

"That's Tan Ai Ling."

"Tell me what you know about her?"

Gimme Lao wore a puzzled look. "What do you mean?"

"She has worked here several years now. Surely you know more than just her name?"

Gimme Lao found himself at a loss for words. He really didn't know a single thing about Tan Ai Ling. She was just one of a team of staff nurses who happened to work in the Communicable Disease Division.

"Let me help you out," Gordon smiled, almost benevolently. "Surely her handwriting left an impression?"

Gimme Lao nodded as he recalled. "Yes, she has the neatest handwriting among the nurses."

"She has beautiful handwriting," Gordon extolled. "She is a devoted student of Chinese calligraphy. She takes part in competitions, but has yet to win any."

"Really?" Gimme Lao had to admit he was surprised.

"She is also an avid reader. And I am not talking about paperback romance," Gordon continued. "I have caught her reading translated works of Bertrand Russell. Apparently she has a better command of Chinese than English. And she hides a book of Sudoku inside the reception desk drawer."

"I must say you are very observant," Gimme Lao conceded.

"I am observant because I care. I am genuinely interested to get to know people." He pointed at the web of scribbling on his cast and said, "They like me, not because I'm good-looking, but because they know I care. If you start showing nurse Tan Ai Ling some tender loving care, in no time you will be able to convert her into a fan. Trust me."

Gimme Lao shrugged. He had never needed anyone to like him, least of all his subordinates. But the new information Gordon provided triggered an idea. Dr Liew Kim Keong's birthday was coming up, and Tan Ai Ling's calligraphic skills could come in handy.

Three days later, Gimme Lao summoned Tan Ai Ling. He had purchased a Chinese wood scholar's tray and requested her help in personalising the gift by copying an honorary couplet onto the base of the tray in Chinese calligraphy. Tan Ai Ling went into a mild state of shock. The scholar's tray looked like an expensive antique replica. What if she fumbled and smeared the surface? Gimme Lao laughed and assured her he would not hold her accountable. He made it sound as though he had full confidence in her. The truth was Gimme Lao had a backup plan. If Tan Ai Ling fumbled, he could always pay an artist to paint over her blunder.

But Tan Ai Ling did not fumble. Despite his limited comprehension of Chinese calligraphy, Gimme Lao could tell that Tan

Ai Ling delivered excellent work. He was pleased and lavished praises on her. The next day, Gimme Lao came back from lunch with a book of Sudoku and passed it to her at the reception counter. He was rather amused to see her blush deeply. What he failed to notice were the collective looks of shock the other nurses shared.

In the weeks that followed, Gimme Lao began to notice traces of Tan Ai Ling in his office. The first item to appear was a new coaster for his tea mug. The print on the coaster, in Chinese, proclaimed those born in the year of the snake to be intelligent and enigmatic. Gimme Lao peeped into the wastepaper bin and spotted the stained and soggy coaster he had been using for years. It was one out of a set of five pieces that he had bought while on holiday in New Zealand with his family many years ago. It was indeed time to get it replaced.

The second item to appear was an exquisite lacquer pen holder in the shape of a coffin. Gimme Lao smiled to himself. The Chinese idiom 'Sheng Guan Fa Cai' was a play on words that linked the word coffin to prospects of promotion. Gimme Lao wondered if he should step out and thank her in person. But that did not feel right. He admired the stealthy grace at play in the way Tan Ai Ling left these tiny gifts around to surprise him. Gimme Lao thought he should reciprocate in the same manner. After lunch, he bought two pieces of curry puff and left them inside the drawer at the reception counter next to her book of Sudoku. He could play stealthy too.

A few days later, Gimme Lao found the third item hooked onto the hanger he used for hanging his coat. It was a sandalwood carving in the shape of a lion head that gave off a distinct whiff of fragrance. The inscription on the back declared that those born under the Leo zodiac sign were extraordinarily gifted children who would grow up to achieve great things.

Gimme Lao was secretly amazed at how pleased he felt. He knew most of the nurses kept their distance because they were a little fearful of him. Tan Ai Ling had behaved much the same way until the episode with the Chinese wood scholar's tray broke the ice. That marked the turning point. The bold change in her behaviour surprised him as much as the thoughtfulness that went into her gift selections touched him. Gimme Lao was not entirely sure what she had in mind. And he found that element of mystery to be rather alluring.

The next day, Gimme Lao snooped around the reception counter hoping to spot a clue. As luck would have it, Tan Ai Ling had left a Chinese entertainment magazine opened at a particular page. It was one of those multiple-choice questionnaires that purportedly assessed the reader's personality. One of the questions required the reader to pick her favourite movie director from among a few, and Tan Ai Ling had circled the name Wong Kar Wai with a blue pen. That was the clue Gimme Lao needed.

The following Monday, Gimme Lao slipped a gift-wrapped DVD into the drawer at the reception counter. He had picked *In the Mood for Love*, director Wong Kar Wai's latest masterpiece. The unmistakable sense of bliss he detected in Tan Ai Ling's demeanour brought Gimme Lao an inexplicable sense of delight. Over the next few days, both of them had to make the concerted effort to hide their smiles whenever their eyes met. It was as though they were back in secondary school, trying hard to camouflage a teenage romance and keep it a secret from the rest of the class.

One morning, Gimme Lao received a text message from Tan Ai Ling asking him to skip breakfast, as she had bought him a packet of wanton noodles. Gimme Lao texted to thank her. But when the wanton noodles appeared on his desk three days in a row, Gimme Lao began to panic. It was obvious that the repetitive breakfast carried a message, but the message itself was not at all obvious. What did the daily packets of wanton noodles mean?

On the fourth morning, Tan Ai Ling left an envelope underneath the packet of wanton noodles. There was a movie ticket inside for a Thursday night screening. Thursday was Tan Ai Ling's rest day. The movie was *Hero*, a swordfighting epic starring the same actors who had appeared in *In the Mood for Love*.

That gave Gimme Lao the clue he needed. After work, he dropped by a video shop and bought the DVD. He told Wei Wen that he needed to rush a project and locked himself in the study after dinner. At 100 minutes long, *In the Mood for Love* was a rather short movie. But the torturously languid pace at which the narrative crawled made it seem twice as long. Gimme Lao persevered. There was a clue embedded somewhere in this arthouse romance, and he was determined to uncover it.

When the pertinent scene finally rolled around, Gimme Lao gave a silent shout of triumph in his heart. In the scene, Tony Leung stood waiting under the street lamp for Maggie Cheung to walk past him on her way to buy wanton noodles every night. Both characters were hurting. Should they succumb to temptation and sink into the mud of adultery as their spouses did? Or should they rise above their carnal yearnings and remain irreproachable? Tan Ai Ling's message was finally clear to Gimme Lao. If he met her at the cinema on Thursday, he would be accepting her invitation to step into the mud.

Gimme Lao lost sleep. He had never paid Tan Ai Ling any attention until Gordon pried his eyes open. Once he did, he found himself mesmerised by her sensitivity and grace. While other nurses frittered their tea breaks gossiping away, she read philosophical essays and played Sudoku. Her choice of gifts for him showed an attention to detail that he found flattering. With the movie ticket, Tan Ai Ling had sent him a clear and bold message. The ball was now in his court.

Gimme Lao could not tell if he was feeling nervous or excited when he stepped into the cinema. He did not remember much of the movie either. He vaguely recalled Maggie Cheung on a rooftop warding off wave after wave of incessant arrows as Tan Ai Ling's fingers brushed across the back of his hand. He believed Maggie Cheung might have stabbed Tony Leung with a dagger when he felt Tan Ai Ling slip her hand into his palm. Someone later told him there was a memorable scene when the two committed suicide standing atop a spectacular desert cliff. But Gimme Lao missed that scene. He had his eyes shut because Tan Ai Ling was engaging him in a long and wet kiss.

Two days later, Gimme Lao told Wei Wen he had to attend an overnight team building session organised by the Staff

Welfare Club. That was the first night Gimme Lao checked into Hotel 81 at Chinatown with Tan Ai Ling. He was touched when he found out that Tan Ai Ling had never been kissed till the night at the cinema and that she had never taken her clothes off in front of a man till then. Afterwards, he held her tightly and did not feel strange at all when she whispered softly that she thought she might be falling in love.

Hotel 81 at Chinatown became the regular spot for their weekly encounters. Gimme Lao told Wei Wen that he wanted to join Gordon for his badminton training on Thursday nights and would sleep over at Gordon's apartment after the game. At the hospital, the two continued their game of surreptitious gift exchanges. He would reach for his cabinet keys and find a pyramid tea bag of Yunnan pu-erh flavour tied to the key chain. Conversely, he would tape a lollipop to a pair of scissors inside her drawer and leave it there to surprise her. It felt like they were stealing kisses right under the noses of unsuspecting colleagues. The necessary cloak of secrecy merely added to the fun and excitement.

Eventually, they got caught.

It was a regular Thursday night. The two had collected their room key and taken the elevator up to the third level. They were walking along the corridor when a door to their right opened and a familiar face emerged. It was Shemin, a nurse from their office. There was a suspended moment as the three stood rooted, unable to move. And then a man shouted from within the room to remind Shemin he did not want any sugar in his cup of Teh C. As Shemin turned to reply, Gimme Lao and Tan Ai

Ling marched on with pounding hearts. They both recognised the voice from within the room. It was Dr Gordon Hoh, who naturally had no idea he was supposed to be playing badminton with Dr Gimme Lao.

Gimme Lao had to fly off for a weekend conference in Jakarta the very next morning. While he was there, Tan Ai Ling texted to share that Shemin and herself went about their shifts at the hospital pretending nothing out of the ordinary had occurred. But she was worried for Gimme Lao. What if the two gossiped and word reached his wife? Gimme Lao did his best to reassure her; he would talk to Gordon upon his return on Monday. But at the back of his mind, Gimme Lao had to admit that Shemin surprised him. He would never have guessed that out of all the nurses who had a crush on Dr Gordon, it was Shemin who had pulled the longest straw.

In truth, the possibility of Wei Wen finding out about his affair was not what kept him awake. Gimme Lao was far more concerned about the gossip mill at the hospital. When he brought Dr Liew Kim Keong and his wife Professor Eleanor Moh out for an abalone treat several weeks before to celebrate Dr Liew's birthday, the couple had revealed that the time was ripe for Gimme Lao to increase his visibility. The prime minister had earlier invited the cabinet ministers to surface potential candidates and groom them to run for the upcoming elections. Gimme Lao's name was first on Dr Liew's list, which meant Gimme Lao was officially on the radar. It was Dr Liew's intention to progressively feed Gimme Lao to the media by putting him in charge of various star events in his constituency.

Gimme Lao ought to be prepared for some limelight.

Lounging by the pool at his Jakarta hotel after the conference, Gimme Lao wondered what had made him wade into the murky waters of an affair with a member of hospital staff right after he was told to be prepared for some limelight. He understood the risk of exposure. But he also understood that if he did not take the risk now, he would never get another chance.

Gimme Lao could not remember ever taking any risks. In school, he excelled academically because he was intelligent, diligent and abided by the rules. During his medical training, the same aptitude and attitude carried him safely through. Gimme adapted, but he would never push the boundaries or show his superiors any disrespect. This attribute could only be an imprint from his father. Like Lao Sheng Yang, Gimme Lao obeyed the system.

As much as he was excited about the months ahead, Gimme Lao was also wary. Once the incumbent party introduced him as a political candidate, he would have to learn to live life under a constant spotlight. Any statement he uttered might be subjected to misinterpretation or malicious distortion. Any behaviour caught on camera or video might be misread or misinterpreted. The margin of error permitted would be razor-thin. Taking risks would be a luxury he could no more afford.

Tan Ai Ling was his one and only chance to disobey the system. He needed to have that one cherished item in his life that was not dictated by others. No one but him should decide if the time had come to terminate the relationship. Till that moment arrived, he would manage the risks.

Gimme Lao did not have to go looking for Gordon on Monday. The man was waiting for him in his office wearing a perturbed look. The main wing at Tan Tok Seng Hospital had referred a female patient to Gordon over the weekend. Recently returned from a trip to Hong Kong, she had fallen very ill. Based on initial test results, Gordon feared that they might be looking at their first case of the virulent atypical pneumonia that the World Health Organisation had earlier identified in southern China. Gordon urgently needed Gimme Lao to verify his suspicions.

Gordon had been right. SARS had washed up on their shores. Tan Tock Seng Hospital became the designated hospital to front the battle against the epidemic. Everyone plunged into combat mode, and everything else became secondary.

When Gordon came down quickly with a fever and tested positive for the SARS virus, the entire team at the Communicable Disease Division went into shock. He was the first case of a comrade crossing the line to join the casualties. Gordon struggled for three weeks before he succumbed to the virus. Tan Ai Ling told Gimme Lao that Shemin was in terrible shape. She would break down midway through her rounds and sob horribly into the N95 mask she was wearing. Someone would have to relieve her duty so that she might rush off to the toilet to remove her mask and wash up. The poor girl was putting herself in danger.

As Gimme Lao was one of the key personnel on the battleground, he was allotted a single room to rest so as to minimise the chances of infection. Tan Ai Ling joined him whenever her rest hours coincided with his. They locked the door, drew the curtains and huddled closely on the single bed. These were stolen hours of freedom the two treasured. Once, Tan Ai Ling started to weep softly. When Gimme Lao drew her close and kissed her tenderly on her forehead, she whispered that she was crying because she felt happy. If she did not survive the SARS epidemic, at least she had experienced romance and the touch of a man. She would be really bitter if her life had ended before that happened.

Gimme Lao was touched. He did not understand how he could have made such a difference in someone's life. But he was deeply pleased to learn that there was one person to whom he represented the precious chance to love and be loved in return.

The two discussed and agreed that it would be too risky to keep meeting at Hotel 81. Tan Ai Ling would persuade her cousin to let them rent a room above his hair salon. Gimme Lao would pay the rent. It was to be their very own place.

The SARS epidemic did eventually blow over. On the day that the Tan Tock Seng Hospital executive director announced that they could all go home, Professor Eleanor Moh summoned Gimme Lao. She locked the office door and told him she had some important news. Her husband had convinced the prime minister that Gimme Lao should be fielded for the very next election. This SARS crisis was as much a challenge as an opportunity. They planned to portray Gimme Lao as a national SARS hero. This would allow him to leapfrog from virtual unknown to instant celebrity, miles ahead of the other new political candidates.

Gimme Lao had to clench his fists under the table to hide his excitement. He had not expected things to proceed so speedily. But he was ready. He had known his entire life that he was meant for something extraordinary.

However, the information that Professor Eleanor Moh next shared shook him up a little. With the backing of the executive director, she had made a deal with the doctor who headed the operation to track down all the cases of infection on the island. The hospital would make it known that it was Dr Gimme Lao, and not Dr Zhang Lei, who had headed the task force. They would also acknowledge and honour Gimme Lao as the very doctor who correctly identified and diagnosed the first SARS patient in Singapore. After all, the late Dr Gordon Hoh was no longer around to receive the accolades. It would be a crime to let the honour go to waste.

Professor Eleanor Moh ended by reminding Gimme Lao not to share the details of the arrangements with his wife. For a politician, a supportive spouse was an invaluable asset. But if the relationship soured further down the road, the same spouse could prove to be the most fearsome enemy. Her advice was to build the trust, but limit the sharing.

Gimme Lao's heart skipped a beat. He wondered if he had shared too much with Wei Wen already.

In the months that followed, Gimme Lao was caught in a whirlwind of private briefings by the Prime Minister's Office and public appearances at constituency events. The next election would only take place three years down the road, but the upper echelons of the incumbent political party wanted Gimme Lao to start working the ground right away. They were nervous about an up-and-coming opposition party member who was both sharp and eloquent and were eager to crush her by pitting the national SARS hero against her.

Gimme Lao was initially unfazed. His targeted opponent was inferior when it came to educational qualifications and professional achievements. The opposition party she represented was underfunded and disorganised. In contrast, not only was he better qualified, he was also backed by a political party that had dominated the Parliament over the last 40 years. It was inconceivable that their stronghold could be challenged.

However, Gimme Lao soon found out that he had underestimated his opponent. Jowene Tay was a fiery candidate on a passionate mission. She was campaigning as a single mother who found herself penalised and oppressed by the system that was put in place by the government. While married couples with double incomes were given housing and child care subsidies, she and her child received none. Her efforts to petition a change in housing policies were met with bureaucratic indifference. Singapore was, in general, a conservative society, the authorities explained with dispassion. It would not do to use public funds to subsidise citizens like her, who chose an alternative lifestyle.

Jowene Tay was infuriated. She tapped on social media to share her frustrations and was astounded when a huge wave of support rolled in. There were middle-income earners who were angry that their elderly parents chalked up astronomical hospital bills but could not qualify for assistance because they were home owners. There were low-income singles who were unhappy that they had to stay with their parents because there were limited public housing options available for them. There were gay couples who were frustrated that the legal system provided them with no recognition, support or protection. All of them claimed to feel Jowene Tay's pain.

To Gimme Lao's horror, his opponent turned her weakness into her strength. Jowene Tay rode on the wave of support she received from marginalised groups who felt they too had been slighted by the system. By the time the general election was announced for 2006, Jowene Tay was leading Gimme Lao in the unofficial polls.

Gimme Lao fought hard. He attended baby shows and kissed as many babies as he could. He visited nursing homes and handfed toothless residents spoonfuls of congee. His political party made sure that his campaign was featured prominently on the front page of *The Straits Times*. Yet it was to no avail. The electorate was inclined to root for Jowene Tay the underdog, and Gimme Lao lost his first election.

After the vote count was over, Gimme Lao sent Wei Wen a message to inform her that he was not going home yet. There were bound to be some reporters lying in ambush and he did not feel ready to talk to them. He next sent Tan Ai Ling a message to ask to meet her at their little hideout above the hair salon. He told her he missed her terribly.

Gimme Lao had not seen Tan Ai Ling for over three months. He had taken a leave of absence from the hospital to focus on the election campaign. And he did not dare arrange to meet her clandestinely either, not when the media spotlight was trained on him. In truth, he hadn't really missed her that much. He had been too busy to think of her.

The first thing that caught Gimme Lao's attention when he stepped into the room was the scroll laid out on the bed. It was an original by pioneer Singaporean calligraphy artist Tan Siah Kwee. Gimme Lao's heart sank. He had gotten it as a birthday gift for Tan Ai Ling two years ago.

There was a letter placed next to the scroll. It was dated the day before. In her exquisite handwriting, Tan Ai Ling explained that she had decided to break up with him. It had not escaped her that his love had diminished over time. Even when they did spend time together, his attention was never on her. She could understand when he said it was too risky to meet up during the election period. But was it so risky to send a text message of concern? Was that why she received a miserable total of five messages from him over the last three months? If she was no more on his mind, she did not wish to remain in his life either. She had arranged for a transfer to another hospital. And she would like him to leave the room key with the hair salon lady downstairs.

Gimme Lao slumped onto the sofa. For a moment he was unsure how he felt. Was he devastated? Tan Ai Ling was right when she observed that his love for her had diminished. Snuggling with her in their little hideout had become as much a routine as his dinners back home with Wei Wen and Skye. Perhaps this breakup was for the better. He ought to be glad that neither his career nor his family life had suffered any repercussions.

Gimme Lao checked his watch and decided that he had ample time to catch a nap. That was what he should do; get rested, go home to his family and pick up from where he left off. Nobody would suspect anything.

Unbeknown to Gimme Lao, Wei Wen had moved past mere suspicion. She knew. She had hired a private detective and held a docket of photographs and video footage of Gimme Lao and Tan Ai Ling at their little hideout above the hair salon. But Wei Wen had yet to decide what to do with the evidence gathered.

For the past two years, Wei Wen had been stretched thin by the demands on her as a daughter and a granddaughter. When her mother called her up crying on the phone one day, she could not make sense of her incoherent babble and so had to rush over in person. It turned out that her parents had had a squabble and her father hit her mother for the first time in the 42 years of their marriage. The squabble concerned a woman that they had recently hired to help them out at their hawker stall. Her mother was convinced that the woman had seduced her father.

When Wei Wen confronted her father, the old man denied it. The China stall assistant was a hardworking single mother making an honest living. Was it wrong of him to be kind and fatherly to her? There were no grounds for her mother's accusations. Why should he give in to the unreasonable demands of a jealous wife and deprive an innocent woman of her job? He refused to fire the suspect.

Wei Wen's mother continued her accusations through tears. Her father was blind to the China woman's agenda. He was turning 65 soon, by which time he would be eligible to draw out monthly payments from his CPF retirement account. That was what she was after. The tabloids had published countless tales of gullible Singapore men who were swindled out of their retirement nest egg by scheming, manipulative China women. Her father was just too bull-headed to acknowledge his own stupidity.

It took weeks for Wei Wen to settle the dispute. Eventually, she helped the China stall assistant secure another job in a different hawker centre across town. She also made sure that the next stall assistant her parents hired was an elderly woman who did not have what it took to arouse her mother's suspicions or jealousy.

During the period leading up to the election, Wei Wen's grandmother began to display signs of dementia. She kept forgetting to take her showers, but insisted that she had when she was queried. Twice she lost her balance and fell while trying to put on her pants. When she eventually urged the family to stock up on rice and hide it from the Japanese soldiers, they knew it was time to seek professional help. It fell upon Wei Wen to sign her grandmother up for a programme in a dementia daycare centre and to ferry her to her various medical appointments. This routine continued for more than a year before her grandmother finally succumbed to pneumonia and passed away.

Wei Wen felt relieved. Finally free from caregiver duties, she arranged for her parents to go on a vacation in Vietnam. But she was unprepared for the devastating news that came three days later. Wei Wen's business contacts in Vietnam had signed her parents up for an overnighter on a tourist boat that went on to catch fire and sink. Subsequent investigations after the accident traced the fire on the boat to a cooking gas tank explosion. It was likely that her parents panicked and jumped off the boat. Their bodies were found the next day near Trong Mai Rocks.

After the initial shock, Wei Wen beat herself up over her parents' untimely demise. It did not help that she had to fly over to Vietnam alone to collect the remains. Gimme Lao had a paper to present at a conference and could not avail himself, whereas Skye was recuperating from an injury he had sustained in camp. As she sat alone in the waiting lounge in Noi Bai International Airport holding her parents' urns on her lap, Wei Wen felt disconsolate. Within two months she had lost her grandmother and both her parents. And neither her husband nor her son was at hand to offer her support and solace. That was the moment it struck her: there was nobody she could count on.

Wei Wen had a fierce argument with Gimme Lao over the issue of custody for her brother Too Sexy. There was no reason why they could not take him in; they had a spare bedroom. The family maid could sleep on a rolled out mattress next to the bed. But Gimme Lao was adamant that Too Sexy should not live with them. He was even willing to foot half the bill for the nursing home.

Eventually, it was Gimme Lao's brutal honesty that won the argument. If something untoward were to happen to Wei Wen tomorrow, Gimme Lao was unwilling to take over custody of her brother. It was best that Too Sexy was placed in a nursing home right away.

Wei Wen gave in. On the day she helped Too Sexy move in to the Assisi Lodge, she sat in the garden with him and held his hand, crying. He needed to understand that her hands were tied. She was married to a man who was unwilling to share her burden. In fact, she began to wonder if Gimme Lao would act in the same callous manner when her time came. At the worst she still had Skye, Wei Wen contemplated as she dried her tears.

Skye hated that he could not be discharged from hospital in time to accompany his mother to Vietnam. He lost sleep thinking of Wei Wen all alone, handling the red tape and processes necessary to bring the remains of his grandparents home. But that was not the only thing keeping him awake. Skye was also worried about KC Kok.

After Skye broke up with Jason, he withdrew from the swim team. He felt he needed to keep a distance for the healing to begin. Although it hurt to be on the receiving end of Jason's cold animosity, the pain brought about a startling clarity. His first love was flawless only because he had wilfully imagined it to be. He had allowed the shine of Green Lantern's light to blind him to that which he did not wish to see. Jason was capable of cruelty and hypocrisy.

The distance he now kept from the swim team also illuminated another blind spot of his. This was a pack of alpha males who regarded their physical prowess with narcissism. The adoration they received from lesser creatures like KC Kok further convinced them they were a caste worthy of reverence. Skye shuddered when he realised he had behaved very much the same way. He would never in a million years pick a scrawny, creepy teenager like KC Kok as a friend.

That was precisely what Skye decided he would do.

Skye kept a lookout for KC Kok. In the student cafeteria, he sat down opposite the teenager uninvited and started a conversation. Although his initial efforts were met with suspicion, Skye persevered. Over time, KC Kok began to let down his guard. When he eventually permitted Skye to browse through his treasured portfolio of photographs, Skye knew he had hacked through the firewall of distrust, for KC Kok had been too shy to show it to anyone else.

The photographs in the portfolio took Skye's breath away. There were portraits of people, many of whom Skye knew in college. KC Kok's lens brought out a singularity to their mood and personality that he would otherwise have missed. There was the look of annoyance the cleaner wore as she approached to clean a messy table while the occupants laughed heartily. A lone girl sat looking dejected, surrounded by other cheerful students chatting away in the cafeteria. A heavily pregnant lecturer held on to the handrail for support as she manoeuvred up the stairs clumsily. The swim team did their warm-up stretches by the pool, their vivacity vibrantly illuminated by the morning rays. KC Kok had been able to imbue these suspended moments with meaning and significance. It was then that Skye learnt to look beyond KC's social awkwardness to see the incredible sensitivity with which the teenager viewed the world.

The two became fast friends. Now that Skye had dropped out of the swim team, he needed a new sport. He urged KC Kok to join him for his afternoon jogs, but KC Kok could not keep up. So the two compromised and took up cycling instead. After their lectures ended, they would pedal their way to West Coast Park, grab a drink from McDonald's and settle down on the embankment to chitchat. They grumbled about tutors who bored them to death and tutorial assignments that inspired suicidal thoughts. They shared gaffes they committed or witnessed and scandals they overheard. No topic was taboo between them.

Once, Skye looked KC Kok in the eyes and asked point blank if he was gay. KC Kok fidgeted and hurled the question back at Skye. When Skye nodded firmly, KC Kok looked relieved and nodded too. That was how the two came out to one another.

KC Kok admitted that he had never kissed or touched a man before. When he learnt that Skye had recently ended a relationship, he became inexorably inquisitive. Was it anybody in college? How did it start? How did the two connect? How far did Skye go? Was it painful? Why did it end? He was awfully disappointed when Skye kept a tight lip over the identity of his mysterious ex-lover. But Skye felt he owed it to Jason to keep him safely in the closet.

When the time came for enlistment, Skye and KC Kok were excited to find themselves posted to the same infantry unit. They held the title of specialists in the same platoon and commanded a section of six riflemen each. Skye slipped into his role easily. He managed his section with a firm hand and made it clear right from the start that he would not tolerate any disobedience. KC Kok on the other hand was unable to control his riflemen. They blatantly disobeyed his orders and scoffed at him when he could not keep up with them on road marches and fitness runs. Skye often had to cross over and help KC Kok discipline his unruly bunch.

After training ended for the day, most of the specialists liked to hang out at the clubhouse to play cards or carom or shoot some pool. Skye and KC Kok however preferred to hole up in their bunk and surf the Internet. The two conjoined their beds so that they could browse on their phones side by side. It did not take them long to discover chat rooms and discussion boards for the local gay community. They gasped at the brazen displays of lust and lechery in the personals and leered at the spread of muscles and pulchritude. KC Kok was especially mesmerised. It seemed he had found a safe space where he could explore the depths of his sexuality and end his inexperience with just a tap of his finger.

By the end of the first year, Skye was itching for more than just a screen connection. He eschewed guys who were looking for sex buddies and picked the ones who were looking for something more. Skye missed the element of intimacy he once had with Jason. He was certain he would not find satisfaction in casual flings and one-night stands. He wanted to meet someone he could build a future with. Although some of his dates were enticing, the chemistry never seemed right. It took six months of serial dating before he met a suitable candidate.

Skye knew there was something special about Kuan Eng the first time they met. The man had a gaze that suggested a sharp intelligence without the accompanying arrogance and an air of assurance that could only come from someone who was deeply in touch with himself. On his part, Kuan Eng liked that Skye was not intimidated by his being 10 years older, or that he worked as a corporate lawyer. Before the first date was over, both of them knew they wanted more.

The more Skye learnt about Kuan Eng, the more amazed he

became. Despite the demanding career that had him ploughing a 50-hour work week, Kuan Eng found time to volunteer regularly and take part in social activism. Skye was delighted that he had hooked up with Clark Kent but landed himself Superman. Through Kuan Eng, Skye was able to discover a part of Singapore that he had never known existed. As for Kuan Eng, he watched Skye blossom with a mentor's satisfaction. The two quickly became a couple.

That was the period Skye and KC Kok drifted apart. During the stage when he was serial dating, Skye was happy to indulge KC Kok's curiosity and had no qualms sharing the details of his encounters. But once Skye's relationship with Kuan Eng had stabilised, KC Kok's incessant probing came across as an intrusion into his privacy. His replies watered down to uninspired one-liners. Very soon, KC Kok stopped probing and retreated to his reclusive demeanour. Bathed in the bliss of a new relationship himself, Skye was blind to the depth of dejection his friend had sunk into.

KC Kok felt betrayed. His best friend had shut him out the moment he landed himself a catch. With no more access to Skye's tales of debauchery, KC Kok took it upon himself to create his own adventures. Once he clicked on the mouse, there was no turning back. He went from one casual encounter to another, and as he grew bolder he began to take fewer precautions. It didn't take long before he landed himself in trouble. KC Kok had somehow contracted an STD.

Once the riflemen figured it out, their attitude towards KC Kok went from disrespect to disdain; the incompetent specialist was also a cock sucker. It did not help that the other specialists were just as likely to mock KC Kok behind his back. More than once Skye picked a quarrel with them and admonished them for their insensitivity. It was in that perturbed state of mind that Skye became distracted during an assault drill and suffered a bad fall. Lying in the hospital bed with a dislocated shoulder, Skye wondered how KC Kok would cope without him around to fend off the malice and cruelty of the others.

Throughout his hospitalisation, Skye constantly texted KC Kok to check on his progress. Although the replies were brief and distanced, KC Kok did share that the antiviral pills were working and that the cold sores had all but receded. He also informed Skye that he had successfully secured a transfer and would be out of the infantry unit before Skye's discharge.

Skye did not get to meet KC Kok for the remaining six months of their national service. Despite his repeated attempts to arrange for a meet up, KC Kok kept turning him down. After the army stint ended, Skye went on to university while KC Kok enrolled in a diploma programme at the Lasalle College of the Arts. The two effectively lost touch.

When the news came one year later, Skye went into a state of shock. KC Kok had overdosed on sleeping pills.

The intensity of what transpired that fateful evening was deeply etched in Skye's mind. Kuan Eng had dropped him off after a dinner gathering with friends. As he stepped into the apartment, he was slightly surprised to see that the family had guests. There was a lady who looked to be his mother's age and a teenage girl, around 16 or 17. Both of them tilted their heads and nailed him with a steely gaze as he stepped in. His mother had a perturbed look on her face. It was as though she was fearful for him.

"This is Mrs Kok and her daughter," Wei Wen introduced. "They are here to inform you that your friend KC passed away last Wednesday. He took his own life."

Skye stood paralysed. He had to struggle to digest what he had just heard. Wei Wen came forward and guided him to sit down on the sofa.

"My brother left you a letter." The teenage girl gestured at a sheet of paper on the table. It was folded twice to fit neatly into an envelope addressed to him, but had since been extracted and unfurled. It was obvious that all three present had already read it.

KC Kok had taken his time to pen his last letter; the handwriting was deliberate and beautiful. Skye read through the letter thrice, not merely because he could not digest it properly in his muddled state of mind, but also because he needed time to prepare himself. He was almost certain that whatever Mrs Kok had to say to him next would not be pleasant. Despite the foreboding, that was not the reason he was distressed. The guests would eventually leave. It was Wei Wen's unknown response that struck panic in his heart. His mother now knew his secret. There was no more hiding.

"Mrs Kok has something to say to you." Wei Wen leaned forward and gently pried the letter from Skye's hands. "You can read this again later."

Skye nodded and looked straight at KC Kok's mother. "I am so sorry."

"My son says he does not blame you," Mrs Kok began. Her tone was calm. "I will try not to blame you, too. You are just as young as Kheng Chye. But I want you to know, your words and your behaviour have an impact on others, especially people who trust you. What you do is wrong. You are not my son, so I am in no position to lecture you. But I want you to remember this. Behind every young man who does wrong is a mother who will have her heart broken. I feel sorry for what your mother has to go through tonight. But she still has a chance to make things right. For me, I don't even get that chance. My son is gone."

Skye could feel tears welling up. If his mother or Mrs Kok thought he was fighting tears of shame and sorrow, they were mistaken. These were tears of bitterness. It was the bitter indignation over Mrs Kok's unassailable stance that what he did was wrong. It was also the bitter understanding that this was not the time to defend himself. Her child had died. If she needed Skye's culpability to reach a closure, Skye would have to grant her that.

After Mrs Kok and her daughter left, Skye tensed. He was now all alone in the room with his mother. He knew it must have come as a shock for her. What he did not know was the sense of helplessness his mother felt not being able to come to his defence when Mrs Kok had laid it out for him. Yet how could she, when her son did not trust her enough to share with her his deepest and darkest secret?

Skye answered his mother's string of questions in a daze. Yes, he was certain. No, he was not promiscuous. He had met someone and was in a monogamous relationship. No, he was not ready to tell his father yet. Could they discuss this another day? He was really, really tired.

Skye texted Kuan Eng furiously once he was alone in his bedroom. His mother knew. She might ask to meet him. Was he ready? Kuan Eng's affirmation when it came almost instantly was the solace he sought. They discussed their strategy over the next hour. Kuan Eng knew a counsellor who conducted a monthly session with parents whose children had come out. He would find out details of the upcoming session so that Skye could invite his mother. It would help tremendously to have a professional counsellor ease her mind.

After Skye switched off his handphone for the night, he laid supine in bed, spent. That was the moment it hit him. KC Kok, the reclusive gay teenager he had goaded out of the closet and then carelessly abandoned, had killed himself. Skye cupped his mouth as he began to whimper uncontrollably.

Wei Wen pretended to be asleep when Gimme Lao came in after midnight. Though she lay unmoving, the torrent of anxious rumination tormented her the entire night. How could she have not detected the signs? Would it have made a difference if he had come to her in the beginning? Why did he not trust her? Wei Wen felt as though she was going mad. In the end, she convinced herself that there was only one question she needed to focus on: how could she now help him?

The next morning, she left the apartment at dawn and went for a swim in the condo pool. She continued to contemplate as she covered her laps. Skye had always been independent in spirit and mind. If he identified himself as a gay man, Wei

Wen was inclined to believe him. But it was going to be such an arduous journey for him. There were people out there who made it their fanatical mission to shame and denounce gay men. Her boy would have to suffer the bigotry of these people. Her heart ached. Skye could have had a much easier journey were he straight.

When a group of elderly residents descended upon the pool for their regular aqua aerobic workout, Wei Wen retired to the deck chair to tan herself. The warm rays toasting her skin would normally induce her to doze off, but she had too much on her mind that morning. Her thoughts meandered till they landed on her brother. He, too, had to suffer the prejudice of society at large, not least from her very husband. She was powerless to protect him when he needed her most. She would not let that happen to her son.

Skye's message reached her as she was getting ready to head home. There was a counselling session on Thursday conducted by an organisation for parents of LGBT youths. Would she come with him? Wei Wen texted her reply without hesitation. She would love to.

The session was held at the Ulu Pandan Community Club. As Wei Wen stepped in after Skye, she immediately recognised someone she knew from university. Try as she might, she could not recall her name. But the woman spotted her, beamed and approached quickly. "You are Wei Wen, aren't you? My goodness, we haven't met in like…two decades?"

"Has it been that long?" Wei Wen laughed, a little too shrilly. It was a desperate attempt to hide her embarrassment.

"And this is your son?"

Skye returned the smile and took the woman's hand as she offered it. He was surprised at how resolute her handshake was.

"I am Omala, the counsellor for this evening's session. I used to know your mother in university."

It all came gushing back to Wei Wen instantly. Omala, the student leader known for her fiery passion. They had a nickname for her—The Tornado.

One week later, Omala arranged to meet Wei Wen for coffee. She was astonished to learn that Wei Wen was married to Gimme Lao. Laughingly, she admitted she had not kept up with the gossip mill among their university friends. Wei Wen vaguely remembered Gimme Lao mentioning that he and Omala had some sort of a falling out, and so did not suggest the two get together. Instead, she asked Omala to fill her in on the missing decades.

Omala had plunged into work life right after she attained her degree in sociology. Over the years, she worked for various NGOs, finally settling down as the assistant director of operations for an organisation working with migrant workers. She was the only one among her siblings and cousins who remained unmarried. Omala relished her image as the bold and adventurous aunt that her 12 nephews and nieces adored. They knew no one else who had flown over the Victoria Falls in Zambia in a microlight, ridden a camel into the Merzuga desert in Morocco and paraglided over ancient ruins in Romania. Omala loved her life.

Moving forward, Omala was excited about a significant event

she was spearheading together with a group of activists. Come June the following year, they intended to organise an afternoon of festivity at Hong Lim Park. The event, in support of the LGBT community, would be the first of its kind in Singapore.

"A gay pride parade? Here?" Wei Wen gasped. She could not imagine the conservative government giving the green light for such a controversial event. "Can you get the permit to run it?"

"We have people working on that," Omala enthused. "And it's not exactly gay pride. The focus is not on the LGBT community's clamour for recognition, but the acceptance, support and love from allies in the community. The friends and families would stand in support of their gay sons, daughters and buddies."

Watching Omala speak, Wei Wen realised that her old friend had not lost her passion all these years. In contrast, Wei Wen herself felt jaded. When was she ever passionate about anything?

"I would like to invite you to be a part of it," Omala said.

Wei Wen was about to reply that she would give it some thought when she remembered her resolution to be there for Skye. "Yes. I will attend the event."

"That is not what I meant." Omala shook her head. "We need lots of hands on deck to organise this. Come in and help us. It would also give you the opportunity to get to know your son's boyfriend better. Kuan Eng is on the main organising committee."

Wei Wen felt a wave of gratitude wash over her.

The following week, Wei Wen turned up for the volunteer briefing session. She watched as Kuan Eng shared the newest updates with the group of over a hundred. All the attendees would be asked to turn up in pink. At the appointed hour, everyone would gather to form a gigantic pink dot in the middle of the park. Photographs and video clips of the formation of the pink dot could then be circulated online to create awareness and branding. The event would become the inaugural 'Pink Dot 2009'.

When Skye arranged for Wei Wen and Kuan Eng to meet over dinner two nights later, she admitted that she was rather taken by Kuan Eng's eloquence and presence on stage. Kuan Eng laughed and said he ought to be thankful for all the mock court trials he had to undergo during his undergraduate days. On his decision to go into corporate law, Kuan Eng tickled both Wei Wen and Skye with his whimsical theorising. The law enforcement agencies in Singapore were so efficient that the crooks and criminals could never grow their illicit businesses to any respectable size. The virtual absence of deep-pocketed clients who could pay defence attorneys good money led to an exodus of the best lawyers from the courtrooms to the corporate meeting rooms. This unfortunate imbalance in the legal and criminal ecosystem was disastrous for any aspiring lawyer. It was a good thing the Attorney-General's Office was not as efficient as the law enforcement agencies. Otherwise, corporate lawyers would starve too.

Wei Wen and Skye both laughed heartily; Wei Wen because she was happy that Kuan Eng was intelligent, charming and in a strong position financially to give Skye a comfortable lifestyle, and Skye because he was glad that his mother approved of his boyfriend. To all parties concerned, the first meeting was a resounding success.

Wei Wen was roped in to help coordinate the various agencies setting up booths at the event. Over the next few months, she became familiar with the language and personalities in the community. At one point, a gay stand-up comedian even gave her free tickets to his performance. When she invited Skye to come along, he laughed and said Wei Wen probably knew more people in the community than he did now.

As Pink Dot drew near, Skye asked Wei Wen if she thought it would be a good idea to invite Gimme Lao to the event. Wei Wen secretly thought that even if Gimme Lao could come to terms with the fact that Skye was gay, he would surely not be too keen to be spotted at such an event. But she knew that if Skye was ready, she would give him her full support.

The day of the event finally arrived. As Wei Wen sat across from Skye in the café waiting for Gimme Lao, she could tell that he was nervous. She was about to reassure him when a call came in from Kuan Eng. A logistical emergency had arisen on site and they desperately needed a few extra pairs of hand. Could Skye hop over?

"Go," Wei Wen urged. "I will handle Dad."

From where she was seated, Wei Wen had a good view of Hong Lim Park. A handful of people had started to stream in. They laid out picnic mats near the main stage to book their spots before retreating to the shade by the fringe. The programme would not begin for another two hours; it was simply too hot to be sitting under the sun. Someone was testing the mike, but Wei Wen could not make out the announcements.

"Is that the gay pride event? I did not realise it was today."

Wei Wen turned around startled. The thick carpeting in the café had allowed Gimme Lao to sneak up undetected. She gestured for him to take up Skye's vacated seat and pointed at the slice of chocolate banana cake. "You can have that. Skye had to rush off to tend to an emergency."

"What emergency?"

Wei Wen tapped on the window pane to draw his attention to the park. "He is helping out with the set-up."

A glint of suspicion registered in Gimme Lao's eyes. "Why is Skye involved?"

Wei Wen did not immediately reply. She gently tapped on her mobile phone screen to bring it back to life before handing it over to Gimme Lao. It was a photo of Skye standing next to another man. The two were beaming ear to ear in a seemingly invincible state of bliss.

"That's Kuan Eng. He and Skye have been together for three years now."

It took Gimme Lao mere seconds to register the multiple layers of truth and implication. His wife was telling him that his son was gay and had been in a gay relationship for the last three years. That was the obvious. Embedded in this was the incrimination that he was so removed from his only son, he was blind to his affairs. For that he felt a pinch of shame. That Skye trusted his mother more to share the truth with her first did not surprise Gimme Lao. What surprised him was Wei Wen's betrayal. She knew he was running for election within the next two years. She must surely know it would hurt his political ambition to be seen championing the gay cause? For that he felt annoyed.

"You know I can't be attending this. I will speak to Skye when he gets home tonight."

"I know this is a shock to you. And I know Skye should be the one defending himself here. It is unfortunate that he got held up," Wei Wen continued in her measured tone. "But this event is important to him."

"I am not saying that I am against it," Gimme Lao reasoned. "I am just saying it is not a good idea for me to be seen publicly supporting the cause. That will lose me tons of votes."

"I don't care what your voters think," Wei Wen remarked coldly. "I care what our son thinks."

Gimme Lao was taken aback. It was uncharacteristic of Wei Wen to take on such a resolute stance. "You and Skye have been plotting this for a while now, haven't you?"

Wei Wen clenched her fist and pressed it against her lips, quivering a little. For a while, neither spoke.

"You can't drop this on me and expect me to come to terms with it instantly," Gimme Lao finally said. "I will talk to him eventually. But not here, not this gay pride event. I have to skip this."

Wei Wen was silent as she locked in her gaze. Gimme Lao knew that meant she was trying to come to a momentous decision. It perturbed him that he had no inkling what was on her mind right now. "What is it?"

"I will make you a deal." Wei Wen switched back to her measured tone. "If you attend Pink Dot with me today, I promise I will not sabotage your campaign when you run for election."

"What do you mean?" Gimme Lao felt a chill.

"If I do eventually decide to get a divorce, I will keep my mouth shut when the media come knocking on my door and not mention the name Tan Ai Ling."

Gimme Lao felt his head spin. All these years sharing a bed and he had no idea she knew.

"That is over," he muttered weakly. "We are no longer together."

"I know."

An awkward silence ensued.

"Why are you contemplating divorce only now, when you have known all along?" Gimme Lao finally asked.

Wei Wen maintained her gaze at the picnickers out on the lawn. "After Skye came out to me one year ago and introduced me to Kuan Eng, I saw in them what we once had. The passion. The romance. The optimism focusing on a future together. We have lost that, Gimme. I don't look forward to growing old with you anymore."

Gimme Lao felt shaken. "We can work on the marriage, Wen. There was no woman before Tan Ai Ling and no woman after. I swear."

"Come to this event with me." Wei Wen turned to face Gimme Lao. "We can discuss our issue later. Let today be about our son, all right?"

Gimme Lao nodded feebly. The consecutive waves of surprises this afternoon had worn him out.

Skye had reserved a picnic spot near the stage and stood up to wave them over. He was brimming with tears when he went up to Gimme Lao and hugged him tightly. "I love you, Dad.

This means a lot to me."

Gimme Lao felt a wave of emotion wash over him. He could not remember the last time Skye hugged him. As a toddler, Skye was a devoted thigh hugger. Coming home from work, Gimme Lao always looked forward to the toddler shrieking with delight and rushing forth to hug his thigh. He had missed that badly when his son outgrew the phase. At this moment, as Skye embraced and pressed himself hard against him, Gimme Lao was reminded of his role. He was, first and foremost, a father to his son, and a husband to his wife. For many years he had relegated his primary role to the periphery as he focused on his secondary roles as a doctor and a politician. Those had brought him prestige and fed his ego. He realised now that he had taken his family's support for granted. He was so removed from Skye and Wei Wen he had no idea his son was in a committed gay relationship, and his wife was contemplating divorce. Gimme Lao wondered if it was too late for him to salvage his marriage.

"Kuan Eng is manning the sound system behind the stage. He will join us after the event," Skye explained, his face flushed with the excitement of finally introducing his boyfriend to his father. "You will love him, Dad. I promise."

The three settled down on the picnic mat as the emcee announced that Pink Dot 2009 would officially begin. The lawn instantly erupted into a madhouse of ear-piercing whistles and celebratory cheers. The emcee introduced the three Pink Dot ambassadors in the line-up. He was proud to present the first speaker among them, the resident playwright of The Queer Stage, Mr Hasim Hassan.

Gimme Lao sat up straight upon hearing the name. Surely it could not be the same man? And then Gimme Lao caught sight of him as he strode onto the stage, the teacher he had not seen for close to three decades. The oddity of it all sent chills down Gimme Lao's spine.

Mr Hasim Hassan had aged visibly. His hair was grey, his goatee was speckled with white and he stooped a little. But as he started to address the crowd, Gimme Lao noted that the man had not lost his fire. Mr Hasim Hassan spoke passionately about his early years struggling with the dichotomy of hiding in the shadows while forging a gay identity he was proud of. He was a literature teacher in a local secondary school. He was known among his students to be upfront and vocal about a multitude of issues and topics. Yet he felt it necessary to hide the fact that he was gay. The school authorities then were not ready to acknowledge the presence, let alone the contribution, of gay teachers. If it were not for a student who publicly outed him in class, he might have continued to be part of the contingent of gay men unable to contribute openly to the gay cause because they felt they could not step out of the shadows.

Gimme Lao blushed as Mr Hasim Hassan proceeded to share, in detail, the episode that was pivotal in his stepping out of the closet. It was deeply traumatic. He tendered his resignation and went into a state of depression. It was his partner's devotion and support that helped him pull through. His partner rightly pointed out that he had no reason, now he had been outed, to continue with his shadowy existence. In fact, he ought to leverage on the new freedom. That remark turned Mr Hasim

Hassan around. He devoted himself to his passion for stage plays and subsequently became the resident playwright for The Queer Stage. It was there that he found his calling.

Mr Hasim Hassan concluded with a personal confession. He used to bear a grudge against the student who outed him publicly. That boy had caused him to be derailed from his career as a teacher. In retrospect however, the chain of events triggered by the outing had actually pushed him to new heights in his journey. Thus he would like to make it known that wherever the boy was today, he wanted to thank him. It was that pivotal push out of the closet that had given him the courage to live a full, open life as a proud gay man.

As Hong Lim Park thundered with applause, Gimme Lao fell into a troubled reflection. He had been vindictive when he outed Mr Hasim Hassan 30 years ago, all because he resented losing Omala to Mr Hasim Hassan's camp. It wasn't till this very moment that he realised how injurious his actions had been. Had someone ambushed his upcoming election campaign and confronted him with his extramarital affair when he least expected it, he would have been devastated.

Gimme Lao remained in a daze throughout the Pink Dot celebration. A part of him wanted to go up to Mr Hasim Hassan and apologise for the hurt and harm he had caused. Yet he could not. Not when he was running for election soon. He had to abide by the stance his political party took on major social issues. He could not be seen advocating for LGBT rights and equality. That would be political suicide.

It was a similar dilemma he had with Skye. Even if he

was ready to accept that his son was gay, he knew he would be gunned down by the conservatives for sitting down to an amicable dinner with his gay son and his partner. He had to strike a delicate balance between his public and private stance.

With this thought in mind, Gimme Lao was polite but distant when Skye introduced Kuan Eng to him after the event was over. Skye was disappointed that his father failed to show any warmth, but Wei Wen pulled him aside and told him to be patient. His father needed more time.

The next evening, the three of them arrived on time for their fortnightly dinner with Mary Lao and her husband. Ever since her husband suffered a minor stroke two years ago, Mary Lao conceded that they needed a domestic helper. It was by a stroke of luck that the Javanese help they picked happened to be an excellent cook. Both Mary Lao and her husband had put on considerable weight and were often teased in church for exemplifying the plenitude of God's grace. The teasing was done in good nature, for Mary Lao had become a respected elder of the church. She sat on the church's executive committee and gave the occasional sermon. The congregation looked up to her.

Skye waited for dinner to be over and the Javanese help to finish serving them pandan cake and oolong tea before breaking the news to his grandparents.

Gimme Lao was amazed at how composed Skye was. It would appear that his son was completely comfortable in his skin as a young gay man. Wei Wen was the one who was obviously nervous and looked ready to pounce in Skye's defence were Mary Lao to flare up and attack. To everyone's surprise, the attack did not come from her.

It was Lao Sheng Yang who exploded.

"Being gay is an abomination in the eyes of the Lord!" was his opening volley, followed by accusations of defilement, condemnations of sexual impurity and a miserable lament that there was a reprobate in the family. The outburst was so uncharacteristic of the reticent old man that everyone at the table sat in shock. Even the Javanese help dropped her dishes and ran out of the kitchen to investigate the commotion.

Skye blushed fiercely. He had been prepared to reason things out with his grandmother, but this unexpected tirade from his grandfather caught him off guard. He had a pocket full of ammunition against Christian haters who were ever ready to condemn gay men in the name of the Lord, but he held this tongue. This was after all his grandfather. Stealing a glance at his grandmother, Skye was surprised to catch her holding his grandfather in a condescending gaze.

Mary Lao was indeed gazing at her husband with mixed feelings, not the least of which were pity, annoyance and condescension. He had remained the timid man incapable of original thought or personal stance all these years. When they both joined Pastor Kong's church two decades ago, she saw it as a platform to grow her influence and extend her reach. He saw it as the obedience school he had always yearned for, where independent thinking was removed from the syllabus and strict adherence to the sermons and scripture the only qualifying factor. Lao Sheng Yang was an excellent follower. Back in the era of witch hunting, he would be brandishing his pitchfork right behind Pastor Kong and clamouring for the noose to be tightened. Mary Lao had no illusions about her husband. Neither had she any qualms leveraging on his unquestioning fanaticism to extend her reach in church all these years. But right now, when the family was gathered for a serious discussion, his self-righteous clamouring was simply annoying.

"Leave the room please."

Mary Lao had not raised her voice, but her husband stared at her with incredulity, as though she had threatened to expel him from church in front of the entire congregation.

"If you cannot behave civilly, leave the room."

The chair was knocked over as Lao Sheng Yang stood up abruptly. He gave the tabletop a half-hearted bang as he shuffled away. Just before he disappeared round the bend, he glanced back at Skye and hissed with vehemence, "I don't even want to be in the same room as you."

Mary Lao looked Skye squarely in the eye and asked, "Are you all right?"

A little taken aback, Skye could only nod.

Mary Lao nodded too. "You know you are precious to me, Skye. This road you have chosen, it is going to be tough. But it has to be your choice. No one else should decide how you live your life."

Skye suddenly found himself on the brink of tears. He had not anticipated the ready acceptance by his grandmother. "I want Kuan Eng to meet you. You will be so proud of him. He works as a corporate lawyer and does great work for the LGBT community."

Mary Lao shook her head with a poignant smile. "I will not

be inviting him to this house."

Skye was again caught off guard. "But why?"

Mary Lao sighed. "To you, I am merely your grandmother. To the church congregation, I am their church elder. They look up to me for leadership. I cannot preach against deviant sexuality and yet condone it in my family. I have to align my public stance with that of the church."

"So you are saying that you don't accept me and my boyfriend?" Skye asked, perplexed.

"I am saying that I will publicly condemn your behaviour in church, if need be," Mary Lao explained carefully. "You will always be welcome at my house as a grandson I love very much. But your boyfriend will not be allowed here. I hope I am making this very clear."

Skye felt Wei Wen's hand on his arm and turned around to catch her gently shaking her head. Mary Lao had made known her stance. Wei Wen did not want Skye to pursue the matter.

"What about you?" Mary Lao swivelled to Gimme Lao and asked. "The prime minister is fielding you for the next election. If word gets out that your only son is gay, how are you going to handle it?"

Gimme Lao could feel both his wife and his son's eyes bearing down on him. "I haven't had time to think it through."

"You had better," Mary Lao cautioned. "You never know when they will find out. You do not want to be caught without a ready answer."

"Dad, you have to lend us a voice," Skye became alarmed. "Both Kuan Eng and I have talked about it. If need be, we will step forth and be visible in your campaign. 377A has got to go."

"If your father chooses to champion your cause, there is a very high chance the prime minister will drop him from the election team," Mary Lao turned to confront Skye. "Is that what you want? Your father's political career stamped out just so you can get to say your piece? Don't you think it is a little selfish?"

Skye blushed. He had not looked at the matter in that light.

"There is no need to rush Gimme into a decision," Wei Wen interrupted. She knew how persuasive Mary Lao could be. "We should leave now. Thank you for the wonderful dinner, Mum."

Wei Wen volunteered to take over the wheel when they reached the car. She knew Gimme Lao had a lot on his mind and snapped at Skye when he tried to bring up the issue again on the drive home. "Give your dad a break. He's had enough surprises over the last two days."

What Wei Wen did not know was that Gimme Lao had received a text message from Mary Lao, which he chose not to share with her. The message simply read, "You are meant for great things, Gimme. Don't you forget that."

TEN

THIS WAS TURNING out to be the worst day of his life.

At three in the morning, Gimme Lao woke up abruptly with a squeezing sensation in his chest. For a while, he had difficulty catching his breath. He reached out to grab Wei Wen's arm, but there was no one lying beside him. And then he remembered. Wei Wen had moved out three years ago. She did not share his bed anymore.

The tightness soon subsided, and Gimme Lao could breathe again. Was it a nightmare that triggered the response? He could not tell. Gimme Lao could never recall his dreams.

Rolling onto his left, Gimme Lao propped himself up and reached for the glass of honey lemon on the nightstand. This was one of the habits Wei Wen managed to inculcate in him. She used to prepare one each for the both of them before bedtime and would chide Gimme Lao if he left his untouched in the morning. Now that Wei Wen was gone, Gimme Lao had taken to preparing the glass of honey lemon religiously every night. It made him feel as though he was still married and not the 50-year-old divorcee that he had become.

Gimme Lao was grateful that Wei Wen waited another year after he assumed office before filing for divorce. In the cacophony of post-election fanfare, the media did not pick up on the news bite. Except for the cabinet ministers and a select group of parliamentarians, no one else knew about the divorce.

Prior to the 2011 elections, Gimme Lao came clean with Dr Liew Kim Keong. There were two personal issues that might work against him. His wife was contemplating divorce, and his son was in an openly gay relationship. Dr Liew Kim Keong frowned. The Party was fielding Gimme Lao for election under the Bukit Panjang Group Representation Constituency ticket, together with two other new candidates. If any of them came under attack, it would directly affect his chances of re-election.

Dr Liew Kim Keong discussed the matter with his wife Professor Eleanor Moh and came to the consensus that Gimme Lao was too invaluable a candidate to drop. The party had been strategically grooming him since the SARS crisis eight years ago. There were plans to make him cabinet minister further down the road. They would simply have to exercise damage control.

The two set up a private dinner meeting with Gimme Lao and Wei Wen. They wanted to be assured that the divorce was going to be amicable and that there was no third party involved. Wei Wen said that there wasn't. When they urged Wei Wen to delay divorce proceedings till after the election, they were relieved that she readily agreed. That meant they did not have to execute plan B. In her graciousness to be accommodating, Wei Wen had spared herself the character assassi-nation the Party was prepared to launch. It could have gotten ugly.

As for the issue of the gay son, Dr Liew Kim Keong explained to Gimme Lao privately that it was a double-edged sword. If the inconvenient truth surfaced, Gimme Lao could turn it to his advantage by taking a resolute, personal stance as the aggrieved father. The sympathy votes from the conservatives would far outnumber the votes lost from the minority camp who were proponents of LGBT recognition. Whatever his relationship with his gay son was in private, he must not be seen advocating for LGBT rights. That would go against the Party stance.

As it turned out, the issue never surfaced. Dr Liew Kim Keong decided to fire the first volley when he found out one of the opposition candidates was highly active in the LGBT outfit Oogachaga. He got hold of a video clip featuring a discussion forum held by Oogachaga, which captured the opposition candidate advocating for LGBT rights. After the candidacy was announced, he made sure the clip was leaked through social media. The furore that followed diverted media attention. Accusations that the opposition candidate was harbouring a gay agenda proved too hot to handle, and the man was dropped by his own party. No one looked in Gimme Lao's direction.

After the election in 2011, Dr Liew Kim Keong continued to groom Gimme Lao. Among the cohort of newly elected parliamentarians, Gimme Lao led the pack in approval ratings. The only one who came close was Sharon Shi. She became the darling of the media when she championed the fight to save the Red Brick Hospice at Stamford Road from demolition against an aggressive private developer eyeing the piece of prime land. The photograph of her giving a foot rub to an elderly resident dying of cancer went viral. But neither Dr Liew Kim Keong nor Gimme Lao was worried. No one could possibly top the SARS coup.

Three days ago, the entire nation was dismayed when they read in *The Straits Times* that the founding prime minister of Singapore had been admitted to the ICU. It became apparent that the end was near for the nonagenarian. A working committee was set up to prepare for the impending state funeral. Dr Liew Kim Keong, who sat on the committee, fought for Gimme Lao to be one of the six parliamentary representatives in the funeral cortege procession. The spots should not be exclusively reserved for pioneer parliamentarians, Dr Liew argued. Someone had to represent new blood, and there was no better candidate than Gimme Lao.

The glass of honey lemon having soothed his parched throat, Gimme Lao sighed with satisfaction. There was a briefing by the working committee scheduled for 10 in the morning. He ought to catch some sleep. Returning the glass to the nightstand, he caught sight of the soft blink on his mobile screen. There was a message from Dr Liew Kim Keong.

"Skip 10am briefing. Sharon Shi will replace you."

Gimme Lao was stunned. He wondered what had gone wrong. Two days ago, he had arranged for an electric double boiler stew pot to be delivered along with a gift pack of premium bird's nest to the family of the founding prime minister. He had received a texted message to thank him for his concern. Had he overstepped? Or had he not done enough? Gimme Lao racked his brain to re-examine his actions over the last two days. He had a media conference the day before and was mindful in deflecting media enquiries about the founding prime minister's condition in the hospital. Had he been careless and let slip sensitive information?

As much as he was tempted to text and ask Dr Liew Kim Keong for an explanation, Gimme Lao did not want to come across as being importunate. He decided that patience should be exercised. He would wait till the briefing was over.

Now that sleep had all but eluded him, Gimme Lao fired up his laptop to clear his emails. A quick glance down the inbox caused his heart to skip a beat. There was a request for an interview by *The Huffington Post*! Gimme Lao could not for his life imagine how he ended up on the radar of the Pulitzer Prize-winning online news portal. Eagerly, he tapped on the email and quickly browsed through. Just as quickly, his heart sank.

The Huffington Post was in the process of publishing an interview with an up and coming medical researcher at Johns Hopkins, a Dr Zhang Lei. Dr Zhang had a recent breakthrough identifying three specific biomarkers, which accurately measured the severity of chikungunya fever. When the interviewer brought up his involvement in the SARS crisis while working for Tan Tock Seng Hospital in Singapore back in 2003, Dr Zhang Lei was dismissive of the experience. He shared that he was pressured into surrendering his contribution to a political aspirant backed by the incumbent party. He was robbed of his rightful recognition. Now *The Huffington Post* wanted to seek Gimme Lao's response.

Gimme Lao slammed his laptop shut. That ungrateful

bastard! The man had enjoyed the generosity of a research scholarship from the Singapore government when he was an unknown. Now that he was soaring, he had turned around and pecked at the hand that fed and groomed him. Was this the reason Dr Liew Kim Keong was dropping him in favour of Sharon Shi? But how could they have known? There were too many unanswered questions. Gimme Lao texted a message to Dr Liew Kim Keong's personal assistant. He needed to set up a meeting in the afternoon. They had to coordinate their responses to *The Huffington Post* enquiry.

Flustered, Gimme Lao lay sleepless for the next three hours. At daybreak, he showered and drove over to River Valley Road to buy Mary Lao's favourite bak kut teh. Since he had the morning free, Gimme Lao decided to join his mother for breakfast.

Mary Lao was reading the papers when he walked in. She held a magnifying glass in her hand as she pored over the tiny print. Her head of hair was uncombed, a wild fuzz of unruly white. Gimme Lao frowned. Retirement had not sat well with his mother. After she fell out with Pastor Kong two years ago and stopped attending church altogether, she became practically scruffy. It was as though she did not care anymore.

"Pastor Kong is up to one of his tricks again. Did you read about it in the papers?" Mary Lao clicked her tongue dismissively.

Gimme Lao could not help but smile. Where once Mary Lao used to be Pastor Kong's most trusted church elder, she had now become his most vehement critic. The bad blood could be traced back to the library book saga that had divided the church committee. Elizabeth was the one who raised the alarm when she came across a particular library book for children. The story was about two male chinstrap penguins in New York Central Park Zoo who behaved as a courting couple and raised a baby chick by themselves. Horrified, Elizabeth brought it to the attention of the church executive committee.

"Our children are reading about gay penguins!" she exclaimed. "Their minds will be poisoned. How can the National Library Board be so careless? We have to do something!"

Pastor Kong agreed. He would raise the issue at Sunday service and urge everyone in the congregation to write in to the National Library Board to protest.

"Aren't churches in Singapore forbidden from interfering with policymaking in the secular sector?" Mary Lao frowned.

"You have a point," Pastor Kong nodded. He turned to the committee secretary and gave specific instructions that she should draft several samples of protest letters to be circulated via the mass email list. There should be no mention of the church or the Lord in the contents. Every letter should be signed off with the likes of 'indignant parent' or 'concerned citizen'. The recipient must not be able to trace it back to the church.

"That is not my point," Mary Lao clarified. "The library is for everyone. How can we as a church impose our restrictions on non-churchgoers? Parents should be free to make their own decision on what their children can or cannot read."

The committee gasped. For decades, no one had questioned Pastor Kong's judgment.

"Mary, God needs us to do his work, not only within the church walls, but outside these walls too," Pastor Kong patiently explained. "It would be irresponsible of us to do nothing when the sexual deviants roll out their gay agenda to recruit the young. This storybook is a tool of sexual grooming. They are grooming our children to believe that gay marriage and gay lifestyle are acceptable. For us to remain silent is to be complicit."

Mary Lao remained unconvinced. "We can preach and enforce all we want within these walls, but there has to be a restriction on what we can preach and enforce outside the church. I have Buddhist friends who are vegetarians because they are against killing. Surely they cannot be allowed to write in and demand a stop to the import of meat? Would our congregation agree to that?"

Pastor Kong was displeased when he spotted two other executive committee members nodding in agreement. Over the next 30 minutes, the two of them continued to debate the issue. When it became clear that Mary Lao would not give in, Pastor Kong decided to get personal. "Mary, it is bad enough that you have failed the Lord and not made any effort to save the soul of your own grandchild. Please don't stop us from saving ours."

Infuriated, Mary Lao stood up and left the meeting. The next day, she tendered her letter of resignation to the executive committee. She vowed never to step in to Pastor Kong's church again and kept her word.

"What is Pastor Kong up to now?" Gimme Lao enquired as he laid out the soup spoons and chopsticks and dished out the packet of bak kut teh.

"He is applying for a permit to hold a Family Day Festival and picked the Padang as his preferred venue, on the very same day that Pink Dot is to be held at Hong Lim Park one street away. He wants everyone attending to wear red. This is nothing if not a war cry." Mary Lao flicked her finger at the newspaper. "Of course the authorities would reject his application. I would! Now he is crying foul!

Gimme Lao nodded. "I am aware. There is worse, though it hasn't made it to the media yet."

"What is it?" Mary Lao raised an eyebrow, intrigued.

"There is this fiery ustaz who is spearheading a Wear White Campaign among the Muslim community on the same date. Pink Dot happens to clash with the first day of Ramadan this year, so it is going to be a volatile situation."

Mary Lao whistled. "Pink versus red versus white; things are getting interesting! If your father were still around, he would find all these intimidating. In a way, Pastor Kong's church was good for him. It removed the need for him to think. All he ever wanted was to obey and follow instructions."

Gimme Lao studied his mother as she chewed on a succulent piece of pork rib. He remembered how well she took it when his father unexpectedly succumbed to a heart attack the year he was elected into Parliament. Mary Lao carried on with her daily routine as a new widow as though she had been preparing for it. Gimme Lao suspected that his father had ceased to be an important part of his mother's life many years prior to his death.

"I almost forgot. I found something interesting among your father's belongings. I think you should have it."

Mary Lao disappeared into the bedroom and returned with a tote bag. She extracted a copy of yellowing newspapers wrapped in plastic and handed it over. The date at the corner read 1971.

"You don't remember it, do you?" There was a twinkle of mischief in her eyes as she caught his frown of confusion. "Unwrap it."

Gimme Lao chortled when he flipped through and spotted a picture of himself on page 17. He was six. His kindergarten teacher had alerted the tabloids that her star student had come up with an ingenious method to save water. Over 20 classmates queued up in front of the trough to demonstrate the tiered method of washing their hands. The article praised the wonder boy and predicted he would grow up to be a star citizen.

"I can't believe Dad kept this," Gimme Lao laughed.

"Yes, he did. He was really happy when the article got published. He said you missed your chance six years earlier, when you could have been featured as the first baby born in independent Singapore. It's too bad that a baby girl beat you by one miserable minute."

"I remember. He even told Professor Eleanor Moh that story when he came to my convocation. It was embarrassing!"

"Your father loved you," Mary Lao said quietly. "He may have been intimidated by me and my achievements, but he was very proud of you and yours."

Gimme Lao was surprised to find himself moved. Mary Lao had always been his role model, the parent he looked up to for inspiration. In contrast, his father lurked in the shadows. The man did not aspire nor amount to much in life. But now Gimme Lao realised that the lack of personal achievement had not detracted from his capacity to love his son. All these years Gimme Lao had been cruel when he judged his father to be underachieving.

He must have been aware that his son looked down on him. Nevertheless, it did not stop him from loving his son.

"Skye dropped by for dinner two nights ago, together with Kuan Eng," Mary Lao suddenly announced.

Gimme Lao was taken aback. He had not met Skye for over a year now.

"When was the last time you had a sit-down dinner with Skye?"

Gimme Lao shrugged. "You know the story, Mum. The boy insists that he will not meet me for dinner unless I invite Kuan Eng too. But I can't be seen having dinner with my son and his gay partner. Someone could take a picture and hit me with it at a media conference."

"First of all, Skye is 29 years old, hardly a boy," Mary Lao said. "He has been with Kuan Eng for close to a decade now. Can you blame him for insisting that his own father recognise his partner?"

Gimme Lao remained silent. He had missed Skye as much as he had missed Wei Wen.

"When you were busy with your career in the early years, Wei Wen was the one who kept your family intact. Now that you are divorced, you have to make an effort to keep in touch. Otherwise, you and Skye will end up strangers."

Gimme Lao frowned. "I am quite sure that wasn't the advice you gave me back when Skye first came out to us."

"You are right," Mary Lao nodded emphatically. "Back then I was looking out for your political career and my leadership role in church. I was being selfish. Now where did that lead us? Alone. You and me. With all our impeccable achievements to flaunt and no one dear to celebrate with us."

Gimme Lao flinched. He had not been willing to admit it, but he felt lonely. There were nights he lay awake and wondered if anybody would miss him if he were gone. Mary Lao must have felt the same way too. That was probably the reason she had stopped her personal grooming routine.

"I will give Skye a call this afternoon," Gimme Lao finally said. "We'll work out an arrangement."

"Too late. Skye and Kuan Eng left for Vietnam yesterday. They are taking part in a 500km cycling challenge along the coast to raise funds for one of those gay causes they champion. I donated," Mary Lao smiled, "as I am not beneath spending some money to keep in touch with my only grandchild."

Gimme Lao felt his heart sink. There was no denying the disconnection. He had no idea what was going on in his son's life.

Mary Lao reached out to stroke his arm. "Your son is not in town, but your ex-wife is. Go have lunch with her."

"I don't know her schedule," Gimme Lao said. "It's rude to intrude without an appointment."

"Today is Thursday. Wei Wen will be at the Ren Ci Community Hospital from 10 till noon to help out with her brother's physical therapy session," Mary Lao said. "Go surprise her."

Mary Lao was right. When Gimme Lao turned up at 11, Wei Wen was seated in the therapy room guiding her brother through a series of exercise. "This is a nice surprise!" She seemed happy to see him.

"How's my Too Sexy?" Gimme Lao beamed as he patted Wei Wen's brother on his shoulder. Focused on the task of fitting blocks with irregular shapes into the wooden frame, Too Sexy chose to ignore him.

"Not too good," Wei Wen explained. "He is hard of hearing and has blurred vision. That makes him really irritable. The nurse told me that he is also losing his appetite and complaining of pain in the abdomen."

Gimme Lao sat down and examined Too Sexy. He was losing his head of hair and looked way older than his age. "Do you know what they feed him for breakfast?"

"Cereal, I think."

"I am guessing it is coeliac disease, which is common among adults with Down's syndrome," Gimme Lao said. "The body cannot digest wheat gluten and the intestine linings get damaged. That will cause pain in the abdomen. I will ask the nurse to arrange for a blood test. If need be, a biopsy. We can put him on a wheat-free diet in the meantime."

Wei Wen kept her gaze on him for a moment before smiling, "The perks of being married to a doctor. Free medical consultation. Thank you for extending the freebies beyond the marriage."

Gimme Lao laughed. The two of them continued bantering as they watched over Too Sexy. The irony did not escape Gimme

Lao that they had become almost the best of old friends now that they were amicably divorced. There was this wealth of memory he shared with her and no one else. He secretly wondered if it was possible for him to court Wei Wen again.

"I am hoping that I won't have to eat lunch alone," Gimme Lao put on his best smile. "There's this great Katong laksa stall down the road. Please join me."

"Oh, I wish I could," Wei Wen lamented. "But I have a lunch appointment."

"Business lunch?"

"Not quite," Wei Wen hesitated a little. "One of my Vietnamese clients set me up on a date with her brother last week. It went well, thus the follow-up lunch date."

"I am so disappointed. You actually have a life after me." Gimme Lao scrunched up his face and made a show of whining. He hoped his disappointment was veiled.

"He is picking me up at noon. Do you want to meet him?" Wei Wen asked tentatively.

"It's okay. I don't want to set the benchmark too high for him," Gimme Lao winked. "I guess it will be lunch alone for me then."

Gimme Lao did not enjoy dining out by himself. He gave his secretary permission to arrange work lunches and dinners throughout the week. On the rare occasion that a slot was unfilled, he had difficulty thinking of anyone to invite. He had a long list of professional contacts, but an exceedingly short list of friends. The dire situation only became apparent after his divorce. He had not made any effort to keep in touch with his old friends.

Gimme Lao was almost happy when he received a text message from his secretary midway through his bowl of Katong laksa.

"Committee briefing over? Reporters waiting."

"Why reporters?" Gimme Lao texted, alarmed.

"Come in back door. Will brief you." his secretary cautioned.

Gimme Lao knew there was major trouble the moment he spotted his secretary. She suffered from hyperhidrosis and perspired profusely when she was tense. Right now, there were two damp patches on her blouse conspicuously radiating from her armpits.

"Do you remember how you replied to one of the questions during the media conference two days ago? The one about ministerial salaries?"

"Well, I remember the man who challenged me about ministerial salaries was very sarcastic," Gimme Lao frowned as he recalled. "He claimed that our cabinet ministers were greedy public servants who gave themselves million-dollar salaries. He said that the reason why Singapore government has a near zero corruption record is that we factor the corruption into our official wages."

"Him being sarcastic is beside the point," his secretary said. "How did you reply?"

"I quoted the example of Dr Liew's appointment as the Minister of Information and the Arts. If his salary was merely half a million, how is he going to stand tall and discuss policy formulation and implementation with media CEOs who earn millions of dollars themselves? They won't pay him any attention.

He needs to have equivalent pay to maintain his dignity on the negotiation table."

As Gimme Lao heard himself explain, a chill ran down his spine. It suddenly dawned on him that he might have made the biggest blunder of his political career.

"Social media had a field day yesterday attacking your statement. I have bookmarked some of them," his secretary remarked as she jiggled the mouse and brought the screen to life.

Gimme Lao slumped into his swivel chair and browsed through the bookmarked sites with dread. *The Online Citizen* claimed that henceforth if a police officer stopped you on the street, ask the officer for his pay slip. If he earned less than you, you had the right to ignore him. *The Real Singapore* came up with a bar chart to compare the salary package of political leaders all over the world. The article highlighted the glaring fact that even if the prime minister of Singapore took a 70 per cent pay cut, he would still take home more money than anyone else, the president of the United States and the German chancellor included. *New Nation* featured a GIF where Gimme Lao's head was transplanted onto an inflatable figure that kept ballooning as a moving queue of stick figures continuously fed him money. Superimposed on the image was the text 'Gimme Now! Gimme Now!'.

"Are you all right?" his secretary suddenly asked, alarmed.

Gimme Lao was not feeling all right. The tight squeeze in his chest had returned, and a sharp pain was shooting up his arm. "I think I might be having a heart attack. Call an ambulance, quickly."

After his secretary made the call, Gimme Lao gave her instructions to push him to the lift lobby on his swivel chair. Meeting the paramedics at the main entrance would save valuable time. In his panic, he had forgotten that there were reporters camping at the lobby waiting to ambush him. Almost immediately, they crowded around him, pushing the recording devices in his face and bombarding him with questions.

"Please make way! Dr Gimme Lao is having a heart attack!" His secretary screamed as she tried to bulldoze her way through.

When the reporters realised that Gimme Lao was indeed perspiring profusely and looking unusually pale, they quickly whipped out their cameras and mobile phones and went to work. The entourage shadowed him all the way down to the main lobby and filmed the paramedics loading him onto the ambulance. Thereafter, it was a wild race to their vehicles and a mad dash to the nearest hospital. The Accident and Emergency Department staff was shocked to see the contingent of reporters barging into the room and asking for Gimme Lao. The security team had to be brought in to chase the intruders out of the restricted area.

Gimme Lao was curtained off in one corner of the Accident and Emergency Department. There was only an intern on hand, who apologised and explained that the doctors had carpooled for lunch earlier and had met with a bad accident; they were receiving treatment themselves even as he spoke. Gimme Lao assured the intern that the worst spell had passed and he could wait a little. He then turned to his secretary to dictate instructions. She was to notify both his ex-wife and his mother first, followed by Dr Liew Kim Keong and Professor Eleanor Moh. After that, she was to buy drinks and buns from the cafeteria and distribute them to the reporters. Inform them that Gimme Lao's condition appeared to be stabilised. Advise them against reporting the incident.

After the intern and his secretary left, Gimme Lao shut his eyes to ponder the situation. Now he understood the reason Dr Liew Kim Keong was dropping him in favour of Sharon Shi. How stupid could he be? To quote Dr Liew as an example was to shine the spotlight on him, something he would not appreciate. During the media conference, Gimme Lao had been irked by the sarcasm of the man who challenged him. He was focused on winning the argument. In his haste, Gimme Lao had made an unwise analogy and portrayed himself as the greedy politician the people would love to hate. Nothing short of a public apology could save him now.

As Gimme Lao pondered, he became aware that a documentary was being aired on the television screen hanging over the bed. The camera followed a local woman as she brought the crew on a tour of her flat. Like 80 per cent of the Singapore population, she was housed in a public housing unit built by the Housing Development Board. She and her husband shared a room, while her elderly mother and her teenage daughter shared another. She remarked that she wished her daughter could have a room to herself, but the family could not afford to upgrade to a bigger flat. Property prices had skyrocketed the last two decades and were out of reach for single-income families like hers.

The interviewer interrupted and asked if the woman's family had not benefitted from the astronomical rise in their asset value as homeowners. Was it not true that the Singapore government's asset enhancement programme was one of the most successful public housing programmes in the world? The woman grinned sheepishly and said yes, she was very grateful to the Singapore government.

The interviewer continued to prompt and ask what else made her proud to be a Singaporean. The woman stammered. It was painfully obvious to Gimme Lao that not only was the woman ineloquent; she was very uncomfortable in front of the camera. Whatever the theme of the documentary was, the producer could not have picked a less suitable interviewee.

The interviewer had to practically spoon-feed the woman. Was she not grateful living in a city with one of the lowest crime rates in the world? Her teenage daughter could come home in the dead of the night and she need not worry about her safety. Did she not agree that the extensive public transport system in Singapore made life easy for families like hers who did not own a car? In comparison, the traffic conditions in neighbouring countries were horrendous. Did she not feel lucky that the meritocratic system in practice meant that her daughter had as much opportunity as the next teenager to rise up in life? She did not have to know the right people to get her child into the best schools.

Gimme Lao cringed as he watched the woman nod and agree unfailingly to everything the interviewer suggested. This was a terrible interview! Why on earth would the producer pick such an unintelligent woman who held no opinion or view of her own as the subject? Who was she? Gimme Lao struggled to sit upright for a better view, but the caption on the screen was too tiny. He flipped himself onto all fours, crawled to the edge of the bed and knelt on his knees. Only then was he close enough to read the caption.

The woman's name was Giam Mei Mei. Gimme Lao vaguely remembered there had been a mousy little girl called Mei Mei back in kindergarten. The girl was taciturn and non-participatory in class. More than once she had embarrassed herself by wetting her panties when she became nervous. This timid and nondescript woman on television could well be the grown up version of the girl back in kindergarten. But the question remained. What was the documentary about and why did the producer pick Madam Giam Mei Mei?

The mystery was solved when the documentary came to an end. The interviewer explained that it was his pleasure to interview the first baby born in independent Singapore. Madam Giam Mei Mei was born six minutes past midnight on 9 August 1965. She grew up a beneficiary of the Singapore system and enjoyed a safe and stable life that many people in other nations would envy. She was rightfully proud to be the nation's firstborn.

Gimme Lao could hardly believe his ears. This was the woman who had stolen his queue number! Gimme Lao knew unequivocally that he was born seven minutes past midnight on the day Singapore became independent. He knew because Grandma Toh, who used to babysit him, often betted on the number 6507. Twice the winning number turned out to be 6501. Grandma Toh cursed and said Gimme Lao was too stingy to bless her with a windfall.

The irony did not escape Gimme Lao that he himself was a thousand times more qualified than Giam Mei Mei to be showcased as the nation's firstborn. All-round excellence in his academic record. A national hero during the SARS crisis. Voted into public office by voters who trusted him. Given enough time, he could well make cabinet minister.

Gimme Lao cried out when a sharp pain suddenly tore through his chest. Bending over with the excruciating affliction, he swung his arms wildly as the bed skidded and sent him crashing onto the floor. Just before his head hit the ceramic tiles and he was knocked out cold, an irrelevant thought crossed his mind.

He would have made a wonderful poster child for the nation.

ACKNOWLEDGEMENTS

I would like to express my gratitude to the team at Epigram Books who made this novel possible, especially to Lan who was a most agreeable editor to work with.

I would like to thank Dr Lens Lee and Hui Chee Hong for allowing me to pick their brains.

The play in chapter five was inspired by *Porcelain*, written by Chay Yew in the early 90s. I am proud of his impressive achievements as a Singaporean playwright.

ABOUT THE AUTHOR

Sebastian Sim grew up in a two-room HDB flat with parents who were part of the pioneer generation of independent Singapore. Not one to shy away from the road less taken, he has tried his hand in different industries and travelled around the world to soak up different experiences and cultures. He was variously a bartender at Boat Quay, an assistant outlet manager at McDonald's, an insurance salesman, a prison officer in a maximum security prison and a croupier in a casino. *Let's Give It Up for Gimme Lao!* is Sebastian's first English novel.

Also by Sebastian Sim: (writing as 岳观铭)

《天厨记》
《蝠泣录》
《欢乐咒》

INHERITANCE
BALLI KAUR JASWAL

A NOVEL

INHERITANCE BY BALLI KAUR JASWAL

- Winner of the 2014 Best Young Australian Novelist Award -

In 1971, a teenage girl briefly disappears from her house in the middle of the night, only to return a different person, causing fissures that threaten to fracture her Punjabi Sikh family. As Singapore's political and social landscapes evolve, the family must cope with shifting attitudes towards castes, youth culture, sex and gender roles, identity and belonging. Inheritance examines each family member's struggles to either preserve or buck tradition in the face of a changing nation.

ISBN: 978-191-2098-00-2
PUBLICATION DATE: MAY 2017

KAPPA QUARTET

A NOVEL

DARYL QILIN YAM

KAPPA QUARTET BY DARYL QILIN YAM

Kevin is a young man without a soul, holidaying in Tokyo; Mr Five, the enigmatic kappa, is the man he happens to meet. Little does Kevin know that kappas—the river demons of Japanese folklore—desire nothing more than the souls of other humans. Set between Singapore and Japan, *Kappa Quartet* is split into eight discrete sections, tracing the rippling effects of this chance encounter across a host of other characters, connected and bound to one another in ways both strange and serendipitous.

ISBN: 978-191-2098-72-9
PUBLICATION DATE: MAY 2017

NOW THAT IT'S

a novel

OVER

O THIAM CHIN

NOW THAT IT'S OVER BY O THIAM CHIN

- Winner of the 2015 Epigram Books Fiction Prize -

During the Christmas holidays in 2004, an earthquake in the Indian Ocean triggers a tsunami that devastates fourteen countries. Two couples from Singapore are vacationing in Phuket when the tsunami strikes. Alternating between the aftermath of the catastrophe and past events that led these characters to that fateful moment, *Now That It's Over* weaves a tapestry of causality and regret, and chronicles the physical and emotional wreckage wrought by natural and man-made disasters.

ISBN: 978-191-2098-69-9
PUBLICATION DATE: JULY 2017

THE LAST
LESSON
of
MRS DE
SOUZA

A NOVEL

CYRIL WONG

***THE LAST LESSON OF MRS DE SOUZA* BY CYRIL WONG**

One last time and on her birthday, Rose de Souza is returning to school to give a final lesson to her classroom of secondary school boys before retiring from her long teaching career. What ensues is an unexpected confession in which she recounts the tragic and traumatic story of Amir, a student from her past who overturned the way she saw herself as a teacher, and changed her life forever.

ISBN: 978-191-2098-70-5
PUBLICATION DATE: JULY 2017

SUGARBREAD
BALLI KAUR JASWAL

A NOVEL

SUGARBREAD BY BALLI KAUR JASWAL

- Finalist of the 2015 Epigram Books Fiction Prize -

Pin must not become like her mother, but nobody will tell her why. She seeks clues in Ma's cooking and when she's not fighting other battles — being a bursary girl at an elite school and facing racial taunts from the bus uncle. Then her meddlesome grandmother moves in, installing a portrait of a watchful Sikh guru and a new set of house rules. Old secrets begin to surface, but can Pin handle the truth?

ISBN: 978-191-2098-66-8
PUBLICATION DATE: SEPTEMBER 2017

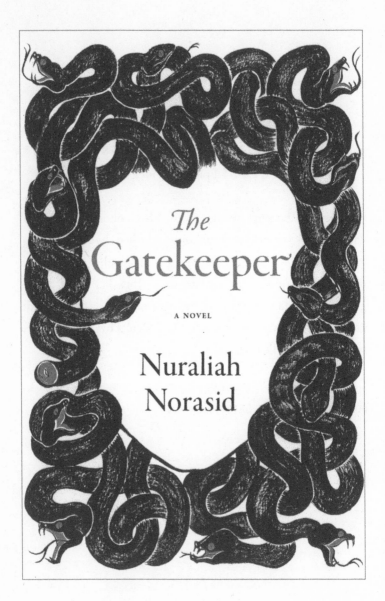

The
Gatekeeper

A NOVEL

Nuraliah
Norasid

THE GATEKEEPER BY NURALIAH NORASID

- Winner of the 2016 Epigram Books Fiction Prize -

The Gatekeeper tells the story of a ten-year-old Gorgon girl named Ria, who petrifies an entire village of innocents with her gaze. Together with her sister, she flees the jungle of Manticura to the underground city of Nelroote, where society's marginalised members live. Years later, the subterranean habitat is threatened when Ria, now the gatekeeper, befriends a man from the outside.

ISBN: 978-191-2098-68-2
PUBLICATION DATE: SEPTEMBER 2017

STATE OF EMERGENCY

A NOVEL

JEREMY TIANG

Author of *It Never Rains on National Day*

STATE OF EMERGENCY BY JEREMY TIANG

- Finalist of the 2016 Epigram Books Fiction Prize -

A woman finds herself questioned for a conspiracy she did not take part in. A son flees to London to escape from a father, wracked by betrayal. A journalist seeks to uncover the truth of the place she once called home. A young wife leaves her husband and children behind to fight for freedom in the jungles of Malaya. *State of Emergency* traces the leftist movements of Singapore and Malaysia from the 1940s to the present day, centring on a family trying to navigate the choppy political currents of the region.

ISBN: 978-191-2098-65-1
PUBLICATION DATE: NOVEMBER 2017